Lynette Lowthian has worked as a journalist and editor all her professional life, and she also teaches creative writing and journalism. She's met and interviewed an incredibly diverse range of people in her career—from politicians, authors, actors and TV personalities to families in crisis and campaigners for disability rights. 'I'm obsessed with people, what haunts them, what drives them and why they do the things they do. And I love to write about them,' she says. *The Gene Genie* is her first novel, and she's now at work on her second.

To Rob – thanks for everything you do, but especially for giving so generously of your time in editing and proofing my first novel and for encouraging and believing in me throughout.

Lynette Lowthian

THE GENE GENIE

AUSTIN MACAULEY PUBLISHERS™

LONDON • CAMBRIDGE • NEW YORK • SHARJAH

A CIP catalogue record for this title is available from the British Library.

ISBN 9781398469679 (Paperback)
ISBN 9781398469686 (ePub e-book)

www.austinmacauley.com

First Published 2023
Austin Macauley Publishers Ltd®
1 Canada Square
Canary Wharf
London
E14 5AA

Part 1
The Past Imperfect

Chapter 1
Toby Summerfield, 2013

It's one of those midsummer evenings special to London, when hot sun filters through dirty city air to form a gauze of golden motes. For Toby Summerfield, it is an evening redolent of the past.

Toby sits in his north London garden scanning *The Ham and High*. Not a newspaper he habitually reads, but he has an affection for it, for giving him a job when he was just another graduate who thought he could write. God knows, as editor-in-chief of the foremost liberal left-leaning daily in the country, he should read all the newspapers he can, if only to keep an eye on the competition. His wife Clara does a great job in keeping him abreast, especially of the human-interest stuff. After a week of print, he'd sooner get out his headphones and listen to music.

He's not much interested in what *The Ham and High* has to say about national politics: he can pretty much pre-guess it. He shuffles through to a page of local stories. His go-to pub is getting a makeover and will be closed for the summer. A girl at his son Theo's school has won a national handwriting competition. Local residents are up in arms over their rubbish collection being cut. All of mild interest, but Toby's keen editor's eye is drawn to a name in the lead story, a report of a domestic incident not far away in West Hampstead.

The name in the story is Enderbie and it turns Toby's mouth dry. There's no mistaking the name and its unusual spelling, with the unexpected 'ie' at the end. Toby senses a rising anxiety in his chest and his vision waves and blurs as he reads on.

From The Hampstead & Highgate Express, October 22, 2013

Mystery surrounds the identity of an assailant, following an incident in a house in West Hampstead this week.

After an alert, paramedics arrived at the scene to find two women, believed to be identical twins. One had received a serious blow to the head and was unconscious. She was taken by ambulance to hospital in a critical condition. The other woman, described as 'uninjured', is unable or unwilling to verify her identity. Police were called to the hospital to interview both women, but no further information has been released as yet.

Jasmine Poole, who lives next door to the house where the suspected attack took place, told The Ham and High: 'I moved in three months ago. Anna Enderbie and her partner and child live next door. They seem a pleasant enough couple, though I only pass the time of day with them. Just a normal happy family. One thing I do remember as odd. I was in the front garden not long ago and Anna came out of her front door. Her beautiful black hair had been dyed bright honey-blonde. It gave me a shock, but to be polite I called out "like the new hairdo." She stared back at me as if she'd never seen me before in her life. It's not like Annie to ignore people. I'm wondering now if that was the other twin. I wasn't aware Anna had a twin, let alone an identical one.'

Police are unable to comment until investigations are complete.

Toby believes himself to be a mild-mannered man. In editorial meetings, he doesn't bang his fist on the table and insist: he listens. When his son steps out of line, he doesn't shout and order: he reasons. Not a man to make a fuss. So, in his usual manner, he quietly folds the newspaper, removes his Panama and reading glasses and places everything neatly on his deckchair. He doesn't cry out for his wife, or falter, as he crosses his lawn in long strides, to reach the dim recesses of the house.

In the little cracked mirror in the cloakroom, he peers at his face. It has squared out: gone are the planes and hollows of boyhood, replaced by the surplus skin and air of complacency of a moderately long life, lived well. Staring intently at his fallen face in the mirror, Toby lets out a silent howl of anguish. For what he loved and lost. For the deceptions and lies. And for the babies, stolen from him, that he would never hold.

Chapter 2
Emily Enderbie's Memory Book, 1978

Dear reader

My babies have taken over my life. I'm only just 18, it's not fair. One is tough enough, but twins are crazy bad luck.

I'm going to write everything down because I haven't got anyone to talk to. My mother has barely spoken to me since I fell pregnant. She and my father think I've brought shame on the family.

So this will be my Memory Book. Or it could be a diary. It can actually be whatever I want it to be. I'm not sure anyone will ever read it. If by chance you're reading it now, you'll already know that it's a ring binder with a sticker saying 'Emily Enderbie's Memory Book' on the front and a stars and planets design. I was thinking of 'reaching for the stars' or something corny like that. I might put it in a box and make it a time capsule when I'm done with it. Or there again, I might hide it under the bed or behind the wardrobe and someone will find it in about the year 2000! Whatever, I'm sure if I write down all the stuff that's going around in my head, I'll feel better.

I guess my bad luck began when I was born. I've read books about girls raised on farms, with ponies, a big garden and lots of brothers and sisters. No such luck for me. I've lived in 101 Elm Avenue, Tooting Bec all my life. It's a narrow terrace and though there are only three of us—well, five now, if you count the twins—everywhere you go, you're squashed in.

Let me tell you a bit about the inhabitants of number 101.

My dad is Clive—I call him creepy Clive, though not to his face. I prefer to call both my parents by their real names, not mum and dad. It makes the gulf between us feel bigger, which is fine by me. Truth is, they're nothing like my idea of a mum and dad. Clive is a skinny little man with a gnome-shaped head and wire specs. Small he may be, but he's got a loud mouth, a big temper and a high opinion of himself. He's a mechanic so, as he loves to point out, he's more than a cut above someone like me who has never worked in a proper job at all.

One thing I've always wanted, along with a pony, a brother or sister and a big garden, is the sort of mum you can have a heart-to-heart, or even just a laugh, with. I've tried so hard to get Norma to do girly things with me. But it's as if someone switched off her inner light bulb. Some people might call her strong and silent, but to me she's more silent and deadly. She's tall and Clive's tiny, so the two of them look ridiculous as a pair. God knows how they ever got it together to create me.

If I said Norma and Clive never wanted me, you'd probably think I was making it up. But I truly believe they didn't. Norma doesn't shout, she glares. But Clive gets so mad that he turns purple and all the veins in his neck stick out. I can see why they didn't bother with a brother or sister for me. Which is pretty much how I feel about the twins, if I'm honest, although I'm trying hard to be an okay mum, even if I'm not a good one. I'm 18 and supposed to be having fun, not spending my days flipping out boobs and bottles so the babies can get fat on me.

I'm struggling to think of much to say about the twins because they're just babies who cry, eat and sleep in that order and then need a nappy change. It would be easier if they looked different, but they're identical from the tops of their fuzzy heads to the tips of their fat, pink toes. Annie and Bea. Two peas in a pod.

But wait, there is a difference. Annie is my firstborn. In the cot, she waves her hands in the air and studies them thoughtfully. When I pick her up to feed, she gurgles happily even if I'm frowning. Her eyes seek out mine as she sucks away at my breast. Bea is my difficult one. She hates the cot and cries bitterly to be lifted out. She avoids my face and I have never yet seen her smile. Annie smiles all the time. Or what passes for a smile in a three-month-old. A sort of gummy grimace.

If someone is out there reading this, you're probably wondering how I got myself in this fix, stuck in a skinny tube of a house with two babies who are sucking me dry and parents who would rather I was somewhere else—or nowhere at all. To get where I'm coming from, you need to know a bit more about me. So here's me in a snapshot. You may get more than you wished for.

I'm an only child and it's hard work. I deal with my parents' dreams and disappointments all on my own—if they ever had dreams. They had a shotgun wedding and then Norma had a bad birth from which she's never fully recovered. Or so she says. She's told me often enough that it 'might' have been better if I'd never come along. She might not have stuck with Clive and they might have had better lives. I am the big disappointment. I get that.

So what do they do with their lives, so badly diminished by me? Norma likes housework and what she calls 'make do and mend'. Anything from crocheted cushion covers to horrid homemade 'frocks' made from tissue patterns. Clive likes mechanical stuff, paper airplanes and shouting—which takes up a lot of his energy.

I did have dreams, but they are long dead. One was to be a writer. You see, I always loved reading and writing and my teachers even talked of university. When I was still in school, I read *Jane Eyre.* Jane felt a bit like me. She had no love, no certainty, nothing to tie her to a person or place: and then something changed and everything fell into place for her. *Dear reader, I married him.*

Maybe that'll happen for me someday. I thought if I could just have someone to love and be loved by…and that's when Toby Summerfield, with his soft lips and floppy hair, stepped in.

Be careful what you wish for.

Chapter 3
Norma Enderbie, 1978

Having a baby again in the house at 101 Elm Avenue was never going to be easy. But really, Norma had completely underestimated the havoc it—or they—would bring. What on earth is her feckless daughter doing upstairs in the attic bedroom with not one but two babies, both born out of wedlock?

Norma doesn't consider herself unkind. She hasn't kicked the girl out. She is providing Emily with shelter and food. What more can be expected? But this constant crying is too much. She cradles her mug of morning tea and watches the ice gently melting on the inside of the bedroom window. At least the twins haven't disturbed Clive yet. He's snoring away happily in the single bed next to hers. How does he sleep through it?

Two nights ago, the twins woke Clive in the small hours and he couldn't get back to sleep. By 6 a.m., he'd had enough. He'd burst in to Emily's room, picked up one of the twins (Norma guesses it was Bea because she cries hardest and longest) and started shaking her. Norma wasn't sure what she feared most: Clive having a heart attack or a dead baby on her hands. He was puce in the face and all his veins were sticking out, but the baby did stop crying.

In any case, Norma has seen a lot worse than Clive in her time. She takes a deep breath and tries, unsuccessfully, to steer her thoughts in a better direction. Memories have a habit of jumping out of the cabinet, even when you think you have them securely filed away. It's always at this time of the morning that they get to you. Even a morning cuppa is haunted by the past. By childhood.

She pictures the bleak pebble-dashed West Country cottage, five streets back from the beach. Growing up without a mum, without even the memory of a mum. The father who detested her because he blamed her for losing his wife in childbirth. Then, when she got to 13, the loathing turned to lust.

Norma sits up sharp and pulls up the eiderdown. Quickly rearranges the images in her head. Now, she's picturing herself on the windswept pebble beach, 13 years old, looking out to sea for German warships. Praying for them to come and rescue her, invade this small isle and set her free.

Norma gathers her eiderdown around her once more and concentrates hard on a single lump of ice on its meandering journey down the windowpane. But nothing can stop the images that define her childhood, returning to her sometimes by day and often by night to taunt her equilibrium. The first time.

She sees herself, hair whipped by the sea breeze, in her flower-print dress with the grubby peter pan collar. The fabric barely covers her lean brown thighs: she's already growing into the statuesque woman she will become. She is standing on the cliff path, watching for Germans in the cobalt sea, but something—a sense of impending threat or perhaps just the wind in the gorse— makes her turn round. Behind her, a broad meadow dotted with daisies and buttercups slopes gently upwards towards the blue, blue sky. Seagulls swoop and somewhere, she thinks she hears a skylark.

She spots *him* at the top of the meadow, where the land meets the sky. With his ragged farm clothes flapping in the wind, he looks from a distance like an overfed scarecrow in silhouette. He stands motionless, scanning the meadow before marching towards her. She has nowhere to go but towards the cliff edge.

By the time he catches up with her, Norma's father is breathless and red in the face. 'What do you think you doing? You should be setting supper,' he says.

'I didn't know what time it was. I haven't got a watch.'

'Well it's time to get back girl.' He pushes her in the small of the back.

Norma flinches. Why does he always call her 'girl', never 'Norma', although he was the one who gave her the name. Now he's gazing at her legs.

'That dress is too short.'

'Well, get me another,' she retorts. He scares her most of the time, but she's made a pact with herself not to show it. As they trudge side by side up the hill, she keeps a careful distance. Her father slides odd glances at her.

'Should you be wearing a you-know?'

'A what?' she snaps back.

'You know, a corset.'

She nearly sniggers. 'You mean a brassiere, father.' Her words are layered with barely-concealed contempt.

'Yes, that.'

He's gazing fixedly at her emergent breasts and she instinctively covers them with her elbows.

'Well you need to buy me one then.'

'I can't do that girl. You'll need to get Nance to do it.'

Norma's great aunt Nance is always sent for to help with what her Father calls 'women things'. Recently Nance, who is 84, unmarried and wears callipers, was called on to assist with rags. She is dubious that Nance will even know what a brassiere is.

'Yes father.' Norma spins a dandelion clock in her fingers as they return in silence to the cottage. She prepares supper as she's done every evening since she turned 10. After their plates of spam, hard-boiled eggs and some leaves of home-grown lettuce soaked in vinegar, sugar and salt, she escapes to her bedroom. She doesn't like light evenings, which leave hours with nothing to do except sleep. It's better in winter when she can gaze out at the stars. She reaches under her pillow and pulls out a book. It's *The Girl from the Limberlost* and she stole it from school. She loves stories, but she's never told anyone as she's afraid it might be a sin. Norma adores the resourceful Elnora Comstock and plans to make a getaway one day, just like Elnora did.

Shadows are falling and Norma is nearly asleep, the book discarded on her bedspread, when footsteps come tap-tapping up the stairs. Suddenly wideawake, she hears them approach her door. 'What is it?' she calls out. 'What do you need?'

Her father opens the door a crack and lets himself in. Approaching the end of the bed, so he is towering over her, he removes his shirt. 'What are you doing, you're in the wrong room,' she says.

He doesn't speak, but his eyes don't leave Norma's face as he begins to pull down his trousers and then his underwear. Now he is naked, his body luminous in the moonlight. He sits on the edge of the bed. 'Go away, *father*.' Norma spits the word in his face. But she has nowhere to run and nowhere to hide, just the dark garden, the empty fields and the village beyond, where the villagers will turn their heads in scorn.

'Take off your night-dress, girl.' She freezes. Though she only dimly understands what's about to happen, she recognises that, for her, the earth will never again tilt in quite the same way. She loathes and fears her father in equal measure. Wordlessly, she obeys.

This is the first night that Norma's father visits her room. The first of many, stretching into the remainder of her childhood like a row of tin soldiers. As time wears on, she starts to understand that confiding—in a kindly teacher or a trusted friend—would be as much a betrayal of herself as an indictment of her father. She learns words like Used Goods and Whore. She is not, she will not be, that person.

Well, in the end, it wasn't the Germans who rescued her, it was Clive. The thought almost makes her laugh out loud. If her father killed her capacity for love, then Clive hardly re-ignited it. But he's put a roof over her head, kept her in tea and biscuits—and even brassieres.

Norma learnt young to be a survivor and the only time she feels she might get knocked off her perch is when she's around babies. Something about them—their innocence, their vulnerability, their trust. All the things she lost. She sighs as another piercing scream rips through the ceiling.

Something must be done.

Chapter 4
Emily's Memory Book, 1978

Toby Summerfield. The skinny feel of him in my arms. His fingers in my hair. The taste of him on my tongue. I promised you, dear reader, that I'd get to Toby. So here goes.

He's way out of my league, Toby Summerfield. That's the first thing to say about him. He lives on the far side of the dog-ended, pooh-infested area of grass they call a common. We both live next to it, almost overlooking it, but that's not the point. Our side of the common is made up of row on row of narrow terraced houses, some split into two. Most of the roads are at right angles to one another—there are hardly any curves or corners—I guess you can get more houses crammed in that way. And there are no trees. You have to cross the common to find one of them.

Toby's side is way different. The Victorian houses are big and slightly crumbly, but in a good way. Some have walled gardens with apple trees tippling over the walls. You can't see inside, but you can imagine a secret family life going on in there. Mums sunbathing, Dads reading the Sunday papers or mowing the lawn and kids having fun hanging out. I've got no way of proving it, but I know in my gut it's a different way of life from ours, over here in Elm Avenue.

So we have (or had, in my case) this weird situation at my comprehensive school: a mix of kids from both sides of the common. Perhaps it's some sort of experiment they're doing with their kids over there on the other side. A lot of them put even Labour Party stickers up in their windows. Why do that when rich people vote Conservative? And why send their kids to our grubby old comp when they could be going to a smart private school?

I asked Toby about it, one hazy, lazy Sunday afternoon, as we lay entangled together in my single bed in the attic room, with Norma and Clive safely out of range at Clive's mum's. 'Why don't they send you to a private school?'

'Because they don't want me to be an elitist,' murmured Toby, nuzzling my ear. I was about to say: 'What's an elitist?' but I didn't want to look stupid and Toby sensed it. He always knew what I was thinking, often before I did.

'It's someone who thinks they're better than other people because they're wealthier, cleverer, or have a higher social status. So they want me to meet lots of people from different backgrounds, ethnic backgrounds, social backgrounds, you name it...' he tailed off.

Toby is going to be an architect. Or a film director. He hasn't quite decided, but his parents definitely want him to be an architect. His dad Rupe (it's actually Rupert but no one ever calls him that) is a human rights lawyer and his mum Maddy is something high up in the probation service. I'm slightly in love and in awe of them both. Toby must have been around all the time I was at the comp, but I didn't notice him until fifth form. I struck lucky: they'd just put the school-leaving age up so it was harder for Norma and Clive to get me to leave—although they would much rather me bringing in some bacon. We were in the middle of exams and I was expected to do well, especially in English, which Clive says is a time-waster.

At school, I felt like a misfit. I didn't really fit into either camp, you see. Too clever by half for my own lot and not enough airs and graces for the others. Skinny, scrawny loner with jet black hair, a beaky nose and a glum look on my face. Maybe I had a bit of attitude back then. Maybe that's what Toby liked in me. You'd have to ask him.

We'd been discussing *To Kill A Mockingbird* in class and all the rights and wrongs of it were going around in my head. I noticed Toby, by himself in a corner of the cafeteria, head slumped over his book.

'Hey Emily. Good book, isn't it? 'he said in his posh voice which always made me feel like laughing. I nodded. It probably looked more like a curtsey bob than a head nod, I was so stiff with nerves and I don't know what. 'Sit down,' he said. 'I'll get you a coke.'

'Flash.' I thought, but I sat down. And that was it. The start and the end of everything.

Chapter 5
Norma, 1947

At 16, Norma Jackson was almost a beauty, with her wasp waist, lean limbs and curtain of raven hair. But she was damaged goods. As a child she had been shy and introspective, now she was aloof and bitter. She'd been clever, now she was calculating. The village girls were scared of her and the boys ignored her. She liked it that way.

After she left school at 15, she found employment in Allens, the village butcher's shop. It was the sort of job that most girls of her age would find distasteful. But Norma really didn't mind how many slabs of raw meat she boned and chopped, or how many rabbits she strung up. She wasn't squeamish about blood and gore. After three years of her father's nightly attentions, there was little left to love, hate or be squeamish about.

The villagers thought Norma and her father an odd pair. He was small and stout, while she was tall, slender and almost queenly in her way. You rarely saw them together, but if you did, they never spoke. Even the nosiest neighbour had long ago given up speculating about the nature of their relationship. If only the mother hadn't died in childbirth. But they'd stopped feeling sympathy for Norma when the shy but eager little girl was replaced by a woman who seemed to have too many airs and graces for her own good.

One sleety winter morning, Norma was wiping down the counter when Clive Enderbie stepped into the shop. She wiped her hands and gave him her vacant stare. He looked like a war casualty, though the war was over two years ago. Everyone knew how to spot a war casualty: they looked pale, wan and slightly brain-dead. But Norma suspected Clive was not much older than she was.

'What can I do for you?' Her questions tended to sound like challenges.

'For now, I'd like a meat pie, but I'm also looking for a job and somewhere to board, if you're asking.'

It turned out that Clive had been a 'lucky' one. He'd signed up for the army at 17 and survived the bloodbath in France. Back home in London, his luck ran out when he couldn't find a job. He wanted to get out of the city, so he'd packed his bags and set off in search of work. Quite why he had hit on this desolate coastal spot was a mystery, even to him.

Norma eyed him up and down speculatively. He was puny, with wire-rimmed spectacles and a head that reminded her of a turnip. Could he be her ticket to freedom? She couldn't imagine him in a stand-off with her father, but at least he was a man. 'There could be some farm work at our place,' she said. 'I would need to talk to my father. And we might have a spare room. It's a sort of outhouse downstairs next to the kitchen.'

Two red spots appeared on Clive's pallid cheeks. He's keen, thought Norma. Now all I need to do is to talk father around which shouldn't be too hard. Since she'd begun work in the shop, her father badly needed extra help, even if it was only casual labour. What mattered was getting Clive in as a boarder.

When she got home, Norma unwrapped two lamb cutlets she'd brought as a treat from the butchers' and put them on to sizzle. 'Supper's ready,' she called to her father when she'd assembled the cutlets and mash on plates. Once he was settled down chewing on his lamb, she plucked up courage. 'I met someone looking for work today.'

'Oh yeah,' said her father, sucking juice from his fingers.

'Yes, he'd be happy with any work he can get. I thought you could do with some extra help now I'm at the shop. And he needs to find lodgings too, so we could make a bit extra boarding out the outhouse.'

'Hmm.' Her father might sound reluctant but Norma could see he was tempted, not so much by the extra help as by the cash.

And so Clive Enderbie moved into the hastily tarted-up outhouse. The extra rent money quickly burned a hole in Norma's father's pocket and by the third week, the arrangement hit a snag. Clive, a city lad, couldn't stand the farmyard smells and noises in the outhouse, or the cold and damp.

Little did Clive know that Norma had been hard at work while he'd been labouring in the fields. Each day she'd pop home in her lunch hour and open the outhouse windows to let the icy winter wind in. Then she'd take a bucket of water and liberally splash the whitewashed walls. And finally, she'd check there was always a big bucketful of fresh dung concealed around the side of the outhouse, right under the window.

Within a fortnight, Clive said he'd had enough of the dank, smelly room and threatened to move out, confident he'd find another place in the village. 'No, no, don't do that!' said Norma. 'You can have my room upstairs instead. I don't mind swapping. Can't he, father?'

She couldn't tell if either man had picked up the heavy sarcasm she put on 'father'. And she wasn't confident her father would agree. She couldn't imagine him visiting the damp and chilly outhouse and in any case he wouldn't want to risk Clive putting two and two together. Would her father be prepared to give up his night-time visits? After all, she was used goods now, even by his standards. And the extra rent money would be a lure. Would greed outweigh his need? There was a moment's silence.

'Righto, sort it out between yourselves,' her father said. 'Make sure the rent is always a week in advance and it'll be getting on for double for the upstairs room.'

And so Norma Jackson moved to the outhouse where she could lock herself in and feel safe in the cold and damp. After three years of nightly abuse, she set herself free.

Chapter 6
Emily's Memory Book, 1978

I probably make it sound like a whirlwind romance, the sort of thing that happens in those rubbish magazines Norma reads, but it wasn't like that. What with me being a bit bolshie and Toby being shy, we took it slow.

We had so much to talk about. I'd only had two boyfriends before Toby and it was all about snogging from day one. It got boring. They'd take me to the cinema and I'd be craning my neck to watch the film while they tried to swallow my face whole!

Toby wasn't like that. He could be quite distant, which I like. He loved to talk about music and play the guitar. Punk was his thing, but you'd never know it. He always wore very simple stuff—jeans and a T-shirt—as if clothes didn't matter. No bondage trousers or metal studs. It's thanks to Toby that I stopped thinking of schoolwork as something to be endured. I could do it well and easily, but I'd been brainwashed into thinking it was boring. He put a new spin on it.

We were always arguing about Holden Caulfield in *The Catcher in the Rye*. Toby thought he was a spoilt brat. I disagreed. I could see why Holden was jaded and cynical. I thought he was angry inside and understood how that felt. It was hard to imagine Toby angry.

One day he arrived in class late. As he trundled in with his heavy backpack of books, his caramel-brown eyes sought mine. He pushed back his floppy fringe and gave me just the slightest smile. My heart did a flip, sending a warm rush through my stomach all the way to the tops of my legs. I knew this was something.

On a sweet summer afternoon, we lay under a tree in the shade on the posh part of the common, arguing about nauseating Nancy and how much influence she had on Sid Vicious and whether she really was a psycho. I thought she was fake, but in his gentle way Toby tried to explain why she was maybe a troubled soul.

'My Mum and Dad would love to meet you,' he said, out of the blue. 'How do you feel about that?' I was thrilled and scared at once. Thrilled because at last I'd get to see what life was really like inside one of those houses on the other side of the common. Scared because I knew I wouldn't fit into it. But I agreed, partly out of curiosity and partly for Toby.

That summer of 1976 was endless love and sunshine. I arrived at Toby's house on the dot of 3 p.m. and knocked on the big brass doorknocker. The door opened a crack to reveal a little girl with a halo of white-blonde hair.

'Could you be Chloe?' I asked. I'd brought her a box of Smarties which suddenly seemed all wrong. But her eyes popped out in delight when I handed them over and she hugged them to her tummy.

'Toby, it's Emily here,' she shouted up the broad staircase. Clearly Toby's sister, and probably everyone else in the family, knew all about me already. I was tempted to run away down the chequered garden path. Too late. Chloe had already danced off to find her mum. Maddy—which Toby had explained was short for Madeleine—was already at the door. Wearing an enormous butchers' block apron, she wiped her floury hands down it and tried to shake mine at the same time. Giving up, she enveloped me in a hug.

'Lovely to meet you at last, Emily. Welcome, welcome. Sorry about the floury hands. I've been trying to bake a cake, but I'm not the world's best baker. Chloe, where did you get those sweets? You know you're not allowed artificial colours. Put them away please. There's some fresh fruit on the kitchen counter.'

My first gaff. I knew I wouldn't fit. But somehow it didn't matter. I knew right away that Maddy Summerfield was the mother of my dreams. The lost mother in all the childhood stories I'd picked out at the library and read under the bedclothes at night: *Little Women, What Katy Did, A Little Princess*. Even the mum in *The Famous Five* with her spectacular picnic teas. I fell in love with Maddy's messy topknot and her dreadful home cooking and the way she talked to me, so gentle and yet direct. She had a knack of making everyone feel special, but I never got long enough to discover if it was real.

Toby came tripping down the stairs and I was steered through to the sitting room to meet Rupe, who was hiding behind the Sunday papers. Not my idea of what a proper dad should look like at all. I have these images, you see, of what families should look like. Norma, Clive and I don't match up to them. Parents should be like the ones in Enid Blyton books. Maddy was pretty close with her pinny, floury hands and gentle ways.

But Rupe didn't come near it. He looked like James Taylor, only old, with flat, straight salt-and-pepper hair hanging down from a centre parting. And he wore black-framed glasses which made him look intense. I thought he must be an ex-hippy. Definitely not like a dad.

Now the talk was all about what qualifications you need to be an architect and where my choices might lead me. Yeah, *me*. But it was also about the heatwave, the drought and what the government was doing about the falling pound. Everyone chipping in, even Chloe who wanted to know if she could have a paddling pool. Would there be enough water? This family could talk for England, as Clive would say. No wonder Toby was so quiet with me. He got more than enough talk at home.

And then, suddenly, they all had to be somewhere else. Maddy was taking Chloe to see her grandma in Finchley and Rupe was popping into the office to prepare for a case. With the final slam of the front door, a dreamy silence descended on the house. Toby took my hand. 'Come and see my space.'

It was just as I'd imagined. Scruffy. Music sheets, discs and books everywhere. Not one, but two guitars propped up in the corner alongside a tennis racquet with hardly any strings. Black and white posters of The Sex Pistols and Blondie on the walls. On the windowsill, a primary school photo of Toby with gap teeth and another of him holding a baby violin.

Apple tree branches curved around the edge of the window and when I looked out, there it was, the scene in my head. In next door's walled garden, two kids lounged on a blanket arguing over a magna doodle. Mum lay on a sunbed, a floppy straw hat over her face, while dad messed around half-heartedly in the flower border. My perfect family.

Toby turned me around and steered me towards the unmade bed.

'Your mum and dad...' I said. Toby nodded and as his hands moved gently over me, further and further upwards and downwards, it all stopped mattering. I pushed his floppy hair back from his forehead and told him, 'I'm ready'. It was the first time for both of us, but he didn't know that. I think he thought I was experienced, being as I was from the wrong side of the common.

As it turned out, it wasn't important. We learned from each other.

Chapter 7
Norma, 1951

For four years, Norma held off both her father and her lodger. By day, she cut and chopped and boned and by night she lay on her narrow bed in the outhouse, watching stars and listening to familiar farmhouse sounds.

For a while it was enough not to have to endure the nightly visits, the creaking of the floorboards, the turn of the door handle, her lumpen father covering her, the smell of supper still on his breath.

Clive grew stronger as he took on more farm work and he stopped looking like a war victim. He lost his lassitude, but it was replaced by anger. Clive was furious at the world. He was angry with the politicians who sent him off to war and didn't welcome him back. Angry with the cows because they didn't produce enough milk. And furious with Norma's father for not paying him enough.

One evening, early in 1951, it came to a head. Norma's father accused Clive of not paying his rent. Clive said he had and Norma knew this to be true. Her father was losing his memory. At supper, the two men had a face-off and Clive stormed out.

Next morning he returned for his belongings and an ultimatum for Norma: 'I'm leaving. Back to London where I belong. Come with me and marry me.' Or the unspoken: 'Stay here'.

'Give me a day to think. If I want to come with you, I'll be ready by noon tomorrow.' Norma didn't think to ask for details of what Clive had in mind in London.

She locked the outhouse door, lay down on her unmade bed and considered. The prospect of London was attractive. It would mean an escape from this deadbeat village and her abusive father. She thought of the endless days stretching ahead, working at the butchers' and coming back to her forlorn outhouse. As time passed and her father aged, the farm would go to seed and she wouldn't have the will to save it. She took a certain pleasure in imagining how he and the Farm would deteriorate if she and Clive defected.

Clive was not an especially bad man, just not a likeable one. But marriage? Could she tolerate a new wave of nightly visits from a man who was not much more appealing to her than her father? She balanced her life on the farm against a voyage into the unknown with Clive.

Next day, packed and ready, bag in hand, she met Clive on the doorstep at lunchtime. Over his shoulder, in the distance, she could see her father in a field of rape, his body bent, staring into the acid yellow flowers as if they could tell him something. He's losing it, she thought. She shut the front door without hesitation and she and Clive trundled down the narrow country lane with their cardboard suitcases to catch the branch line. Clive bought third class tickets for the GWR steam train to London.

Many hours later, as the great train rolled into Paddington station, Norma was shocked by the towering dwellings that ran along both sides of the track. It was dark now, but from the train window she could see a patchwork of illuminated rectangular windows, some with strange faces peering out at the train through the evaporating steam. At Royal Oak, she saw her first black face. Framed in the window, the man seemed to be intently watching her, cocooned in the carriage, as the train rattled by.

'Like the golliwog on the jam,' she said, turning away from the window.

Clive chuckled. 'You'll be seeing a lot more of them where we're heading. And others like them.'

Their destination was Tooting, where Clive's uncle had agreed to put them up while they sorted themselves out. It was, officially, their first night as a couple. Norma battled with a queasy sensation in the pit of her stomach. She wondered if she would be able to hold payback time off until they were officially married.

As it happened, she needn't have worried. Despite his testosterone-fuelled bouts of anger, Clive turned out to have a low sex drive. She wasn't bothered very often.

Chapter 8
Emily's Memory Book, 1978

We got very little time together. I was stupid to think it could go on forever, although for a while it looked as if it might.

I'd been working hard at school. Hanging out with Toby and his family opened my eyes to things I'd never thought possible. They encouraged me to consider staying on in the sixth form. I didn't think for one minute that Norma and Clive would be very happy about that idea. They were already dreaming about a third wage coming in.

But no one could plan anything until we got our exam results. It was like being in a time capsule. The heat beat down on the common, the trees as still as soldiers. Toby and I made love in my stifling attic, sometimes at dusk in a corner of the common and twice in the bath at his place. We listened to music, swigged pop and argued over *The Magus* (I loved it, he said it was pretentious-moi)! We both knew a big change was coming.

On the day of the exam results, I went along to school to see the list. I went straight to the Es in the alphabet. When I finally found Enderbie, I thought they'd got it wrong: I had a top grade in every single one of my 10 subjects. I was elated, but also weirdly anxious. It was great getting these results, but what on earth would I do with them? Looking down the column, I found Toby's. What I saw made me feel sick. He had nine top grades all right, but he'd dropped a grade in his top subject, English Literature. How could that be?

As I skirted back around the common, I was on a rollercoaster, feeling bad for Toby. In helping me, he must have picked up some of my way-out ideas. Like Hamlet being a really young person—not much more than a teenager like us—rather than a noble prince of Denmark. Toby must have listened to what I said and used some of it, while all the time it was me that was supposed to be learning from him.

We'd agreed to meet that evening on the common. It was getting towards dusk and I saw Toby before he saw me. This was always a treat. I loved looking at him when he didn't know he was being looked out. He was sitting cross-legged, head bowed, trying to read though the light was fading fast.

'Toby, I'm so sorry.'

His head jerked up. 'Why?'

'Well, your English Lit. You dropped a grade. You should be the one with the top grade, not me. I don't get it.'

Toby stood up and cupped his hands around my face. 'Emily, we're celebrating. Look what *you* did, what a way you've come. Dropping one grade isn't going to change my life. But not dropping a single grade could change yours.'

'But all that silly stuff I came out with about Hamlet. You didn't put any of it in your answer to the Hamlet question, did you?' Tears filled my eyes. 'I'm never going to have an opinion about a character in a book again. Well, I'm not going to say it even if I think it.'

'Emily, you think *you're* to blame for my single dropped grade. That's crazy stuff. Actually, I didn't even choose the Hamlet question. Did you?'

'No. I chose another because I thought my Hamlet theory was so off-the-wall that I'd fail.'

'Probably a good thing. If you'd answered it, they might have had to invent a super-super top grade just for you.' Both of us were laughing now.

That evening, when we made love it was more intense than before, lying under the stars on a carpet of tinder-dry grass. We clung to each other fiercely. It felt almost like anger, but I knew it wasn't. It was simply that slow and sweet was no longer enough, we were too hungry. Love and hate. So close, I think. Like twins.

Back home, Norma was at the door wanting to know where I'd been. 'It's dark.' Not 'Where have you been?' or 'We were worried.' They don't normally fuss about my comings and goings.

'I went to see a friend. Her family invited me over for a pizza to celebrate our results.' I nearly laughed as I said it. The idea of me, stuck-up Emily Enderbie the loner, getting invited out for a family pizza was pretty far out.

'What result?' Norma had forgotten. Naturally.

'My exams. I got top grade, an A, in all 10.'

'Well done.'

I was pleased she'd said it and was about to try a small hug, but she looked as if the words had filled up her mouth with pebbles.

'So you won't be needing anymore schooling. That's good news, isn't it? We'll start looking at the job ads tomorrow.'

Silently, I trundled up the steps to my attic room, lay down on the bed and cried into my pillow.

Next day, I told Norma and Clive I was going to school to collect my belongings. Then something happened that turned out to be a game changer. I was rummaging around in my locker, stashing old exercise books into my duffel, when our English teacher Mr McFadden walked past. He paused when he saw me.

'Great results, Emily. Look forward to seeing you in sixth form next year. You'll be signing up for Eng Lit, I assume?'

I felt dull and tired and tears were welling up again, making my eyelids itchy and full. 'I'm not coming back, Mr McFadden. My parents won't allow it.'

'Why?' His eyebrows shot up.

'They need me to get a job and they don't think schoolwork will get me anywhere.'

Mr McFadden muttered something under his breath. It sounded like *is this the second half of the twentieth century or what?* But then he seemed to pull himself together. 'Do you want to stay on, Emily?' He fished a greyish hanky out of his trouser pocket and handed it to me. I was crying properly by then.

'I really do.'

'Then leave it with me. I'll see what we can do.' And he strode off on his bow legs, trousers flapping around his ankles. Two days later, sitting cross-legged on my bed looking at job ads, I heard the bell ring and a bit of a kerfuffle in the hall. Hanging over the banisters, I saw the top of our headmaster's shiny bald pate. Unmistakable! Norma shooed me back upstairs with one of her daggers-at-dawn looks and they disappeared into the front room. They were in there for a very long time. When I heard the head's bumbling voice on the doorstep, I crept back to the banister.

'Come down,' commanded Norma, slamming the front door on the headmaster's back. She guided me into the front room and told me to sit. Clive was in his favourite chair in the bay window, legs akimbo and gnome-head nodding along to everything she said.

'We are going to allow you to remain at school.' Norma looked as if it pained her to say it. I nearly jumped up and threw my arms around her, but one look at her face told me it wasn't a good idea.

'These are the conditions. You'll have a Saturday job, of course, and you will contribute all your earnings to the household budget. We also expect you to get an after-school job for a few hours each day.'

'But when will I do schoolwork?'

Norma can look pretty forbidding when she wants to. She drew herself up to her full height and began to speak a bit like the Queen. 'You will have Sundays, of course. Perhaps this is the moment to think about all the time you are wasting with that lovesick boy of yours. In any case, I'm not especially interested in how you spend your time as long as you stick to the conditions.'

What more can I say? Reader, I agreed to everything. Weekday evenings and Saturdays, I would sit at a supermarket checkout ringing up fish fingers and angel delight and marmite and tinned peaches and loading them into bags for hungry customers, while dreaming of Kafka and James Joyce and Sylvia Plath. Deep into the night, working in my attic bedroom by my little Woolworths reading lamp, I would structure essays, deconstruct poetry, struggle with syntax. And Sunday was just for Toby and me. I couldn't have wished for more.

Chapter 9
Norma, 1960

Norma Enderbie sat on a park bench, legs stretched out, contemplating her bloated ankles. How had she come so far without falling pregnant? She'd assumed it would never happen. This year, she'd turn 30 and though there was still time, she and Clive slept in separate beds now and she was rarely visited by him in the night—only when he'd had too much drink. In which case he couldn't perform anyway.

Giggling to herself, Norma brought to mind another reason for one of Clive's nightly visitations: her famous lemon meringue pie. In the early days of marriage, she would bake them for him as a special treat. A lemon meringue pie on the supper table would prompt wild promises from him. Norma had secured several new frocks, a budgie in a cage and even one of the new fridges, in the warm afterglow of a lemon meringue pie. The pie baking had to stop, though, when Clive began to celebrate his mealtime afterglow with something more physical, urgent and invasive.

A woman walked by, pushing one of those enormous prams favoured by the Royal family. Norma doubted that even lemon meringue pie would get her one of those. Tottering slightly in her court heels, the woman peered down at Norma: 'Not long to go now.'

She wasn't going to move on until she'd got a response, that was clear. It pained Norma to give one. Other women were so nosy, had they nothing better to do? 'Any minute now, actually,' she spat out. That should put Nosy Parker off. Blood and gore were clearly not her style.

'Where do you live?' asked Nosy Parker, taking three steps back and glancing at her watch.

'Up there,' Norma jerked her head in a vague direction encompassing both dreary Elm Avenue and the more salubrious Carisbrooke Close. 'Actually, I should be getting back right now.' As she staggered upright, she felt more fluid draining into her bloated ankles. When she looked up again, the woman was gone, tap tapping in her high heel shoes along the tarmac path in the direction of the common.

Lumbering up Elm Avenue under a beating sun, Norma considered once more her feelings about the coming baby. A few years back, she'd begun to believe she would never be a mother. Mostly, it was a relief. Deep inside herself, Norma understood that she had a limited capacity to love. Many years later, with help from her beloved women's weekly problem page, she would begin to see that the deadness she carried around like a dark cloak didn't need to define her. She would recognise herself as a victim, rather than a woman unable to love. For the time being, she kept her daily anger and despair closely 33raped up inside. Even Clive would never know.

She'd do her best by this child. She would feed and clothe it. She knew that mothers were supposed to be madly in love with their babies, but she didn't know how love was supposed to feel. Maybe it would feel like a warm rush in the pit of her stomach, or the sun coming out from behind a cloud. Maybe she *would* feel it, but she wasn't counting her chickens.

As she edged into her narrow hallway, Norma felt a stab of pain in her belly and a burst of warm liquid down her leg. On the pink and black lino, she saw a widening pool of water. Like it or not, the baby was on its way. Norma had rehearsed the drill in her head many times over, but she was terrified. How on earth would this massive lump be removed without ripping her apart? After towelling herself dry, Norma hobbled next door and, ignoring the bell, banged loudly with her fist on the door.

It opened a crack and Marcia Grimes' nose peeked out. A dough-faced woman in a stained housecoat, Marcia had no particular affection for Norma, but knew about doing the right thing.

'Okay, I'll get the midwife.' She quickly removed her housecoat, smearing her face with a gash of lipstick and grabbing her house keys. 'You go home and try to relax.'

As Norma watched Marcia's ample behind swaying down the street towards the T junction, she experienced a stab of pure terror. How long would Marcia take? Would she find the midwife? What if the baby started coming out before they got back? But she did as she was told. Safely back on her own bed, she groaned, rubbing the mound of her abdomen which was lurching around like wobbly jelly. The pain settled into rhythmic waves. Norma counted to 50, then 42 between each wave—they were getting closer together.

She thought about Clive, safely closeted in his workplace. Men! She'd heard that expectant fathers sometimes hovered nearby when their babies were born. Some even dared to enter the birth room, although they were generally shooed briskly out. Clive had shown not a speck of interest in being there and Norma was glad of it. As if she didn't have enough to deal with.

The atmosphere changed abruptly with the arrival of the midwife and Marcia Grimes, who was desperate for a peek. Norma felt she had been riding a rough sea on a solitary raft, with no one and nothing in sight. Suddenly, it was all hustle, bustle and no-nonsense.

'Open your legs, dearie,' snapped the midwife, arms akimbo.

Norma had removed her soaking knickers after her waters broke and not thought to replace them. Did the midwife know she was not wearing knickers? Clearly this wasn't an issue. Without hesitation, the midwife knelt at the end of the bed and prised Norma's reluctant legs apart. Desperately trying to hold on to what was left of her dignity, she hitched her frock down. With one hand, the midwife jerked it back up again. In the other hand, she brandished a razor. 'What's that for?' Norma asked.

'To keep baby and everything nice and clean and hygienic.' The midwife was now busy shaving into Norma's pubic hair. That done to her satisfaction, she peered into her insides, feeling around with a plastic-gloved hand.

'We need to get her to hospital and quick.' The midwife turned to Marcia. 'Do you have a neighbour with a telephone? Can you find someone and call for an ambulance?' Marcia scurried towards the door, pleased to be part of the action but also relieved to be out of it.

'What's wrong?' Norma couldn't believe it was her voice. It sounded so faint and far away.

'Baby's all the wrong way and the cord's around its neck too, by the looks of it.'

Norma felt hot tears stinging her eyes. She'd never even asked for this baby.

'It'll be okay, dearie,' soothed the midwife. 'You just need to be in hospital.' She went downstairs to the kitchen and returned with a damp flannel.

Sitting on the edge of the bed, she dabbed Norma's brow and her cheeks. Then she took Norma's hand in her own large and raw one and stroked it calmly. Norma couldn't help noticing that it was the same hand, minus the plastic glove, that had been up her insides a few moments ago. Every now and again, the midwife anxiously consulted her watch.

Norma was grateful for the rest of her life that she remembered almost nothing about being carried down her narrow staircase, slotted into an ambulance and jolted through the city streets with the claxon clanging. But she will always remember the poking and prodding and pushing, her body reduced to a vessel in a sea of pain.

She woke to a dull ache in the pit of her stomach and somewhere way off, a baby crying. A smiley young nurse in a starched white cap bent over her and gently stroked her hair from her eyes. 'You're with us. Good. Tea? And of course, the best thing. You have a little girl. A healthy little girl. Would you like to see her?' Norma shrugged herself down the bed and turned her face to the wall. Go away, she begged silently.

But the nurse was not to be put off. Minutes later, she appeared at the end of the bed with a white cellular bundle snuggled in her arms. 'Your husband's on his way. Let's introduce you to baby.'

Norma peered through a haze of sweat and tears at the little face encased in blanket. Same olive skin, same shock of black hair, same neat nose and little mouth with a cupid's bow. It was the image of her and it had the same aura or neediness about it that it hadn't yet learnt to disguise.

'Take it away. Maybe later. I'm tired now.'

'But wouldn't you like to hold her? You could give her a little cuddle. You could try to feed her.'

'I shan't be feeding. Please give her a bottle if that's what's needed. And don't disturb me. Tell my husband I'm asleep. I'm so tired.'

Norma turned her face to the wall and drifted into a world where there were no babies and nobody to make demands of her when she really had very little to give.

Chapter 10
Emily's Memory Book, 1978

I'd always been 'the swot' or 'the weirdo', but in the sixth form things began to change. Most of the kids were swots—they acted cool, but you could tell they wanted to do well. Some were there for a fun ride and a few had parents who'd forced them to stay on at school. But they were the minority.

I was on a mission to discover longer words and bigger concepts, although I'd no idea how I was going to use them. I guessed I'd still end up in Woolworths because that's what I was destined for. University was out of the question: Norma and Clive just wouldn't buy it. What I didn't bargain for was ending up as a single mum with not one, but two, small babies.

One morning I was late for school. I'd worked overtime at the shop the night before and then stayed up late working on an essay. I felt so sick it was hard to get out of bed. Thinking it must have been Norma's disgusting fish pie leftovers, I stumbled down the attic stairs and bumped into Clive on the landing. He was wearing his string vest and looked all pink and raw from his shave, a bit like a peeled prawn. It made me feel sicker.

'What's up with you? You look like death warmed up,' he said. I nearly vomited in his face. Once I'd managed to wash and dress and get into the outdoor air, the sickness began to wear off. Instead, I was ravenously hungry. For the next week, I was either sick or starving and my body seemed to be taking on a life of its own. I dragged myself out of bed later and later each day. Running for the school bus, I noticed my boobs were hurting.

It's hard to believe all this stuff happened little more than a year ago. I was naïve. It didn't occur to me that I might be pregnant. One of Norma's favourite complaints about me is that I have 'too much imagination' and for once she may have been right. I was overcome with fear that I had a terrible illness that was making me tired, hungry-sick and achy all over. I must have cancer, I thought. I would lie flat out in the bath, stare at my near-perfect body floating below the water and imagine it riddled inside with cancer. At night, I tossed and turned thinking of how far I'd come, only to have it all taken from me.

Toby noticed the difference in me. 'Emily, what is it?' he'd ask me gently as I turned away from him. I loved him so much, but I didn't want him to touch my aching boobs or stroke my diseased body.

Three weeks after I fell ill, I began to vomit. I was just about to go off to school. I retched loudly and when I raised my head from the toilet bowl, dizzy and depleted, I knew I had to tell someone there was something wrong. It wasn't going to go away on its own.

Norma was stationed outside the bathroom door, toothbrush in hand, waiting impatiently for me to finish. The look she gave me was bleak, even by her standards.

'Now you've gone and done it,' she said through her tight-lipped grimace.

'Done what?'

'Gone and got yourself up the duff by the sound of it.'

I must have looked blank. 'Pregnant? Baby?' she snapped. 'Have you been a naughty girl?'

It all fell into place. Toby had been using rubbers, but sometimes, when we got too caught up in the moment, we forgot. I didn't know whether to be relieved that I probably wasn't dying, or terrified of what the future might hold.

'Wh-what do I do?' I stuttered.

For a moment, I thought I saw a fleeting look of sympathy cross Norma's face. I wanted to run to her, hide my face in her lap. I wanted her to be a mum. For a split second, it felt like it could happen. Then she pushed me gently away. 'I'll book you an appointment with the doctor,' she said.

The surgery is in a tall, grey Victorian villa on the South Circular Road. From the outside, it looks forbidding, but the reception area is cheerful with magazines, bright plastic toys and posters on the walls reminding mums about baby clinics and 10 Reasons Why Your Baby Needs to See the Doctor. My stomach did a weird flip.

Sitting beside me, Norma was buried deep in a True Romance (free-magazine bonanza time for her). Opposite, a little boy with dirty knees sat on his mother's lap and picked his nose. An old lady, dressed in beige from head to toe, sat in the corner jerking her head up every now and again like a bird.

Norma stood stock-still in the corner of the surgery while a kindly doctor with wild grey curly hair examined me. It didn't talk long to confirm the news. But there was more to come. 'Looking at you, I think there's just a chance there's more than one,' said the doctor as he retreated from between my open legs.

'What, you mean, two?' snapped Norma, alarmed. If it hadn't been so tragic, I would have laughed. What did she think he meant, that I had an army of six in there!

'Possibly twins,' said the doctor, handing us a note for a referral to the hospital down the road in Tooting. 'They'll be able to confirm and can give you a care plan.' He gave me a nod and a wink as Norma and I almost collided in our rush to the surgery door. 'Bad luck,' he said. 'Rather too early in life for you, huh? But remember every baby is a blessing, even if it doesn't seem so right now.'

Norma managed to hold on to silent-but-deadly mode until we were safely behind the front door of number 101. 'What-were-you-thinking-off?' she spluttered in my face. 'Who was it? Was it that skinny kid you've been loping around with? The one that looks like butter wouldn't melt? Moons around like a sick calf?'

I never thought faster, or harder, in my life. I couldn't quite believe what came out of my mouth. 'No, it wasn't him. It could have been any one of a number of the boys at school. I really like it, sex that is, and I didn't want to stop. They did use rubbers though…'

Norma stared as if she was seeing me for the first time. A strong, rebellious, defiant me—not someone either of us had met before. Maybe a bit more like her, someone feisty she could admire. 'Go to your room and stay there,' she ordered. 'I shall need to tell your father. Do not leave your room until I say so.'

A glint came into her eye: 'Of course, you know this means the end of your schooling.' I nodded dumbly, but I kept my chin up. The new Emily. Experience was changing me so fast that I hardly recognised myself from one moment to the next.

Late that evening, towards midnight, I did something risky. I waited until I was sure Norma and Clive were fast asleep. That's easy, because Clive snores like a pig and Norma does the odd whinny in her sleep, catching her breath as if it's her last. I took the torch from my wardrobe, threw on my jeans, sweater and shoes and tiptoed downstairs. Toby and I had a plan. If ever I needed him urgently in the middle of the night, I would cross the common, creep down the side of his house through the garden gate that was always left open and flash the torch directly at his bedroom window. As the rest of the family sleep at the front of the house, we judged this fairly safe. In any case, it wasn't something we ever seriously expected to do.

It was a breezy night on the Common. The old oak tree we'd laid under that summer rustled and billowed in the wind. My torch lit up the way ahead as I kept a wary eye out for sinister shapes in the blackness, but I stuck to the concrete cross path and soon I was at Toby's. I turned off my torch and trod stealthily across the wide gravel drive and down through the side gate to the garden, picking up a handful of gravel and stuffing it in my jacket pocket.

In the still garden, I beamed my torch up at Toby's window. Nothing. I took the gravel from my pocket and hurled it at the windowpane. A moment later, Toby's face appeared, white in the darkness. 'Emily, wait right there.' It gave me a pang that he didn't even question me or why I was there, waking him in the middle of the night. He was always just there for me. But I summoned up my resolve. I tried to think of myself as the new Emily: the one with less to give and more to take, with a harder edge and tougher, shinier surfaces. Like Norma.

I knew I had to get in first. Before he came to me or held me. 'Toby, I'm pregnant,' I said. His expression didn't shut down, not for a second. He looked excited and scared and full of questions, all at once. He opened his arms, but I stayed rooted to the spot.

'It's almost certainly not yours. Even if it is yours, it has to end here. I'm not ready for this. I'm too young.'

I begged him not to tell anyone and never to contact me again. I made him swear to it. I told him it wasn't fair. He almost certainly wasn't the one who got me pregnant, being around me would only cost him extra pain and would make life difficult for me too. I spelt it out in so many ways. Toby sat on the wet grass with his head in his hands. He didn't look at me, or try to make me change my mind. I must have been that forceful. I thought of Norma. I am, after all, her daughter.

Dear reader, it was the biggest act of love of my life. I want for Toby all the things I will never have now. Oxford, the world. Babies born in the right time and place with the right person, who will love him and be loved back.

When I turned my back on Toby, I walked out on Maddy, Rupe and Chloe too. The closest thing to family I'd got. I'm looking out of my window. It's sheeting rain today, kids are jumping in the puddles and cars are splashing up mud on Commonside Road. I could bundle the twins up, put them in the Moses basket, shelter them inside my big plastic raincoat and struggle across the damp common. Couldn't I? Would they welcome us over there? Would they take in the two babies that I can't seem to care for? It's not going to happen, anyway. The Summerfields closed up their foursquare house and left months ago. And it's best if I don't know where.

Toby Summerfield is the love of my life, but he's a closed book to me now. I have vowed never, ever, to tell him he is the father of my twins. Bear witness to this, dear reader. He will never know. God knows it's been hard, but he'll be at university soon and he'll forget. I don't think they take boys who get girls pregnant at Oxford University. But I'll never forget how everything felt, for that very short time I loved and was loved in return.

Chapter 11
Toby, 1978

Toby is gazing across the rooftops of Muswell Hill from the sanctuary of his new attic bedroom. It's not unlike Emily's attic space in Tooting, though the view's better. He's sitting cross-legged on the bed, headphones on, listening to an old Joni Mitchell track, *I Wish I Had a River*. Punk used to be his thing and he still loves the crashing energy of it. But he's become more reflective since losing Emily. Ah, how he longs for her, her quirkiness, her mane of shiny black hair tickling his face.

His mum runs up the stairs and bangs hard on his door. 'Toby, breakfast. French toast.' It's his favourite. Toby sighs. He won't be around much longer for her to make French toast for him. He'll be gone, to Oxford. He loves them all, his mum, his dad and Chloe. But he's changed. French toast and playing hide and seek in the back garden to amuse Chloe doesn't do it for him anymore.

Rupe has started asking him out for the odd pint, which he loves because he's always interested to hear his dad's take on the world. But the one person he really wants—needs—is Emily. And he can't have her. *Why* can't he have her? 'Shut up,' Toby tells himself silently as he pulls off his headphones.

Downstairs, it's the usual Sunday morning breakfast chaos. Toby finds a plate with only a few crumbs on it that Chloe's left around, grabs his breakfast and steers a course between his mum at the stovetop and his dad who's hogging the breakfast bar with his Sunday newspapers as usual.

'Morning darling,' says Maddy tentatively. Rupe grunts in his direction and Chloe offers him a high-five, which he declines.

Maddy is talking to Rupe about a case she's working on. 'The CPS are dragging their heels,' she complains. 'I need to know a little more about this guy before I can make any recommendations.' She drones on, sounding indignant, but Rupe is clearly more interested in the falling pound and Chloe has disappeared under the table to play dens with her doll.

'Why did we move?' asks Toby. It's a question that's been going round and round in his head for weeks. Maddy stops talking abruptly. Rupe peers over the top of his newspaper. Only Chloe carries on with what she's doing, putting dolly to bed under a grubby table napkin.

Rupe looks at Maddy who looks back at Rupe. 'Well darling,' she says. 'The schools are better for Chloe in north London. And the house is easier to run. And it'll be easier to get to see you in Oxford…' she trails off.

'That's rubbish,' says Toby.

Rupe looks at his son intently. 'Why is it rubbish?' he asks gently.

'It's because of Emily. You wanted to get me away from Emily.'

Maddy takes his free hand in hers and rubs it gently, a gesture he finds annoying even though he loves his mum to bits. 'That's not entirely true, Toby,' she says.

'What does "entirely" mean?' It comes out sarcastic. Toby is hardly ever sarcastic. He shocks himself by the way he sounds.

'It means we wanted to live in north London because of the schools and because it's easier for Oxford. But we were also concerned for you,' Maddy adds lamely.

Toby thinks of all those times he spent skirting the common looking for Emily. Summer evenings, the sun a hot golden ball hanging over the trees. The times he took a blanket, a book and his headphones and sat huddled on the grass, close enough to Emily's house to detect comings and goings, but not so close it would be weird. Maybe his mum had spotted him from her bedroom window? Maybe it did look weird…and compulsive. He doesn't go to the common now. Instead, he sits in his bedroom, where Blondie gazes down petulantly at him from the wall and his guitars lie untouched in a corner.

'You didn't want me to be with Emily because she's from the wrong side of the common,' he spits out. It's been welling up in him a long time and strangely he feels better now it's out in the open.

Maddy looks shocked. 'Of course not, Toby. We'd never think that. It's just that you were—are—so young and Emily was your first girlfriend. And to be honest, she let you down rather badly, didn't she?'

'She could have treated you better,' adds Rupe. 'She could at least have given you an explanation as to why she dropped you like a stone. You're young, Toby and so is she. But we think you deserve more.'

Toby is still haunted by the look in Emily's eyes that last night. She'd loved him, he knows it. He'd been drifting off to sleep when he heard the gravel hitting the window. At first he'd thought it was the branches of the apple tree in a gust of wind. Then he'd seen the beam of the torch. He'd pulled on some clothes and crept downstairs through the kitchen into the dark garden. Emily had been acting strangely for a while. She didn't want to be kissed or hugged, or even touched really.

Toby recalls Emily standing in the middle of the damp lawn. She looked messed up. 'What's up? You're scaring me!' he'd said.

He strode across the lawn, ready to gather her in a big hug, when she blurted out: 'Toby, I'm pregnant.' He'd stopped in his tracks, struggling to come to terms with what was happening. He didn't know whether to be elated—*could* he be a dad at his age? Or scared—what would happen to Oxford and his dreams for the future? He did know one thing: he would always be there for Emily. But then came the five words that had rocked his world.

'It's almost certainly not yours. I'm sorry, there've been a few boys. You've been lovely. We've been good together. But even if I knew it was yours, it would have to end here, this relationship. I'm not ready for it. I'm too young. Please don't tell your family. Let's keep it between us. I don't want them to think badly of me.'

'This can't be for real,' he'd said. 'You don't mean it.' He'd pulled her into him, held her tight and tipped up her chin so he could look right into her eyes. All he could see there was sadness and confusion. This wasn't the face of a girl who'd cheated on him.

But she'd struggled out of his arms and made a space between them. Now there was something else in her expression: a hint of determination that was almost ruthless and hit him like a shard of ice.

'I'm so so sorry, Tobe. But I won't be coming back to school. I don't want to see you again, ever. It's over. Please don't try to get in touch with me.' She turned away from him and walked fast towards the garden gate, plucking anxiously at her jacket. She didn't look back.

Rooted to the spot, he watched until she faded into the blackness at the end of the lawn. He curses himself for this. Why didn't he run after her, stop her?

Why, even now, doesn't he hop on a tube, go to her house, bang on the door and demand to speak to her? This is the start of Toby's lifetime conviction that he lacks courage. But, years later, he will recognise that there was a little worm of something else in his lack of fight for Emily. He didn't dare to disturb the universe. His universe. His glittering future.

Toby drags himself back to the present. Maddy is plucking at her ring finger, her nervous habit. Rupe has his face in his hands. Mercifully, Chloe is still talking to her dolls under the table. Toby doesn't know how to tell them that he feels angry and sad and lost. So instead, he adopts what will become the habit of a lifetime. He puts a spin on it: 'You're right. We were too young. And now I've got Oxford coming up. Oxford here I come!' He punches the air in anger, mixed with resignation. He hopes they don't notice that he's broken inside.

Chapter 12
Julia Howard, 1978

Upstairs in her sunny study, Julia is working on illustrations for a new series of children's picture books when she hears the phone ring persistently down in the hall. She sighs. Working at home is hard, with constant distractions. Even before the morning begins, she feels compelled to clear up the breakfast things, make the bed, put out the garbage and load up the washing machine. With a deadline looming, she's promised herself not the answer the phone until at least mid-day.

The phone stops abruptly, but by now she needs a break. Tripping down the bare wood stairs, she pauses to remind herself once again. This house is hers. Or hers and Sean's, of course. Not that it's anything particularly grand, just a knocked-around-the-edges Edwardian terrace. But oh my God, does she love it!

They found it quite by chance one wintry day. They'd been out walking on the Heath, planning their joint future. From the front, Number 10 Rose Garden Walk looked as if it was winking at them, enticing them in. Tiny square panes of coloured glass in the wooden door glinted in the sunshine. They never thought they'd get it, but they struck lucky with an injection of extra cash from both sets of parents.

Julia loves the long sitting room with its big sash windows, stripped floors and ancient fireplace. She even tolerates the tumbledown kitchen, although she's itching to get rid of the Formica cupboards and counters, real fifties stuff.

Filling the house is their biggest challenge. Every room looks slightly under-furnished—years later, Julia will remember this and shake her head at the clutter they went on to acquire. She knows there's one way to fill up a house quickly, but it hasn't happened for them. Julia is painfully aware that their likelihood of having a baby is closing down.

She sits on a packing case in the bay window, sipping her mug of tea and wondering what Sean's thinking. Now it's confirmed he's the problem, not her, they don't talk much about it. Though Julia would deny that she thinks of Sean as 'the problem', he is the one with a low sperm count.

But she loves Sean, she does. Nothing alters that. She imagines him in his lecture theatre, strutting back and forth, imparting knowledge to students who, for the most part, adore him. Over the past few years, she's been in danger of seeing him more as a provider of sperm than a well-loved husband. She never ceases to ask herself, why. Why him? Why them?

Something that attracts her to Sean, ironically, is his look of virility. With his nut-brown hair, ruddy complexion and long, skinny legs, he reminds her of a racehorse. Sean's good friend Joe looks wimpish by comparison, but he and his partner Cora have already managed to produce two under-fives.

Julia looks at her watch—it's only noon so she has several hours to blast on with her work before Sean gets back. As a freelance, it's so much easier to get on when the house in empty. Even Sean mooching around downstairs is a distraction. So how on earth would she manage with a baby?

She's putting the final touches to an illustration depicting a small blonde boy and a little girl with ebony curls playing with a beach ball in a sunlit garden. The family dog—with suitably bright eyes and floppy ears—looks on. She gazes at her work and realises she's just drawn her own fantasy, children and dogs filling her life. The phone rings again, but she ignores it, caught in her own dreams which had once seemed fairly achievable but now feel fragile and achingly out of reach.

Why does she have this overwhelming need to be secure, surrounded by family, friends and four sturdy walls, when so many of her friends are busy throwing off the shackles of conventional life? When she had such a sunny, uneventful childhood herself? Julia thinks she knows. She does something she often finds herself doing when she is between illustrations, or alone in the house and reflecting. It's a reminder of who she is, her real place in the universe.

The phone trills again, eight rings this time. Julia ignores it, opens the bottom drawer of her dresser and takes out a large, well-worn buff envelope. Inside are pages of handwritten script and a sepia photograph, tattered around the edges. She perches on the side of the bed and begins to read, once again, the words that shaped her childhood.

Chapter 13
Julia, 1959

Julia grew up in a large, draughty and comfortably shabby house in North London, not far from the busy North Circular Road. It was a tight little family unit: Julia, her younger brother Peter and her parents. For Julia, it was a carefree childhood. Her father Ernest was kindly, a little distant, but that was because he had an important job to do in the city. Her mother Sara did all the things that mothers are meant to do. When Julia fell off her first bicycle and grazed both knees, Sara was there to administer 'magic' lotion and dry her tears. She was at the finishing line at Julia's first school sports day and won the Egg and Spoon race. She was there to comfort and console when toys got lost, or friends didn't want to play, or shadows in the curtains turned into monsters in the middle of the night.

Sometimes Sara seemed to withdraw into herself and that was generally when she was busy with her writing. She would disappear into her tiny study overlooking the garden and the children were discouraged from interrupting unless they had a solid reason. It was a ramshackle room, fusty with old books and Julia didn't need much encouragement to stay out.

Julia and Peter would play for hours in their overgrown garden—neither parent was a keen gardener. Sometimes Sara would take both children on a day trip to London. They'd pick up pastries just out of the oven from Grodzinski's bakery down the road, then board the underground at Golders Green to emerge at exciting places like the Zoo or the Science Museum. Or they'd head up the hill to the Heath, filling a basket with picnic treats at the deli on the way. Then there was school and ballet and swimming. Life was full and it wasn't until Julia was nine that she started comparing her family with the families of her friends.

Her loss of faith in her small, secure universe began the day her friend Hannah announced that she was going on a family holiday to Devon.

'Where's Devon?' Julia asked Hannah.

'Well, we're going to Salcombe actually,' explained Hannah, who wasn't entirely clear about the location of Devon although they'd done the British Isles in geography.

'Where's Salcombe then?'

'It's the seaside. Well actually, it's not real seaside because you can see land on the other side of the estuary. But there are lots of beaches and there are boats to take you across and anywhere you want to go,' explained Hannah.

'It sounds fun…' Julia had never been to the seaside—for some reason her mother wasn't keen—so she decided to change tack. 'Who's going?'

'Oh, loads of us, all the family. Mum, Dad, Gran and Grandpa, both sets of aunties and uncles and my cousins of course.' Hannah started counting on her fingers. 'I think 12?'

Julia had always felt a little superior to Hannah because of having a brother, despite how irritating Peter could be. This changed things. Hannah had more than enough relatives to make up for one small brother. In the old days, Julia would have gone running straight to her mother and asked why Hannah had such a big family when there was only the four of them. But instinct told her to hold back. In any case, she was getting too big to keep running to her mother with questions.

But she did begin to notice odd things. Family photographs, for instance. There were plenty of Peter and herself, but no cousins or aunties or uncles. Neither her mother nor her father seemed to have any relatives at all Her mother had Oma and Opa of course, but no brothers, sisters, aunties, uncles, or even the odd cousin. Surely most people had a cousin, at the very least. Every Sunday afternoon, promptly at 3 p.m., Hannah's grandparents arrived at their family home for tea. She liked to boast that there were at least 20 of them, all crammed into the tiny front parlour. Julia thought it might get a bit of a bore, week in, week out. But a cousin or two, now that would be something else. Especially a girl cousin.

Shortly before Julia's tenth birthday, she came home from school with a project. 'You'll need help from your parents with this, but everyone should learn as much as they can about where they came from,' said her teacher as she handed it out to the class. The task was to create a family tree, with as many names, dates, photographs and little memories as you could muster.

Finally Julia had the excuse she needed to ask her parents where her relatives had gone. Had they all had a terrible row and never spoken again? Or were they swept away in an epidemic which only her parents and grandparents had survived? Julia felt ready to find out more, even if it was bad. One afternoon after school, she tapped quietly on her mother's study door.

'Mummy, can I come in? I need to ask you some things to help me with my school project.'

'Come in Julia.' As Julia pushed the door open, she was struck by her mother's pose. A bundle of paper lay on Sara's desk but the top was on the pen and she didn't appear to have been writing for some time. Instead she was gazing out of the window, her face gaunt in the late afternoon light. Her dark blonde hair, which usually sat on the top of her head in a neat bun, fell across one shoulder in a fat plait.

'What can I do for you?' Sara's tone was gentle, but somehow not as welcoming as Julia would have liked.

'I have a project, Mummy,' she said. 'It's a Family Tree. We have to fill in as much as we can about our family history and we need to get help from our parents. I know it's your writing time, but I need to get started,' she finished lamely.

'Need, need—what do you know about need?' muttered Sara under her breath. But her smile was kind. 'I don't think I can help you.'

Julia didn't know what to say. Why couldn't her mother help? Had there been such a big family row that she couldn't bring herself to talk about them? Had she been adopted or run away? 'Well, shall I ask Daddy then? I do need to know. Hannah's got pictures, but there aren't any pictures of our relatives. What shall I tell them at school...' her voice trailed off.

'Julia, come here.' Sara took her daughter in her arms pressing her face into Julia's neck. When she released Julia, her cheeks were streaked with tears. She set her daughter down on what she called her casting couch and went to the bureau. From the bottom drawer, she drew out a big envelope containing some of her writing and a sepia photograph. 'I was just 11 when it happened. You're nearly 10 now, old enough to know.' She handed the photograph to Julia.

'This is your family. We don't have pictures or records for Daddy, but this was my family.'

Julia stared at the faces in the picture, which had been taken on a beach. Two older people, rather stout, looked like they could be grandparents. Julia was struck by the four youngish grown-ups, two men and two women. They looked like people in old newsreels about the war she'd seen at Hendon Cinema when she was taken to *The King and I*. They were all laughing at the camera as if someone told them to say cheese. Two of them were wrapped in a hug as if they couldn't bear to let each other go. Then there was a young boy, the sort Julia dreamt about, when she thought about boys, with sharp cheekbones and a crinkly smile.

'But Mummy, is that you?' she asked, pointing to a little girl crouched at the front of the group, face daubed in ice cream.

Her mother sighed. 'Yes, that is me'. She pointed to the older couple. 'Here are your great grandparents. And those two canoodling are of course my parents who would have been your grandparents. This is my aunt Lotte and my Uncle Lars and their son Pieter, my cousin.'

'But where are they now, Mummy? Did you have a quarrel with them? They can't all be dead. Pieter isn't much older than you.'

'I'm going to give you a story I wrote before you were born, child,' said Sara. She opened the bottom drawer of her writing desk and pulled out a folder with handwritten sheets inside. Turning to Julia, she said: 'I want you to take it away and read it carefully. When you have done so, come to me and ask as many questions as you need. I will try to answer them. This is my story and now it's yours too.'

Chapter 14
Sara Kaplinski's Story, 1941

Sunday is Sara's day for remembering. She goes to her tallboy, removes the sepia photograph and takes it to the window where there's more light. It's creased and faded, but each member of her family is still visible. There are Oma and Opa, with their kindly but rather heavy Dutch faces, reclining in their stripy deckchairs. Mama and Papa, so young, are crouched in front, windswept and laughing at each other. Aunt Lotte and Uncle Lars gaze out from behind her cousin Pieter who is as usual squinting rather anxiously at the camera, sand in his hair and traces of ice cream around his mouth.

And here she is, that girl she was so long ago, the girl they called Sara. She has a round face, skinny legs and a mop of blonde hair. It's her birthday and she is 11 years old.

The image distorts through the blur of her tears. It's no longer a photograph. She's there, standing on the promenade in front of the vast sweep of Zandvoort beach on an unexpectedly warm Sunday in mid-May. 'Mama,' she squeals. 'I can see a sailboat'. And sure enough, there it is, bobbing along determinedly, a shock of bright yellow and red in the deep, deep blue.

Overhead, gulls caw and wheel. Lovers stretch out on the warm sand while children play catch-up with the waves and the elderly huddle in their beach huts watching the world go by.

The Van Essens come to the beach well-equipped. They take the tram from Haarlem, but still manage to load up deckchairs for Oma and Opa, rugs and a picnic of sorts—although food is getting harder to source. Still, it's Sara's birthday and despite the hardships Mama has produced some homemade lemonade and a stick of her favourite liquorice. And Uncle Lars has promised her an ice cream.

Going to the beach is a great adventure for Sara, but she's noticed that grown-ups always do the same boring thing when they get there. Oma and Opa pretend to be looking at the sea, but actually they are nodding off and will soon be fast asleep. Mama and Papa get locked into a conversation of their own which used to look like canoodling, but seems to have become a lot more serious—and now Mama frowns instead of giggling and Papa puts his arm around her but in a worried rather than a canoodling way.

Uncle Lars is always tucked behind a newspaper. Sometimes you hear him grunting and he even swore once. Aunt Lotte, who is the kindest aunty in the world, is usually on hand to help build sandcastles and play tag, but she looks sad today. So that leaves Pieter.

Sara isn't sure what she thinks about Pieter. He is her cousin and she has grown up with him which should make it all fine. And now the whole family live together in one apartment on Nieuwe Keizersgracht which she loves because everyone's together.

But Pieter is 14 and he's a boy and he has very, very long muscular legs with a smatter of downy hair on them. His voice sounds a bit croaky, which Mama says means it's breaking and he talks a lot of stuff Sara doesn't really understand. Pieter is always nice to her, but he makes her feel odd—she's not sure if it's good odd or bad odd.

At the sea edge, Sara squidges her toes into the wet sand and watches the imprint fade. And here is Pieter, right behind her, casting a long shadow.

'Wanna walk along the beach?' he asks.

'Are we allowed?'

'You're allowed if you stay with me, but suit yourself. Just look at the waves all afternoon if that's what you like to do.'

'No, I'll come.'

She scuttles along beside him, her feet slapping in the wet sand. They walk a long way fast and soon Mama, Papa and the rest are just two more tiny dots on the beach. There are fewer people here, but they keep on walking, not speaking at all, until they reach a rocky outcrop.

'I found a little cave last time we came,' says Pieter. 'You want to see it?'

'Sure,' she says, although she's not really. She's got that feeling in her stomach like she's sick and hungry at the same time.

They creep into the mouth of the cave and Pieter turns to her. 'Can I kiss you?' he asks. She must look very startled because he begins to explain.

'I might never kiss a girl,' he says. 'I want to know how it feels. Might only happen once.'

'Why?' she asks, feeling stupid. Pieter is tall and handsome and clever. Lots of girls will love him, surely?

'Just because,' he says.

Instinctively, she lifts her face and his lips are warm salty and sandy on hers. It stops mattering that Papa is always worried and Mama tearful and she can't see some of her friends anymore. Or that people give her funny looks on the street as if she's not a very nice person, which she knows is untrue. Everything melts away in Pieter's kiss. Then he pulls away: 'Come on, kid, better get you back,' he says.

They return to the family, as they went, in silence. Mama is coaxing Oma and Opa out of their deckchairs and Papa is folding up the windbreak. Aunt Lotte has made a sandcastle with a big moat for them, but for once it looks a bit childish. Uncle Lars hands them both ice creams and gets out his pride and joy, the Kodak Box Camera, for one last picture.

'But you must be in the picture,' protests Aunt Lotte. 'Don't be silly, it won't be the same without you in it.' Suddenly, it feels imperative that everyone is in the picture, so Lars reluctantly hands over his beloved camera to a passer-by and pops around to Aunt Lotte's side, grinning broadly.

The bang on the door comes not so many nights later. Sara is snuggled under the blankets, dreaming of Pieter's kiss. Downstairs, there's a huge commotion. Could they be having a row? Sometimes they get a bit noisy when they've been listening to the radio because they can't agree on what should, or might, happen next. Perhaps Opa is ill? He is very frail.

Sara creeps down the staircase into the sitting room in her long nightdress. Three men in in the dreaded black uniform of the SS, are ordering Mama, Papa, Aunt Lotte and Uncle Lars towards the front door. As they pass, she notices with a chill the emblem of the skull and crossbones glinting on their insignia.

Her family go quietly, heads bowed. Why aren't they making more fuss? Opa is arthritic and seems to be having trouble rising from the chair, but a man in uniform pulls him up and shoves him towards the door. Pieter is angry and shouting and then—the most terrible thing—one man in uniform raises a stick and beats him around the head. Blood pours from Pieter's nose, but now he's doing what he's told and joining his parents near the door.

Sara stays quiet as a mouse, but she stumbles on the hem of her nightdress and trips on the stairs. Like a spotlight beaming on you in the school show when you've forgotten your lines, the three men in uniform turn their gaze in unison on her.

'Leave the girl!' shrieks Oma. Her grey hair has escaped from its Kirby grips making her look as wild as a witch. The tallest soldier, who seems to be the leader, casually reaches for the stick again and pokes her hard in the middle.

'Bring her here,' he snaps at the youngest-looking soldier who has blonde hair rather like Pieter's. The soldier looks scared, but seizes Sara's arm.

'Put her next to him,' the first soldier commands, pointing at Pieter. Sara is dragged across the floor. When she reaches Pieter's side, she grabs hold of him.

The tall soldier turns to Oma. 'You choose,' he says. Oma looks confused. 'You choose which one,' he repeats.

Oma releases a terrible wail and hides her face in her hands. The others look on, silent and frozen. Time stops. Then Pieter steps forward.

'I'll go,' he says. 'It should be me.'

But this isn't enough for the soldier. He pulls Oma up from the floor and shakes her. 'You. Choose,' he spits in her face.

Oma doesn't seem able to speak. 'Just point at me, Oma,' says Pieter in his gentle voice. And Oma does. She raises a crooked forefinger at Pieter and now the soldiers are in a hurry. Everyone except Sara is herded through the front door. None of them look back.

She doesn't see any of them ever again. And so these are her memories. Her 11th birthday. Gulls cawing in the sky. Wet sand under her feet. The taste of homemade lemonade, liquorice and ice cream. A salty-sandy kiss. And one photograph to remind her it did all happen, although the image is fading fast and who knows what will happen to it when she is gone…

This is the way Julia discovers that her mother's family, every last one, was murdered by the Nazis somewhere between 1941 and 1945. She returned the buff folder to her mother. She has so many questions, but just now she has no appetite to ask them.

Chapter 15
Sara, 1941

After her parents were rounded up, Sara stayed rooted in the apartment for a long time. Rigid with fear, she curled herself up into a ball on the stairs. The only sound was the ticking of the big brown clock on the mantelpiece. At 2 a.m., she stretched her wobbly legs and spoke into the silence to see if her voice would work. All she could manage was a low croaking sound. Perhaps she would never be able to speak again?

At daybreak, she peered cautiously out of the window. Out in the street, she saw a huge crowd of men, women and children being rounded up and pushed into order by soldiers. It looked as if they were expected to form a crocodile, a bit like school. Most were doing just what they were told, but one man was shouting at the soldiers, throwing his arms around wildly. Within seconds, a soldier clipped him sharply on the side of the head with the barrel of his gun. The man staggered backwards, blood trickling down his neck and on to his shirt collar.

Sara spotted their neighbours, the Wolffs, with their two small children Lotte and Luuk. Only the other day, she'd sat with them while their mother went looking for shoes. With shoes rationed, hardly anyone in Holland had a pair that fit anymore. Both three-year-old Luuk and five-year-old Lotte were getting squidgy toes. Mrs Wolff was worried their feet would become misshapen.

Mr Wolff worked in a bank and always seemed in control of things. Now, he was raking his fingers through his hair and clutching his single brown suitcase for dear life. Would one suitcase be enough to see them all through the war, Sara wondered. Luuk was clinging to his mother who kept wiping her face with her sleeve. It looked as if she was crying. Meanwhile, Lotte was whooping around, playing tag with two other girls. The soldiers raised guns at them. Sara shut her eyes and turned away. Thankfully, she heard no gunshot. When she dared to look again, Lotte was being carried along the road by her father, in a slow procession leading to the square.

Surely Sara's parents, or some members of her family, must be there? She looked hard, but she couldn't see them. Perhaps they had already been taken somewhere else, like prison. Sara knew that Jews like herself were disappearing daily. Her parents had warned her over and over again about a load of things, like curfew. But she wasn't sure where people went when they disappeared. Her parents didn't seem to know either, or wouldn't tell her. So she'd decided that it must be prison. She'd heard some huge new camps had been outside the cities. She hated the idea of her family being locked up in prison, but hoped they might stay safely in a camp—even if it meant being under lock and key—until the war ended. That could be just a matter of months, Papa said so. Food might be in short supply and they'd hate being locked up. Papa might not even be allowed his beloved books. But at least they would be free of the curfews, the round-ups, the soldiers on the street and most of all everyone hating them for being Jewish.

At twilight next evening, Sara made her escape. It was past curfew for Jews, but being blonde and blue-eyed she hoped not to be stopped. Surely if you were Jewish, no one would even expect you to be wandering in the streets after curfew? She reasoned she had more chance of slipping through the net if she brazened it out, instead of looking as if she had something to hide.

Wrapping up in as many clothes as she could and armed with a hunk of bread and some cheese she found in the cupboard, she tiptoed into the hallway. Uncle Lars' beloved Brownie camera was there on the hallstand so she tucked it safely underneath her big woolly sweater. Pulling on her overcoat, she slipped through the front door.

Instinctively, she wanted to merge into the shadows close to the buildings. Instead, she strode along the pavement, her bright blonde hair poking out of her woolly hat, blue eyes looking this way and that, sharply observant. She didn't have far to go. Her parents had friends close by: the Jonkers treated Sara as a daughter. Should turn her away, she had no plan.

She screwed up her eyes to hold back the tears and shut down images of her mother being cuffed in the head, Pieter beaten with a stick and her father, head bowed, going along with it. Their friends, the Jonkers, would know what to do, where her family had been taken and how to get them back.

But it was with trepidation that she knocked on the Jonkers' heavy front door. They weren't Jewish, but would *anyone* answer their front door after curfew?

And would they help her? Sara had always been a fiercely independent child, but for once she longed for a grown-up to take over and do the worrying for her.

One look into Elise Jonkers' eyes and Sara knew she had reached a place of safety. She collapsed into the haven of Elise's well-upholstered chest, while Mr Jonkers rustled around producing hot milk and biscuits. They took Sara in and guarded her as if she was one of their own.

But the arrangement couldn't last. When the round-ups intensified, the Jonkers' smuggled Sara out of the city to a family living remotely in the countryside. They had agreed to take her in, hide her and keep her safe, even though she was Jewish.

It was at this safe house that Sara met Ernest who was also in hiding. His well-to-do family had owned a large house in Rotterdam. In 1940, when the Germans bombed Rotterdam to rubble, Ernest was lucky. He was an adventurous and curious child and just before the bombs fell, he decided to investigate the cellars below his house—naturally, without the permission of his parents. He was crawling around with his torch, looking for bugs, of all things. He wanted to be an entomologist when he grew up. All his family in the house perished in the bombings, but down in the cellar he survived.

Sara was nearly 14 when she met Ernest: he was 16, the same age that Pieter would have been. Clever, brave—sometimes rash—Ernest was a survivor, like her, and they made an instant connection. Sara thought she was in love with Pieter but came to recognise that as a silly dream she had to leave behind. A moment in a cave at the seaside, shared by an 11-year-old girl and a 13-year-old boy.

Like Ernest, Sara learned quickly that there was little place for imagination or wit in hiding. Days, weeks went by in stultifying boredom in that isolated farm perched on a dike near the sea, although you were never free of that prickly sense of unease. Had a stranger cycled by? Was that a black car bumping along the horizon? Surrounded by flat land, sky and sea, Sara felt exposed and vulnerable.

Then there were the trapdoor days. Early on in the war the Van Smits, who owned the farm, had dug a large rectangular trench at the back of their property. It was just high enough for Sara and Ernest to sit up in and sufficiently long and wide for them both to lie flat out, side by side. The base was lined with old tiles, but the sides were bare earth and across the top lay an ancient trapdoor. If the Van Smits were expecting any untoward visitors, or if there was a red alert, Sara and Ernest got straight into the trench. The Van Smits would then replace the trapdoor across the top and conceal it under a layer of grey dirt to match the rest of the farmyard.

Sara suffered from claustrophobia and it was hell for her. Terrified she might suffocate, she had to be calmed by Ernest, even though the Van Smits supplied them with torches, food and drink and were careful to show them where the air holes were located. Most times, they were only in there for an hour or two, maybe when a nosey neighbour insisted on a visit or someone dropped off farm product. But for Sara, even five minutes underground felt like an eternity. Once, someone in heavy boots stomped right over the trapdoor and across the farmyard. Sara lay in terror, waiting for the dirt walls to crumble or the rotten trapdoor to give way.

The Van Smits were an odd couple. Sara spent many solitary hours trying to work out what motivated them in their dangerous war work. Was it simple Christian charity? Surely not greed: as far are she knew, they received no financial recompense. Years later, Sara learnt more about the Van Smits and wished she had known then what she discovered later.

In what would become the final year of the war, Ernest found sweeter ways of quieting Sara. It started with a surprise touch of hands in the pitch black and ended in a mutual need so intense that it took her breath away. Passion mingled with the love, comfort and touch they'd both been so long denied. Now, for Sara, the trench became the cave: but then Pieter's sunny, blonde 13-year-old face began to fade and in its place was Ernest's: anxious, bespectacled, intense.

Chapter 16
Sara, 1948

When she stepped on to English ground in January 1948, all 18-year-old Sara carried with her, apart from the clothes she stood up in, was a battered Brownie camera. Little did she know that she was already pregnant with Julia. Her formal education had stopped abruptly when she was 10. Her two safe houses had provided shelter, but for four years she had barely been outdoors. After the war was won, she and Ernest had spent many months in a displaced persons' camp, hanging on by their fingernails to a belief that they could build a good post-war life. The clever, gregarious child had been replaced by a rabbit in the headlights.

But she had *survived*; that was the point. And now she had a whole new country to discover and a resourceful young man to share the experience with. They even had somewhere to stay. Ernest's father's boyhood friend and business partner Solomon had used his share of family money to get out of Holland before the war and now lived in Brooke Road, Stoke Newington. He had been good enough to forward them some money for the journey and promised a room in his home for as long as they needed it.

Many years later, the teenage Julia would ask to hear the story of her parents' early years in England over and over again. 'We were so poor to begin with,' Sara told her. 'Your father's mother—your grandmother—had stitched a large wodge of money into a pair of his thick winter trousers. Needless to say, your father wore them most days even in the summer months!'

Julia loved to hear her mother's first impressions of England. 'Solomon and Hester were our saviours. Without them, we wouldn't be where we are now. We were all cramped together in their little house in Brooke Road. It was hard for them, less so for us because we were used to the trench! I felt very sick, from the moment I woke up until bedtime. Nauseous and so, so exhausted. I was naïve and didn't even suspect I might be pregnant. I thought it was all to do with missing my family and my home.

'You are a true British baby, Julia! The National Health was getting into its heyday the year you were born and Hester insisted on taking me along to see our new GP because she was worried for me. It turned out I was five months pregnant already. I thought I'd managed to gain a few curves on rationing! As you grew inside me, I was ravenous all the time and even though I had a special green book with bigger rations, it was never enough.

'Your father worked day and night to provide for us. Mostly it was manual work, helping to build all the new houses they needed in England after the war. He became a big, strong man, not the skinny, bespectacled scholar he was at 16. That's probably thanks to all the lifting and shovelling he did in those early years in England!

'He got the chance to go to night school where he wisely chose to study accountancy. He'd dreamt of being an entomologist back in Rotterdam. But doing accountancy led him into banking, where he finally got the chance to use his formidable abilities. He was working around the clock, on the buildings by day then back to Brooke Road for a quick bite to eat and on to night school. And of course, he had to fit in home study too.

'Meanwhile I was getting bigger daily. Hester did her best to look after me and often gave me bits of her food ration. I tried to help around the house, but I wasn't much use. Hester would send me off for a nap and when she thought I was asleep, she'd cover me up with a warm, woolly blanket.'

Did it feel good, being safe in England after all they'd been through, Julia would ask. At first, Sara was careful with the truth, but as Julia grew, she felt able to be more honest.

'We had some good times. When Ernest had one of his rare free days, we'd take the number 73 bus which trundled all the way from Stoke Newington to Richmond. It took hours, but we didn't mind a bit. We'd take sandwiches wrapped in greased paper and have a picnic in the park. From our vantage point on the top deck, we saw lots of London as the bus rumbled along past beautiful St Pancras Station, down Tottenham Court Road into Oxford Street and then towards Knightsbridge where we got a tempting peek into Harrods windows!

'But as Jews, we didn't feel particularly welcome in England. It was odd. We thought we were coming to this promised land where we would be welcome for no other reason than what we'd endured. But people felt they'd suffered enough in the war and they'd turned their faces to the future. We needed to tell our stories to make some sort of peace with ourselves, but people didn't want to hear about suffering.

'Solomon and Hester were liberal Jews, as we had been back in Holland. We don't wear our religion on our sleeve, although we quietly observe it at home, as you know. Some people avoided us, but others were welcoming. In time we found friends and became part of the community, as Solomon and Hester had done before us.

'It didn't help that I was pregnant with you. I was only 18 and had done nothing with my life except survive. My dream of being a teacher was over. Something I will always regret. And here's a little secret I probably shouldn't share, but I'm not ashamed. We weren't married! We wouldn't have known *how* to get married in England. But, don't worry Julia, you are properly your father's daughter! We married very quietly in 1951 before Peter was born. We didn't want anyone to know.'

Julia always saved the best bit of the story until last. Tell me again, Mama, about what it was like when I was born, she would demand.

'It was a good birth at home in Brooke Road, with the midwife and Hester in attendance and Ernest chewing his nails in the front room downstairs. Not easy. Is giving birth ever easy? But it felt good and right, especially meeting you at the end of it,' Sara tells her. 'Your shock of dark honey hair and tiny pursed-up lips. It was love at first sight, Julia. After all the losses, it was wonderful for me to bring you, my own flesh and blood, into the world.'

'Was I an *adorable* baby, Mama?' Julia liked to ask at this point in the story. And Sara always gave the same reply: 'Adorable and adored, little one! Ernest and I lost just about everyone in Holland and here you were, our joint flesh and blood. We all doted on you. Your father would rock you in his arms when you woke in the night. Hester wore her fingers to bits knitting tiny jackets and bootees for you. Even Solomon, who is not a natural with babies, would burp you and rub your back when you got wind.

'On your second birthday, Ernest announced that we had saved enough deposit and could apply for a mortgage on a house of our own. We planned to stay close to Hester and Solomon, but this house came up. It was a frosty winter's day so we bundled you up in woollies, hat, coat and leggings and the three of us set off for the 73 bus. You were waddling along on your stout little legs, fascinated by everything from the cracks in the pavement to the frost on the puddles. Ernest wanted to carry you, but you insisted on walking all the way to the bus and climbing up to the top deck *all by myself*!

'We took the underground from Euston. It seemed like a huge expedition. But when we emerged into the light just before our station stop, it was worthwhile. Big houses, each with a private garden running down to the rail track—we couldn't believe how much space was lavished! We were used to being crammed in, but everything here looked as if it had been spread out to fill the space. We wandered past a parade of pleasant shops and into a network of suburban roads, circling and rolling up the hillside to the park. Finally we saw our house, cream stucco, with its big bay window and arched brick porch. But do you know what I loved most? The apple trees, two of them at the bottom of the lawn in the back garden. They were sprinkled with hoar frost, but I pictured them in late summer, the fruit hanging low in the branches and me and you sitting on a rug underneath.

'Thanks to your father, we were able to buy this house and Peter was born here. We became a proper family and I was finally able to let go, just a little, of the past. I was proud to call him Peter.'

Chapter 17
Emily's Memory Book, 1978

So it's one of those dog-day Saturday afternoons when the light is bleached beige and the people on the pavement look as if they're moving in dazed slow motion. The twins are napping peacefully and I'm reading the problem page in Norma's pink-and-blue women's weekly, when I hear footsteps stonking up the attic stairs. It's rare for Norma to pay a visit to the attic. For a moment, I let myself dream it's someone else. But who, apart from Clive—and Toby, of course—knows I'm here?

She opens the door a crack and pokes a beaky nose through. 'You're awake.'

I feel like saying: 'Do feel free to state the obvious' but something stops me. She's not acting like Norma. She seems almost afraid of something—surely not me.

Cautiously she pushes open the door and perches on the edge of my bed. 'How are you?' A question so weird by Norma standards that I feel like blurting out the truth.

Which is this.

'You told me that giving birth is hell and brimstone, Norma, and you're right. I'm a shadow person. Sometimes I study the mirror to remind myself I exist.

Why did you leave me alone in that great gothic pile of a hospital? It made me think of Jane Eyre's orphanage. When I walked through its yawning mouth of an entrance, I thought it would gobble me up and spit me out. I went in as Emily and left eight days later as this freaky person with a crying baby tucked under each arm.

It wasn't only the birth that destroyed me, it was the 'afterbirth'. Being poked and pummelled and called 'dearie' by nurses who insisted on me feeding both babies until they were full up. Which never happened, of course.

'Where were you, Norma, when all this was happening?'

But I don't say it, or anything like it. Instead: 'As you're asking, I'd feel a lot better if I could get some fresh air. I haven't been out much since the twins were born and that was over a month ago. Could we get a second-hand pram so I can take them for a walk?'

Norma sighs and twiddles her finger in her hair. 'It's hard with two. Being honest, it's not really manageable, is it?'

I can't see where this is going. So I turn my face to the wall and ask her, please to let me get some rest while the twins are napping. Or find me a pram from somewhere, so I can get some fresh air.

But now she's looming over me: 'We need to talk about this. One of them has to go. I, we, can't support all three of you.'

I twist around and stare straight into her black eyes. 'What do you mean, one has to go? Are you turfing us out?'

'No, not you—and not both twins. But one has to go. You should choose which.'

I think she's mad, I really do. But I sense a distorted logic in it. It's true: loving just one would be so much easier. I picture a morning where I change, dress and feed *just one*. I could take *just one* to the park, without a pram even, carrying her in my arms. *Just one* mightn't scream relentlessly when I change her nappy. At night, *just one* wouldn't wake the other and we'd all get some sleep.

'You're mad,' I say. For once, she doesn't answer back. She knows her words have hit home. She sidles towards the door, twisting the knob back and forth as she delivers her final shot.

'Think about it. You've time to decide. Let's say until tomorrow. I think it's best done quickly. Dragging out decisions like this is never a good idea.' She's talking as if she knows my decision is already made. It's just a question of me coming to terms with it.

'But where?' I ask.

'Leave it to me. We'll put her up for adoption. A lot of women would be thrilled to have a healthy baby with a pair of lungs like Bea's. She'll likely end up in a much better home than this one. I'll take it all out of your hands.'

Bea. Must it be Bea? It's down to me. I have to choose between Annie and Bea. Or I could choose both, or neither. The door clicks shut and I am left with my babies. I lean over the cot. As usual, they are lying head to toe. Annie is napping peacefully on her side, eyelids resting on her chubby cheek. She looks as if she would like to put her thumb in her mouth, but isn't quite ready yet. Her wispy hair is the colour of caramel, like Toby's. On the other side of the cot, Bea is writhing.

I watch them for a long time, thinking about their future and mine. I'm not giving the three of us a chance. I'm in survival mode. Is this how everyone feels after giving birth? The afternoon ticks on and the bleached-beige light at my attic window darkens to a muddy grey. It's 4 p.m. and still the twins are sleeping.

There's a timid tap and Clive sticks his head around my bedroom door. Of course, he's off work today. 'What is it?' I ask irritably. I really can't face Clive right now.

'Something for you. I can't bring it up. You have to come down.'

I reluctantly crawl off the bed and follow him downstairs. By the front door, almost blocking our narrow hallway, is the most extraordinary sight: a huge, shiny black pram, the sort the royals use.

'I saw it in a second-hand shop, but it was as dusty as hell and needed doing-up,' says Clive. 'Ted Grimes let me keep it in his lock-up while I did some work on it. I wanted it to be a surprise.'

His face is flushed beetroot with excitement. Who'd have thought that he, of all people, would be the one to grant me an exit card? I don't know what to say. No one ever taught me the language of gratitude. So I gently rock the chassis, pull up the hood and bend down to check out the roomy storage tray below.

'I'm getting the girls,' I say. 'I'm taking them shopping.' Clive follows me upstairs and grabs a handful of bedding while I pick up a still-sleeping baby in each arm.

The commotion disturbs Norma's afternoon feet-up session. 'What the heck?' Her face falls at the sight of the pram. 'Did you do this, Clive?'

He nods. For a moment Norma looks as if she might hit him, but she quickly regains her equilibrium. 'You can't get two of them in there.'

'Yes, you can. Easy peasy.' I place the twins, side by side, into the nest of blankets. 'I'm going out.' I run upstairs for my shoes and coat.

When I get back, Norma has disappeared but Clive is waiting with the twins. He slips a banknote into my hands. 'Get yourselves a little something. On me.' He looks anxiously at the sitting room door.

Together, we manhandle the pram through the front door and down the step. On the pavement, I am flooded with a sense of freedom, my feet barely touching the ground. I can do this thing. The pram feels like an ocean liner. *Sail on, silver girl*. Humming to myself, I steer it towards the shops.

We head to our shiny new local branch of Baby&Co, where I meet my first challenge. I can't get the pram through the shop door. I try this way and that and I'm beginning to get agitated when a shop assistant rushes from behind the counter to give a hand. It's a struggle and we make a dent in one of the wheel spokes. But finally, I steer the pram into a visible position on the pavement, near the door and put the brake on.

I'm about to run into the shop when an elderly lady steps across my path. 'Not a good place to leave the pram, dearie, is it?' Her chicken neck shakes with indignation. 'How am I supposed to get past that great hulk of a pram into the shop?'

It's tempting to say: 'Try losing some weight, grandma' but sweat beads are breaking out on her powdered nose. I move the pram six inches down the pavement, which leaves the shop door clear but means I can't see the twins.

Running into the shop, I feel like one of those people in that new reality TV show, Smash and Grab, where you have 30 seconds to raid the shop shelves and get to keep whatever you can carry away. I'm in luck. Right in front of me is a discount range of 'baby accessories'. I pick up a cute bonnet adorned with an embroidered bumblebee for Bea and a bib in the shape of an apple for Annie. Rushing to the counter, I pull out Clive's banknote.

'Is that your baby crying?' asks the assistant as she wraps up the bonnet. I sprint out of the shop.

Sure enough, Bea is screaming for England and the pram is rocking like an ocean liner in a stormy sea. Annie is waking too. I haven't brought formula or even a dummy. I can't walk all the way back down my road with Bea crying like that. What to do?

Opposite is the church. If I can make it over the busy road, I could maybe breastfeed Bea in the churchyard. But I can't get across. It's close on rush hour and the cars are coming thick and fast. Nobody wants to spare the time to let me safely over. It's a few minutes' walk to the nearest Belisha beacon crossing and as I head towards it, Bea's cries ricochet off the shop fronts.

Finally, I make it to the churchyard wall, but I forgot the steps. Six tall, narrow, slippery ones. I try to bump the pram up, but that sets Annie off. In the end, I park it on the pavement, pick Bea out, sit on the lowest step and pull out a boob.

The step is cold and damp, Bea is grappling hungrily with my nipple and Annie is growing more restless by the minute. Worse still, I am getting evil looks from passers-by as if I am the world's worst mum. I perform a stop-start feed and put Bea back in the pram ready to head home.

Halfway down Elm Avenue, I detect a strong smell in the air. I sniff cautiously. Could it be pooh? Sure enough, it looks like Bea has done a tsunami in her nappy. It's around her legs, up her back, sinking into the blankets—and the fallout is heading straight in Annie's direction. Tears well in my eyes. So much for freedom.

Back at number 101, Norma is still glued to the TV and Clive has gone out for an early evening pint. I manoeuvre the pram into the hall, rescue Annie from the gooey blankets and take her upstairs to her cot. Bea needs the bathroom, but she's hungry again. It's a battle to clean and feed her.

It takes two hours to settle both girls. When I'm done, beyond exhaustion, I tiptoe down the stairs and gently prise open the living room door. Norma has a tray on her lap and silently offers me one of her corned beef sandwiches.

'No thank you, I'm not very hungry.' For a nano-second, I hesitate in the doorway. Then I turn and, looking her directly in the eye: 'It's Bea. Take Bea.'

Now I know this much is true. Norma and I share something: we are both in the business of survival.

Chapter 18
Norma, 1978

There was never any question of taking the child to an adoption agency. Norma's experiences with authority have taught her to avoid it. She knows little about adoption agencies, but she's suspicious. They might charge for their services. They might investigate 'donor' families in a way that Norma would find invasive. Worse, they leave the way open for further contact down the line. There will be official records and witnesses to the baby changeover. It's messy and distressing and Norma wants a clean break.

She outlines her plan to Clive. 'We need some sanity back into the house,' she explains as they sit opposite each other at the fold-down breakfast table, eating boiled eggs. It's mercifully quiet upstairs. Emily and the twins are still fast asleep.

Clive nods his gnome head sagely. 'Is Emily okay with the idea?' he asks. Norma's been dreading this question. She'd prefer to leave Clive out of the loop, but she doesn't think she can pull this off alone. She tries to remember the last time Clive disagreed with her. She can't. He's angry with the world, but in thrall to her. She clears her throat.

'Actually, I haven't told her. I've said we'll take the child to an adoption agency. She was quite reluctant at first, but I think she'll cave in. She tried taking them out yesterday and hardly got past the front door. Bea was screaming, she was weeping. It was awful. Good job you were out.'

'Mmm.' Clive frowns at his egg. Norma can see he's considering Emily. It dawns on her: he's not like me. He's an angry man, but not without feeling. All these years, Clive has been a shadow figure in her life, supplying respectability, a roof over her head and Emily. But who is he?

She will need to rely on her powers of reasoning. 'I know it sounds cruel. But it's less messy. It's a cleaner break. With an agency, you never know what sort of comeback there might be further down the line. There's the paperwork—everything's on record.'

'Mmm.' Clive's carefully cleaning up the last vestiges of egg yolk with a greasy forefinger and Norma is starting to feel exasperated.

'Clive, you do understand that if I do this thing, no one, but no one must ever know? You must back me up—and if it comes out in the newspapers, which is possible, we'll need to keep Emily away from them. The less she knows, the better.'

'How will you do it?'

Norma lets out a cautious sigh of relief. It seems she's over the first hurdle. 'You know, I think it's best if I keep it all to myself. The less you and Emily know, the better. Just carry on as normal if I need your help, I'll ask for it.'

'Okay, I'll leave it to you,' says Clive. 'Just don't get the law involved and try to look after Emily.'

Norma suspects he has a notion that he should have done more to protect and nurture his daughter in the last 18 years. Could the war and living in a sham marriage have blunted his better nature?

'When?' he asks as an afterthought.

'Within the next week if I can. Just look forward to a good night's sleep.'

Norma makes her plan with military precision. Her first challenge is—where? She considers a shopping precinct—warm and indoors—but they all shut down and lock up at night. Wandsworth Town Hall is grand and she briefly considers the steps there, but it's too close to home. Churchyards seem to be popular for this sort of thing, but she'll worry about the cold and wind. In any case, she's not a religious observer. She doesn't want God to have an opportunity to wreak vengeance on her.

Finally, after settling on north London—easy to get to, yet far enough to discourage suspicion—Norma pays a visit to the local library. Pulling out a tattered copy of the *London A to Z* from the shelf, she turns to the sections served by the Northern Line. Her eye is drawn to Highgate Cemetery. A quick scan of *Visitors' Guide to London* confirms she has stumbled across somewhere quite grand! It seems that the cemetery, after falling into disrepair for many years, has been rejuvenated and is now packed with flora and fauna. Not only that, it is the final resting place of some very distinguished people indeed.

'Following its opening in 1839, Highgate Cemetery quickly became a fashionable place for burials and was much admired and visited. There are approximately 170,000 people buried in around 53,000 graves in the East and West cemetery' she reads. *'The cemetery's grounds are full of trees, shrubbery and wildflowers and are a haven for birds and small animals such as foxes.'*

The list of celebrities who are buried there is impressive. A lot of them, admittedly, she's never heard of. But she's certainly heard of Karl Marx. She notes the cemetery opening times.

Fortunately, Norma didn't find any reading matter on supernatural experiences at the cemetery. If she had, it might have given her pause for thought. *'On Christmas Eve 1969, a local gentleman reported seeing "a grey figure" and other visitors to the cemetery described spotting various ghosts: a tall man in a hat, a spectral cyclist, a woman in white, a face glaring through the bars of a gate, a figure wading into a pond, a pale gliding form, bells ringing and voices calling.'*

But Highgate Cemetery ticks the boxes. It's far enough from Tooting. It's anonymous. It's buzzing with ghost-and-vampire hungry tourists most days and it sounds like there are lots of nooks and crannies where a child can be lightly concealed without actually disappearing.

Emily's in the kitchen making up bottles when Norma gets back from the library.

'I went to see the adoption agency.' Norma disguises her lie by making a fuss about hanging up her coat and scarf. 'They'd like me to take the baby in on Monday.'

'Didn't they want to see me? Do I have to speak to them direct? Or fill in paperwork?'

'No, no, they understand that would be painful for you,' Norma's lies are beginning to sound preposterous, even to her. But Emily's been off the planet since giving birth. She's hardly in a state to pick up on lies.

'Can you have her ready early, around 8:30 a.m. tomorrow? They've asked me to get her to the agency bright and early, then they'll take it from there.'

'What will happen to her then?'

'Well, I'm assuming they'll find a good home for her and that will be it. You'll be free to work at bringing up one twin properly.' Norma nearly adds, 'and we'll all get some peace at night,' but stops herself in time.

70

'You'll be surprised how much simpler it'll be raising just the one. You'll be able to take her out, give her more attention and there'll be more money to go round. It'll be easier, you'll see and the other one will get a better life too.'

Emily looks unconvinced. 'How can you be sure of that?'

'Because I am. I've got faith in the agency. They'll take care of everything. Now, go and sort out which twin is going. You don't even need to tell me if you don't want to. I won't know the difference and neither will anyone else.'

But Emily *has* discovered a difference—one that she's never told anyone. Bea has a small port wine birthmark on the inside of her ankle. As if she's marked out for something, although you'd have to look closely to notice it.

Next morning, Norma finds the Moses basket on the kitchen table, with one twin tucked snugly inside wearing the fluffy bumblebee bonnet Emily bought and Baby&Co.

'Must be Bea,' she reasons. There's no sign of Emily, just muffled sobs coming from upstairs. Norma sighs in exasperation. She has to lug the basket all the way to the underground at the T Junction, then down at Baby&Co, countless steps before she even gets on the train. With any luck, the commuters will have cleared off by then. Good job she's got strong arms from all that meat hacking.

She feels like a criminal as she trots stealthily up Elm Avenue, but at least Bea is sleeping and they don't run into any neighbours. Once she's found a seat on the northbound train, she breathes a sigh of relief. Sitting next to her, a pimply boy dressed in black from head to toe is fast asleep, his head nodding on his chest to the motion of the carriage.

As the train heads towards King's Cross, it gains speed, rattling and screeching through a tunnel. Bea wakes and lets out a wail like a banshee. The pimply boy's head jerks up. Bea pushes into full throttle, her cheeks an angry red.

A middle-aged woman opposite Norma leans forward. 'Can I help?' she asks. 'Does she want to feed?'

She leans in closer, her grey utility coat almost brushing Norma's knee. 'It's so hard for mums, isn't it? To breastfeed I mean. But you should do it if you have to, dear. Don't mind us.' Pimple Face has shifted in his seat and it feels to Norma like the whole carriage is waiting to see what she will do next.

'Oh no,' she says. 'I'm not the mother. I'm just looking after it. And the mother forgot to give me a bottle. Or water…' Bea is screaming louder, or so it seems. In mounting horror, Norma considers her options. Get off at the next stop?

71

That would just replace one crime scene with another. Pick Bea up and try cuddling her? Not her preferred option. Then she has a brainwave.

From the depths of her coat pocket, she recovers an ancient cough sweet. Prising away the gunky wrapping, she pops it in her mouth, gives it an enthusiastic suck and slathers the lozenge all over her little finger. Tentatively, she pokes her finger through Bea's angry gums.

It works like magic. Bea can't get enough of menthol, eucalyptus and artificial cherry flavour. It keeps her happy until they alight at Archway and Norma finds a corner shop to buy another pack of lozenges—just in case. They arrive at the Eastern entrance to the cemetery at opening time, just as planned. There aren't many people about, but with any luck there are enough for someone to notice an abandoned baby and sort it out.

As she wanders along one of the main pathways, Norma is stuck by the difference between this cemetery and the bare, windswept ones of her West Country childhood. She's turned into a narrower path now. Underfoot, grass and weeds are growing unchecked and her feet make a sucking sound in the sodden earth. Above, an arc of trees blocks the sky. Everywhere is the drip, drip of moisture from the turning leaves. Some graves are coated in moss and lichen, others are shiny new with posies of freshly-laid flowers. Norma stops by a gravestone.

It's newish compared with most of the stones in this part of the cemetery, but not so showy as to attract attention. A simple grey headstone, without adornment. There are no flowers or cellophane-encased photographs, or any evidence that the grave has been recently visited. Norma scans the carved lettering on the stone.

'In memory of our darling Lillian Rose Dempsey
Taken from us October 8, 1940
Age 4 years
May the angels care for one of their own'

A child, thinks Norma. Not much younger than I was then. Could it have been a bombing raid? Or one of the many fatal illnesses children succumbed to before we got the NHS? Why isn't someone tending the grave? Norma feels her heart expand and shift in her chest and she doesn't like the sensation. Pulling herself together, she assesses the suitability of the grave. It's on a well-trodden route, not too hidden and there's a bench just around the corner which makes a perfect viewpoint. Perhaps it's a sign—out of the ashes and all that.

Norma folds the sleeping Bea firmly into her blankets. Fortunately it's not raining and the wind has dropped to a gentle whisper in the trees. Carefully checking there's no one on the track, she tucks the Moses basket beside the grave and moves stealthily towards the bench. Putting on her reading glasses and adjusting her headscarf, she takes a cheese and pickle sandwich wrapped in greaseproof from her coat pocket and begins to eat. She hopes she looks like what she is: a lonely middle-aged woman, past sensible childbearing age, killing time in a cemetery.

Within minutes, she hears footsteps at the end of the track, near the junction with the main pathway. She holds her breath, but it's a cemetery attendant carrying a garden rake and he doesn't even glance at her. Ten minutes later, there are more footsteps. A hooded figure appears through a gap in the foliage: it looks like a teenage girl and as she gets closer, Norma can hear her snuffling. Must have had a row with her boyfriend. The girl passes right by without noticing either the Moses basket or the baby inside it.

A while later Norma has stopped looking at her watch, it's making her nervous – two figures emerge through the trees. A man and a woman, maybe mid-forties, well-dressed. She's wearing a camel coat and heels and her blonde hair falls in a neat bob. Norma guesses the man must be her husband. He looks smart and affluent too, in a heavy overcoat with the sort of black, shiny shoes you can see your face in. They are within 12 feet of the Moses basket. Norma's heart lurches and thumps. The woman seems to be drawn to the basket as if by a magnet.

'My God, Mike, what's this? Surely it's not a baby?' She speaks in a weird twang and it takes Norma a few moments to realise she is American. They both peer into the basket. 'It is, it's a baby.' she cries. 'Oh, Mike. Do you think someone has abandoned it? You couldn't lose your baby, could you? It must have been left deliberately.'

The man called Mike is dubious. As he looks into the basket, Bea kicks a tiny leg, disturbing the blankets. 'My God, Libby we don't want to get involved in something like this. We've a plane to catch this evening. I'm sure it'll be found by one of the park people soon.'

'Mike, this is an abandoned baby. We have to do something.' She looks up at her husband in shock. 'We can't just leave it here.'

Sighing, Mike picked up the basket. 'Let's take it to the ticket office. They'll know what do to. I wonder if it's a boy or a girl.' He looks at Bea's bumblebee hat. 'You can't really tell.'

Gently, his wife scoops Bea out, cradling her in the crook of one arm. 'You know, I have this feeling she's a girl. But I don't think we should do the obvious and check right now. We don't want her getting cold. Oh look, I think I see someone through the trees there.'

They both turn to see Norma huddled on the bench, picking at her cheese and pickle sandwich. The woman scurries in her direction, Bea in her arms. 'Do you know anything about this baby? We found it, just around there, by a grave. We think it's abandoned...'

Norma turns her inscrutable gaze on the woman. 'Goodness me, I've no idea. I've only been sitting here a few minutes eating my sandwiches. I've not seen anyone come and go. You could maybe take it to the ticket office? I'm sure they'll know what to do.'

Mike is on the point of suggesting that maybe she could do the honours. They've got a plane to catch, a life to lead for God's sake. Which clearly this sad-looking lady past her peak does not. But that's going to give him no end of grief with Libby. And prick his well-buffed conscience too.

'Don't worry,' he says. 'Please. Get on with your lunch. We'll take it from here. If the child *has* been abandoned, I'm sure the park authorities will know what to do.'

Norma's eyes behind her reading glasses are like black glass pebbles. The job is done. 'There's no accounting for folk, is there?'

'Indeed,' says Mike. 'Look, we must go—we have a plane to catch. We'll take the baby and make sure it's sorted out. Don't let this distressing business spoil your day.'

'I won't.' Norma watches them stumbling cautiously down the path, Mike carrying the basket and Libby cuddling Bea. As they round the corner, the child lets out a piercing wail.

They didn't even notice Lillian, cold and alone in her mossy grave, thinks Norma, with a flash of sadness.

Chapter 19
Sean Howard, 1978

Sean is a decent man, but he does have a weakness: a liking for ladies. Now he's married to Julia, he wouldn't dream of acting on it, of course. It's not altogether a sexual urge, though he'd be lying if he claimed there was no sexual content. It's more that he's in touch with his feminine side. He's not an overtly masculine man, favouring music, books and theatre to sport and other traditional manly pursuits. Among his media students, he's a legend. But it's the girls who flock to him like pigeons.

Now he fears his popularity is coming to haunt him. It's the end of a teaching session and he's shuffling papers around on his desk. Why do media studies generate so much more paper than any other discipline? If you can call it a discipline. It's a fairly new subject, so it demands to be taken extra seriously. The college doesn't want to be seen as going lightweight. Not so many years ago, Sean made his academic choices from an enticing selection ranging from Eng Lit through History to Geography. He'd have killed to spend his student years comparing newspaper headlines and evaluating page 3 girls for gender representation.

Today, they've been studying stereotypes. Sean has delivered his usual thought-provoking 'facilitation' but he privately suspects that the entire media shebang is based on stereotypes. The hard left activist, the right-wing fascist, the vulnerable elderly, the cocky teen, the strong, silent dad, the grieving mum. Are there *any* nuanced people out there?

All his students have left, except one. Amber Kerslake is sitting at the back in a despondent heap, apparently doodling on the desk. Her blonde hair falls in rivulets over her pear-shaped breasts which seem to be forced upwards and outwards by some mysterious force of nature. As Sean picks up his bag to leave, Amber smiles coyly up at him through slack raspberry lips.

'You off then,' Mr Howard?'

Sean is tempted to say: 'What does it look like?' but stops himself just in time. Best to be nice to the students so that further down the line you can rely on them being nice to you. Something about Amber reeks of litigation. Like a concealed landmine, lurking in harmless-looking terrain.

'Yes, off home now, Amber. Looking forward to dinner, putting my feet up and a spot of TV.' Sean hopes he's selling an image of an idyllic domestic fortress, whose walls stand proud against invasion from pear-shaped breasts and raspberry lips. But as he speaks, he feels his eyes sliding downwards to Amber's ample breasts. She is quick to pick up the vibe.

'I think I need some extra tuition, Mr Howard,' she simpers. 'I don't quite get all this stereotypes stuff. I need help understanding how it all works.'

Sean is known to his colleagues for his speedy, soothing and benign response rate. He can think on his feet. It's one of the things that make him so good with his students. He really should have been a politician.

'Well, Amber, actually, what you're telling me is great. The message I'm getting is: you don't see stereotypes in society. Ergo, you don't stereotype. Ergo, you are well on the path to enlightenment.'

Sean falters here. Will Amber know what 'ergo' means? Probably not, but maybe that's not a bad thing. A little judicial language-masking may be just what's needed to edge them gently out of the classroom. She will surely be too embarrassed to ask what 'ergo' means and just drop it.

As if by magic, Sean's hastily concocted strategy works. A po-faced Amber sidles off, leaving a vapour trail of Boots My-Man-and-I eau de toilette in her wake. He recognises the smell because Julia bought some once and then threw it out after a few puffs, complaining it had an undertone of uncooked meat. Five minutes later, he's safely in his car, sailing along the North Circular with Baker Street blaring on the radio. If only he had an open top. One day.

He stops at the pedestrian lights to let a young girl across the road. She's battling with her hair in the wind. It's long, brown and dead straight under her floppy patchwork hat. Her legs rise from her DMs, gloriously firm and shapely in purple tights. She grins ruefully at Sean. Freckled nose, translucent skin, no make-up. She's more his type than Amber really. Sean sighs. Time for a reality check.

Sean met Julia in the Tate Gallery and fell in love in an instant. He was killing time. She was doing art. He'd been wandering around aimlessly, wondering what to look at next, when he noticed a tall, almost-thin woman of about his age gazing fixedly at a painting of some children on a windswept beach. Feigning an interest in the painting that he didn't necessarily feel, he made a move in her direction. She turned towards him.

'Don't you love the movement in it?' she asked. Dressed in black, her dark hair escaped like storm clouds from a small grey cloche hat, framing a pale, sculpted face. Her smile was uncertain, beginning in her eyes and taking its time to reach her lips. And so it began.

Sean is good with words. After all, he works in media and is trained to conjure up just the right one, or as near as damn it, at the right time. He has many words that he associates with Julia. She is gentle, earnest, fragile, loving. She can be funny and she is a devastating exponent of lavatorial jokes. But even at her funniest, sadness lurks below the surface. Sean hesitates to say the word, or even think it, because it feels like a betrayal. But here it is: she is *tragic*. Tragedy hangs around Julia, like a black cat mewling at her ankles.

By the time Julia told Sean her family history, they were madly in love. Sean gazed into her limpid eyes and swore he would take the sadness away. He failed to appreciate how the burden of loss is passed from one generation to the next. His own eventful childhood was spent in a pleasant but unpretentious thirties semi in one of the leafier parts of Birmingham, where his father worked in the council offices. His mum 'worked around the boys' as she liked to say. Sean was the middle one of three and they all muddled along fine. He recalls feeling like piggy-in-the-middle because he could never get enough of his mum's attention. And he got teased a bit at school because he was rubbish at sport. Nothing more awful than that, which is why he feels completely ill-equipped to deal with Julia's loss.

And now there is a fresh loss to deal with: their failure to have children. Sean blames himself for this. He is the one with the low sperm count and perhaps he should have got himself checked out before they married. But do other couples do that? Sean thinks not. Would they have gone ahead with the marriage in any case? He believes so. His love for Julia is deep and wide and he's sure she feels the same way about him. But he's conscious that her childhood was wreathed in shadows and he has added yet another. And there is a price to pay.

Sean has begun to feel like a sperm machine. Love-making, which once was magic, has become mechanical. The trouble is, he's the mechanism and doesn't work properly. If Julia had a leaky tap in the kitchen, she'd probably push and pull and pummel it. Eventually she'd get angry and, somewhere down the line, she'd give up and go and buy another. Sean doesn't like to think along these lines because sometimes he sees himself as that tap. It doesn't matter how hard Julia tries, he's not going to work. Now, it's official. Sean has a low sperm count and is unlikely to produce children.

Just this summer, a miracle occurred. Louise Brown, the world's first baby conceived by IVF was born in a Manchester hospital. But this is cutting edge stuff. Sean doesn't think it will happen for them. He worries that he is past thirty. A few months ago, they decided to try for adoption.

Since that decision, he's felt better. It seems like a proactive step, to acknowledge his shortcoming and to make an active move towards creating the family they both want. He's unsure how Julia feels. He suspects she would prefer her own flesh and blood to help replace her annihilated family.

What he does know is that since they signed up for adoption, Julia is like a cat on a hot tin roof. She is always first at the letterbox in the morning, scanning for letters with an adoption agency stamp. When the telephone trills in their empty hall, she jumps, turns pale and—if Sean is around—refuses to answer it. It's been months since they signed up at the agency and there's been nothing. Sean guesses it's a bit like selling houses: you have to wait for the right one to come along.

As he pulls into his driveway, Sean sees Julia, in her favourite 'work' outfit of Levi's and floppy black pullover, hovering on the doorstep. He feels that familiar tug of guilt and overwhelming love. How will she be tonight? He can never second-guess. On a bad day, she will be nervous and needy. If work has gone well and she's held on to her focus, she may be quiet, but serene. She rarely discusses her work but Sean can always tell when she's pleased with it.

Today, Julia is neither of these things, her face flushed with animation. She's rubbing her fingers up and down her bobbly pullover, almost in glee. And her feet won't stay still: doing a little dance of their own on the doorstep.

'Sean, I thought you'd never get back. Look, look at this.' She digs into her apron pocket, pulling out an official letter. He drops his briefcase on the doorstep and grabs it.

It's from the adoption agency. They have a possible baby. Would Julia and Sean contact them immediately, preferably by telephone? Sean hurls the letter into the dusty city air and waves his fist as it flutters down to rest on the privet hedge.

'We're having a baby,' he hollers as he lifts Julia and carries her over the threshold.

Part 2
Double Lives

Chapter 20
Julia and Sean, 1978

Julia gazes at her reflection in the long oval mirror and sighs. Thanks to the rain, her hair is frizzy and she can see a budding pimple on the tip of her nose. Just like a real mum, she thinks with perverse satisfaction. She's seen mums pushing buggies in the street and noted their tired skin and unwashed hair. Beleaguered is quite the look for young mums.

They're meeting with the adoption agency today, another step on the long ladder to having a baby of their own. Julia thinks back to all those meetings, having their lives examined in a way that felt almost ruthless. The times they've relayed their hopes, fears and expectations to jaded social workers. The intimacies they've been forced to share. The unexpected truths they've been obliged to hear from each other's lips. Would she ever have known that Sean had a dream he'd been adopted when he was seven? Would he have learnt that rarely a day passes without her thinking of her lost family in the Netherlands?

She is grateful to Camille, their cheery and ever-neutral social worker, for steering them through 10 months of gruelling self-examination. Or maybe self-flagellation is a better word. Like picking meat from an exposed carcass. As to Sean, she's not quite sure how he feels. Which is ironic, considering the amount they've told a third party about themselves and each other.

Today is significant, a huge step forward. They're meeting with the panel and if all goes well, perhaps even their baby. First impressions count. Julia's staple wardrobe of Levi's and black sweater for home and a black shift with statement jewellery for work isn't going to cut the mustard. She rummages around in her wardrobe and pulls out an A-Line midi in deep red and a creamy print blouse with a ruffled neck. Teamed together, it looks a bit Laura Ashley, but at least it's modest and mumsy. Out come her best zip-up boots and her voluminous charcoal trench coat. She layers everything on together and examines the end result. Hmm, she thinks: a well-dressed tramp.

Sean is bellowing from the hall, telling her to hurry up. She trips down the stairs, trying to avoid getting tangled in her trench coat. Sean gazes at her with an expression somewhere between admiration and horror.

'What the f ***?' he asks. 'Is this a new look? Meryl Streep meets Karen Carpenter?'

Julia is crestfallen, but doesn't respond. It's something she has in common with her mother. Pain, anxiety, anger: they're all kept carefully in a box where Julia also stores her family history.

'Just joking. It's perfect.' He puts his arm around her protectively. What the heck if they're five minutes late. Julia's more important. 'You look like the most gorgeous…most sexy…most *mumsy* mum ever.'

'I don't want to look sexy, Sean. That's not the point.' But Julia has brightened and now she's twitching his collar and tie. Sean rarely wears a tie and he's feeling slightly asphyxiated.

'Let's get going,' he says. 'We'll be late.'

He revs up his battered mustard-coloured Datsun and heads towards Hampstead High Street. The adoption agency is in Haringey, a journey of little more than five miles that can take more than 30 minutes. Plenty of time for apprehension to turn into full-blown anxiety. Sean winds down his window though it's breezy and the clouds are matt grey and glances at Julia.

She's pale and still as a statue in the British Museum. With blunt cheekbones, smudged kohl eyes and shocking gash of bright lipstick, she looks exotic. Not like his idea of a mum, he thinks ruefully. Her hands quiver as she clasps the drawstrings of her mirrored bag.

The adoption agency occupies part of a concrete block that also houses the council offices, library and a Citizens' Advice Bureau. Built in the brave new world of the early sixties, it's already showing its age. Within the revolving doors, they find a thin corridor painted in shiny lime green with doors leading off at regular intervals. A smell like stewed apples lingers in the air. At the end of the corridor, Camille awaits them. Her afro mop is tamed into a head of magnificent cornrows and her big, wide smile radiates confidence.

'Come on in, guys. We're going to nail this thing.'

Inside Door 14, the adoption panel presides behind a long beige table. The woman who seems to be in charge leans across and envelops them in handshakes.

'Mr and Mrs Howard, good to meet you. I'm Geraldine Lilley, head of adoption services.' Julia's small white hand shakes visibly as it's seized and pumped by Geraldine's beefy one.

The rest of the panel seem indifferent to handshaking, but do at least have nameplates. Brian Bunt is sitting on Geraldine's right, frowning through bushy eyebrows at a pile of reports marked 'Howard'. What on earth can he be reading about them in that file, Julia wonders. Next to Brian is Maisie Tuckey, a young woman with a complexion of deathly pallor. Winding her colourless hair compulsively around her index finger, she gives Sean a small, lopsided grin. And finally, there's Adam Turner who might be a graduate trainee, in his tight floral shirt and shiny maroon flares. Sean can see muscular legs spread wide beneath the desk and chest hair sprouting through a gaping button on Adam's shirt. He senses that Adam is cocky and smart: the loose cannon and possibly the most threatening.

'Please, do take a seat down,' says Geraldine. They sit directly opposite the panel like opposing forces in a trench war. Sean tries to break the pattern by twisting his chair to a 30-degree angle and rocking it gently on its back two legs.

'Do be careful with the legs on that chair, Mr Howard,' warns Geraldine. Like a meek schoolboy, Sean rights the chair and twitches his tie. The grilling begins.

Two hours down the line, it feels like the panel have extracted and examined every aspect of the Howards' lives. Aspects they were barely aware of themselves. Just when they think there is nothing else to expose, Geraldine delivers her killer blow.

'Now, Mr Howard, we note that you—erm—have a fertility issue. Can you tell us a little more?'

Sean's head shoots up. He thought they knew this. He *knows* they know it. It's in the reports. Surely he's not expected to talk about this in front of two strange men and three women, one of them his wife?

'Yes, I believe it's all there in the report,' he says.

'But we'd like to hear about it in your words, Mr Howard. How it impacts on you. How, for instance, it makes you feel about fathering a child that is not your own.'

Sean swallows hard. Maisie is gazing out of the window, either bored or embarrassed. Julia is plucking at the little mirrors on her bag. Brian is still silently scanning the papers, as he's done all morning. But Adam Turner is looking straight at Sean. His bright, mocking eyes feel like an assault on Sean's manhood.

'You can rest assured that 1, or rather we, have considered this issue most carefully,' says Sean. 'My wife and I have worked through the pain of knowing we are almost certainly unable to conceive and we have come to terms with my infertility. We are keen and ready to move forward with adoption.'

Sean's speech is met with a momentary stunned silence. Then Adam Turner pipes up: 'Mrs Howard, would you agree?'

Julia pictures their lovemaking, how mechanical it's become, although of course they do really love each other. She thinks of the nightly struggle to reassure Sean that everything is all right—although clearly it isn't. 'I, 1, yes I've accepted it. We've accepted it,' she mutters, finally tugging one tiny mirror off her bag.

But Adam Turner isn't ready to let them off the hook. His eyes bore into Sean like hot coals and the trace of a smirk hovers around his mouth. 'So, to clarify things. You've accepted it as a couple. And Mrs Howard says she's accepted it. But what about you, Mr Howard? Can you share your sense of acceptance of it with us?'

Sean fixes Adam Turner with a blandly cordial mask. 'Of course, Mr Turner. 'You don't need to procreate to consider yourself a man.' He feels like adding that you don't need leg muscles or copious chest hair either. The tension between the two men crackles for a moment and then passes like a summer thunderstorm.

'I think we're ready to conclude,' says Geraldine. 'We're all aware that Mr and Mrs Howard have been talking to Camille over a period. Camille has reported back to us on these conversations. We now need to discuss this as a panel and reach a decision.' Brian Bunt snaps the Howard file shut and Maisie transfers her pale gaze from the window to her fingernails. Adam Turner does a spot of man-preening, fiddling with his wicker belt buckle and raking his hands through his heavy hair.

'Would you step outside, Mr and Mrs Howard? We need to discuss your case as a team but it really shouldn't take too long.' Geraldine smiles, briefly but encouragingly. 'My judgment is that you will make excellent parents.'

Sean and Julia wait in the hall. Somewhere, a clock is ticking but otherwise it's utter silence. The rooms must be soundproofed. Julia looks at her watch: it's been 26 minutes. She plays a game with herself. If it gets to 30 minutes, it's a no. At 28 minutes on the dot, the doors open and Geraldine's broad red face peeps through. 'Do come in again, Mr and Mrs Howard. We have a little someone we'd like to talk to you about.'

As they file back into the room, Geraldine seems almost as thrilled as they are. The rest of the panel are doing whatever they were doing before the world turned on its axis: Maisie examining her nails, Brian reading files through his bushy eyebrows and Adam Turner admiring his shapely thighs. For Geraldine it's still a vocation, while for the rest of them it's already just a job, thinks Sean. Even cocky Adam Turner who's barely got started in life.

'I'm delighted to say that you can, if you wish, meet our little girl. We've called her Bea just for now, for reasons I will explain to you shortly.'

Sean looks at Julia and they nod in unison. Does this mean they've passed all the tests? It's scarcely believable and they dare not ask.

'I'm going to tell you what we know about Bea but I'm afraid it's not much,' Geraldine pauses and clears her throat. 'She was abandoned several weeks ago and taken in temporarily by a foster family.'

'Where?' asks Sean. 'Where was she abandoned?'

'In a cemetery. Highgate cemetery.' Geraldine gulps and pauses again. Best to leave a few moments for this to sink in. It's a macabre case and she can't help wondering how Mrs Howard will take it, given her close relationship with death. Some couples would run a mile at this point. The upside is that abandoned babies are often the easiest to place. Most likely they weren't wanted in the first place, so there's less chance of them being wanted back. Not having a known back story can be an asset. She waits to see how the Howards will react.

Julia has turned the colour of parchment and Sean is clutching her hands. Geraldine hesitates.

'I'm going to tell you all I know,' she says when she is certain they are not about to get up and go. 'Several weeks ago, an American couple, tourists we believe, were visiting the cemetery and found a Moses basket half-concealed behind one of the gravestones. The little girl was asleep and wrapped up warmly in the basket. It didn't look as if she had been there for very long.

'Not knowing what to do, the American couple took the child to the main gate at the cemetery and from there she was taken in by social services. They found her to be healthy and well looked after, so she was transferred to temporary foster care. We judge her to be around three months old. Do you have questions at this point?'

'Which gravestone? Whose gravestone?' asks Sean. It's a crazy question, but it's suddenly crucial for him to know. A bit like everyone having the right to know their place of birth.

'Gosh, that's something I don't know. But I'm sure I can find out for you.'

'Who are the American couple? Can you give us their names? Why did they just dump her at the gate?' asks Julia.

'I'm afraid I can't divulge their names or contact details because they want to remain anonymous. But I can reassure you on one point. They didn't just dump Bea. They acted responsibly. They clearly cared what happened to her and left her in good hands.

'We are keen to keep Bea's details confidential. Nothing will be gained from the newspapers getting hold of this. Notoriety is likely to have an adverse effect on Bea's future development and that's what we would like to avoid. At some point much further down the line, it may be necessary to share the details with Bea. But that's a long time away. For now, we must observe what's best for Bea. We would expect co-operation from the adoptive parents in this respect.

'There's something more I can tell you—it's only a small thing,' Geraldine adds apologetically. 'She was wearing a little hat in the shape of a bumblebee when we found her. That's why we named her Bea. Her adoptive parents, whether you or anyone else, will naturally be free to change that.'

Geraldine pauses. 'This is a lot to take in. Would you like to meet Bea. Do you need more time? Or would you prefer, in the light of the background, to reconsider?'

'Of course we want to see her,' Julia says. They are led back down the lime-green corridor to a door at the far end. Inside is a makeshift nursery of sorts. Faded images of apple-cheeked babies beam down from the walls. In one corner is a Formica table with a beige changing mat, a pile of grey nappies, milk bottles and several bright plastic rattles.

The cot is placed ceremoniously in the centre of the room. Julia approaches it in a daze, while Geraldine and Sean hang back, caught up in a procedural sort of conversation about dates and forms. For Julia, their talk is white noise: she's transfixed by the baby in the cot. Bea is fast asleep, snuggled down in cellular blankets. All Julia can see is a Mohican shock of black hair and a tiny squeezed-up face with a puckered mouth and long dark lashes.

'Do pick her out. Give her a cuddle. Here, let me help.' Geraldine lifts the fragile bundle from the cot. Snuggling Bea into her shoulder, Julia is intoxicated by baby smell: a mix of skin, powder and milk. Underneath, she sniffs something acrid. Could the baby need changing? She drifts into a gentle rocking motion, crooning into the side of Bea's head, whispering into her velvety ears.

Something about Julia's whispering disturbs Bea. As she wakes, she beats the air with her little fists and her head nods furiously against Julia's chest. Then she starts to cry. Although Julia has heard babies cry many times—in shops and supermarkets and on the underground—she never heard anything like this. She feels completely in thrall to the sound. And also helpless, as if it's her job to fix it, but she lacks the skill or emotional energy to do so.

Bea's cries reach a crescendo. 'Shall I take her?' Geraldine offers tentatively. 'I think she wants feeding. That bobbing motion—that's what they often do when they're hungry.'

Settled in Geraldine's expert grip, Bea's cries subside. By the time she's passed to Sean, she is emitting the odd shivery hiccup. He wraps her tight to his chest and she snuggles in close like a kitten. Julia watches. She's never felt such a terrifying mix of emotions. She is falling in love with Sean all over again, seeing him with the baby. But she hates him too, for calming Bea when she couldn't. Geraldine, who seemed like a perfectly pleasant woman just an hour before, is now hateful because she can handle the baby. And Julia despises herself for being so inept. She, who has always been capable—to be honest, a bit of an over-achiever—can't even soothe a baby. And *they* can. Those mums on the high street, the ones who look so pale and distracted and despairing. Is this how they feel?

'Could I try again?' Julia takes Bea in the crook of her arm and is once again hit by the sweet and acrid baby smell. She examines her cupid lips and perfect button nose. Then she looks into Bea's eyes. They are black, opaque and inscrutable. Julia feels hollow. But like the good mother she has promised herself she'll be, she kisses the baby on the cheek, stroking her Mohican gently back off her brow.'

'Take her now, please Geraldine. We'll be in touch soon.'

Chapter 21
Julia and Sean, 1978

It's the big day. The papers are signed, the meetings completed, the promises made. Julia lies in bed, a knot of apprehension in her stomach. Today they will bring their daughter home. She nudges the still sleeping Sean. How can he be so calm?

'Sean, Sean, please wake up.'

He grunts and rubs his eyes. It's a late November morning and the alarm hasn't gone off. He's truly desperate for a little more sleep, just 10 minutes would do it. 'How're you doing?' He fumbles for his specs. He hates waking up to a blur in the morning.

'I'm okay. Good.' Julia wonders if she should mention that the knot in her stomach feels more like dread than excitement. Since that first meeting at the agency they've kept to the party line that they're delighted—elated to be adopting Bea. Any individual doubts are kept firmly under wraps.

'Did you remember the nappy liners?' she asks Sean. Since becoming a mother—that's how she's trying hard to think of herself—she's obsessed with practicalities. The small nursery is crammed with plastic product in tones ranging from tomato red to what the marketing men like to call café au lait. This is the colour palette of seventies babies, Julia thinks ruefully. She's painted the nursery a tasteful dusky rose, paying homage to Bea's gender but avoiding those horrid 'traditional' baby pinks that make her wince.

Sean is roaming around the bedroom, repeating the 'essential product' list like a mantra. 'Baby wipes, liners, Babygro, bottles, sterilising solution. Um, I think we forgot cotton wool,' he adds. The list is endless, with a mountain of beige and white plastic invading their empty spaces. Julia worries he's beginning to feel a bit pushed out.

'Mustn't forget to put the Moses basket in the car. Oh and a bottle in case Beatrix needs feeding,' Julia shouts up the stairs. Sean trundles barefoot downstairs to join her. It's freezing, but he's not a man to wear slippers, or a dressing gown for that matter. He always says he's still far too young for such things.

Julia is dressed and ready and has dropped her mumsy Karen Carpenter look. She's transformed back into a magnificent witch, draped in silver grey to the ankles, her black lace-ups peeping out below. She's added a harlequin scarf and a porkpie hat in maroon, from which her hair streams in a dark river.

On the familiar route to the adoption agency, she gazes through the car window at the rain-splattered shops with their garish frontages and silly names. Passing Veggie Rama, she thinks: I shall be a proper mother next time I buy potatoes from there. She laughs inwardly and it releases the tension in her stomach. They arrive at least 15 minutes early and argue about whether to wait in the car park or go in regardless. Julia wins. At the very end of the puke-green corridor, Beatrix awaits, like a baby princess in a tower, impatient to be set free.

Geraldine Lilley takes them straight to the nursery. At the door, she hesitates. 'I meant to say…I'm not sure if it's appropriate at this stage, but I appreciate you were keen to know. I found out more about the circumstances of Bea's desertion.'

'Yes, we want to know,' says Sean, although Julia is less sure.

'Well, I spoke to the staff at the cemetery. We managed to track down the member of staff who attended to the couple who found her. As I said, I can't divulge anything about the couple. But I do know the date.'

'Which was?' asks Sean.

Geraldine peers at them over her mannish spectacles and clears her throat. 'It was the 31st,' she says. 'October 31st.'

'Halloween,' replies Sean.

'That's right.' Geraldine's face is a mask of professionalism. But she's clearly unsettled by the details surrounding Bea. 'We were also able to pinpoint the exact location where she was found. It's close to the eastern entrance. You take the main pathway to the right for about 100 yards, then turn left on to a narrow-overgrown track. About halfway along, on your left, you find a child's grave. The name on the gravestone is Lillian Rose Dempsey. Sadly, she was only four years old when she died in 1940. Bea's Moses basket was tucked down beside that gravestone. As I told you, she was warm and well cared for. She can't have been there for so very long. It's a little macabre, I know...' Geraldine's voice trails off.

Removing her specs, she clears her throat and the mask falls away. 'Look, I know it doesn't sound good. A baby found deserted on a gravestone on Halloween—well, it's enough to give anyone pause for thought. But Bea is a baby, an innocent victim in all this. She's *your* baby now. Yours to love and nurture and cherish. My advice to you is to put this disturbing back story behind you, leave it in a box and get on with your lives. As a family.'

'Of course,' says Julia. 'This is what we must do, Geraldine. We appreciate you sharing it with us, but we will not allow it to define Bea or our perception of her.' The lime green walls are pulsating and her stomach is crawling. What are we taking on, she asks herself.

In her shabby nursery, Bea slumbers peacefully, but now it's time to pick her out. Julia prays that the child won't cry, or start that weird pecking motion she does when she's hungry. Not in front of Geraldine and the staff at the agency. She reaches in to the cot and gathers the tiny bundle into her arms. Sean is behind her, stroking the small of her back. Bea's puckered face is peeping through her white cellular blanket and Julia breathes in the sweet powdery baby-smell. A wave of protectiveness sweeps over her. 'Our daughter,' she says and she feels something like love warming the pit of her stomach, replacing the pangs of anxiety.

Bea opens her eyes and looks directly into Julia's. They are very dark brown, almost black and they are impenetrable. It's unsettling. They seem to be looking into Julia's very soul. Mother and daughter stare at each other like soon-to-be lovers meeting for the first time. Then Bea opens her tiny mouth and lets out a sharp cry. Her face grows angry and Julia hands her hastily to Sean.

Enveloped in Sean's arms, she begins to settle. 'A daddy's girl, do you think?' observes Geraldine.

Her tone is light, but Julia is wounded. 'A bit early to tell, wouldn't you say?'

'All the ladies love me,' says Sean, rocking Bea gently and cooing into her ear.

'Hmm.' Julia shoots him a withering look and Geraldine busies herself with the carrycot they've brought. 'Would you like this to keep for her when she's older?' she asks, holding up the bumblebee hat. 'At some point, if her past becomes an issue and you do feel it's right to tell her what happened, it might make a nice keepsake.'

'Mmm,' says Julia. 'Why don't you just keep it? We want to focus on our family, going forward.'

'It's the only significant belonging Bea possesses from her other life. I quite understand why you might not want it. But you never know…in the future. It might help her.'

'Okay, we'll take it.' Julia stuffs the bumblebee hat in her bag. 'We'll give it to her when she's bigger. Maybe we can tell her she wore it as a new-born. We don't have to mention the other life.'

The atmosphere could be cut with a knife. It's a relief to everyone when they've said their goodbyes and the Howards, plus their new addition, are headed out to the car.

'I should sit in the back,' suggests Julia. She gets carsick and never travels in the back, but the thought of Bea crying all the way home and not being able to stop it fills her with foreboding. Bea seems to like the motion of the car. Julia notices that Sean is watching them both anxiously in the rear-view mirror, so she closes her eyes and allows herself to relax into her own personal space.

This is hard, she admits, though Bea is beautiful. Harder than she ever imagined. She worries that she hasn't carried Bea inside her for nine months. How can she compete with a birth mother? Nor can she feed Bea. She will never breastfeed her own baby, so how will they develop the close bond she longs for? Is she destined to be an inadequate mother?

Bea shudders as if dreaming and Julia is flooded with what feels like love— and pity. Is she missing her birth mother? Stroking Bea's cheek with her little finger, Julia makes a vow. *Your name is Beatrix now and you belong to us. And I promise that you will never, ever feel that you belonged anywhere else.*

Undisturbed, Beatrix sleeps on. Julia sniffs her powdery smell, strokes the Mohican off her forehead and tucks her in securely once more.

She's glad Beatrix doesn't open her eyes.

Chapter 22
Julia, 1979

October 31 is Beatrix's 'official' birthday and the aroma of baking cake is wafting from the Howards' authentically retro kitchen. Sean's pinned happy first birthday streamers in the porch and the hall is festooned with balloons in shades of baby pink, blue and lilac. Upstairs, Julia is coaxing her daughter into a tiny peach party dress, complete with smocking and peter pan collars.

'Come on Beatrix,' she pleads. 'Grandma and Grandpa will be here any minute.' Beatrix probably doesn't understand a word, but Julia's sure she gets the message. Why can't she sit still for a moment? Julia picks her up by the armpits and lowers her on to the changing mat, but Beatrix won't lie flat. Recalling the health visitor's advice not to let things turn into a battle, Julia decides that dressing her in an upright position is the only option. Like a soldier on enemy alert, she waits for the moment when Beatrix will be distracted and battle can commence.

When the doorbell rings, Julia is still busy negotiating her daughter into starry sky tights and Beatrix is producing a thin wail of protest. She has excellent hearing, or so the health visitor says. Everyday background noises, like birdsong, wake her and she is visibly shaken by sharp, unexpected sounds. She hates the babble of water running into the bath, or the coffee grinder, or even the car door slamming shut, although she hears these sounds daily and must be accustomed to them.

While Julia clears up the debris, Beatrix is busy trying to climb the chest of drawers via her toddler stool, to see out of the window. 'Beatrix. No.' Julia remembers the advice about clear commands in the face of danger. Ignoring her, Beatrix wriggles up on top of the chest of drawers: one more push and she'll be in danger of falling straight through the window or on to the floor. 'Beatrix, let's get you back down now.'

Standing upright on the chest of drawers on her wobbly little legs, Beatrix stares blankly, almost defiantly, at the opposite wall. It's as if I'm transparent, Julia thinks. Grabbing the child, she lifts her like a sack of potatoes to the floor. Mother and daughter remain locked in combative embrace for a moment. Julia nuzzles her face into Beatrix's neck and finds her endearing baby creases. 'Baby, when oh when will you start to listen to me?' she whispers into her ear.

This is Julia's conundrum. At 12 months old, Beatrix can walk, climb the stairs and most of the furniture, feed herself with a spoon and almost open her own buggy clasp. But what she can't, or won't do is speak. For Julia, language is a sacred tool: if she could just speak with Beatrix surely all misunderstandings would melt away as if by magic. She could explain *why* climbing furniture is all wrong. And *why* we have to dress in the morning, eat three meals a day and go to bed and sleep without protest. But Beatrix is not having any of it.

'How's it going up there?' Sara shouts from the bottom of the stairs. 'Shall I come up?'

'Please do.' Julia's utterly defeated and the party hasn't even begun. There's a lot of rattling downstairs as Sara negotiates the staircase.

'Get Sean to do that,' Julia shouts down. 'It's really fiddly.'

'I can't. He's at the end of the garden with Ernest, in the shed.'

Julia groans inwardly. She calculates the time it will take her to open two stairgates, one at the top and one at the bottom of the stairs. Surely she can do it in 30 seconds, 45 tops? Beatrix is doing something vaguely constructive with her building bricks. Julia holds her breath and makes a run for it.

But by the time both women are back upstairs, Beatrix has discovered a stray wax crayon under her cot. Her peach party dress now has a deep purple line daubed across the bodice. 'Beatrix! What have you done?' Julia cries.

'Let me take her a moment,' suggests Sara.

'You're welcome.'

Cradling Beatrix firmly in the crook of her arm, Sara mutters into her ear. 'Hello, little one. What have you been up to now?'

Beatrix gives Sara her implacable gaze. Her black, almost opaque, eyes give little indication of what she's feeling. Julia shivers. What could this child's history be? What has she seen—or lost?

'Let's not worry about the dress. She looks so pretty. Let's just have a lovely day, shall we?' Sara cuddles Beatrix tighter to stop her wriggling.

'She doesn't really like being cuddled, Mama. She prefers to be on the go.'

Downstairs, Sean and Ernest are opening a bottle of bubbly. Thank God, thinks Julia. She's become over-reliant on alcohol in the past year, but she hasn't the strength to resist it. It takes away that nasty cold knot of anxiety in the pit of her stomach.

Taking a big gulp, Julia watches her mother and father jiggle Beatrix between them, singing Happy Birthday in Dutch. Ernest, in particular, has such a way with her. He's wearing his trademark double-breasted, suit complete with tie and shiny black shoes, while Sara is formally dressed in a russet two-piece with belted jacket and flared trousers. They don't seem to care a lot about getting creased or sicky. So solid, so dependable, both of them. Her own flesh and blood.

Sean is giving her the look that says: I can see you're at the end of your tether. He's right. She's been up since 5:45 a.m., while he slept on. Things had gone reasonably smoothly until mid-day when it was time for lunch and nap. This is usually an oasis, but today Beatrix was having none of it. After refusing carrot puree, she resisted Julia's efforts to get her to lie flat in the cot, arching her back and emitting a pitiful wail. Julia prayed the neighbours couldn't hear it. Now, she's overwrought and grumpy. Not the happy family idyll Julia had wanted her parents to see.

'You're right. I'm exhausted. I'll take half an hour.' As she climbs the stairs, she gazes wistfully at Beatrix who is now cuddled up on Ernest's lap while Sara sings Hush a Bye Baby. The little so-and-so is going to drop off to sleep, she just knows it.

Lying down with a sigh of relief on the big marital bed, Julia hears footsteps and a moment later Sean appears. 'Having a challenging day?' he asks, sitting on the edge of the bed and sweeping her up in his arms.

'Oh Sean, I love her so much but it's *so* hard.'

'Yes, I guess babies are harder than we thought. And we didn't get nine months training either. It does feel like being pushed off a precipice. But I never heard of an eight-year-old crying all night or throwing a wobbly over carrot puree. It's got to get better.'

'Eight years, Sean?' I'm not sure I can take eight more days of sleepless nights and daytime meltdowns. I need her to be eight years old *now*.'

Sean nuzzles the top of Julia's head. 'What do you imagine she'll be like when she turns into a real person?'

'I have no idea. Quite likely, she won't be like me and she won't be like you either.' Sean has hit on a sore point.

'I sort of imagine her as a free spirit. Maybe someone artistic like Frida Kahlo. Or powerful like Germaine Greer. It's not all about nature, is it? Nurture comes into it too.'

'All I want is for her to be happy.' But even as Julia says it, she knows it's not the whole truth. She wants her daughter to be clever and resourceful, articulate and civilised like her parents—or actually adoptive parents. But where does Beatrix come from? Found abandoned in a graveyard on a cold autumn day. What sort of a woman could her birth mother be? It's playing with Julia's head all the time. Who is Beatrix?

'It's the not knowing,' she tells Sean. 'I'd just like it if she cocked her head to one side to listen attentively, like you do. Or if she tugged at her fringe when she was nervous, like me.'

'She'll learn to copy us, you'll see. She'll pick up our good habits—and our bad ones. She'll soon pick her nose when she thinks no one's looking like me and wag her finger in the air when she's being bossy like you.'

'You know, you can look at her birth history in a positive way, as well as a negative one,' adds Sean. 'It's actually rather romantic, like the beautiful princess imprisoned in the tower until she's rescued by the hero and heroine of the tale. Us, of course.' He tilts Julia's chin and kisses her gently.

'Mmm.' She's dropping off to sleep and Sean's tiptoeing towards the bedroom door when there's a commotion downstairs.

In the sitting room, Sara has a flailing Beatrix grasped firmly in her lap. Ernest is bent over near the sideboard clutching his hand and blood is dripping on to the floor.

'What the?'

'It's fine, it's okay. Ernest cut his finger rather deeply. He needs a tissue and we'll clean it up,' says Sara.

'How on earth did he do that?' Sean wonders how many ways can you cut yourself in an under-furnished sitting room?

'It was an accident. A wineglass fell on the floor and broke. Ernest was picking up the pieces.'

Sean looks at the three remaining wineglasses sitting on the low sideboard, waiting to be filled with bubbly to toast Beatrix's birthday. 'But they're on the sideboard. Of course, it's no one's fault, but I don't get how one of them fell off.'

'Well, actually, it was Beatrix.' Sara sounds sheepish. 'She was crawling around the floor one minute and the next she'd pulled herself upright using the sideboard. I ran over, but it was too late. She'd already taken a swipe at the wineglasses and one of them tippled over.'

Sean notices smears of blood on the stripped floorboards beneath him. Beatrix has already crawled through it and added bright red smudges to the purple gash on her party dress. She waves her arms in delight, like a director who has masterminded a spectacularly gory crime scene.

'Well, Beatrix is happy enough. She does seem to like to take centre stage!' says Sara.

At that moment, Julia steps in. She takes in the shattered glass and the blood, her injured father and a jubilant Beatrix in a ruined peach dress. 'Beatrix, what will we do with you?' She gathers the squirming child in her arms. Beatrix looks into her mother's face and lets out a high-pitched scream. As her rage gathers momentum, her little face contorts and she beats her fists.

'Sssh, sssh now,' says Julia. But nothing will deflect Beatrix's screams. As her little daughter's rage intensifies, Julia hands her, like an unwanted gift, to her mother.

'You take her please. I can't deal with this right now.'

Chapter 23
Julia, 1985

Jacob Theodore Howard, born on Christmas Day 1984, was the miracle no one believed could happen. It's 3 p.m. on one of those grey March afternoons when winter is reluctant to loosen its grip. Julia is lying with three-month-old Jake in the crook of her arm and they are both supposed to be napping. She watches him intently as he studies his starlike fingers. Still, she can't believe he's real. Soon Beatrix will arrive home from school and their special time will end.

Jake takes after his maternal grandmother, Sara, with tufts of fuzzy blonde hair and bright blue eyes. Julia is convinced she knows the moment he was conceived. After the adoption, life was tough. She and Sean grew apart. She was constantly stressed by Beatrix's needs and grew introspective and self-absorbed. Sean turned outwards, finding solace in his work, colleagues and students. A gulf developed between them, which neither seemed able to bridge.

Then Beatrix started full-time school and Julia got some me-time back. She began work on her illustrations. She would visit clients, donning her gypsy velvets and high boots and pulling her hair into an artfully messy topknot. One spring afternoon, Sean arrived home early from work. In her study, Julia was working on an illustration involving a muddy puppy and a fat-cheeked toddler. The sun shone like sherbet through the 99lated blinds. Julia looked up as Sean walked in and smiled in the guarded way he loved. He took her in his arms and guided her to the couch. Lovemaking felt real, urgent, alive as it had in the beginning. Julia marked the day with a primrose that she pressed and dried in her diary.

After that, they regained much of their lost closeness, though even now it ebbs and flows. Some weeks after that afternoon, Julia noticed changes in her body. Her small breasts felt sore and swollen and her face lost its angles. She was nauseous and couldn't even eat her favourite chocolates. Feeling it was playing with fate to take a pregnancy test, she made an appointment with the GP. When pregnancy was confirmed, she pressed another flower, this time a daisy, into her diary.

Julia rejoiced in being pregnant. She gloried in her fecund body and her abundant head of hair. She would talk to the baby and very soon he would 'answer' with a gentle kick of his tiny foot or hand. It was a happy time and an easy birth. Despite this, Julia can't escape from a sense of unease that there will be a price to pay for such good fortune.

She hears the front door open: Beatrix and Sara are back from school. 'Come on up. We're both awake. I'm just about to feed him.'

They clatter up the bare staircase, Beatrix trailing a few steps behind Sara as usual. This is one of several things about Beatrix that Julia finds disconcerting. She doesn't behave in a predictably childlike way. In Julia's experience, seven-year-old children romp in ahead of the queue and bounce on the bed. They don't loiter in the background. But Beatrix has a quality of reserve, which Julia has learnt to accept. Response must be teased from her.

'Come and say hi to baby Jake.' She pats the bed for Beatrix to sit with them. 'It's okay, he's awake. You could tickle his chin. He likes that.'

Beatrix edges closer to Jake and reaches out her hand, but is reluctant to touch him. 'Go on, tickle his chin, Beatrix, he won't break,' Sara urges.

'Shall I, Grandma? He might cry.' And sure enough, as Beatrix begins to stroke Jake's neck, he lets out a plaintive wail.

'No, Beatrix, you're being too rough with him,' says Julia, pushing her hand away.

'I thought he liked it.'

'Of course he does, darling. You just have to be ever so gentle with babies,' says Sara. 'Why don't we show mummy what you've been doing in art today?'

Beatrix drags a crumpled sheet of paper from her blazer pocket. 'We all did a picture of our family today. So this is what I did.' She hands it to Julia.

It's a conventional drawing of a mum, dad, big sister and baby brother. Beatrix has exaggerated Julia's long flowing dresses, her rainbow colours and bright lipstick. Sean's pictured close beside her, head to toe in trademark black. Beatrix is standing a little apart and, as an illustrator, Julia has to admire the way she's captured herself: olive complexion, black eyes, curtain of dark hair and skinny arms and legs. But there is something very odd about the way that Beatrix has depicted Jake. Lying in a crib at Julia's feet, he dominates the picture—a big, fat, nude cherub drawn larger than his big sister and almost as large as his parents. It's sinister, thinks Julia, hating herself for thinking it and feeling guilty about her lack of enthusiasm.

'It's lovely, darling,' she says. 'You look so like you and I love the way you've done Daddy and me. But why is Jake so big?'

'He's big because he's most important. The most important thing in a picture should be the biggest. Mrs O'Connell told us that.'

'But he's not most important, Beatrix. You're just as important. You're equally important.' Even as the words are formed, Julia is examining her conscience and persuading herself it's true.

'Okay.' Beatrix shrugs.

'Perhaps we'll go downstairs now and leave Mummy to get more rest,' suggests Sara. But Beatrix is already plodding across the landing in her heavy-footed way and soon there's a cacophony of cartoon voices floating up from the TV.

She'll soon be in her familiar screen-shutdown mode. Once locked in to a favourite show, she's transfixed, sitting for an hour or more, apparently without moving a muscle. Julia doesn't think it's healthy, but it's better than the alternatives. If any attempt is made to turn off the TV, Beatrix will either fight for the controls, or cover her ears and scream very loudly until it's switched on again. Or there's her silent and deadly mode, where she walks wordlessly from the room and makes for her bedroom. Once inside, she slams the door hard and barricades it with furniture. That may be the last anyone will see of her until the following morning. Julia thinks this reaction, though the least disruptive, is the most disturbing. She finds Beatrix's capacity for self-containment chilling.

'Let her go. It's best. She needs to sort her feelings out in her own space,' suggests Sara.

Julia hesitates. She wants to confide in someone, but instinctively feels that Sean isn't the best person. Should she burden her Mama with this? Sara is generous and wise, but Julia has grown up from the age of 10 with an instinct to protect her. From what, she wonders. Beatrix isn't a Jewish child growing up in Nazi Germany. She isn't even Jewish, as far as they know. That's the thing, they don't know.

'Mama, while you're here and it's just the two of us—apart from Jakey of course—I wanted to ask you something. About Beatrix.' Julia plants a kiss on Jake's tufty head.

101

'Yes.' It's a question and a statement at once.

'Where do *you* think Beatrix came from?'

'Well, you would know more about that than me, child.'

'It's just, she's seven now and I know she was a high-maintenance toddler but I seem to find her as challenging as ever. Could it be something to do with her background?'

Sara seems to choose her words with care. 'I can only speak from my experience with you and Peter. I can remember myself being seven too, but not much. And soon after that, there's a huge blank until I was 18 and pregnant with you. Yes, Beatrix is different from how I remember you being as children. I'll be straight with you. Your expectations were so high when you adopted her, but when she came to you as a baby, things didn't seem to turn out quite the way you hoped. Now, I sense a certain distance there.'

'You're right. Perhaps we never quite bonded as we should. Having Jake has made me realise something of what I should have felt with Bea. But how do I mend that? What can I do?'

'I think, child, you must resolve this uncertainty you have about her past. Yes, she was found in the cemetery. Yes, she has a way about her that's different and can be unsettling. But you must put that in a box and forget where you hid the key. Or, there's another way.'

'Which would be?'

'Take the bull by the horns. Find out, finally, who she is. Where she comes from. I believe it may be easier to track down such details nowadays. Start with the adoption agency and see if they can provide more detail. They may be less reluctant now that Beatrix is, on the surface of it, settled. You said an American couple was involved. Perhaps the agency can supply an address. This thing haunts you. So attack it, Julia, don't let it overwhelm you. Don't let Beatrix grow up a stranger.'

'Thanks Mama.' Julia gently gathers up Jake and takes him to his nursery, a cheerful den of palm trees, exotic flowers and jungle animals. He's sleeping soundly and she places him gently in his cot, kissing his head which smells blissfully of her own milk.

Downstairs, Sara is trying to coax Beatrix from the TV set. 'How about some of your favourite cheese on toast with spaghetti hoops on the side?'

'No!' Beatrix is a fussy eater, so food enticements fall on deaf ears. If only Sean were here, thinks Sara. He'd get her to eat something. They've developed a bond, Sean and Beatrix, and he can coax her to do things that no one else seems able to.

But when Julia comes down, the tension lessens. 'Tea, Beatrix.' Without even discussing choices, she puts fish fingers and alphabet fries under the grill. 'Thanks Mum. I'll take over now. You're right, I need to know. And I'm going to find out. But please keep Sean out of it.'

Later that evening, Julia tiptoes up the stairs to check on Jake. Beatrix's door is firmly closed but there's a sliver of light around the doorframe. Perhaps she's fallen asleep with her book? Julia gently opens the door and sees that the duvet is mussed up, the bed empty. With a pounding heart, she checks the big wardrobe. Could Beatrix be playing tricks on her?

Back on the landing, Julia notices that Jake's door, always left ajar, is firmly shut. Anxiety mounting, she bursts into his animal kingdom. The nightlight is projecting coloured stars across the ceiling and emitting white noise that sounds like the sea in a shell. It takes a moment for her eyes to adjust to the dimness and then she sees them.

Jake is lying in his king-size cot, on his tummy with his bottom in the air. Beatrix is in the cot too, deeply asleep.

But the strange thing is that, instead of lying next to Jake, she has arranged herself so they are head to toe, with Beatrix's legs tucked close to his tummy and his head reaching just above her knees. If she'd wanted to lie close to Jake, why point herself in the wrong direction.

Julia doesn't have the heart to move them—Sean can carry Beatrix back to her own bed when he gets home soon. But she can't rid herself of the feeling that this strange configuration is a clue to Beatrix's past. She tells herself to stop being silly. 'Too much imagination, Julia,' she hears her mother say. Gently shutting the door, she tiptoes back downstairs.

Chapter 24
Julia, 1985

Do adopted children have half-formed memories and leftover behaviours from their early lives? This question haunts Julia. Since her conversation with her mother, she's been obsessed with the worry that she hasn't bonded with her daughter. And part of the problem, she reasons, could be that Beatrix hasn't properly let go of her former life.

Julia can't get out of her mind that night she found Beatrix lying upside down in the cot, head to toe with Jake. She can understand a toddler lying upside down in a cot. But why a seven-year-old?

Carefully hidden in a locked metal file in the outhouse is a collection of other 'evidence' she's amassing. Not even Sean is allowed to see it. On her study desk is a pile of reference books with titles like *The Psychology of the Early Years* and *Interpreting Childhood Memories*.

Sara has been enlisted to help and today they're planning a visit to Highgate cemetery. Julia has the adoption papers, but they really tell her nothing more than she knew when Beatrix was adopted. The only tangible piece of her past is the bumblebee hat. Julia's beginning to feel the task is insurmountable.

'I wish I'd kept the Moses basket and the clothes she came in too. They might have held some clues. Where they were bought, for instance. The weird thing is, there are no newspaper cuttings. Or not any I can track down and I've spent hours in the library. Wouldn't you think the press would have picked up on an abandoned baby?'

'Mmm.' Sara is anxious about what they might uncover. Julia can't, or won't let this rest. She doesn't want Sean involved until she has something concrete to show him, so it falls to Sara to provide the support. 'Why don't we get a move on while Jake is well fed and happy. With any luck, the cemetery will hold some clues.'

Julia grabs the baby bag and carrier and settles Jake, who is warm and snuggly after his feed, in the back seat. It's a fresh spring day and when they arrive at the cemetery, Julia thinks it looks more like a burgeoning arboretum—an affirmation of life—than a memorial to death and decay. Her spirits lift a little.

They head straight for the East Cemetery, Jake jogging gently in his baby carrier strapped around Julia's tummy. We're crazy, what are we doing here, she thinks. Anyone who had anything to do with Beatrix's mysterious abandonment probably left years ago. Even if the warden at the time was still here, he might not want to talk about it. He mightn't even remember. This is mission impossible.

But Sara thinks differently. As a 'lost' child herself, the miracle of finding or being found never happened for her. Throughout her life, in every street corner and on every crowded train and boat she has sought a bright blonde head and the guttural tones of her native Dutch. She never found Pieter. But she knows of many who lost everyone, then found just one—an elderly aunt or a long-lost cousin—years later. Some have found long-ago lovers and some have even been reunited with children who were wrested from them in the camps. For Sara, nothing is impossible.

'We're looking for someone,' she says in her accented English to the young man in the ticket office. 'A warden. He would have been working here seven years ago and he was involved with a baby who was abandoned in the cemetery.'

'Right,' says the ticket man guardedly. He looks like he just got out of school and is wearing a peaked cap pulled down over his brow, so it's hard to read his expression. A badge on his jacket identifies him as Sam.

'We're not here to cause trouble, truly,' says Julia. 'You see, that little baby is my daughter—my adopted daughter—and she's seven now and we all feel we need to know a little more about the circumstances. It's just personal, honestly. We'd be so grateful…'

'Are you sure you want to bring all this up? A mate of mine, his mum had an illegitimate son she gave away at birth. This would be 22 years ago because my mate's 20, same as me. A few years back, his mum got it in her head she wanted her boy back. They went to all sorts of trouble to find him. He was a teenager by this time, of course and living with a foster family. Wow, he was trouble that kid. My mate wishes he'd never clapped eyes on him and family life has never been the same since. If you want my opinion, there's nothing to be gained by raking up the past. Why rock the boat?'

'Because my daughter's not right. She has dreams and odd habits. She's solitary. She doesn't make contact easily. It's like she's hiding secrets. We, I, have to get to the bottom of it.'

The clock ticks in the long silence. Sam gazes at his cracked gardener's hands. 'Bill's your man. But he's dead. Died this spring. He was 69 so he had a reasonable innings. Good man—we all miss him. We used to take our lunch breaks together sometimes. He told me about that business with the abandoned baby. It haunted him. I don't think he ever got over it.

'He left a log though,' adds Sam. 'If you can show me some sort of proof you're the adopted mother, I'll let you see it.'

Julia scrabbles in her bag. What will work? In her purse, she has a picture of Beatrix as a toddler but that's probably not enough. Her child benefit book? She throws both on the table, along with Beatrix's library card. 'We named her Beatrix after Bea.'

Sam retreats into a back room. It seems to take forever, but eventually he returns with a yellow folder labelled 'bumblebee baby, 31/10/78'. Inside is a single sheet of lined paper covered in meticulous old-style cursive handwriting. 'He was one of the good uns, old Bill.'

Julia resists the urge to wrest the file from Sam's hands. 'Take it,' he says. 'Read it for yourself. He had good handwriting.'

'Write this down, Mama. It was mid-morning on October 31, 1978. He was manning the ticket office when an American couple came in, carrying a Moses basket. He's given precise directions to where she was found. Remember, we never got that from the adoption agency. Look here, it has their names, Mike and Libby O'Brady. Irish originally, perhaps. They never told us their names either—they said the couple didn't want to be contacted.'

'Yes, well, there's a story behind that too,' says Sam, who is warming to Julia. 'Bill told me. The man was in a rush to catch a plane, but his wife came running back. She was a bit breathless and said she couldn't stop. Seems she'd told hubby that she had to go to the ladies! Anyway, she'd scribbled something down on a scrap of paper—their address. Hubby hadn't wanted to get involved, but she told Bill that if ever there was a problem with that baby and she could help in any way, to please contact her. It's there in the log somewhere.'

Julia scans the log to locate the address: Elizabeth O'Brady, 220 Lauren Avenue South, Westchester, NY. 'She didn't put the zip code in, but who cares! We got it.'

Bill had carefully noted Beatrix's pathetic collection of belongings, which amounted to bedding and the clothes she was wearing, along with the bumblebee hat.

'But there's more,' says Sam. 'Bill was a bit of a sleuth, between you and me. Wasted as a warden. He was curious as to where the baby came from. So you know what he did? He took a look at the labels in her belongings and it turns out they were all purchased at the same place. Well, if it had been somewhere like Marks or Woollies, it wouldn't have got us far because they're all over the place. But guess where they did come from?'

Sara and Julia nod encouragingly in unison.

'Turns out it was a shop called Baby&Co. Big shiny new place opened in the mid-seventies. It means nothing to me. But Bill told me his daughter shopped there for her little one. I'm pretty sure it's not there anymore, gobbled up by Mothercare probably. Now you're going to ask me where this shop was and I think I can help you on that score. Bill's daughter lives in Tooting, so it's more than likely the shop was south London way.'

'Why didn't Bill tell all this to the adoption agency. And why didn't they tell us?'

'No idea. Bill told me they were a funny bunch at the agency. Maybe they wanted to keep it quiet and simple, thought it would be less painful for all concerned that way. They're an adoption agency. I guess they're under no obligation to track down stray birth mothers, d'you see?'

Julia does see. 'Would you show us where she was found?'

Sam nods and they follow him along a broad path, turning on to a narrower track at a junction. Here, the flora and fauna is thicker and acid-yellow primroses are pushing up out of the ground. He stops by the gravestone of Lillian Rose Dempsey. 'Just here. Warmly wrapped up and well-fed, according to what Bill said.'

It is the sight of Lillian Rose's grave that brings Julia to her knees. Is she grieving for the unknown child Lillian? Or for her own daughter who—she now suspects—is weighed down with a sadness she lacks the understanding and language to express? Julia kneels beside a clump of primroses, the heels of her hands to her eyes, Jake hanging from her, still slumbering in the baby carrier. Bending stiffly, Sara tentatively rubs her shoulder. It is a tableau of loss and grief.

Sam shifts from foot to foot. 'I should be getting back. Tickets don't sell themselves.'

'Of course,' says Sara. 'Please leave us here. We may stay awhile. You've been so helpful and so kind.'

'Well, I just hope it didn't make matters worse,' Sam pulls his peaked cap even lower over his eyes and disappears through the undergrowth.

'Mama, we should go.'

'There's no hurry, my darling, if you want to stay a little longer. Plenty of time before school ends.'

'No, no. We must go. I need to make a transatlantic call. Today. Now. It must be getting-up time in New York, right?'

Back at home, Julia gently hands Jake to Sara. 'Please take him, Mama. I need to make this call now, before Beatrix is back and I mustn't be disturbed. Afterwards, we'll put Jake in the pram and walk down together to pick her up.'

In her study, she grabs the phone and asks international directory for an NY number: Michael O'Brady, Lauren Avenue, Westchester. 'No such listing,' chimes the operator. On a hunch, Julia says, 'Try for Elizabeth O'Brady.'

'Got it,' says the operator. 'Shall I put you straight through?'

'No, just give me the number for now, please.' Julia scribbles it down on her pad. She replaces the handset, takes three deep breaths and finally dials. On the fifth ring, it picks up.

'Westchester 58246,' says a sprightly voice.

'Could you be Elizabeth O'Brady?'

'Sure that's me.'

'I'm sorry to disturb you. My name is Julia Howard. I have an adopted child, Beatrix. She was found as a baby in Highgate Cemetery seven years ago. I believe you and your husband found her.'

There is a long silence at the other end of the line, then: 'Jeez.'

'I do apologise for bothering you, but I'm trying to learn as much as I can about Beatrix's experiences before she came to us. I know you weren't with her for long, but sometimes the smallest thing may have a bearing.'

'Is she not well then, the child?' asks Elizabeth in her husky New York drawl.

'Yes, yes, she's fine physically. But she has some issues with behaviour and she seems to be finding it hard to connect. Emotionally, I mean.'

'Oh hey, sorry for that. I guess I was with her for no more than 20 minutes so I don't think there's much I can add. She was such a pretty little thing. Lots of black hair and bright eyes.' Elizabeth clears her throat. 'That whole episode was the start of a pretty bad time in my life.'

'I'm sorry to hear that.' Julia hopes she isn't going to hear the full story.

'Yeah, Mike and I split up and to be honest it all kicked off with that incident with the baby. You see, it showed me how uncaring Mike can be. Ultimately. To think he was just prepared to shimmy off back to NY without even leaving contact details in case that poor baby ran into trouble, didn't get adopted, whatever. I couldn't get my head around it. Mike and I live apart now, which is why it's just me listed at this address.'

'That's awful.' Julia wishes she could be more empathetic towards a disembodied transatlantic voice.

'Yeah. Awful. But it's life. What're you planning to do, going forward? She's seven now, right. Does she know she's adopted?'

'No, but we're considering telling her.' Julia's beginning to feel more comfortable talking to the disembodied voice. It's like unburdening yourself to a therapist who can't see your face. 'She seems to have memories. She wakes up with bad dreams and suchlike. We, I, think perhaps she would be more comfortable in her own skin if she knew.'

'But what can you tell her? That she was abandoned in Highgate Cemetery. That you have no idea what sort of shitty family she comes from. That is so unsettling. Believe me, honey, she's better off in ignorance. You'll get through this troubled time and further down the line, she'll appreciate the wonderful family she's got. She doesn't want to think, "Oh, but hang on. I'm not really a part of it."'

Julia hears the Atlantic Ocean crackle and quiver down the line. Elizabeth is so convincing. What if they do find out something really awful about Beatrix's background? Is that going to help her? Or them, for that matter. The reality of knowing the truth is sinking in.

'You're right. Thank you so much for your advice, Elizabeth. It's the right advice. I need to stop this obsession.'

'You're welcome, honey.' The line goes dead.

Julia runs back down the stairs and takes Jake into her arms. 'We have to stop this,' she tells Sara. 'Let's bin all those books and cuttings. Beatrix belongs to us now. She's part of this family.'

Chapter 25
Sean, 1989

'Images of Men in the Mass Media' is a compulsory strand in the curriculum for Sean's students this term and it's given him pause for thought. Made him think more about who he is and what function he performs. When he was growing up in the late fifties and early sixties, it was all so simple. Men were there to bring in the bacon, mow the lawn, wash the car on a Sunday morning (if you were lucky enough to have a car) and perform light duties with the kids, maybe Saturday mornings and half an hour before bed.

Shoving everything into his briefcase after a day in which he's been verbally challenged by one student and discovered another in tears, he wonders what awaits him at home. It won't be light duties. He has the misfortune—his word—to do a job which finishes formally at 5 p.m. No one counts the hours of preparation and marking.

He's noticed that the epicentre of nuclear family life occurs around 5 p.m. Is that because it's when he walks through the door? Could it possibly have been going on at that tempo all day? Jake is typically throwing a tantrum for one of several reasons: he can't find Teddy, there's no ketchup, his Lego tower has fallen over, or his sister-who-should-know-better has given him a sly dig in the ribs. Beatrix has low blood sugar—Sean wishes this let-out clause for all sorts of bad behaviour had been invented when he was a child. It basically gives her carte blanche to disobey Julia, assault Jake as long as it goes undetected, refuse to eat anything but peas and sit on the sofa in a collapsed heap, glaring. Meanwhile, Julia will be wandering around looking like an unexploded bomb.

Getting into his car, he sees Amanda Cox teetering across the tarmac towards him in her high heels. She's gesticulating in a way he can't ignore. He groans. He just wants this thing to stop.

'Sean, thanks for stopping! Could I get a lift?' Amanda lives in Eggleston Avenue, the next road to his.

''Fraid not, Amanda. I have to stop by the supermarket on the way back.'

'Oh, well...I could wait in the car?'

Now Sean has to think on his feet. 'Aha, it's a big shop. It'll take a while. Plus I have the car seat and my fold-down bike in the boot...Not enough space, sadly.' He prays she doesn't ask to check the boot. The fold-down bike is a barefaced lie. It's at home in the garden shed where it belongs.

Amanda is crestfallen, it's clear. But she's doing a good job of not showing it. 'Okay, no worries. I better run for the bus.'

Revving up his engine, Sean lets out a sigh of relief. Amanda Cox is a red line and he crossed it. And he doesn't want to go there, not now or ever again.

Amanda Cox has always been one of those fixtures around the college. Sean never really noticed her. She was just a bottle blonde head bobbing around in the library, tidying up shelves and signing out books. Until the day Sean's life went pear-shaped. He'd popped into the library to find a book on how media influences social morality. Home had been a war zone that morning, what with Jake throwing up in the marital bed and Beatrix doing her school-refusal bit. It was a relief to gaze into Amanda's sunny, unclouded face and feel the warm wrap of her concerned attention.

'Mmm, not sure we have a title devoted to that topic, Mr Howard,' she said. 'But I'm confident we can find something that touches on it.' Amanda's heels clacked across the parquet floor and as she bent down to a low shelf, Sean admired her breasts, two brown speckled eggs tucked into her low-cut blouse.

'Ah, yes. Here's something,' she pulled out a book called *Adolf Hitler and his Role in the Growth of Mass Media.*

'Well, it wasn't quite what I had in mind.' Sean hunkered down and took a sidelong glance at the brown eggs.

'Well, what did you have in mind?'

Is this a come-on, Sean asked himself. He'd been out of the territory so long that he'd lost his sense of the terrain. A sense of panic overtook him.

'Look, I need to go...errr, Miss Cox. I have a class right now. Maybe I'll try again later.'

'Call me Amanda, please do. And may I call you Sean? Listen, why don't I see if I can drag some material out for you and it'll be ready when you finish classes.'

Sean gulped. A tempting offer, on so many levels. 'Okay. Sounds good. Julia likes me home at teatime though.'

Amanda's expression was unfathomable. Was it pity he saw in her eyes? Or lust? He loped off to his first class. The rest of the day was hard. One student used his *Media and the Moment* textbook as a launchpad to propel an apple core into the air. It hit one of Sean's more sensitive female students right in the eye and they both ended up in the principal's office. The photocopier broke down so he had just 10 minutes to re-think his Images of Men presentation. Predictably, the students picked holes in it. And halfway through the afternoon, the principal's secretary pulled him aside in the corridor to say that Julia had phoned in to ask if he could let her know exactly what time he'd be home. WTF, she knew perfectly well. Without the beguiling images of Amanda's tantalising smile and speckled tits, he wouldn't have got through the day.

For the next couple of weeks, Sean seemed to need a lot of reference books and Amanda was reliably on hand to supply them. One afternoon she told him that she hadn't brought her car. Would he mind giving her a lift back to Eggleston Avenue? Perhaps they could nip in for a quick 'reviver' at the Wellington Arms on the way. No more than half an hour. Her treat. Sean, still in denial that this was about anything bigger than the demand and supply of books, readily agreed. Julia was out at the cinema with a girlfriend anyway and the children were at their grandparents'. If he ever wanted to stay over for a pint with a friend after work, they were always happy to cover. They loved being with Beatrix and Jake and they exerted a mysterious good karma over them. It worked all round.

'Just let me call my in-laws and tell them I'll be a little late. Can I use your phone?' asked Sean, leaning across the desk and breathing in the essence of My Lily, My Lady that exuded from Amanda's cleavage.

Minutes later, they were heading towards The Wellington Arms in Sean's Datsun, *She Drives Me Crazy* beating out over the car radio. Trigger-happy, Sean leant over Amanda's shiny American Tan thighs and reached for his sunglasses. She gazed into the setting sun.

The pub garden was open, but they opted for the womb-like interior where they found a round table in the corner and stared at each other over frothing glasses. Sean felt his cock rise, twitch and stiffen slightly under his tight jeans, so he tucked everything out of sight under the tabletop.

'Shall we?' asked Amanda. It was the end of any form of pretence. They jumped in the car and headed back to Eggleston Avenue. This was dangerously close to home, but by now Sean wasn't thinking straight.

Inside the front door, Sean and Amanda clawed at each other like drowning cats, hurling bits of clothing all over the narrow hallway. Still locked together, they stumbled up the stairs to Amanda's bedroom. She turned on the lamp and Sean stopped in his tracks. The walls were painted baby pink and a group of soft toys sat on the bedspread, gazing up at him mournfully. Above the bed was a giant image of Rod Stewart in snake-hip stance. A kidney-shaped dresser was heaped with glittery things: make-up, jewellery, coins and a silver-backed hairbrush. Beneath the bed he spotted a pair of pink ballet shoes. This was a kid's room for God's sake. A little girl's room. And Amanda must be all of 35. What was he doing here?

He prised Amanda off and held her firmly at a distance. 'This is wrong,' he said. 'I shouldn't be here. I shouldn't be doing this.' A wave of longing for Julia's musk perfume overcame him. Julia would *never* wear pink. He craved her angular body and black clothes and sheer reticence. He ran down the stairs, leaving Amanda with her soft toys. Struggling with his clothes, he picked up his car keys and slammed the front door shut.

Next day came around all too soon. There would be hell to pay, Sean knew it. But he would not evade his responsibilities. Making his way straight to the library, he found Amanda dispensing books, as usual. She was wearing sunglasses and when she removed them her eyes were badly swollen.

'Amanda, I'm so sorry,' he said. 'It's not that I don't find you attractive. It's just that I love my wife. Look we can't talk here. Do you have the car today?'

She nodded dumbly. No.

'Well, at the very least let me drive you home and try to explain to you.' He sensed this was probably a mistake, but as a gentleman what else could he do? She nodded again.

So that was how, on September 26, 1989, at 4:30 p.m., Sean Howard's car came to be parked in Eggleston Avenue. Inside, Sean poured out his soul to Amanda. How he'd thought he could never have children. How, now he has *two* children, family life is driving him crazy. Why he will always be in thrall to Julia, even when she seems absent from him. Amanda held him in her arms, like the mother he never sees, offered a tissue and listened patiently. Neither of them noticed Beatrix, crayons clutched in her hand, rounding the corner into Eggleston

113

Avenue. Nor did they hear her running towards the Datsun shouting: 'Daddy, it's me.'

Then she stopped abruptly. In the car, parked at the kerbside, she saw two heads. In the late afternoon sun, they looked like partially joined-up silhouettes. She hid behind a privet hedge and watched the mysterious silhouettes through her curtain of black hair As the sun began to lower and dip in the sky, two heads came into focus: a blonde head and her father's, dark and close-cropped, leaning into it. Neither Amanda nor Sean noticed her turn and retrace her steps around the corner.

Chapter 26
Beatrix Howard, 1989

When Beatrix is 11 years old, she transfers to Dame Mary Ellen's, a private day school for girls. She's actually 12, but no one speaks about the missing months before the graveyard event. Julia and Sean have picked the school with care. Both agree that Beatrix needs careful handling. Julia usually chooses the word 'different' to describe Beatrix. On a bad day, Sean silently translates that to 'difficult'.

Dame Mary's, as it's known, is a gothic Victorian mansion concealing a big modern block where most learning takes place. The girls wear straw boaters in summer: the black velour winter hats have been phased out. The school motto, which translated from the Latin means 'study leads to freedom' or 'study makes you free' reminds Sean disturbingly of the inscription over the gate at Auschwitz. He wonders what his mother-in-law Sara thinks. Hopefully she can't read Latin. With their mauve stripy ties and regulation black shoes (white socks for summer, grey for winter, compulsory) the girls make quite a show as they saunter through the urban village of Hampstead.

Beatrix has made it clear that she hates the uniform. On her first day, she sets off with white knee socks pooled around her ankles ignoring her mother's pleas to pull them up neatly. She's consulted an old Girl Guides manual belonging to Julia that has a section on tying knots and she's cleverly adapted one of the more bizarre knots to her school tie. It now looks more like a neck brace. Dismissing the 'recommended' school satchel, she's opted for a backpack, over which her long black hair flows like a shiny black glacier.

'Won't you use your new satchel, darling?' asks Julia. 'It's what the school recommends.'

'This is better.' Beatrix only says what's necessary. No explanations, modifications or additions. It means that her mother always has to ask another question to get to the nub of things.

'Why's it better, darling?

'Cos you have to carry a satchel on one shoulder. A backpack spreads the weight. See?' Beatrix points to the Girl Guide Manual and opens it up to a page on trekking. It clearly states: *'Guides should always spread the weight load across the back, rather than carry it on one shoulder. So do use a backpack rather than a shoulder bag when out trekking.'*

Julia sighs. To be fair, she can see the sense of it. What she can't understand is Beatrix's willingness to be different. When she was at school, all she ever wanted to do was blend in. She watches her daughter trudge down the garden path, head bowed. She'd begged to be allowed to walk with her, or even drive, on this the first big day. But Beatrix had been firm: she'd go it alone.

On the pavement, a gaggle of St Mary's girls is passing by, giggling like schoolgirls do. Beatrix studiously ignores them. One of the girls, a year or two older, was at her primary school. Her name is Candice: Beatrix remembers it well because all the other girls were envious of the name. Not Beatrix though. Why would you want to be named after a sweet?

Raising a hand and almost blocking the pavement, Candice says: 'Off to *big* school, huh? Better pull your socks up. Didn't anyone show you how to do your tie right? You look wee-erd, Beatrix Howard. You oughta smarten up before Mrs Pascal sees you.' The others watch, enthralled, to see how Beatrix will react.

Sidestepping Candice, she stomps doggedly down the pavement, without a backward glance. There's a queasy sensation in the pit of her stomach that she's beginning to recognise as anger. Fury at Candice for picking her out. And a relentless dull ache of anger at her mother that she can't make sense of and finds confusing.

Once at school, Beatrix is directed to her new form classroom. There's no assembly on the first day as the head judges it more sensible to get the girls straight into a classroom routine. Beatrix is relieved because she's heard assembly is religious. If they ask her what religion she practises, what should she say? She knows that Grandma and Grandpa are Jewish—although she's not entirely sure what that means—but she has no idea what goes on in her own home. Nobody ever mentions God.

After the girls have been assigned desks and filled them up with brand new exercise books, pens and pencils in neat rows, her form teacher, Mrs Pascal, asks everyone to listen. 'Girls, I'd like every one of you to accustom yourselves to doing a little homework each night. And I have a crafty idea to you get into the habit of it, while helping me to learn more about you all. Now, does everyone have an English language exercise book to work in and a pen?'

There's a rumbling of assent and Mrs Pascal continues.

'Most of you have written stories before. The title of the story I want you to do for me today is *My Family* and I want to hear all about your life at home. Tell me about your parents. Do you have brothers or sisters? And, very important, what is it about *your* family that makes it special. Start now and you may take it home to complete it.'

There's a wave of rustling, whispering, subdued giggling and a few sighs. Mrs Pascal holds up the flat of her hand: 'Quiet, please girls. It only takes one girl to distract the whole class. And that's not fair, is it?'

The hubbub subsides and all Beatrix can hear is the tick, tock of the classroom clock. In the pit of her stomach, the new, raw anger at Candice is still swishing round, along with the old throb of resentment against her mother. She opens her exercise book, puts *My Family* at the top of the page in a decorative script, chews her pen for a long time and begins to write.

My Family by Beatrix Howard

I have a mum, a dad and a baby brother called Jakob. My dad works as a sort of teacher, but it is more importent than a teacher. My mum works at home. She has an office in the bedroom and I am not alowed in there if she is busy. My mum never gets cross but she looks tired when she sees me. She has to look after my brother too. I am trying to love my brother but I dont. It's okay because everyone else loves him a lot. I dont look like my mum and I dont look like my dad either. I read a story about a girl who did not know who her real mum and dad were. It made me think, are these my real mum and dad? They are not like me. Jakob is like them. I like my house but it is a bit empty because we do not have much stuff and we do not have carpets. My dad is nice and he is kind to me. The other day I saw his car quiet near our house. My mum was at a meeting and grandma was looking after us and I was walking home from the shops, My grandma said I could go there to one shop only to buy some new crayons for my

project. My dad and another lady were in the car. She was sat next to him in the
car. He reached over and they kissed. I ran away as I did not know what to do. I
hate my life now. My dad is going to leeve us and go to live with that other lady.
Then nobody will love me much because he loved me most and he will be gone.
I am sure my real mum and dad are someone diffarent. They might have a brother
or sister for me. I hope I find them.

Beatrix checks it over: there aren't too many crossings out and although she's unsure of a few spellings, she thinks it will do. No need to take it home. It's done. At the end of the lesson, she hands it in to Mrs Pascal and heads to geography.

The next couple of days at the new school pass uneventfully. Everybody is busy learning the ropes, making new friends and establishing their place in the pecking order. The teachers are bogged down by admin, new curricula and the struggle for names. No one notices the shadow girl with the long black hair and cheap backpack who sits at the back at a desk on her own and barely utters a word.

That changes on Thursday morning. Julia has delivered Jake to his school and is sitting down to work when the phone rings.

'Mrs Howard?'

'Yes, that's me,' says Julia anxiously. She's a terminal catastrophiser. One of them—Sean, Jake or most likely Beatrix—is lying under a bus, she's sure.

'It's Dame Mary Ellen's, Mrs Howard. This is Miss Pattison, the head, speaking. Can we have a moment to talk?'

Julia's heart lurches. 'What's happened to Beatrix? Is she ok?'

'Sorry, let me assure you, Beatrix has not had an accident, Mrs Howard. She's in class right now. But I would like to talk to you about her. Perhaps better not on the telephone. Would you be able to pop down?'

'When?' Julia can feel her heart rate is up. Surely Beatrix can't have done something awful so soon that they're going to expel her.

'I can hear anxiety in your voice, Mrs Howard and I sense that this is a matter best dealt with sooner rather than later, for all concerned. Would you like to pop in later this morning?'

Julia has a deadline at the end of the week and she feels a mountain of work collapsing around her. But Miss Pattison is right: best sooner.

'That works for me, Miss Pattison. Shall we say 11? Or, if you think it better if my husband comes along, we could make it after 4 p.m. sometime?'

There's a pause at the other end of the line. Miss Pattison clears her throat. 'Um, actually, Mrs Howard, it might be best if it was just you.'

'Okay, see you at 11 then.' Julia is slightly mystified, but she guesses it must be because Miss Pattison wants to get off on time. After all, school closes at 4 p.m. That must be it.

Promptly at 11 a.m., Julia is waiting anxiously outside Miss Pattison's office that is, naturally, in the Victorian part of the building. She's abandoned her pretty witch look and gone mumsy, with a simple A-line skirt, print blouse and cardy. The black lace-ups are a bit of a giveaway, but with any luck, Miss Pattison won't look down. The disguise gives her a boost of much-needed confidence. Miss Pattison emerges from her office at 11 on the dot and extends a gnarled, bejewelled hand. She is a vision of perfection, from the tip of her silver head, through her eau-de-nil couture suit to her low beige courts. A whiter shade of pale.

'Do come in, Mrs Howard. Can I offer you a coffee?'

Julia is worried that her hand may shake if she is required to pick up a cup, so she declines. 'No thank you, Miss Pattison. I just had one.'

'Ah yes, too much coffee—not good for the system, is it? I try to limit it to two a day.'

Just get on with it, Julia pleads silently. She can't take much of the small talk. She lets a pause hang in the air.

'Well, Mrs Howard, I expect you're wondering why I asked you in.'

Julia nods, fearing any comment from her will throw Miss Pattison off *piste* again.

'It's about Beatrix's essay,' says Miss Pattison. Julia notices that Beatrix's exercise book is sitting right there on the desk in front of her.

'Yes? I haven't actually seen it myself.'

'Well, Mrs Pascal set the essay assignment, *My Family.* It was intended as an introductory exercise which would tick several boxes in that it would allow her to assess where the girls are at, academically, as well as helping her to get to know each one of them individually.'

'Mmm.' It all sounds perfectly reasonable and Julia can't understand what it has to do with Beatrix.

'Perhaps you should read it, Mrs Howard. I've thought long and hard about the ethics of involving you in this. I have no intention of interfering in the private lives of the families of our girls. But there are issues here that may impact not only on Beatrix's academic performance, but on her psychological health. And clearly, that is my business.'

Julia almost snatches the exercise book off the desk and begins to read. The silence elongates. At length, she looks up, tears in her eyes. 'I see.'

Miss Pattison opens her drawer, brings out a tissue and hands it over the desk. Julia has the impression that it was put there earlier, specifically with her in mind. Now that Miss Pattison is firmly in the ascendency, her tone becomes less unctuous, more condescending.

'I feel there are a couple of issues here, dear. Of course, the state of your marriage is not my business. Only in the way it impacts on Beatrix and her ability to reach her—umm—potential at school. But what does concern me is Beatrix's apparent lack of self-esteem. And at the heart of it appears to be an issue with the way she relates to her—ahem—mother.'

Reaching across the desk, Miss Pattison extends her claw-like hand over Julia's small white one. 'I feel this is painful, my dear. And I don't quite know how to counsel you.'

With a sense of rising claustrophobia, Julia wrests her hand away and pulls herself to her feet so she is towering above Miss Pattison. 'I'm sorry. I can't be here. I have to go.' She makes for the door. Once safely on the other side of it, she doesn't stop running until she's out of the school grounds and around the corner. Glancing furtively behind, she's relieved to see that no one is following. And then the hot tears come, salted with hurt, anger and guilt.

Chapter 27
Beatrix, 1994

School sucks, thinks Bea. But nothing like the way it sucked at Dame Mary Ellen's where the kids were stuck up and made her feel like a weirdo. She flunked GCSEs—well, not exactly, she did pass four. But that wasn't enough to stay on in the sixth form at Dame Mary's.

Done with school, Bea was all for leaving and getting a job. But her parents had other ideas. They made her feel like she couldn't be a proper person if she didn't go on to the sixth form. In the end, they sent her here, to join the sixth form at Gunter Park Comprehensive. It meant that instead of signing up for stuff like Latin and History, she could go for Drama and Eng Lit which she does quite like because she doesn't mind reading. It takes two buses to get here, but there's a good buzz down in Haringey. She loves the rickety little shops with their strange fruits and veg, the noise and bustle and the random people you see wandering around. Hampstead is boring, with its stern, silent villas and oppressive trees.

Bea (as she's now known to everyone, except her parents who still insist on calling her Beatrix) is sitting in her favourite spot on the window seat in the science labs, munching the remains of an apple. She shouldn't be in a lab at all—she gave up science light years ago—but she snuck in here so she could watch the activity at the bike racks down below, where a lot of stuff happens.

Right now, she sees Mr Ellis the science teacher, doodling towards the racks on his ancient bike. So uncool, it even has a basket for Mr Ellis's textbooks. Bea can feel her apple core burning a hole in her fingers. Raising the sash window, she takes aim at Mr Ellis' bald pate. Splat! It hits the shiny part with force, causing macerated bits of apple to slither down his face. His bike is now skittering around, his textbooks are floating in a muddy puddle and he's about to fall off. Dismounting the bike, Mr Ellis waves an angry fist at the lab window, but Bea's face has disappeared from view.

'Go Bea, go!' shout voices behind her. 'Go get 'em!' She turns around to see several classmates cheering her on from the lab benches. For the first time ever, thanks to Gunter Park Comp, she's *almost* popular and basking in it. At Dame Mary's, it seemed like everyone wanted to be teacher's pet. Some of the kids here long to be rebellious, but they're too chicken. Bea, who is fearless, is more than happy to do it for them.

She hears Mr Ellis thundering up the stairs to the labs. Stealthily, she slips into the huge stinky-egg science cupboard where the chemicals are kept. It's a survival technique Bea knows how to use, an ability to blend into nothing when she needs to. She carefully closes the cupboard door on herself. She's in luck: it's slatted which means she doesn't need to worry about being able to breathe.

Through the slats, she spies parts of Eddie Mercer, Cindy Pattison and Matt Hargreaves, all kids in her class. They're sitting at a bench looking down, she guesses at their textbooks. She can see a bit of Willy Harmer too. He seems to be studying a Bunsen burner, although Bea's sure he doesn't know what to do with it. Willy is doing drama, like her. He shouldn't be in the lab at all. What a wanker, she thinks.

Then she hears Mr Ellis's booming voice: 'Who did that? Come on—own up.'

'Not me, Sir,' chorus Eddie Mercer, Cindy Pattison and Matt Hargreaves in unison. All Bea can see of Mr Ellis is his sleeve jacket where apple stalk, pips and flesh form a malevolent cluster at the elbow.

'What're you doing here, Willy? You're not meant to be in the science lab.'

'I come here to eat my lunch sometimes, Sir. It's quiet and I don't get bothered. Usually.'

Willy is definitely an oddball. He gets nicknamed X-ray man because of his other-worldly translucent skin and skinny arms and legs. His big claim to fame is his eyelashes. Bea reckons they're bigger than his hair. He's good at drama, no getting away from it. But he's still a jerk.

From her cupboard hideout, Bea hears a background rustling which she guesses is Mr Ellis bumbling around. She holds her breath. 'What's this?' he says.

'My lunchbox, Sir.'

'And it's empty. So what did your mother provide you with for lunch today?'

'Ham and mustard sandwiches, a tomato, a yogurt and an orange drink,' replies Willy uneasily.

'And? What else?' thunders Mr Ellis. 'Could there have been an apple in there?'

'No, Sir. Honestly, Sir,' replies Willy miserably.

'You lot,' says Mr Ellis, turning to Eddie, Cindy and Matt. 'Get off into the playground until lunch hour ends. And as for you, Harmer, my office *now*.'

Bea can't help clocking that Willy doesn't try to put the blame on anyone else. Impressive, she thinks, but not impressive enough. When she hears Mr Ellis clumping towards the lab door, accompanied by Willy's light pattering step, she cautiously extricates herself from the cupboard.

Safely back in the library, Bea finds herself the quietist spot she can for what's left of lunch hour. From her schoolbag, she pulls a well-thumbed book. The jacket image depicts a Victorian beggar boy gazing wistfully through a set of magnificent wrought-iron gates. In the background is an old country home and in front is a young girl, her hair in blonde ringlets to her shoulders. *Great Expectations* is written in ornate copperplate across the top.

Since two second-year sixth drama students scripted this as a play and the head of drama announced it would be staged at the end of summer term, Bea has become obsessed. She wants to play Estella. In an ideal world, she would *be* Estella: beautiful, proud, clever and irresistible to men. But getting the part will be hard. For starters, she doesn't have blonde ringlets, although she's begun to twist strands of her pancake-flat black hair around a pencil when class is boring.

There are bad things about Estella as well as glamorous ones. She can be cruel, manipulative and heartless. And there's that sense she's all alone in the world. Bea can buy into that. Though not an orphan herself, she sometimes thinks she might as well be, what with Jake eating up all the love in their house.

Bea's just got to the bit near the end where Pip and Estella reunite in the garden of Satis House, when the bell rings. It's not quite clear if they get together and that's worrying her. With two lessons to go before the big audition, she's trying to get inside Estella's head. So much so that she nearly calls Eddie Mercer 'boy' when he passes in the corridor.

At 4 p.m., the Estella auditions begin in the drama workshop room. They are reading a piece from early on in the story when Estella first meets Pip and is at her most arrogant and disdainful. First up is Abigail Riley who is blessed with blonde curls and slightly hooded eyes that give her the appearance of looking disdainfully down her nose. Bea thinks that listening to Abigail read is so full of nothing that it's like bathing in tepid water. Next is Emily Peterson who gets the anger, but none of the angst that Bea feels is such a key part of Estella's character. Katie Burne fluffs her lines, goes very red in the face and walks offstage. Then it's Bea's turn.

Sean once told her that he always takes three deep breaths before beginning a lecture and Bea thinks it's good advice. It has the effect of pitching her voice just a shade lower. Her Estella is a bully, but also a victim; manipulative but needy; haughty but damaged. With her black hair and angular face, no one ever thought of Bea as an Estella. But now they see she *is* Estella. There's a ripple of applause.

Two days later, Bea is called to see the head of drama and offered the part of Estella. It's a big commitment—is she ready for it? he asks. He sees in her a fresh way of looking at the character of Estella, a way which focuses on the character's underlying anguish as well as on her beauty and arrogance. Does that strike a chord? Bea nods: 'I feel like I am Estella. But who will Pip be?' she asks. It suddenly seems very important.

'Oh, didn't you know. We've offered the part to Willy Harmer. He's Pip all over. You'll see. Are you okay with that?'

'I guess so,' says Bea, shrugging on her backpack.

Chapter 28
Bea, 1995

Finally, Bea's making proper friends. She's hanging out with Matt, Cindy and Eddy at Matt's house while his parents are away for the afternoon. They've pooled resources and have two small cans of lager, half a pack of Marlboros, a tube of Smarties and a bar of Cadburys Dairy Milk. Oh and a small quantity of weed carefully wrapped in tin foil. Bea's excited to try it, perhaps a bit scared too.

Since the apple core affair, as they call it, the foursome are bound together like glue. They respect each other, that's what it is, thinks Bea. Nobody snitched on anyone to Mr Ellis, although they did let Willy take the can. But that worked out fine in the end because the drama department was so fixated on him for the part of Pip that they found a let-out way to punish him. Just a detention, which Willy didn't mind at all. It meant he could read in peace and quiet.

The great thing about Matt, Cindy and Eddy is that they're all outsiders, like Bea. Matt comes from a posh family in Hampstead too. His mum and dad seem to think it will do him good to go to the comp. Truth is, Matt's not over-bright and even at the comp he's punching above his weight. He's supposed to be doing medicine at uni, but Bea can tell he won't hack it. Poor Matt. Why can't they just let him get on with being a musician, which is what he wants to be and what he's good at.

Cindy's parents arrived on a boat from Jamaica in 1969 when they were both 19 years old. It took them forever to settle in London because they hated it—the grey, rainy summers and cold winters when frost would lace the insides of their windowpanes. Cindy was born in 1978, the fourth of five children. 'They just kept going to stay warm, like a couple of rabbits,' is how she puts it. Everything Cindy does is about being proudly Caribbean: she wears bright turbans, plays

Bob Marley although he's dead and has even managed to acquire her parents' cool Caribbean lilt though she's never been there herself.

Eddie is the nerd. He's doing maths and science and his teachers are even talking about Oxbridge. He doesn't talk much and he seems more into numbers than people. When he goes into a room, he's more interested in how many people are in there, than who they are. It's weird, thinks Bea, but in some ways she's the same. For all the books she has to read at school and the others she devours by torchlight under her bedclothes at night, she doesn't really get why people do the things they do. It's a code she's always trying to unlock.

They all know what they want to be. Matt is going to be a doctor, although he'd much rather be a musician. Eddy wants to be an astrophysicist and Cindy's dream is to be a midwife. Bea thinks she'll make a good one. What better way for a baby to enter the world than into Cindy's big, warm arms? Bea has a goal too, but she's not telling anyone what it is. Actually, she has told just one person. Someone she knows will never betray her.

'I got an idea.' She raises a hand to get everyone's attention. 'I could get Julia and Sean to let me babysit.' Bea never calls them mum and dad, it sounds naff. 'I'll try for Saturday. If I swing it, you could all come to mine once the coast is clear and we can try out the stuff? We can get Willy over too.'

There's a pause. 'Why does he need to be there?' asks Matt. Because I want him to be, thinks Bea. They all know she's close to Willy and they think it's odd. Whatever. She leads the group and on most issues they come around to her way of thinking sooner or later.

'Well, I suppose it makes sense to have it at yours,' says Matt. 'It's a bit dodgy here. You never know with the olds. I'm never sure when they're getting back.'

'Ask Willy if you must, Bea,' adds Cindy. 'As long as we can be sure he won't snitch on us.'

'Why didn't you get more of the stuff?' asks Matt. They all know that Cindy took the weed from a stash, which is meant to be secret, in her parents' pine dresser.

'Too dodgy. They're not stupid. As it was, I had to bulk out of tobacco, just to be sure they wouldn't notice anything was missing.'

'Okay.' Bea's impatient to get going now that her plan has been endorsed. 'My place, Saturday, half eight unless you hear. They'll have cleared off by then.' She throws the goodies into a plastic bag.

Back home, Julia is sitting at the kitchen table helping 10-year-old Jake with homework. Bea clears her throat and lowers her shoulders. The way she presents this is crucial.

'Mum, you know you said I could babysit Jake when I got to be 17.' Julia loves it when she calls her mum. It always puts her in a good mood. 'Well, I am 17, so can I? I could do with some extra money, for clothes and things. And it would be fun to sit Jake.'

Julia seems distracted, which is good because it means she's more likely to agree to anything. 'Of course, darling. Next time we want to go out, we'll give it a try.'

Bea swallows and thinks fast. 'I thought maybe we could give it a trial this Saturday. You and Sean, dad, haven't been out together on your own for ages. And Willy could pop over. Just for an hour. We could give it a trial run.'

There's a big pause. Including Willy in the plan is a huge, calculated risk. Julia could go one of two ways. Jake adores Willy so that might swing it. But then, Julia might worry about them being up to no good, as she calls it.

'Oh, Mummy, can Willy come? He might do sword fights with me again,' says Jake. Willy has been learning stage-fighting at his drama club and Jake loves the pretend stabbing which always ends up with Willy writhing on the floor in mock agony.

'Would you like that, Jakey? Well, let's try it then,' says Julia.

Bea lets out a sigh. 'I better call Willy right away. Check he's free.'

As she heads towards the house phone, Bea pictures Willy sprawling on his candlewick bedspread in his back bedroom at home. It's cramped in there and every bit of wall is covered with theatre posters, most of productions he never got to see. Nobody gets the connection between Bea and Willy. Her crowd think he's a wimp. They call him 'ghost boy' because he's so thin and pale. Willy, being easy-going, has accepted the nickname as an endearment that Bea finds sad. She wishes he'd stick up for himself.

It seems a lifetime ago that they were onstage playing Pip and Estella. It was a turning point for both of them. When Bea arrived at the first rehearsal, Willy was huddled in a corner devouring the script through owlish specs, looking more wimpish than ever. She couldn't imagine him standing up on stage holding an audience. Even as Pip, who is a soft character.

For their first play reading, they'd been asked to flip to the very end of the script where Pip meets a broken Estella in the 'ruined' garden of Satis House.

Bea thought this might be to test her. She could be haughty and mean to the moon and back, but could she do sad?

'I have been bent and broken but—I hope—into a better shape.' As she said the words, she felt the truth in them: the sadness just beneath the anger and bitterness so familiar to her.

Then Pip spoke: 'I'm sorry for anything that brings you sorrow.' His voice was like treacle and when she looked into his eyes, she thought she saw tears. For the first time, she took in his bee-stung lips and hollowed cheekbones.

The end-of-year production of *Great Expectations* was the talk of the school. Everybody wanted Pip and Estella to get together and have a big romance, but Bea understood that would not happen. On stage, the two of them seemed to spark electricity. This sense of connectivity was new to Bea and she felt her insides warming and shifting.

Then Willy sought her out and explained that he was gay. She'd told him no, that couldn't be right. He could change. *She* would change him. In the empty cloakrooms, after rehearsals, when the others had gone home, she would throw herself at him and steal kisses from his lips. 'It's not going to happen,' he said, stroking her hair. It took a while, but now she's sort of accepted the rejection and they are best friends.

On Saturday night, Julia is fussing and flapping about getting out. Bea suspects it's because she doesn't really trust her to look after Jake. It's crazy, Jake will be able to sit for himself in a couple of years. Julia's anxiety centres on Jake's asthma.

'Don't forget to make sure he takes his puffers if he needs them,' she reminds Bea, who groans inwardly and raises her eyebrows.

'He'll be fine. Look, Willy's here now. You can trust him even if you don't trust me.' She hustles Julia and Sean out of the front door. 'We won't be late,' Julia shouts over her shoulder, but Bea has already shut her out. Jake is upstairs playing with his Game Boy.

'I thought they'd never leave,' Bea offers Willy a peck on the cheek and breathes in his sweet smell. 'I invited a couple of others over, Matt, Eddie and Cindy. They'll be here any minute.'

'Oh, them.' The distrust between Willy and Bea's gang of four is mutual.

'Yeah, but don't worry. I won't let them tease you. It'll be fun, promise. And I have something to make it even funner. Come and see.'

Upstairs, Bea has concealed the goodies for the evening in a Sainsbury's plastic bag hidden under her bed. Beside the lager, chocolate, tobacco and roll-up paper, Willy's eyes light on the wrapped tin foil that clearly contains weed.

'Should we do that when we're sitting Jakey?' he asks.

The doorbell rings so Bea never gets to answer. Not that anything would stop her. She's been looking forward to some fun all week. Matt, Eddy and Cindy crowd in.

'Make yourselves comfortable guys. I got the provisions. Anyone want a chocolate or some lager. Or maybe move on to the other stuff?' Bea holds the plastic bag triumphantly in the air. They slouch on Julia's super-soft leather sofas, looking more comfortable than they feel. This is a rite of passage. No one's admitting it, but they're all nervous.

Willy shifts uneasily. 'Where's Jake?'

'Oh, he's upstairs with his Game Boy. Nothing on earth will disturb him,' says Bea.

'It doesn't feel right with Jake awake upstairs. I've had the stuff before. It can affect your judgment and make you feel weird.'

'Alright, Mr Not-so-cool.' Bea is busy rolling up the weed with the tobacco. 'As you've done it and you're oh-so-experienced, why don't you sit it out? We haven't got that much anyway.'

'Good idea.' Willy, helps himself to a can of lager.

Passing the joint from one to another, the rest of them wait for something to change. It seems a long time coming. Then Cindy starts laughing uncontrollably. No one's made a joke. Within minutes, she's rolling around on the floor giggling. 'Do you remember Mr Ellis and the apple?' she splutters. Matt and Eddy are trying hard to stay sober, but soon they've collapsed into high-pitch giggles. Bea holds out the longest, but at the mention of Mr Ellis's waterlogged textbooks, she lets out an eerie shriek.

'I'm not being a part of this. Not with Jake upstairs.' Willy jumps up and heads towards the hall. Upstairs, Jake turns off his Game Boy and creeps downstairs in his astronaut PJs. 'What's up,' he asks.

In the sitting room, he finds Eddy, Matt, Cindy and his sister rolling around the floor. They keep shouting out random words and giggling. Some of them are swear words. Jake spots the lit roll-up dangling at the edge of the coffee table. They never have cigarettes in the house. And any minute now, it's going to drop and burn the wood floor.

'C'mon, Jakey, have a go,' shouts Matt. Jake hesitates. He's always wanted to try smoking. He knows some of his friends have. 'Okay. I'll just try it.' Everyone seems to be lurching around in slow motion and he's much quicker than they are. He picks up the cigarette and takes a few long drags. The giggling is replaced by a tense silence.

'Jake, you shouldn't have done that,' says Bea, but she is still giggling. 'Get up now. It's past your bedtime. Let's get you to bed.' Negotiating the stairs seems to take an awful long time and Jake has to sit down several times on the way. 'Bea, I feel funny,' he says. 'I feel like I might be getting an asthma attack.'

Guilt and fear are giving Bea more clarity. 'Sit down on your bed,' she commands. 'I'll tell the others to go.' Back downstairs she orders them out of the front door, grabs a plastic bag and sweeps the evening's detritus into it. She runs upstairs, hides it under her bed and checks on Jake. His breathing is raspy and his small face is white and scared under the bedclothes.

'I'm getting mum and dad,' she tells him. She goes to the house phone in the hall. Sean has a mobile which he hardly ever uses, but they always leave the number on the hall table.

It's picked up on the third ring. 'Please come back. Quickly. Jakey's ill.'

'Coming now,' says Sean.

Upstairs, Bea can hear Jake moaning and then a sound like vomiting, but she's too scared to go and see. She sits on the bottom stair with her head in her hands. 'Please come soon,' she whispers into her fingers.

Chapter 29
Julia, 1995

As soon as Julia opens the front door, she can smell it. 'It's weed. They've been smoking weed.'

She nearly stumbles over Bea, still sitting on the bottom stair, head in hands. 'Get out of my way,' she snaps. Upstairs, the piney tang of marijuana mingles with acrid vomit. Jake has thrown up over the duvet and his breathing is uneven and raspy.

'Call an ambulance,' shouts Julia to Sean. She pulls her son into her arms, rubbing his back and muttering into his ear. Bea has crawled up the stairs and is hovering at Jake's bedroom door. 'Stay away!' Julia commands.

Within minutes, they hear the whine of an ambulance coming up the hill and flashing blue lights illuminate Jake's 10-year-old cave like a disco. Jake is lying in bed, half in and out of sleep, caked in vomit, his chest pulsing like a baby bird. Julia and Sean are huddled at the end of the bed, deep in whispered conversation. No one notices Bea sitting outside on the landing, head cocked against the door, straining to hear what's happening.

'How could she let this happen?' mumbles Julia. 'I've always felt there was something not right. After all, how do we know where she comes from?'

'Shush now. Of course you're angry,' whispers Sean. 'And of course she's behaved irresponsibly. But that doesn't mean we should disown her. She is a part of this family. We need to deal with it.'

'You're right. But just at the moment I hate her for what's happened to Jakey. I guess I'd hate her right now even if she was our own. I'm not thinking right, I know. We'll get through it.'

The doorbell rings and they both jump up to answer it, but there's no sign of Bea on the landing and her bedroom door is firmly shut. Best place, thinks Julia. The last person she needs to run into right now is Bea.

Jake is going to be fine, say the paramedics, after they've assessed him and administered oxygen. They want to take him to A&E so he can be stabilised. It's unlikely he'll be admitted, though they can't say for sure. No one asks how a 10-year-old came to be smoking dope: the question hangs in the air like an accusation.

'Who should go with him?' asks Sean. 'I will, if you like. It's going to be a tough few hours.'

'We should both go.'

'But what about Bea? We can't leave her here by herself after something like this has happened.'

'Well, she caused it. But yes, you're right, of course. You're calmer than me. Better for Jake. You go in the ambulance with him. I'll stay here, sort out a few things and follow on in the car if I'm needed. Just call me. And keep calling me.'

Colour is already returning to Jake's cheeks as he's loaded into the ambulance, but he won't let go of Sean's hand. As they move off, Julia notices that the siren has been turned off. She turns to confront the brightly lit house.

Bea is standing in the hallway, blocking the route to the stairs. Something in her stance makes Julia shiver involuntarily. 'I thought you were in bed.'

'No, I haven't been in bed at all. I've been on the landing most of the time actually. How's Jakey?' Bea's expression is deadpan.

'Jakey's going to be okay.' Julia almost says 'no thanks to you' but manages to stop herself just in time. 'Perhaps you should get yourself off to bed and we'll discuss what's happened here tomorrow when Dad is back.'

'I don't want to discuss that. There's something else I want to discuss and we don't need him here to do it.'

'Ok-ay. Make it quick though. I'm tired and I really don't feel much like talking to you right now.' Julia is beginning to feel queasy. What has Bea overheard?

'Right, I'll be quick. I just want the answer to one question. Who am I?'

'What do you mean, who are you?'

Bea looks Julia straight in the eyes. 'You and Sean said you didn't know where I came from. You said I wasn't quite right. And you said that I'm not one of your own.

'You're supposed to be my mother. We're supposed to love each other. But I've seen what love looks like. I've seen you and Jake. What we have isn't like that. We've learned to tolerate each other. Sometimes we even have good times. But you don't feel like my mother. You never have.'

When did Bea get so articulate, so astute and how did Julia miss it?

'You know, you should not have listened in,' she tells her daughter gently. 'That conversation was not meant for you. We thought you were in bed. But yes, you're right. You are nearly 18 now and you are owed the truth. Shall we wait for Dad?'

'No. Tell me now while it's just us. It feels equal now. It's not you, Sean and Jake all cosy together while I'm out of it.'

'Well Bea, it's true you are not my daughter. Or Sean's. And of course that means Jake is not your birth brother either.' Julia is beginning to wonder if Bea might respond better to her sense of displacement when she knows there's a reason for it.

'Whose am I then?'

'You were adopted. We adopted you through an agency.'

'But where was I before that? Who were my family? Why didn't they keep me? What was wrong with me?'

Julia feels her heart soften and tear at the edges. 'Let's sit down together, Bea and I'll tell you everything I know.' She leaves nothing out, but the telling doesn't take long. Bea's history is so slight.

When she's finished, Bea is stony-faced. 'Where can I find my real mother? Would she love me as much as you love Jake? Because she's my birth mother.'

'But we love you, Bea. We do. You are part of our family.' Julia reaches out to stroke her hand, but Bea pushes her away. 'It's a nice thing to say, but it's not true. I'm not really a part of it. I was brought in to make up the numbers.'

Julia is realising, too fast and too late, that she never gave Bea credit for sensitivity. Over the years, she's even begun to regard her as a little simple. As a toddler, Bea reached most milestones late. At school, it was always 'could do better'. There were the exam failures, the chats with teachers that always ended one way: Bea didn't quite cut the mustard. Maybe her birth parents weren't over bright.

Now Julia sees with devastating clarity how far she has been from the truth. All these years, while she has been worrying over her lack of empathy, her communication skills and, yes, her progress at school, Bea has been lost.

'We tried to give you everything.'

133

'Yeah, you gave me nice clothes and books and toys. A good education that I didn't make use of. You even gave me attention, although not the sort I wanted. But tell me, honestly, do you love me the same as Jake?'

'We love you in different ways.'

'You always were clever with words, Julia. Me, not so much. But I picked up some along the way. Enough to use as weapons. Somewhere out there, I'm looking for a birth mother who will love me *most*. Or at least equally. And I'm going to find her.'

'But Bea, I told you. You were abandoned. In a graveyard. Don't you think that says something? That your birth mother probably didn't want to keep you.'

'I'll only know that for sure when I find her. How do you know she didn't want me? She might have been desperate. Or coerced. I might have brothers or sisters.'

Julia sighs. 'I understand, Bea. What do you want from us? How can we help?'

'That's easy. Just tell me all you know. Everything. I'll be 18 in a few months and I'll have rights. Sometime soon I'll be leaving here and I won't be coming back. It was already in my mind. This has just brought it forward. When the time comes, just let me go.'

'But where will you go, Bea? How will you live?'

'That's my business. You'll do this for me if, like you say, you love me. And don't tell Sean or Jake anything. I don't want a fuss. When the time comes, I'll slip out of your lives and I guess everything will get a lot easier for you all.'

Julia puts her hands to her face. This 'daughter' they've raised for nearly 18 years. Who is she? Cantankerous toddler, silent child, difficult teenager. Was that all type-casting? She feels her resentment to Bea melting and in its place there's a new feeling, bordering on respect. Where did this proud, brave almost-woman come from?

'Out of respect—and love—I'll do it, Bea. I'd like to ask you when you're leaving, where you're going and please to stay in touch. But I understand it's not part of the deal. Just know, you will always be welcome and loved here.'

Eight months pass. Bea celebrates her 18th birthday. She seems calmer, more contented. It feels as if she has lost some of her anger. At home, she studies hard for her upcoming exams. She never babysits Jake again, but she does take him to the park to fly his kite and even to the cinema to see *Toy Story*. She visits her grandparents and helps Sean in the garden. She even takes up an interest in cooking and once makes supper for them all. Julia is lulled into a sense of family normality.

Then, one sunny July morning, Julia rises early to get to work. The door to Bea's room is shut—she's probably having a lie-in. Last week, Bea completed her final exam and finished at school, so it's an option. At 10 a.m., Julia knocks gently on the door, the tea tray wobbling in her other hand. No answer. She knocks once more, then cautiously pushes open the door.

Bea's bed is neatly made-up. A few clothes are missing from the wardrobe. The bumblebee hat, which Julia had given Bea after that dreadful evening, is missing from her chest of drawers. Curtains billow in a light breeze from the open window. Surely Bea didn't make her escape through the window? Julia recalls how she always seems to be able to pass silently through space when she doesn't want to draw attention to herself.

In the chest of drawers, in the place where the bumblebee hat would normally be, is a carefully-folded note with Julia's name on it. At the top of the page is a smiley face. Underneath, in her childlike handwriting, Bea has written: 'Have a good life, all of you. Sorry for being hard work. Tell Sean and Jakey I love them. You too. Or I think I do. I'll know for sure when I find out what love really feels like.'

Chapter 30
Emily's Memory Book, 1978

It's the day *after* the day Norma took Bea to the adoption agency. Everything's changed and I'm confused.

After they left, the house was eerily quiet. Annie was sleeping soundly in her cot—I guess it was more peaceful in there without Bea writhing about and more space too. I tiptoed downstairs in search of something to eat. Sitting in the front room behind the newspaper, was Clive.

'What're you doing? I thought you'd be at work.' Clive is obsessive about not missing a day's work. It's probably because he wants to get away from Norma.

He cleared his throat. 'Well, um, it's a big day, isn't it?'

Now it sounds odd, but I'm saying it like it was. This was the first time that the enormity of what I'd done really struck home. I'd cried a bit the night before, but it was the sort of crying you do when you've been to see a sad film or read a tragic book. It didn't feel 100 per cent real. But now it dawned on me. I'd given away one of my daughters.

'It had to happen, didn't it?' I said, though not sure I believed it. If Clive agreed I felt it would somehow make things better. But he didn't say anything, or even nod his head. He stared down at the newspaper and time stood still.

In that moment, everything came flooding back. Bea's unreadable black eyes watching me intently as she fed. Her little fists waving furiously in the air as she demanded love and food. The way she loved me to stroke her back and tickle her tummy. What had I done? In my mind, she'd gone away for a short break, much needed by me. I'd never got my head around forever.

Clive peered at me over the top of his newspaper. 'You okay?'

'I was. But now I'm not sure. Can we get her back?'

'What's done is done. You're right in that respect.' he said. 'I should've said something, maybe warned you, before. I regret that. But we are where we are.'

'But if we tell the agency we want her back, they'll have to agree, won't they? She's my baby. It's my right.'

'It's not as simple as that. It's an adoption agency. Forms have been signed. They might even have new parents in mind. It's too late to stop it, lovey.' He hid his face in the newspaper again.

Clive has never called me 'lovey' before. I was stunned. The closest he ever comes to anything remotely affectionate is 'my lady' and that's usually when he's telling me off.

'Well, I'm going to speak to Norma when she gets back. She'll be able to do something.' I stomped out of the room, but I didn't feel confident. It would be like speaking to a brick wall.

Back upstairs, I jumped into bed, even though it was late morning and huddled the blankets into a nest. Underneath the pillow was a greyish Babygro that Bea had been wearing the day before. I held it to my face and breathed in the Bea-like smell, which oddly, was quite different from Annie's. Why hadn't I noticed this before?

I've heard people say that you never know what you had till it's gone. I got that feeling with Toby. But I guess because it was me that left and I did it to protect him, it wasn't as raw. With Bea, I thought I might be a little sad, but mainly relieved because she was such hard work. But it's not like that at all. Since she was taken away, I've just sat here in my room feeling cold and empty. All I can do is feed and change Annie in a mechanical daze. Wish I could cry, but it's like I've turned to stone.

Norma didn't get home until mid-afternoon. Annie was lying in her cot, gurgling and squirming. She was probably missing Bea. I couldn't bring myself to go to the cot, so I left her there. She looked so like Bea, it broke my heart.

Lurking at the doorway Norma, for once, didn't have much to say. 'All done. The agency will sort everything—it's in their hands now. So we can relax.'

There was a long pause. That's something both Norma and I are good at, leaving pauses. It makes other people feel uncomfortable, I've noticed. When we do it to each other, you could slice the atmosphere with a knife.

'I'm not sure I it was the right decision,' I said eventually. 'I think I want her back.'

'Well, that's not going to work. What do you expect me to do, take Annie and do a swap?'

'No, no. I mean, the twins should stay together. We should all stay together. I wasn't thinking straight. My brain feels foggy and I'm making bad choices. Can we contact the agency and ask about getting her back?'

Norma gave me a withering look. 'It's too late, absolutely too late. We've signed her over. We no longer have rights. She'll be with another family very soon and she'll be better off, believe me.'

Slumping back on the pillow, I shut my eyes. I was beginning to understand what despair feels like. Sadness doesn't describe it: it's emptiness through and through. 'So that's it then?'

Norma sniffed the air. 'What's the smell? Has Annie filled her nappy?'

I'll admit, I hadn't even checked Annie as I couldn't bear to look in the cot and see just one baby. Norma strode over and peered down at her.

'Phew, she needs changing. Get me some wipes and a clean nappy.'

Astonished, I rolled off the bed and stumbled to the cupboard. In no time, Norma had lifted Annie out of her cot and on to the changing mat.

'Give them here,' she commanded. Firmly but gently, she removed the soiled nappy, cleaned Annie up and replaced it with a fresh one. 'All done now.'

'How did you do that? You don't even like babies.'

'Well, I don't dislike them either. I don't feel that much one way or the other. But this one, you know, she's actually quite a good 'un.'

Norma had Annie stretched out in her arms, about to lower her back into the cot. Shaking her little fists, Annie stared intently at Norma. She looked so like Bea it made me shiver. Then an amazing thing happened: a timid smile broke across Annie's face. It was like someone who was learning to smile but hadn't yet got it quite right.

'She looks like she's trying to smile,' I said.

'Yes, she's about the age for it.' Norma was still peering into Annie's face. 'Well, I better get on with dinner. Enjoy the peace and quiet.'

So that was yesterday. I lost Bea and gained Annie's first smile. Today is a new one and I'd better start 'pulling myself together' as Norma would say. I've decided to lock Bea away. I got an old hatbox from the top of the wardrobe and put in everything that would remind me of her. It was pathetic. My inventory ran like this: one Babygro (I kept the others for Annie); a soft yellow caterpillar that Bea had taken a liking to; a hairbrush which only she had used because she had more hair than Annie and some scratch mittens because she had longer nails too. I wished I'd kept the woolly Bea hat and not sent it off with her to the agency. I wondered where the birth certificate was. Then I remembered I'd given it to Norma to take to the agency. She must still have it somewhere.

I wrote 'Bea' on the lid in big letters, lifted Annie out of the cot and we both kissed it. Sort of kissed it, in Annie's case. We put it right at the back of the cupboard, like a time capsule. I don't want to see it again until I feel quite a bit stronger.

Annie is so like Bea that I don't really like looking at her any more. So I've made a promise to myself. I'll feed and change her and even rock her and rub her back. But I'm trying not to look at her. Not into her eyes. Just not for now, while I'm learning how to hold myself together. I can't take the risk of breaking down again. Annie's quite different from Bea in many ways. She's a lot less demanding. There's no staying awake half the day and night, screaming for attention. She doesn't ask for much and I can't give that much, so for now we're getting by just fine.

Chapter 31
Emily's Memory Book, 1979

It's so long since I wrote to you, dear reader. Almost a year. It's felt like coming through a long illness. When I was 14, I had glandular fever and the weeks and months after were a black tunnel. This was the same. Reading was impossible because I couldn't translate the squiggles on the page. My brain fogged over and I barely had the energy to feed Annie.

Every day has been going through the motions. I've done as I'd promised myself and fed, bathed and changed Annie—even rocked her, though it felt mechanical. I haven't been leaving the house much, just to push her up and down Elm Avenue to give us both an airing. It looks as drab out there as it does in here, even on the sunniest day.

I've battled against these feelings, I've really tried hard. I lost my sense of taste, but munched my way through Norma's meat and two veg methodically, thinking it would make me stronger. Every morning I'd wake, get washed and dressed, despite the black hole in the pit of my stomach. Eating, getting dressed and sorting out Annie has been my limit.

What Norma and Clive made of this, I don't know. I've done my best to hide it from them. Clive was pleased to see me pushing the shiny pram up and down dreary Elm Avenue. Little did he know I was sinking under the weight of it. Norma's rough gauge to a person's state of mind is linked to the amount of food they take on board, so I guess I look okay to her.

Then, two days ago, things began to change. Just a little, like a chink of light through a keyhole. Oddly, three good things happened, all on the same day. Let me tell you about it.

I woke as usual with that nasty falling, twisting sensation in my guts. Annie was slumbering, her soft caramel hair mussed up in the cot bumper. She's nearly a year now and she's filling out the cot. Likes to stand on her sturdy little legs, playing peep-o through the cot bars. It was already 8 a.m. and the sun was sloping in through the slatted blinds.

Sitting on the edge of the bed, watching Annie, I realised I *wanted* her to wake up. The swirling sensation in my guts was still there, but it was subsiding. What I really wanted was to wake her, pick her out of the cot and take her down for breakfast. Which I did.

Annie has her own high chair now, so the kitchen is mighty crowded. Thankfully, Norma and Clive haven't complained, which is something. Norma was pecking at her usual toast and tea, while Clive was carefully concealing his fry-up behind the newspaper. He does that out of deference to Norma because he knows she hates it. She can't complain, or he'll remind her he's the breadwinner.

Still sleepy, Annie was clinging on and hiding her face in me as I lowered her into the highchair. 'Here, let me.' Norma seemed to want to help, but she didn't get up from her chair or even hold up her arms. She waited for me to do the running.

'You mean hold Annie?'

'Yes, what else would I mean? Here, give her to me, while you get your breakfast.'

This was so out of character for Norma I almost said no. But then I thought, why look a gift-horse in the mouth?

'Okay, then. But I haven't changed her yet. And she's only just woken so she might be grumpy.'

'I know.' Annie looked very much at home on Norma's bony lap. She snuggled down, putting her thumb in her mouth and nuzzling close to Norma's mauve floral blouse.

'Aren't you worried about your blouse?' I asked.

Clive coughed from behind his newspaper. Norma shot him a glance, but he clearly intended to say what was on his mind.

'The lassie's quite used to her.' Norma looked about to explode, but she had Annie on her lap so she had to bite her lip.

'I don't understand,' I said. Clive shot Norma an anxious look, but he wasn't going to be railroaded.

'She's gone in and nursed the lassie sometimes when you haven't been well. She did it once when the baby was unsettled and you slept right through. She said she'd not do it again, but she couldn't seem to stop. Sometimes in the afternoon. Sometimes at night.'

I didn't know what to think. The idea of Norma having a warm relationship with anyone—especially my own daughter—was unimaginable. Should I be horrified? Or happy?

'You've been unwell, you see, you've been sleeping a lot,' Clive went on. 'She slips in and sits at your desk chair and rocks the baby. Cuddles her until she falls asleep. She told me not to say, but I've always thought you should know.'

Head buried in Annie's soft brown curls, Norma refused to meet my gaze. Then she looked up and our eyes locked. 'I'm sorry,' she said. 'She's your baby. Take her back.'

'No, no, please keep her for a while if she's happy with you. Will you look after her and give me some space? Just for a while.'

Norma nodded. 'Trust her,' said Clive. 'She loves the lassie.'

Grabbing my tea and what was left of my toast, I headed upstairs. I sat on the bed with my head in my hands and thought hard. The clarity seemed to be returning, although it was slow progress. After what seemed a long time in the silence of my room, I heard a commotion and rushed back downstairs. How could I have left Annie down there for so long?

They were all three in the front living room. Clive was sitting on his leatherette rocker in the bay window. No sign of the newspaper. Norma was perched on the settee opposite. Both were flinging their arms around.

And there, in centre of the room, was Annie. I couldn't believe it. 'She's walking!' She managed two steps on her wobbly little legs before falling headfirst into Clive's outstretched arms. 'She's not even one.'

'Now she'll be trouble,' said Norma grimly. 'Someone will be chasing after her all day long keeping her out of mischief. That'll be you, of course. You'll have to keep her out of my kitchen and I don't want any of my ornaments damaged either. You'll need to watch her like a hawk for medicines and suchlike. I can't be held responsible.'

There was a moment's silence while we all took on board the seriousness of my new responsibilities. Then Clive piped up: 'What about a playpen?'

Coming from Clive, I thought it a brilliant idea, but Norma had to get a downer in. 'She'll be climbing the walls in no time at all in one of those.'

'Well, I'm going to look into it. I might try making one myself. I've got some spare wood in the shed. Even if she's only in it for 10 minutes while Emily's in the bath, it's got to help.'

They say that good things—and bad things—come in threes. It was certainly true that day at no 101 Elm Avenue. Norma was still droning on about how hard life was going to be, for me, with Annie on the move. Clive was muttering about wood and screw fixings and Annie was stumbling around like a drunken sailor, when the telephone rang.

Now a ringing telephone is always an event at no 101. We haven't had one for long and it doesn't ring very often. But also, we just got a new phone installed that is Clive's pride and joy. It's a moss green shade and makes a nice click-clicking purr when you turn the dial. If only we knew more people to ring!

So, the phone started trilling and we all jumped up at once. Clive couldn't resist saying this would be a perfect time for the playpen. Norma got to the phone first, of course. We could hear her imperious voice echoing in the hallway. 'Hello. Yes, it is. Yes, she is. May I ask who is calling?' I was sure it would be a wrong number, but we heard her put the phone gently back on the table and in thrilled silence we waited for her to report back.

'Emily, it's for you.' She looked as if she'd just bitten on an acid drop and broken a filling, so I wildly thought it might be Toby. Or perhaps the adoption agency wanting to return Bea to us.

'It's a Mr McFadden.'

I gulped. My old English teacher. Whatever could he want with me? 'Please watch Annie for me, just for a moment.' It was a new luxury, being able to ask.

Grasping the handset in both hands, I forced my voice down to a sub-shrill level. 'Mr McFadden, how can I help you?'

'Emily, hi, how are you? We've missed you, you know. Such a shame you couldn't complete sixth form. But I do hope you've kept up your reading.'

'Mmm, so-so.' I wasn't going to tell Mr McFadden that I spent a lot of my limited time stuffing my head with pink and blue love stories.

'You see, there's a vacancy here and it made me think of you. It's not a lot of time or money, just two mornings a week, but I think it's something you would enjoy. It's manning the sixth form reading library. You'd need to check books in and out, keep the shelves in order, but most importantly we want someone who can make recommendations and actually engage with the students about literature. What do you think?'

'Wow'. It wasn't the right word to use with a teacher, especially as he was considering employing me. Slow down girl, I thought. Keep your options open. One step at a time.

'Thank you so much for thinking of me, Mr McFadden. I'm excited by the offer. But I'll have to consider it. I have other obligations now. Can I come back to you before the end of the week with a firm answer?'

'Of course, Emily. I quite understand. We look forward to hearing from you. And we do hope you'll take us up on it.'

The phone clicked off and I sat on the stairs, arms crossed, rocking. The fog in my head lifted some more. Now I had a chance at a future and I planned to grab it with both hands.

Chapter 32
Norma, 1979

Norma is engaged in a battle between her instinct and her own good sense. All her life, since that long-ago afternoon on the cliff, she's been driven by a need to survive. But now an army of tiny urges is marching on her, knocking at her barricades. And the root of the problem is Annie.

Yesterday, Emily told her about the job offer. Norma was shocked. Why would Emily of all people be chosen by her ex-school teacher to run a library? They must have offered it to her on the cheap, she concluded. She can't make much money from it.

This suspicion was confirmed by Emily. 'It's not many hours,' she'd said. 'And I shan't make much money. It's not enough to pay for a childminder and I can't afford nursery. Seeing you with Annie earlier on, I wondered. Would you take her for the few hours each week? I mean, I'd pay you, totally, all my earnings. I know you're not big on babies, but you seem to have something special with Annie. It's my only option, really, so if you say no I shan't be able to do it, I do understand, it's just that…'

It was a long speech and with every word Norma had felt her barricades rising. Now she's sitting at the fold-down melamine table in the kitchen, thumbing through her pile of magazines. For years, Norma has relied on a regular dose of women's weeklies to explain emotion. It's a bit like reading a manual that you know might be useful—if you can get your head around it.

Clemency Brown's *Between Ourselves* problem page is one of her favourites. She turns to it now to see if she can find any readers' problems that might throw some light on her own. One writes about the affair she has uncovered between her husband and another woman and the pain it is causing her. Then there's the woman who is madly in love with a man at her office, but he doesn't love her back. And one woman writes in to ask if she should grant her lover sexual intercourse before marriage. Ridiculous, thinks Norma, who is fond of telling Clive that she shut up shop years ago and she doesn't intend re-opening now.

There's one letter that offers some links to her own situation and Norma reads it carefully, to see if there's anything she can learn from it.

'Dear Clemency

I was terribly excited to give birth to my first baby, a boy, just over a year ago. It was a difficult birth and he was taken away from me for a time while we both recovered. This was a stressful period for me and I looked forward to falling in love with him when we were reunited. But when he was handed back to me, I felt nothing. I fed, changed and bathed him and still felt nothing. When we took him home, friends and neighbours smiled and cooed and told me he was a beautiful boy, but I felt dead inside. Now, a year on, I still have problems relating to him. I do experience some emotions, but they feel more like anxiety or pity than love. He has a great relationship with my husband. What can be wrong with me? And how do I change?'

'My heart goes out to you and your family,' responds Clemency. 'Let me reassure you that this situation can change, but you will need to work at it. Firstly, accept that this is not your fault. It sounds as if your son's birth was a truly traumatic experience for you. It interests me that you do not use your son's name, which suggests that you have erected barriers that may be hard to pull down. I sense you are burying your memories of this time and it might be worth allowing yourself to recall details, little by little and only when you feel ready. Half-buried trauma is an invisible enemy that can be hard to conquer. In accepting that this situation was none of your fault, you will take the first steps. Understand that you have sealed off your feelings for your son as a defence mechanism. You will need to allow those defences down, little by little, to let your son into your heart. It won't be easy, but it sounds as if, through natural healing, you are already beginning the process. Enlist your husband's help too and in time you will become the loving, united family you wish to be.'

At first, Norma is inclined to dismiss this as mumbo-jumbo, but there's something in it that rings a chord. Can something bad happening to you result in

146

loss of feeling, rather like a tummy bug makes you lose your appetite? Norma barely remembers what happened to her as a child and she doesn't want to. It wouldn't do any good whatsoever to go raking up the past.

Closing up her magazine, Norma peers out of the kitchen window. Her garden isn't much more than the size of a big picnic rug, but Clive has planted a neat herbaceous border along each side of the lawn, which is just about big enough for two stripy deckchairs and a sun umbrella. She rarely ventures out in case she runs into the neighbours who have created their own small garden kingdom, much too visible over the low fence. But now the weather's getting warmer it's Annie's playground and she loves pointing to the flowers, birds and bugs she sees there.

Right now, Annie is tumbling about on the lawn, eagerly perfecting her new walking skills. With intense concentration, she manages three steps on her plump little legs before dropping down on her bottom and raising her arms to Emily to do it all over again. Her dungarees are filthy. And she's even managed to get mud tangled up in her curls. That'll take some brushing out.

Sighing, Norma sits back down at the kitchen table and cups her head in her hands. There's a tug of war inside her and she doesn't like what it's doing. Not one little bit. The temptation to go outside and be with Annie is huge. But imagine the fallout. An encounter with the neighbours? Norma prides herself on being a private person and prefers to keep it that way. A conversation with Emily—to be avoided at all costs. They've never seen eye to eye. A nod to Clive that she *likes* the garden—his pride and joy? That would be stepping down.

A phrase from that problem page has lodged itself in her head: 'Trauma is an invisible enemy that can be hard to conquer'. Earlier in the year her father died, breaking her last fragile link with the past. He'd died alone and in poverty on his ramshackle farm and if the postman hadn't sensed something odd about the stillness of the place, he probably would have been there still. It was the butcher in the village who let her know. She hadn't seen or heard of her father since that long-ago afternoon when she and Clive had set off down the track to board the steamer to London. Fair play, he never tried to contact her. She's no idea how or where he was buried. She would happily dance on his grave.

Two days after Norma learnt of her father's death, she had the first of what she thinks of as her 'encounters' with Annie. After Bea's departure, Annie became fussy, almost as if she missed her sister. But how could she, reasoned

Norma. She was too little to know she had a sister. It was simply attention-seeking.

Annie began crying harder and longer at nights. Clive snored through it like a pig. Norma, a light sleeper, tried covering her head with the eiderdown and even plugging her ears with cotton wool. Nothing worked. One night, when it became unendurable, she dragged herself out of bed, felt for her slippers and dressing gown and trundled upstairs. Emily was sprawled across her bed, a pillow over her head. Norma pursed her lips. Tiptoeing to the cot, she bent over it and gingerly picked Annie out.

In an instant, Annie's cries dissolved into mewling, with a couple of little hiccups followed by intermittent sobs. Sitting on Emily's desk chair, Norma placed Annie facedown across her lap and tentatively rubbed her back. It felt soft and tender to her hand. Soon, Annie lay relaxed, but Norma continued with her rhythmic rubbing.

In the darkness, Norma thought about her own mother who died giving birth to her. Who would have stroked *her* like this had she lived, but didn't get the chance. So where did she, Norma, learn how to do it? Not with Emily. She gathered up the now-sleeping Annie in the crook of her arm, ready to put her back in the cot. Annie's soft, downy head was tucked into the crook of her neck and she breathed in the unfamiliar baby smell—a mix of milk, new flesh and lotion. It smelled good and she sniffed again before tucking Annie back in.

In the months after her father died, Norma regularly returned to the attic room to soothe Annie. It was an odd sensation, as if something had loosened up in her. Last night, as she was sitting there in an almost trance-like state, Clive opened the door a crack and gazed down at her.

'What on earth do you think you're doing?'

'What do you think I'm doing? I'm shutting her up so she doesn't wake the whole household.'

'It's cold up here. Shall I try to soothe her? You go back down to bed.'

'No, it's fine. I seem to have the hang of it. 'She's out for the count.' Norma clutched Annie a little tighter. She didn't want to let go.

'Why don't you bring her downstairs for half an hour. It's warmer down there and she'll probably drop off to sleep in no time. Emily's not going to wake anytime soon.'

Wrapping Annie securely in her cellular blanket, Norma stole from the room. Back in her own bed, she made a nest with the blankets and lay the drowsy baby down next to her. She wondered where Clive had disappeared, but didn't really care. She felt almost content: it was a new sensation for her and she relaxed into it. Once Annie was sleeping soundly, Norma crept back upstairs and tucked her back in her cot, stroking a curl back from her cheek and implanting a gentle kiss.

Downstairs, she found Clive at his favourite spot, sitting on the kitchen step watching the stars. Norma peered down at his bald pate. 'If you think you'll find the answers you want in them twinkly things, then you won't,' she snapped, recalling her hours of stargazing in the draughty outhouse.

Clive turned to her, stars still in his eyes. 'Yeah and you'd know.'

'I have something to tell you.' Norma remained standing. Her unusual height came in useful in situations like this, allowing her to push her point through and get her own way.

'Yes.' Clive reluctantly dragged his eyes back from the stars once more.

'Emily has asked me to look after Annie. Just a couple of half days a week. She has a job. At the school library.'

'Will you do it?'

'Yes. I've decided to do it. Emily will contribute all her earnings to the household budget and Annie is an easy-enough child. It's only two half days.'

'Do you want help?'

'I shall be looking after her when you're at work, of course. But, yes, if and when practical help is needed.'

It cost Norma a lot to talk about help and she realized she felt exhausted. Turning on her heels, she left Clive with his night sky. Gazing upwards, he spotted something he'd never seen before. A shooting star, streaking through the blackness towards the higgledy-piggledy chimney outlines on Oak Road. He might have shouted to Norma to come and see. But it was over too soon and Norma wouldn't welcome the interruption.

Chapter 33
Extract from Emily's Memory Book, 1979

Today was my first day at my new job. Definitely a day worth recording in my Memory Book!

I woke early, stomach churning, awash with nerves. But weirdly, it wasn't such a bad feeling. It was good to feel something, anything, after months of wading through a thick blanket of nothingness. Annie was still asleep, giving me time to think about what to wear.

It probably makes me sound like an oddball, but I've never been one to worry much about looks. We don't have many mirrors at No 101. Norma doesn't approve, but it goes deeper than that. At school, I was always the odd one out. Norma whined enough about the cost of school uniform, so I usually got the cut-price version of everything. And out of school, there was never any money for gypsy blouses, bellbottoms and kinky boots, like the other kids wore. So I psyched myself up not to care.

This morning I discovered something—I do care! I took a searching look at myself in the freckled full-length mirror inside my wardrobe door. Tall, with iron-straight black hair and big eyes in a beaky face, just like Norma. I'd always dreamt of going punk, it would suit my angular body and glacial look. Plus it would help to keep people at a distance. I pulled out my one-and-only pair of black trousers, but they didn't solve the top half. Tossing through my drawer, the best I could find was a pale pink woollen top I'd bought from the charity shop for my first date with Toby. That was when I'd aimed to look vulnerable and cute. I'd moved on.

Then I had a brainwave. A year or two ago, Norma had bought a very simple black dress—she called it a frock—to wear to Clive's works do. To be honest, she did look amazing in it. It was simple and elegant, showing off her long slim neck and lack of curves. The works do turned out to be a disaster. Clive got pissed and Norma ended up walking the streets until daybreak in her elegant dress. My guess was that she'd stuck it away at the back of her bulging wardrobe. Norma is a puritan on my behalf, but trust me, *she* likes to dress up.

I crept on to the landing, testing the water. Clive was nowhere to be seen, he'd probably left for work already. Norma was shuffling around in the kitchen boiling the kettle for her morning cuppa. I nudged stealthily downstairs and into her sacred boudoir. Result. The wardrobe door was open and right at the back was the little black dress.

Upstairs, I flicked off a few dust specks and smoothed it down. It fit me almost perfectly—a little loose here and there, but it hung on me in a way that I can only say looked, yes, elegant! I tried to shut out that fact that I looked scarily like Norma and added a pale grey and white scarf that Toby had given me. Teamed with long black leather boots (courtesy of Oxfam, but just the job for concealing holed tights) the look was perfection. Posh punk! But how was I going to get out of the house in it?

Annie was now awake, so I shot back into my PJs, bundled her up and carried her to Norma. The kitchen was bathed in a grey haze and crawling with the stench of Clive's fry-up. Yuck.

'You're going to be late,' said Norma, more to her magazine than to me.

'Yes, I know. I still have to dress. I don't want breakfast. I'll just get a cup of tea for myself. Can you take her now?'

Norma shot Annie a suspicious look. 'She's not changed and ready.'

'I know, I'm sorry. We overslept. Could you…I'll leave everything on my bed that you'll need for her. And I'll bathe her this evening.'

'I suppose,' said Norma though her teeth. 'But for future, you'll need an alarm.' As I handed over the warm and sleepy Annie, her face softened. I made my getaway.

Upstairs, I pulled on my new disguise and quickly daubed on some lipstick. Concealing my top half with my trusty parka, I sidled out of the front door shouting 'Bye', trying not to sound too cheerful. It felt so good to be just me. I pictured Annie toddling towards me, arms outstretched, cheeks puffy and red with effort. I tested myself with all sorts of Annie images, to see how they might make me feel. Nothing. Truth is, I was like a bird let out of a cage. No regrets for the parts of my life I'd left behind in there.

It wasn't until I arrived at the T-junction at the top of Elm Avenue that it felt safe to slow down and take stock. Checking my look in a shop window, my confidence ebbed. The smart little black dress looked silly poking out of the bottom of a parka festooned with toggles and clusters of fur on every spare bit of army green fabric. I'd forgotten to put up my hair in a neat lady-librarian bun as planned and the hole in my tights was edging into view at the top of my boots.

But then I looked around. A big red bus was trundling along the main road and beyond it was the park with its solemn avenue of trees. I've never been much into nature. A tree is a tree, what's more to say. But after the dark days of winter, either stuck up in my attic or keeping Annie occupied in our pocket-handkerchief garden, the explosion of fresh green leaves was something else.

A woman walked past, pushing a sleeping toddler in a buggy, with a little girl clutching a cabbage patch doll trailing behind. Women with two kids, specially little girls, do something to me. I can't let go of Bea. When I had her, I wanted to be left in peace. From the front bedroom bay window, I'd watched Norma carry her up Elm Avenue. Well before they'd reached the T-junction, I knew I'd made a mistake. I could've run after them, but I didn't. I should have insisted we contact the agency, but I didn't do that either. I didn't have the strength. I'd sunk into a strange state, like wading through mud in your head. And if I'm being honest, I'm taking it out on Annie.

The little girl dropped the cabbage patch doll on the pavement and began to cry. Pausing, her mother calmly picked up it and dusted it off with the hem of her skirt. But her daughter was still tearful, so the mother pulled a hankie out of her pocket, licked it and began wiping the doll's face. Slowly, the little girl began to stop crying. I couldn't hear what they were saying, but the mother was licking the hankie again and very lightly wiping the little girl's cheeks and her own too. The child laughed and the mother pulled her into a big hug. Then they started off down the road again.

That's how mothers and daughters should be, but not how it is with Annie and me. Norma gets it right more than I do. Every time I look at Annie, I think of letting Bea go. And it makes me angry, sad and bitter all at once. I'm angry with myself for not being a mother to Bea and bitter that Annie is here and Bea's not. Like a dark circle, it goes round and round in my head. Perhaps it always will—or maybe today will be the start of something better.

Arriving at my old school, I discovered a manky old scrunchy in one of my parka pockets, so I wound up my hair. It felt strange, crossing the same ground I'd walked with Toby, through the school gates, along the shiny beige corridors to the library, where Mr McFadden was waiting for me.

'Good morning,' Emily. Great to see you. Lovely morning, isn't it? Wow, you've grown up. Definitely one of us, not one of the student riff raff, now!' Mr McFadden nodded towards a gang of sixth formers blocking the corridor. I knew he was joking. Mr McFadden is one of those special teachers who actually respect kids.

It took nearly two hours for him to explain how the library works. He showed me how the books are shelved and filed and spelt out the need to keep an accurate record of outgoing and returning books. He told me how to deal with students who are lax about returning books and even cautioned me about 'book thieves' as he called them. My head was reeling. How was I going to remember all this?

'But these are just the basics,' he said, just as I was thinking about running back to the safety of my attic. 'There is something else this job is crying out for. And I think you, Emily, are especially well placed to bring it. It's about nurturing a love of books. A passion for reading, even if you come from a home without books, even if you're not the star performer in class. It's about telling our more reluctant library-users that we have something to offer and we welcome them in.'

I wasn't at all sure I'd be able to handle checking the books in and out, let alone achieve anything on that scale. But Mr McFadden believed in me and I didn't want to let him down. 'Are we opening up today?' I asked. My stomach churned at the idea of all those scary sixth-formers bursting in and me sitting here like an idiot wondering what to do next.

'No, no. Don't worry. I wouldn't throw you to the lions on your first day. I've asked Alice to come and help out until you're confident you know the ropes. She's second year sixth and she's helped out before. She'll be joining us any minute. Ah, that could be her now.'

There was a timid knock on the library door. 'Emily, meet Alice,' said Mr McFadden.

Alice Underwood. I knew her from before. She'd been a fifth former when I left school. I first noticed her because she seemed like a girl who had everything that I didn't. And then I was aware of her for another, stranger, reason. Something about her gave me the creeps.

'Nice to see you Emily,' she said, in her polite, insincere way. She looked just the same, eager, clear-skinned face and fine blonde hair swept up into an impeccable topknot. She extended a slim, pale hand. In what century did she live, where sixth formers shake hands?

Come to think of it, everything about Alice was pale. Flat, pale hair, pale blue eyes, pale porcelain skin, bloodless lips concealing a formidable set of whiter-than-white teeth. Her blazer looked as if had been ironed and when she spoke it was like the tinkling of ice in a glass.

'Where have you been?' She gave me a supercilious smile.

'Oh, here and there. You?'

'Well, just working hard and getting by, I guess. I have a place next year to do History.'

'Where?' I couldn't imagine her going anywhere but the best.

'Oxford.'

We carried on in silence, shuffling books around the shelves, returning titles to the right categories. 'I think we're nearly done,' she said. 'Do make sure that all the books are in the right place at the start of the day or everything goes pear-shaped. Shall I go over the checking in and out procedure with you again?'

'Yeah, please.' She was trying to be helpful, but I couldn't bring myself to like her.

'Let me just put tickets in this pile first.' As she bent over the books, her stone-carved face was a study in concentration. A wisp of pale hair escaped from the topknot and she pushed it back in irritation.

'Alice,' I said. 'Can I ask you a question?'

'Of course. I'm here to help.'

'It's nothing to do with the books or the library. It's about before. When I was in the sixth form.'

She looked up sharply then and maybe it was my imagination, but I thought I saw a faint blush mottle her colourless cheek. 'I don't see how I can help you with that.'

'Me and Toby,' I insisted. 'Why did you stare at us all the time? You even followed us. You thought I didn't notice, but one time you trailed us across the common. I noticed because I dropped my sunglasses and I ran back along the track to find them while Toby set up our picnic.'

'You must be mistaken. I never use the common. I live quite a way away from it.'

'You're lying. At least do me the favour of telling the truth.'

Alice's mouth gaped open like a fish. 'Okay, I'll tell you. It's all water under the bridge now anyway. Truth is, I liked Toby. I liked him a lot and thought he felt the same about me. Until you came on the scene.'

'Were you together?'

'Not until later. Toby only ever wanted you, really. I was kidding myself. Once you took an interest in him, I might as well have been invisible. It cut me up badly. I thought I was in love. I became a little obsessed.'

'I'm sorry. But you what do you mean, *not until later.*'

'We had a brief fling after you disappeared off the scene. It was never going to work. What *were* you doing all that time, incidentally?'

'You're going to Oxford,' I said.

'Mmm, maybe a second chance. I don't think so though. I saw him a couple of months back when I went up to look round. I still had that feeling when I saw him. You know?' I nodded.

'I could try another charm assault when I get to uni, I suppose. But I'm not counting on it. It's you he's into.'

'You're welcome to him.' I imagined Toby and Alice together, looking perfectly shiny new. Whatever Toby thinks he feels about me, they make a much better pair. I'm not the right fit.

Chapter 34
Norma, 1983

'Grandma, can I help you wash?'

Annie is perched on her stool at the sink while Norma washes the dinner plates. Clive is at his working men's club and, as usual when there are chores to be done, Emily is nowhere to be seen.

'You just want to play with the soap suds. Here, I'll get you a little bowl of your own, full of them.' Norma wipes her own sudsy hands on her hips and burrows in the kitchen cupboard.

'No, no I want to help.'

'Well, get your hands in these bubbles and see if you can manage this, child.' She hands Annie her melamine bunny plate. 'It needs to be sparkling clean, mind.'

'I know, Grandma. I'll make it really clean.' Annie has deft fingers and soon the plate is lying safely on the draining board. 'Can I have a play with the bubblies now, Grandma? Pleeeeease.'

Norma sighs. It's hard to deny her anything, though she undoubtedly needs a firm hand. Dipping her hands into the bowl, Annie gives herself a bubbly beard. 'Would you like one too, Grandma?' She slaps a foamy mess on Norma's chin.

Quick as a flash, Norma scoops up a fistful of suds and aims it at Annie's forehead. 'Oh dear, your hair's turned white now. Just like mine!' They both collapse into giggles, but stop short at the sound of footsteps coming down the stairs.

'It's Milly,' says Annie. 'Is she coming to play with me?' Milly is her word for Mummy.

'I don't believe so,' says Norma grimly. 'She's going out.'

'I want her to read me a story.'

'Well, perhaps I will if you are a good girl between now and bedtime.' Norma's getting accustomed to being parent-substitute, a role she resents and adores in equal measure.

Where's she going?'

'I expect she's going to the pictures, or something like that,' says Norma guardedly. Emily's clandestine comings and goings are not for the ears of a five-year-old.

'Can I brush your hair, Grandma?' It's a routine they've got into and Norma's not quite sure about it. She's sensitive about her hair, which once was black and shiny as coal and hung down to her waist. It's still long enough for Annie to style into pigtails, skinny plaits and even once an ambitious topknot. But it's lost its sheen and turned wispy and grey in patches, a constant reminder to Norma of the youth she squandered.

But there's nothing quite like the sensation of Annie's little fingers brushing her neck and gently lifting and parting her hair as she creates amazing hairdos. One time, they found a pack of elastic bands in Norma's sewing drawer and turned her head into a hedgehog of tiny pigtails.

'You can do it if you go up now, get your nightie on and brush your teeth. Bring the hairbrush and elastic bands back with you. And be quick about it.' Norma hopes that Annie won't run into her mother on the stairs. It'll just mean more questions, explanations and probably lies. She stares down at her bony hands smothered in suds. What is to be done about her Emily?

The problems started a year or so ago when Emily got a proper job in a library over in south Wimbledon. She'd worked at the school library for nearly three years and seemed to make a success of it. Mr McFadden encouraged the school to double her hours and they'd even sent her off on a librarian course, for which they'd paid. It meant more childminding hours for Norma, of course, but Emily still faithfully handed over her wages every week for Norma to divvy up.

It came as a shock to Norma that Emily had summoned up the courage to apply for a new job at all, never mind attend an interview and get an offer. She'd been blind to the changes in Emily going on right under her nose. Somewhere in those years, Emily had lost that rabbit-in-the-headlights look. Once, Norma and Annie had bumped into her on Elm Avenue, walking back from work. Well, it wasn't really walking. More like sashaying—a word Norma stumbled across in one of her true romances and rather likes the sound of. She'd never say it out loud, of course, only in her head.

Emily had been wearing headphones, which she reluctantly unhooked as they approached. A thick French plait swung down her back and she was wearing shiny doc martens with yellow laces. Could that be appropriate for an amateur librarian? Norma sniffed something which smelled like Chanel No5 mixed with cigarette smoke in the air. Altogether an unsettling odour.

Shortly after that, Emily announced she'd been offered the South Wimbledon job. It would be five days a week, school hours, term time only. Annie had recently started school—could Norma tide her over with after-school childminding? Norma's instinct was to say no until Emily revealed how much she would be earning. And she even agreed to continue with their existing financial arrangement, handing over her entire salary, at least for the time being. 'The money isn't the biggest thing for me,' she'd said. Norma was dumbfounded.

Everything went swimmingly until Norma began to suspect that Emily was 'seeing someone'. It was just little things. She'd asked Norma to babysit on odd evenings and even offered to pay extra. That was suspicious. Where would she get the money to go out if, as she claimed, she was handing it all over? One evening she tottered downstairs in knee-high boots, her hair teased into fat sausage waves which hung around her shoulders like a rolling black sea. The air was heavy with scent and Norma felt herself seething with a potent mix of curiosity, anger and envy. What was Emily up to? She still hasn't got to the bottom of it.

'Ready or not, grandma. Here I come.' Annie breaks up Norma's reverie. Dressed in a pink winceyette nightie and rabbit slippers, she carries a basket full of brushes, combs, hairpins and elastic bands. 'What style would you like today?'

'A single plait would be nice.' Recalling Emily's glistening French plait, Norma's hit by another wave of resentment. What's she doing up there in her bedroom? She should be getting Annie to bed before she goes out.

Annie sets to work. Norma can feel her deft fingers parting the long, thin strands of hair. But it's brittle and hard to coax it into a plait. 'You haven't got enough hair, Grandma. Shall I put it in a ponytail instead?'

'You look like you're having fun,' Emily stands in the kitchen doorway, one foot propping the door open, poised for flight. Parted dead straight down the middle, her hair falls past her shoulders in a mass of crimps. It's the perfect framework. Her floppy black top is encrusted with tiny silver pinpricks at the neck and cuffs and her long, long legs are encased in drainpipes.

I could have looked like that, thinks Norma.

'You look lovely, Milly.' Annie gazes at her mother in admiration, before returning to Norma's hair.

'Thanks. You two look as if you're enjoying yourselves. Well, I'm off. Have fun.'

'What time should we expect you back?' Norma's tone is sarcastic. Lately, Emily has been exploiting her childminding services to the limit. They agreed on one babysitting evening a week, but the other night she heard Emily's key turn in the lock at 2 a.m. Stretching goodwill is what Norma calls it.

'Does it make a difference? You should all go to bed and sleep. You don't need to worry about me. You're fine tucked up in bed, aren't you Annie?'

Annie nods. Why are Milly and Grandma angry with each other? She adores Grandma and is in awe of Milly who is so pretty and tells her amazing stories when she has the time. Annie enjoys dreaming up ways of getting Milly and Grandma to like each other. The other day, Milly had her head deep in a book and Grandma had just finished a jigsaw. Annie asked if all three of them could play hide and seek. But it went wrong from the start. Milly hid behind Grandma's best sitting room curtains, the only ones in the whole house that go right down to the floor. Annie spied a moving shape and tugged one of the curtains apart. There was a horrible ripping sound as it tore from the rail and sank in a heap to the ground. Norma had been icy with fury and since then, they haven't done any more games.

'I can't be held responsible for the child until 2 a.m. in the morning. And in any case, where are you until that time? Pubs are closed. There's nowhere open,' snaps Norma.

'I'm with friends,' retorts Emily.

'What friends?' Norma doesn't have friends, not unless you count a few useful people, like her hairdresser and the lady behind the counter at their local convenience store, who both want her business.

'I do have friends. I don't bring them here, is all. Anyway, I'll leave you with that thought. I'm off. I'll be home by midnight tonight, that's a promise.'

As Annie puts finishing touches to the skinny ponytail, Norma racks her brain. Friends? Who can they be? Surely Emily's not seeing that upper crust loser again? Come to think of it, she *has* spotted Emily once or twice with other people, though she assumed they were just acquaintances. Once, returning from school with Annie, she saw Emily leaving McDonalds on the High Road with another young woman who was wearing a bright red turban on her head. Her face looked as if it might be brown, which made Norma feel so agitated that she stopped looking. Another time, she was quite sure she'd seen Emily in a café window with a tall, pale young man in an ill-fitting suit. Emily had her back to the plate glass window and seemed to be laughing her head off at something the young man had said. All very odd.

'I'm finished, Grandma. Close your eyes and I'll get the mirror. now you can look.'

Annie is proud of her ponytail, but what Norma sees is the haggard face, fallen jaw, eyes dragged down by gravity. 'Hmm. Very nice. But now it's bedtime.'

Later that night, when silence and darkness engulf 101 Elm Avenue, Norma lies awake, scanning her bedside alarm clock. Clive is snoring gently on his side of the bed and up in the attic all is quiet. At precisely 11:45 p.m., Norma lowers her legs into her beige fleece slippers and tiptoes downstairs. Carefully pulling aside the torn curtain, she makes a comfy spot for herself, piling a few cushions under the sash window. She checks that the dustbin isn't obscuring her line of vision and waits.

Minutes tick by, then she hears footsteps tapping along the pavement, followed by a gust of laughter which is hastily stifled. Clearly there are two people out there. The footsteps close in and a low male voice murmurs. Whoever it is, he must be saying something funny because there's another burst of suppressed giggles. Norma pulls herself up to get a better view.

Under the lamppost, Emily and a man are clutching each other. It's unmistakably Emily: her hair shines like liquorice in the lamplight. Norma squints hard, but she can't see much of the man. One thing she's fairly sure is that he's not Toby Somerfield. He seems to be imploring her to stay, but she's dodging behind the lamppost, throwing her head back in delight. Each time her hair ripples out like a glistening fan.

Horseplay, thinks Norma. She can hear them snuffling with laughter. Then they come together in a huge bear hug and the unknown man lifts Emily off her feet and swirls her round, making a perfect silhouette against the pool of light. They share a brief kiss before Emily steals up the narrow crazy paving path, blowing kisses behind her. Norma hears the key in the door and crawls behind the torn curtain, holding her breath. She swallows, bile blocking her throat. The doctor tells her she has acid reflux, but she sometimes wonders if it's all the anger and resentment that's got stuck down there over the years. She knows she's a bitter, disappointed and very nearly old woman. She's seen herself in the mirror and she's not stupid.

So, Emily has a man, possibly even a lover. Huddled in the cold sitting room, Norma feels her jealousy swelling. How come Emily gets the chance to love and be loved twice, when all she ever got was a father who abused her and a husband who's damaged goods? The one good thing in her life is Annie and Emily could take her away anytime. Just with a snap of her fingers. Now she has a man, who knows what she might do?

When Norma is quite sure the coast is clear, she tiptoes back to bed, clambers in beside her snoring husband and pulls up the bedclothes tight. She thinks of Annie, curls splayed across her rainbow pillow and a sensation that feels like love starts somewhere in the pit of her stomach. She stares into the darkness until the morning light wiggles through a gap in her bedroom curtains.

Chapter 35
Extract from Emily's Memory Book, 1988

Leo Petrakis. Just the sound of his name warms me. It conjures up navy blue seas dotted with brave little fishing boats. White stucco houses cut out against an azure sky. Dusty tracks thick with the scent of wild thyme and the chirping of cicadas. Leo has told me so much about his homeland that I feel I've been there. Someday, he promises he'll take me.

Leo's family has lived for generations on the Greek island of Spetses. There are no cars and to get there you take a long ferry ride from the port of Athens. Or so he says. Blue and white houses tipple down the steep hillside into the harbour and one of them belongs to the Petrakis family. 'You can't miss it because Metera always hangs out the Greek flag on the washing line when she knows I'm coming home,' he told me. I love how he calls her 'Metera'. It makes her sound special.

I bumped into Leo one rainy early summer afternoon in South Wimbledon. I'd just left the library and was heading to the underground, carrying a stash of books in a dodgy carrier bag. Deep in my own head, I didn't notice a big bear of a man lifting trays of groceries from a white van at the kerbside. Next thing we'd collided, prompting an avalanche of aubergines, tomatoes, garlic heads and books. 'Hey, lady, maybe you should look where you're going.' Bear Man shook a mane of black corkscrew curls lightly frosted grey in my direction.

'What about taking a dose of your own medicine?' I replied.

Bear Man looked at me caustically and I waited for the inevitable earful, but then he changed tactic. 'Whoa, no need to fight over a few spilt eggplants. Here, let me help you with your books. And then, a Greek coffee? Did you ever taste Greek coffee?'

The only coffee I'd tasted until recently was Nescafe, but I wasn't about to admit that. 'Well, I've had a cappuccino, but no, never Greek coffee.'

'Come. Come on in.' He nodded in the direction of one of the tiny restaurants that line Merton Road. The frontage reminded me of a garish and slightly dog-eared travel brochure. A blue and white seascape, daubed across most of the window, concealed the interior. Between the painted ocean and white foam, you could just about make out the name 'Ambrosia' in twirly writing.

'The food of the Gods,' I murmured.

'My sister's name.' There was a long pause. 'She died.'

'Oh, I'm so sorry.' It seemed a strange thing to tell someone you'd just—literally—bumped into. Was he playing with me? If so, it worked.

Inside, the restaurant was a shadowy cave. Blinking in the dimness, I waited for shapes and outlines to shift into focus. There were a few rough wooden tables, each with a simple candelabra stuck with a candle and chairs painted blue and white. A trailing vine sprinkled with fairy lights hung from the ceiling. The walls were lined with black and white photographs of what I guessed was Greece. One was of a man standing in a rickety little boat on a choppy sea. It looked as if he was reeling in a large fish, though it was hard to tell because the print quality was poor. Another showed a man and woman standing very upright outside a rundown store. The woman's dark, narrow face was encased in a black shawl. The man sported a bushy moustache and a trilby that seemed out of place. Both were tight-lipped, as if trying to hold something back. Three children sat on the shop step in front of them. The eldest, a plump little boy squeezed into short trousers and a striped shirt, was the only member of the family to smile directly into the lens. Two small girls, probably sisters, sat beside him, squinting anxiously. The shop sign was in Greek, but beside the children was a big, brash billboard saying 'Marlboros'.

'Yes, that's me. Leo Petrakis.' Bear Man pointed at the little boy. 'And that's my parents' shop, as it was in 1959. They've moved on since. They run a proper store now, a convenience store. And my surviving sister Elena, the one with the ribbon in her hair, is married with kids of her own.'

What about Ambrosia, I wanted to ask, but it wasn't the right moment. Instead, I took a sip of Greek coffee, letting the sweet, intense liquid linger in my mouth. 'Why did you come over to this rainy old country?'

'A long story. Would you like to hear it sometime?' Leo stared at me just a fraction longer than appropriate and raised his eyebrows. It was definitely a come-on.

'I guess. Maybe.' Truth is, I really *did* want to hear Leo's story. His life sounded exotic and daring, but maybe it wasn't like that if you were the one living it. Perhaps it was dull, counting out your days above the tumbledown shop in the narrow street, with a family who looked as lifeless as puppets. Even with the sun rising high above you each day and the sounds of the sea swelling and retreating in your ears. How did he cut those ties and make his escape? It was something I wanted to do too. And I wanted to know more about Ambrosia.

'I have to go.' I had a premonition that meeting Leo would change my life. I'd wished for change for so long. But now it was staring me in the face, it made me anxious. Everything I'd ever known, apart from that flirtation with Toby and his world, was rooted at 101 Elm Avenue. Though it felt like a dull, dead root, it was stubborn.

We met four days later at a pub up on Wimbledon Hill. Not my normal stalking-ground, but I think Leo was aiming to impress. Everything about the Coach and Horses was horsey, from the animals cantering across the curtains to the horseshoe beer mats. As I sat down on a stirrup-style barstool, I banged my head on an olde-worlde beam. Not a good start.

Leo got the drinks in and sat opposite. 'It's one of my favourite pubs.' He glanced around the room, fixating for a nano-second on a petite blonde waitress wearing an apron emblazoned with miniature coaches. Maybe he has a thing for equestrian stuff, I thought. Or perhaps he loves the traditional English vibe because it's so different from where he's from.

He raised his glass. 'Tell me about yourself.'

I gulped. 'So much to tell. Or actually so very little. Why don't you go first? Tell me about your island.'

Life had been hard, growing up on Spetses in the aftermath of the Second World War. Leo's parents had run a tiny grocery in the only town on the island to keep the Petrakis family fed and clothed. But by the time Leo was born in 1953 the island's fortunes were changing. Rich Athenians headed there in ferry loads, attracted by the hidden coves and pine-covered hills. Super-stylish yachts began to bob up and down in the harbour alongside the traditional wooden fishing boats and tavernas sprung up as if by magic to cater for well-off tourists with expensive appetites.

Leo and his parents and sisters lived above the shop and in the summer when school was closed, he would help out in the family business. 'We'd get a big consignment of deep purple eggplant, or tomatoes the size of tennis balls and still on the vine. My favourite thing was to create the fruit and veg display at the front of the shop. I'd line up the blood red oranges against lemons the colour of pale sunshine, then maybe a few grass green lettuces to set it all off. Wonderful.'

I could feel myself falling for Leo. Or was it the island's spell I was falling under? He certainly liked to talk which suited me fine, as I'm the opposite. Least said, soonest mended, as Norma would say.

'What about you?' he finally got around to asking. 'C'mon, you look like a lady who has an interesting tale to tell.'

'Not at all. Very little to say about me. I'm a librarian. Embarrassingly, I still live in the old folks' home with my parents. I'm always looking at ways to make my escape. But I have a 10-year-old daughter and my mother helps with childcare.'

'No way! So do I. Have a 10-year-old daughter, that is. Her name is Sophia. And a 13-year-old son, Dimitri. He helps with Sophia when I am working. But we live over the shop, so I'm usually close by. After-hours are difficult. Dimitri's nearly the age where he'll want to do more exciting things in the evening. Soon he won't want to sit for Sophia.'

'What about your wife?'

'No wife.' Leo nodded his head resignedly. 'Thea, my ex-wife, came over with me to England in the mid-seventies. We didn't know she was pregnant with Dimitri at the time and we tried hard to settle. It wasn't me, or us, that was the trouble. It was the glowering skies and rainy streets. She said living in England was like being stuck in a black-and-white photograph. So when her mum took sick and her dad couldn't cope, she scuttled back to her beloved orange groves and sunshine.'

'What about the children? Why didn't they go with her? How could she leave them?' As I asked the question, I reminded myself: but you left your baby too.

'Dimitri was 10 then and Sophia only six. Thea wanted to take them, but their life is here. We gave them the choice and they chose South Wimbledon and me. Weird, huh? But good for me. They love their holidays with their momma on Spetses, but for their school, their friends and this sort of life, here's where they want to be. With their papa.' Leo raised his beer, took a big swig and smacked his lips.

'Wow.' So much had happened in his life and so little in mine. I decided not to mention the missing twin or my doomed relationship with Toby.

'We're talking a lot of big stuff early on, aren't we? Maybe that's a good thing. What you see is what you will get. But hey, why don't we take three steps back and do some small talk now.'

Clinking glasses, he gazed into my eyes for a few seconds longer than felt proper. I didn't flinch. 'I have till midnight to be back in Tooting,' I said, lowering my eyes. I was getting that hot sense of expectancy in the pit of my stomach that I hadn't felt since Toby. 'That's my curfew. If we can't fill it with small talk, maybe we could take a walk on the common. And look, the weather's with us.'

Bars of pink gold evening sunlight lit up the pub windows like the lure of a better future. We clinked again. 'Another gin?' asked Leo.

'No, let me get these.' While the barman poured the drinks, I twisted around to get an off-the-cuff glimpse of Leo. He was staring out of the window, watching the sun slip to earth, a fiery blood orange ball like the fruit on the shop front of his parents' grocery.

'A penny for them,' I balanced the drinks on the table.

'I was thinking, Dimitri and Sophia are at home. It's bedtime soon, of course, but...'

'Let's have our drinks and take a walk,' I suggested.

We were both waiting for the dark. It seemed forever coming, but we filled it with small talk. When the barman lit the table candles and the rosy light from the window became a dull grey blanket, we both knew it was time to go.

'Ready?' asked Leo.

'I'm ready.'

And now, dear reader, I have a confession to make. I didn't think I was that kind of girl. But I wanted it, so bad, like an ache inside. A long, lonely ache that had been there since Toby.

The pub backed on to Wimbledon Common. We walked away from the houses and towards the dark centre. Glancing behind me, I could see the lit-up squares and rectangles of windows at the edge of the common. Taking my hand, Leo led me towards a clump of trees near some undergrowth.

'Have you been here before?' I poked him in the ribs.

'No, of course I haven't been here before. Well not like that. Are you sure this is what you want?'

'I am.' Once the words were out, I knew it, for sure.

We sank down through the darkness on to the dampish grass and I let my body take over. The things I learnt with Toby, although this was different. Toby and had I felt like two parts of an interlocking puzzle. We were tentative, working each other out for shape and size and fit. When we finally came together it was a match of equals. An entanglement of skinny limbs and wild, tumbling hair. But Leo took control, enveloping me in his big bearlike body and leading me skilfully to the next level of pleasure. All those years of holding myself in and now here was someone gallantly directing me how to let go.

Chapter 36
Annie Enderbie, 1989

At 11 years old, Annie Enderbie is a force to be reckoned with. Even her grandma Norma is slightly in awe of her. Gone is the little girl with the caramel curls and sweetly compliant nature. Now Annie has hair as shiny black as Emily's, although it still tends to curl. Her soft chubbiness has disappeared, replaced by long bones that remind her mother of the dancing skeletons at the funfair stalls on Tooting Bec Common.

Annie's popularity is legendary. 'Out and about every day at other people's houses after school,' her grandma is fond of complaining. 'Who knows what you eat at these places, or what you get up to? Half the time they're not people like us.'

A Pakistani family has taken over the newsagents at the top of Elm Avenue. It's now called Hussein's instead of Bilton's and Annie's new best friend is the youngest daughter, Alaya. The large, noisy Hussein family has embraced Annie and she spends many happy hours hunkered down with Alaya at the back of the shop, reading illicit comics.

'It's enough to bring on one of my migraines, all those bright clothes they wear. And is it true that he has a head of hair down to his waist, all tucked up in that turban affair he wears?'

'Honestly, it's true Grandma. I've seen it myself.'

'But how does he wash and brush it?'

'I don't know,' admits Annie. 'It's always inside the turban. I'll ask Alaya if you like.'

'No, no, best not. I suppose it's up to him what he does with his hair.'

Today's they've been helping Mrs Hussein make pakoras. Annie gives her school blazer a surreptitious sniff to check for the curry smells her grandma abhors. In the kitchen at Number 101, the rank smell of tinned pilchards hangs in the air.

'What on earth have you been eating around at the Husseins, child? Your breath stinks,' Norma chides.

'It's pakora, Grandma. It's what we had for tea, with biriani too. You'd love biriani. There's lots of rice and interesting things in it. Can we try making it here sometime for tea?'

'Over my dead body. Here, I've covered over some pilchard sandwiches for you. You've been off hobnobbing so long, I thought the bread might go stale. There's Angel Delight too, your favourite, strawberry flavour.'

Annie's eyes light up. 'Thanks Grandma. I'm too full for sandwiches, but I would like Angel Delight. Your puddings are the best!'

She's rewarded by one of Norma's fleeting smiles, like a weak sun peeping uncertainly from behind a rainstorm. 'That sounds like your mother at the door. Perhaps she won't be too proud for pilchard sandwiches.'

'Hi. I'm back. How was school, Annikins? Why on earth are you wearing your scarf around your head?' Emily rolls her eyes.

'It's a new fashion. Alaya and I invented it. Don't worry. We didn't do it until we got out of school. But we thought it would be fun, like being part of a secret society.'

'What's that in your hand?'

'Oh, it's a letter. From my teacher. For you.' She's uncertain whether to hand it to Norma or her mother, but Emily reaches forward and grabs it.

'I hope you're not in trouble, Annie.' She raises her eyebrows in a way that makes Annie laugh.

'No. Everyone got one. Not *everyone* could be in trouble.'

'Okay, I believe you. And surprise, surprise, you're not in trouble! It doesn't say so here, anyway. It's a letter offering us an appointment with the teacher. Next week.'

'Why?'

'Well, I should think to discuss *you.*' Emily pulls another funny face. Annie is in thrall to her mother, believing her to be the funniest, cleverest, prettiest person in the world. She just sometimes wishes Emily could be a bit more mum-like. Alaya's mum is always at the school gates at pick-up time. Alaya has been complaining about it because she'd rather like to walk home with Annie. But then Alaya gets to do cooking with her mum and she has help with homework.

If she tripped and grazed her knee, she'd run straight home to her mum. Annie has Norma instead.

At least she's not an orphan. After Norma read *Heidi* to her a couple of years ago, she worried about being sent to an orphanage. Then, after they read *What Katy Did,* she was terrified for ages of becoming a cripple. But now Norma seems to her to be a bit like Heidi's grandfather—gruff, but sound and someone you can rely on.

'Is it on a work day? Should I take her to the appointment?' asks Norma.

'No need. I'll change my shift if necessary.' Emily turns to Annie. 'Hey, Annikins, fancy a little mother and daughter time. We could go down to the playground if you like. I've got something I want to talk to you about.'

'What about tea? She still has Angel Delight to eat. It's ready and waiting,' insists Norma.

'Cover it, if you would. She can just as easily have it when she gets back. We'll only be gone a half hour. Talk is sometimes more pressing than Angel Delight.'

Sensing the tension between her mother and grandmother, Annie makes a beeline for the door.

'Why's talk more important than tea?' she asks, once they're safely outside on the pavement.

'Because tea fills your tum, but talk fills up all of you. If it's the right sort of talk.'

'What did you want to talk to me about?'

'Annikins, there's someone I'd like you to meet.'

Annie stops short. 'Is it my dad?' She's hasn't mentioned her father to Emily in a long while, although she thinks about him a lot. It's hard for her to remember a time when she didn't feel the shadowy presence of her missing dad. Lately, she's become afraid of what she might find out. She knows from stories she's read that parents aren't always good people and she's grown to suspect that her father must be one of the bad ones. Otherwise, why wouldn't they talk about him? She's decided he probably isn't dead, or they'd visit his grave, like Ann Parker in her class whose father died in a road accident. The whole Parker family visit his grave, once a week on a Sunday. If her father *is* dead and something happens to her mum, she'll be an orphan: her biggest fear.

'D'you want to talk about your dad?' asks Emily.

'Sort of. Is he a bad person?'

'No, no. He's not a bad person, quite the opposite. But he lives a long way from here, in another country. His life is very different from ours. We shan't see him again so we must accept that, get on with our lives and be happy that we have each other. And Grandma and Grandpa, of course.'

'O-kay.' Annie is not sure how you do that. Forget you have a missing father and get on with your life? She's relieved to hear he's not dead or a bad person, though.'

'What does he look like?'

'Oh, you know, a little bit like you, I think. He has kind brown eyes and a nice smile.'

'Mmm,' Annie wishes she could see him for herself. 'Will I ever meet him?'

'No. He has another life now. And we have our lives too. Which is what I wanted to talk to you about. There's someone I'd like you to meet.'

Still reeling with shock at learning more about her father in five minutes than she's known in the last 11 years, Annie's reluctant to change the subject. She suspects this other person is going to be a lot less interesting—one of her mum's work friends, probably.

'Yes,' continues Emily firmly. 'He's a very nice new friend of mine and I think you're going to like him. His name is Leo and he comes from a beautiful island in Greece. He has two children, Dimitri, who is 13 and Sophia who is the same age as you. They all live above a Greek restaurant not far from here, which Leo runs and owns. They've invited us for lunch. It'll be interesting. All sorts of exciting and unusual food, like you get around at the Husseins.'

'Okay.' It does sound fun, but Annie doesn't really want to talk about it right now. She'd like to talk about her father, but she can see the topic's closed. What she really needs to do is go somewhere quiet, like the shed in the garden, where she can think about him. She calls it 'shed thinking'. 'When is the meeting with my teacher? Am I coming as well?'

'Yes, Wednesday after school. And, yes, they want you to come along too. I must see if I can change my shift...' But Annie has bounded ahead of her and is already at the gate of No 101. 'I'm doing some shed thinking, Tell Grandma I'll be in for my tea very soon.'

For the next few days, Annie is distracted. At school, the teacher pulls her up for daydreaming and at home she forgets to collect Norma's pink and blue magazine from the newsagents, which is annoying because she likes reading the problem page too. Worry about the meeting with her teacher nags away at the pit of her stomach and she's started to nibble her fingernails again. She tries to shut everything off by thinking about her dad and his brown eyes and kind smile. She's relieved when Wednesday arrives and she can get the meeting over with.

'Perk up,' says Emily as they go through the school gate. 'You're not in trouble. They just want to talk us through your options.'

Annie knows what 'options' are, but doesn't think they apply to her. She's heading for the comp, that great grey box of a building with windows that look like spiteful slit eyes.

'Come in, come in and sit down,' intones the Head who is a vision of lilac, in an unstructured linen suit and blue and grey courts. 'Miss Enderbie, lovely to see you.'

'Thank you, Mrs Cameron. A pleasure to see you too.' Annie notices that her mum isn't the least bit fazed by the head, even though she's posh and a bit scary.

'Well, Miss Enderbie, I am pleased to be able to say that Annie is one of our most able pupils. She excels in some areas, written composition for instance, but she is a competent all-rounder. She enjoys her studies, don't you Annie' (Mrs Cameron doesn't pause for a response) 'and it's a pleasure to educate a pupil who is so positive about work and play.'

'I suspected this, Mrs Cameron, but it's good to hear you confirm it,' replies Emily. 'So we can expect her to do well at the comprehensive.'

'Ah, well, that is what I wanted to talk to you about. You see, Annie's teachers and I feel that she might—ahem—wish to aim higher.'

'To where?'

'Well, as I intimated to you in my letter, there are options available to bright children from—ahem—less financially advantaged homes. St Winifred's, for instance, offers one full scholarship each year—a free place for a girl deemed able enough to take advantage of it. Or, if you prefer a mixed environment, there are similar scholarships available at Audley Grange.'

'And you think she's capable of this?' Annie notices that her mum's jaw has dropped open.

'Miss Enderbie, I wouldn't suggest it if I didn't believe that Annie is abundantly capable of it.'

There follows a stunned pause. Annie stares down at her scuffed T-bar shoes and dares to hope. Though she's not quite sure what she's hoping for. To stay with her friends and bumble along in the big grey box that is Becside Comp. To know she can go unchallenged, excelling in class, surviving on the sports field and staying with a gang of kids she's known since she could walk, amongst whom she is legend. Or, take a nosedive into the daunting unknown, where she risks losing everything.

Mrs Cameron breaks the silence. 'So, what are your thoughts? Miss Enderbie? Annie?'

Annie is expecting her mum to look at her, maybe give her a tiny yes or no nod, or even ask her what she thinks. Instead she looks direct at the head. 'I don't think so, Mrs Cameron. What Annie will need to learn at school, in addition to book learning, is to live in the real world. Not an ivory castle. At Becside, she will thrive, but more importantly she will learn to survive. Which, as you say, she is abundantly capable of doing.'

Chapter 37
Annie, 1992

You can hang around at school as long as you like, let several buses go by and even drag your feet along the pavement. But sooner or later, you must go home. Annie has lived in the flat over the Greek restaurant on Merton High Street for more than a year now, since her mother married Leo Petrakis in a wedding marked by noisy plate-smashing and wild dancing on tables. But still she slows her pace as she approaches it.

Annie's within spitting distance of the garish Ambrosia shop-front. To postpone her arrival, she steps in to one of the little antique shops that cluster like limpets in the streets of South Wimbledon. In the window, she examines a large UFO-shaped object in sickly pink which she guesses is an ancient bedpan. A tin soldier with a cracked painted face leers at her with his one good eye. Huddled in the shop doorway, she consults her watch. How long can she delay? Five minutes too late and it's a punishable offence. A minute too early is one more minute to endure. Who would believe what goes on behind the rolling seas and cheerful sailboats daubed on Ambrosia's dust-encrusted windows? Annie's only 14, but sometimes she thinks she's seen too much.

Back at Ambrosia, Emily is in the restaurant madly wiping down tables, chipping off congealed scarlet candle wax with her one good nail.

'Hi Annikins, you're late. Better get yourself upstairs and ready. It's family dinner night, remember.'

Family dinner night happens every Friday and it's Annie's most hated ritual. Such a furore. No wonder her mum usually ends up with Gaviscon and an early night.

In the flat upstairs, Leo is cooking up a storm. His vast torso, encased in an under-size Mama Mia apron, blocks the tiny kitchen. One countertop is groaning with ladies' fingers, Florina peppers and courgettes. On the other are the bare bones of a lamb kleftiko and a half-prepared Rizogalo. Leo's face is a picture of concentration as he tosses herbs in olive oil on the stovetop. Sweat dribbles down from his oily black hair and drips into the hot pan.

I should love this, thinks Annie. This is what people mean when they talk about family. Eating together, coming together. But thinking about the stodgy Rizogalo rice pudding makes her stomach twist. And how is she going to 'do justice' to it all. This expression of Leo's is perfectly calculated to make her feel guilty. She thinks with longing of one of Norma's tinned ham sandwiches.

'Go go, get yourself ready. Family supper in one hour. Smarten yourself up. Wear that pretty dress we got you.' Leo waves his hands theatrically in the air, then wipes his glistening pores with the back of his hand. 'Okay,' says Annie. This is not a choice.

She shares a bedroom with Dimitri and Sophia. Shared is not quite accurate, as the girls' area takes up one third of the floor space and is screened off by a black and brown mosaic blanket which would be more at home on the back of an ancient Greek horse. Dimitri has no hesitation in pushing it aside whenever he feels like it, usually when Annie is getting undressed.

Sophia, pale and wan, is lying on her bed reading *True Romance*. Dimitri has taken over their mirror and is rubbing pomade into his thick black hair. It smells like coconut, with hints of rotting meat.

'Oh, here you are. You're late as usual.' Dimitri doesn't bother to turn around, but continues to admire his chiselled Mediterranean features in the mirror.

'Yes. I know. I need to get changed now. So can you please go back to your own bit of the room.'

'Why? What have you got to show?'

'Stop taunting me please, Dimitri and let me get ready. I don't want to be in trouble again tonight.'

Annie rakes through the wardrobe shared with Sophia and pulls out the dress Leo has decreed. She loathes dresses, especially pastel ones with frills. This particular one makes her look like one of those china shepherdesses that Leo has lined up on the lounge windowsill gathering dust. But if it will get them through the meal peacefully, so be it.

What are *you* wearing?' she asks Sophia.

'Oh, Papa never said. I'd better wear that light blue skirt he bought me and maybe the blue and pink blouse. I think he likes it.' She turns her listless eyes on

Annie. 'I wish I could stay up here and just lie on my bed. I got my period today and it's giving me cramps.'

'Are you worried you won't be able to eat?' Sophia shakes her head. 'Well, stay up here and get some rest. I'll tell Leo you're ill. It's Kleftiko and that rice pudding stuff he makes. Heavy stuff. You won't be able to eat it.'

'No, I'm coming. I don't want any bother.' Sophia swings her legs off the bed. She's as white as a sheet.

Downstairs, Emily and Dimitri are already seated around the table and Leo is consulting his watch. We look like a bunch of Mormons, thinks Annie, who recently watched a TV show about them and was struck by the similarity to life at Ambrosia.

'Come. Sit. The Kleftiko is ready to eat right now,' says Leo. It's an order, not an invitation.

Fraught with pitholes, the evening yawns ahead. Emily's managed to finish her wiping, dusting and polishing and has re-invented herself in a simple black dress with demure three-quarter sleeves and a boat neckline that shows off her delicate clavicle. She looks stunning, thinks Annie. What is she doing here, in this tinpot little flat above a 2-star eatery? Dimitri is spruced up in shirt and tie, with neatly pomaded hair, just as his father likes it. Sophia stares at her reflection in the cutlery. The silence is deafening.

'Conversation. Conversation, please,' insists Leo. 'What is family mealtime for?' He piles the Kleftiko high on everyone's plate and passes around the vegetables. Everything is slick with oil.

The monochrome Greek relatives frown down from their picture frames, frozen in time. Annie gazes at the two little girls squinting at the sunlight in the shabby shop doorway. 'Leo, you never told us. What happened to your little sister? Ambrosia.'

Annie is the only one of the children allowed to call Leo by his name. Dimitri and Sophia are expected to call him Papa. She knows very well that it drives him crazy, but it was a right she fought hard for. He is not *her* father.

A ruddy hue is creeping up Leo's neck towards his jowls. 'She died. And now the subject is closed.'

'But *how* did she die?' presses Annie. Emily shoots her a warning glance and Dimitri plays compulsively with a lamb bone on his plate. Sophia keeps her head bowed.

'This isn't talk for a family mealtime,' thunders Leo.

'But it's about family. And it happened such a very long time ago. Aren't you always saying we should continue to celebrate family, even those who are no longer with us? I'm sorry if it's painful for you.'

In the tense pause that follows, Emily raises her eyes and gazes directly at Annie. It's a look that overflows with solicitude. 'Dimitri very kindly bought you girls some special lemonade. Because he knows you don't drink wine. Would you like a glass each? I'll get it from the fridge.'

'Was that a good idea, Papa?' Dimitri asks his father. To Annie, it sounds like a finely judged smirk.

'Absolutely, young man. Always good to keep the ladies well provided for. Isn't that right, Emily? Don't I keep you well provided for?'

'Of course. Abundantly well provided for. Where on earth did you buy this lemonade, Dimitri? It looks like a one-off. Very posh.' The bottle has a narrow neck and bulbous body adorned with a label promising 'Malloney's REAL Homemade Lemonade' in ornate italics. 'Here, Annie, try a sip.'

Annie, who's never tried real lemonade, thinks it has an odd acrid taste. Perhaps that's because it's made with real lemons and less sugar. She knows better than to comment. 'Very nice. Thank you Dimitri.'

At last, the mangled remains of the lamb are tidied away and it's time for Emily to serve up pudding. 'Get a move on with clearing the table, Emily,' bellows Leo in the direction of the kitchen. 'That pudding'll be overdone.'

'Coming. Coming right now.' Emily scuttles in. 'Sorry to keep you all waiting.'

'Okay, just serve it out now, why don't you?' Leo grins at everyone as if he's said something particularly clever. 'Children, I've told your mother it's time she gave up that day job of hers. There's plenty for her to be getting on with here at Ambrosia. She doesn't need to leave the house to work, eh Emily?'

Grimacing, Emily sets the pudding dish, overflowing with beige froth, in the centre of the table. Leo raises his hands to heaven as if serving up manna and orders everyone to get stuck in. Dimitri takes a big helping, winning a grin of approval. 'That's my boy'. Annie spoons as little as she can get away with on to her plate.

'Come on girls,' intones Leo. 'You're never going to grow those nice lady curves with portions like that.'

'I think both girls are tired,' Emily intervenes. 'And they still have homework to do. Can they be allowed to go to their room?'

Leo nods, jerking a fleshy index finger at the door. 'Go get your beauty sleep, girls. You'll need it soon enough. Beauty, that is, not sleep.'

Annie, shoots her mother a glance of gratitude. Everyone kowtows to Leo, but Emily does seem to have him over a bit of a barrel. But it's too little, too late. Over this past year, Annie has felt horribly exposed in this alien house with her benign bully of a step-dad and his provocative son. Milly's tried and she appreciates it, but it isn't enough.

Later that night, the two girls lie in their narrow beds just an arm's length apart. 'Annie,' whispers Sophia into the darkness. 'I know what happened to Ambrosia.'

'Really.' It's rare for Sophia to speak without prompting. Usually, she is bound up in her own silent struggle to survive life at home.

'Yes, but if I tell, you mustn't repeat it. It's a big family secret. My Aunt Elena told me when I was staying in Spetses with Mama last summer.'

'Why are you telling me?'

'Because I want to share it with someone. Every time I look at that picture downstairs, it makes me sad. And anxious too. I want to know what you think.'

'Okay,' says Annie. 'Tell all.'

'You have to take your mind back to when my dad was seven. It must've been about 1960. I'll tell you just how it happened as my aunt Elena described it to me.'

It had been one of those strangely turbulent days that mark the arrival of high summer on Spetses. At mid-day, the overhead sun scorched the rooftops. Wilting under the shop-front canopy, Leo begged his parents to give him an hour off sorting vegetables to go down to the cool of the harbour.

'Yes, so long as you take the girls with you,' his Papa agreed. 'And don't let them out of your sight,' added Metera. 'The wind's coming up any time now, mark my words.'

The thought of dragging his little sisters along with him was annoying. Elena, at five, wasn't so bad, but Ambrosia was only three and quite a liability. But he could see it was his only exit ticket. 'Okay. We'll all be back in an hour, promise,' he said. Down on the tiny beach by the harbour, his little sisters dug their toes into the wet sand and squealed with delight. They wanted to collect shells for their Metera, but Leo had spotted something much more exciting: an ancient wooden fishing boat batting against the gentle waves hitting the shoreline.

'Look at that! It's an abandoned boat. Let's have a go in it,' he commanded his sisters. Elena and Ambrosia hovered on the shoreline while Leo waded into the sea, secured the rope and managed to pull the boat on to the beach. 'It's even got its own paddle. Get in both of you. Let's ride!'

'We shouldn't,' said Elena. 'Remember what Metera said. There's a big wind coming.'

'Nonsense. She always thinks the weather is turning bad. Look at the sky, not a cloud. Get in, or I'll leave you here all alone until I get back.'

'No, don't do that. We'll be scared. We're not meant to be at the harbour by ourselves. Someone might see us and tell Papa. We'll have to come with you.'

Reluctantly, Elena and Ambrosia clambered into the boat and sat on the wooden plank bench, clutching each other for comfort. Leo rowed out into the bay. No one noticed the storm clouds gathering until it was too late. Leo paddled hard to get them back on course towards the shore, but by now the wind was up and a seven-year-old had no chance against the tide. As the boat rocked violently to and fro, Leo shouted towards the shoreline. But everyone had retreated indoors and even the little café on the water's edge was empty.

When a violent wave nearly overturned the boat, both little girls screamed. Leo managed to right it, but they were knocked by a smaller wave from the opposite direction. Terrified, Ambrosia let go of her big sister's hand and tried to stand up on the bench to attract Leo's attention. But it was slick with seawater and the other two children watched in horror as she lost her balance and disappeared over the side.

'Aunt Elena told me that she saw Ambrosia in the waves, flailing about like a puppy. She was only three years old and hadn't learnt to swim. The last Aunt Elena saw was her blonde plait trailing in the water. It's an image she's never forgotten,' says Sophia. 'Her body was never found. The sea took her and didn't give her back.

'Papa and Elena were lucky. Someone in one of the harbour cottages spotted the boat tossing around and rushed to the rescue. But that's why Papa wants to control everyone and everything, according to Aunt Elena. Because he couldn't save his little sister.

'The worst of it was that Papa tried to offload the blame on Aunt Elena. That's what she told me, anyway,' adds Sophia. 'He said she hadn't kept tight enough hold of her sister. But everyone knew it was Papa, he was the one who took the boat out and forced the girls to go on it. Elena told me that life was never quite the same for him after that, either at home or in the village. People avoided him, like he was a bad omen. Even his own family couldn't look him in the eye. He left as soon as he could, taking my Mama with him. But don't let him fool you that Mama left him because she couldn't live away from the island. It was him she couldn't abide. The way he is, you know.'

Annie nods. She does know.

'You should get away,' whispers Sophia. 'And maybe your mum too. You could go back to your Grandma's, maybe? He's not a bad man, my Papa. He tries. But he's toxic. And Dimitri, he's growing into Papa too. Ssshh, he's coming now.'

Both girls dive under the bedclothes as Dimitri opens the door to the bedroom. 'Hi girls, I know you're hiding. Come on, I want to talk to you.' His tone is taunting.

Annie emerges first from the safety of the bedclothes. 'What do you want, Dimitri? We're trying to sleep.'

'Well for starters I want to know if you enjoyed the very special bottle of lemonade I bought for you.'

'Yes, it tasted different.' Annie, chooses her words carefully. 'I expect that's because it was proper lemon and I've only had squash before.'

'Ha, well yes I expect it would taste different as it was made up of eight parts squash and two parts pee. My pee, naturally.'

'That's truly, truly horrible, Dimitri. And anyway, I don't believe it. You wouldn't dare. You're too chicken to play a dirty trick like that.' Already, Annie's stomach is gurgling.

'Well, that's for me to know and for you to guess. Think on it, girls. Or should I say drink on it. Nighty night, both. Sweet dreams.' With that, Dimitri disappears behind the horsehair blanket.

Sophia emerges, tears in her eyes. 'I feel sick.'

'So do I, Sophia. But I'm quite sure he's made it up.' Annie sounds more convinced than she feels, but she resolutely smoothes out her pillow and tucks herself down. 'Tomorrow is another day. Sleep now.'

Next day, Annie has a lie-in, pleading a migraine. Dimitri has left for football practice, Sophia is nowhere to be seen and Leo has taken the van to the wholesaler. Annie creeps down the stairs to the restaurant, where Milly is busy unstacking chairs and setting tables ready for busy Saturday night business.

'Annikins! How're you feeling?'

'Better. My headache's going. But Milly, there's something I need to talk to you about. Just you. Can we go somewhere else, for half an hour? Anywhere but here.'

'Well, okay. What a mystery.' Emily wriggles out of her apron and teases her hair in the mirrored fish eye on the wall. 'I'd better be back before Leo though. You know what he's like.'

In the coffee shop down the road, Milly orders two lattes and sits opposite Annie. 'Shoot.'

'Milly, I don't want to live here at Ambrosia any more. It's not a happy place for me. I want to go back to live with Grandma and Grandpa, if they'll have me.'

Emily sighs. 'I know, Annikins. It's not easy for you here. Leo can be controlling and Dimitri is acting like a little so-and-so at the moment. But we'd miss each other a lot. I'd be so sad without you!'

'But Milly, I want you to come too. I know Leo can be kind, but both of them are bullies. I can't breathe here, always being told what to do and how to do it. You must feel that too. Please, come with me.'

'It's not that simple, Annie. For starters, I'm a married woman now. I can't just walk away from my marriage at the snap of my fingers. And some things here are good, for me. I don't have the same happy memories of Elm Avenue and don't want to go back.'

Annie hangs her head. 'I'll try not to think this is because you care more about them than me. I'll try to understand it's more complex than that. But you can't live *there* and I can't live *here*. That's it, isn't it?'

'That's right, Annikins. I'd like to persuade you to stay, but I understand why you must leave. I would've been the same at your age. And look, it's only a bus ride away. We can see each other loads, probably more than we do now.'

'If they'll have me—Grandma and Grandpa, I mean.'

'Of course they'll have you! They'll have the Welcome Home banner strung across the front door and Norma will be on the step waiting with a plate of covered pilchard sandwiches, just for you. Seriously, Annie, they adore you! Me, not quite so much.' Emily pulls the wry little face that always makes Annie laugh. 'Come on, let's get back before we're both in trouble!'

Chapter 38
Annie, 1996

Annie feels as if she's reached not just a crossroads, but a staggered junction in her life. On so many levels. She's off to university in September and she's grappling with the luxury of choice. Should she take up the offer of a place at Bristol to study Psychology? Or stay close to home and opt for Eng Lit at London? It's lovely to be in demand, but making choices is tough.

Grandma is gunning for London of course. 'You could live here. Save rent. Keep an eye on us two old codgers,' she pleads. And thereby hangs Annie's other dilemma. It feels like roles are being swapped and she's becoming the one looking after Grandma and Grandpa. Especially Grandpa.

Since retirement, Clive has spent much of his time huddled in his brown leatherette armchair in the bay window. With part of his golden handshake, they bought one of the new and preposterously large flatscreen TVs and it flickers and drones all day long while Clive mindlessly flicks channels. Sometimes he doesn't even bother to change out of his PJs. Annie remembers her Grandpa always busy at his place of work, or making things: a spice rack for the kitchen, a shoe shelf for under the stairs. Or he'd be hidden in the newspaper, emerging every now and again to complain bitterly about the state of the world.

Now Clive seems to have lost his convictions, along with his handyman skills. He can't even follow the plot of his favourite soap without prompting. 'If he was a public toilet, he would be marked vacant,' sniffs Norma.

One morning. Clive got up and puts two odd socks on. 'It wouldn't be so bad, but one was bright blue and the other white,' reported Norma. At breakfast, he made his traditional fry-up, but forgot to include his favourite ingredient—two rashers of streaky bacon—and then complained to Norma when he couldn't find it on his plate. As the final straw, he forgot to switch the electric ring off.

'Do you think he should see the doctor?' she asked Annie. 'I'm worried what he'll forget next.'

'Yeah, maybe.' Annie was trying to mug up on her psychology textbook and eat a slice of her favourite lemon-curd-smeared toast at the same time.

'Well, would you be able to take him along?'

Here we go again, thought Annie. I'm the new carer. She sighed. 'Of course. Just make the appointment. Here's your chance to use that lovely green phone, Grandma.'

Today's the day. Grandpa has an ambulatory gait and Annie is trying hard to steer him to the surgery at the top of Elm Avenue. She's given up with conversation. The expression on Grandpa's face rolls anxiety, expectancy and grumpiness all into one. But no evidence of comprehension. It's taking every last scrap of brainpower for him to put one foot in front of the other.

At the surgery, they're called in to see Dr Wright. When Annie was six and had measles, he arrived at No 101 after surgery hours just to check on her. And when she was nine and went over her handlebars, he was first on the scene to tend her broken wrist. She deems him gentle and wise.

'Well, Mr Enderbie. What can we do for you today?' Dr Wright doesn't glare directly at you, like some doctors, when he asks a question. Instead, he's shuffling stuff around on his desk and polishing up his specs in the long silence that follows. Annie finds this oddly comforting, especially as she's not quite sure if she should answer the question on Grandpa's behalf, or continue in this horrible silent void.

Eventually, Clive clears his throat. 'Umm, I'm not quite sure. Norma thought I should...'

'Not to worry, Mr Enderbie. Why don't we give you a quick once over.' He checks Clive's blood pressure and pulse. 'That all looks fine. I'll take a blood test and a sample too, if you don't mind.'

Clive gazes listlessly back at him.

'I tell you what, Mr Enderbie. I have a few questions to ask you. Nothing to worry about, they're just designed to keep our long-suffering patients on their toes.' Dr Wright clears his throat. 'Ahem, can you tell me your birthday?'

'It's in the summer,' replies Clive helpfully. 'I know that because we usually have tea in the garden.'

'Good, good—let's try another. I have to say, they do get a bit more silly and difficult as you go along. Can you remember the name of our wonderful prime minister?'

There is a tense hiatus while Clive struggles. 'Lloyd George?' Annie glances at Dr Wright in trepidation but his expression doesn't alter by a hair's breadth.

'Okay, just one more and we'll give you a rest. Can you take seven from 100 and let me know what that number would be?'

'That's a silly question,' says Clive. 'Why ever would I need to do that? Anyway, normally I could do it, but I just can't get my head around figures at the moment.'

'Of course. I do understand. Let's wait for the test results and see what they tell us. In the meantime, I'd like to make an appointment for Mrs Enderbie to come along and have a quick chat with me too and we'll try to resolve this.'

On the way out, Annie feels like every single person in the reception area is looking at them, but it must be her imagination. 'Why don't we walk back through the park, Grandpa?'

She takes Clive's arm and rubs his brown, speckled hand. As they falter down the avenue of trees, Clive scans the familiar landscape of the park in bewilderment. 'I'm losing it, aren't I, Annie?'

She struggles to answer. Should she be truthful and honourable—or deceitful and kind? 'I'm sure that's not so, Grandpa. They just need to check you over and find out what's wrong.'

'Well, if I am losing it, Annie, there's something I need to say.'

'Shush, now, Grandpa. There'll be all the time you need to say all the things you want. Enjoy your walk in the sunshine for now.'

'No, no. I have to say it.' Clive is getting agitated, his veins throbbing at his temples.'

'Okay, Grandpa. What is it you need to say?'

'You have a sister. A twin sister. Her name is Bea.' Clive is spluttering with the effort of getting the words out.

'Don't be daft, Grandpa. If I have a sister, where would she be?'

'She was taken. I can't remember any more.' For a moment Clive stares straight into Annie's eyes and a chill goes through her. Then he seems to deflate.

'Was there anything more about this you wanted to tell me, Grandpa?'

'No. I can't remember anything more. I must have got it wrong. Please can we go home now.'

Grandpa is turning into a frightened little old man before Annie's eyes. They scurry home to find Norma on the doorstep. 'What on earth is wrong with you two? You both look as if you've seen a ghost.'

'I'm going to water my plants. If I can remember where I put my watering can.' Clive lurches down the hallway, head pecking like a chicken.

'It's true, isn't it? He's losing his marbles,' demands Norma.

'Grandma, we don't know that yet. The doctor gave him a memory test and he didn't do well. But he's getting more tests and I'm sure Dr Wright will get to the bottom of it. He wants you to make an appointment with him to discuss things.'

'There was something else though.' Annie has examined her conscience as to whether she should bring this up, but it feels like an imperative. 'When we were walking back through the park, he blurted out something very strange. He told me I have a twin sister. He even said her name was Bea.'

Norma's olive complexion has turned as pale as milk. But then, Annie reasons, it would come as a shock that the dementia is much more advanced than they'd thought.

'Delusional. He must be delusional as well as demented. I'll go and tell him to stop making up silly stories that will upset everyone. We may even need to consider his future.' Norma is looking angrier than Annie has ever seen her. Someone has to be the grown-up here. It will have to be her, again.

'Grandma, don't talk about sending him to one of those awful homes. It terrifies him. He'll be fine here, with us. It's not as if he's aggressive. He's just got some fantasy fixed in his head and yes, maybe he'll have other fantasies as time goes by. But they're harmless. And he needs us. I don't think he'll ever speak of this again. He's forgotten it already.'

'Well, I'm going right out there now to tell him that if he ever comes out with nonsense like that again, I'll put him in a home. And then we'll say no more about it.'

'Please don't, Grandma.' But Norma is already halfway up the garden path, gesticulating at Clive who is clutching his watering can in self-defence.

Later that night, when Clive and Annie are both fast asleep, Norma lifts the moss green telephone handset from its cradle and dials out.

Down the road in South Wimbledon, Emily's finished laying restaurant tables for the next day and is settling down to watch a late-night comedy show. 'What is it, Norma? It's late.' She yawns, audibly.

'There's something you need to know. Clive's spilled the beans about Bea.'

There's a sharp intake of breath at the other end of the line. 'Why would he do that? We swore it would never happen.'

'It looks like he's losing his marbles. He'd just been to see the doctor and he was walking home through the park with Annie.'

'How could this happen?'

'Don't worry. I'm handling it. I told Clive I'd send him to a care home if he mentions it again. I think he got the message. He's scared shitless of that. And Annie just assumed that poor Grandpa is delusional with his dementia, bless her heart. For now, anyway. She might start asking you questions. I'm warning you.'

'Mmm. How do you think I should handle it?' Emily can't remember ever before asking her mother for advice.

'Just completely poo poo it. Clive's going to get a firm diagnosis any time now, I'm sure of it. He'll get worse, not better. Before long, no one will believe a word that comes out of his mouth. Consider the consequences if Annie finds out. She'll think we're both rubbish. It's not a good look. A grandmother and a mother who connived to give her baby sister away.'

'Well, it wasn't quite like that. But I see what you mean.' Emily is amazed at how the words slip off her tongue. Time, the great healer, she thinks with some bitterness

Part 3
Shadow of a Doubt

Chapter 39
Annie, 2013

As the No 49 double-decker grinds to a halt at the top of Elm Avenue, Annie is blindsided by memories. Here is the very spot where, age four, she was scooped up by her grandma just before she tried to board a big red bus into London. And there is the reincarnation of Husseins Newsagents, where she and Alaya spent happy hours reading comics and raiding the sweet counter. Now it's a shiny new estate agents, the prices in the window reflecting Tooting's dramatically changed demographic. With a wry grin, Annie notes that her grandparents would now be just about half-millionaires!

Superficially, not much has changed in Elm Avenue. Just a long line of modest London brick terraced houses marching up the long slope towards Colliers Wood. Every so often, a gap in the row like a gaping tooth is a reminder of the war: a family lost at number 66 and another buried beneath number 293. Random acts of violence. Don't ask for whom the bell tolls. Some of the gaps have been plugged in, a granny annexe here, a builders' yard there. In 21st century Tooting, the ground beneath your feet is gold dust.

It's only when you start walking down Elm Avenue, avoiding the familiar bad luck cracks in the pavement, that you see the subtle changes. Gone are the net curtains and china ornaments that once embellished every self-respecting bay window. Many homeowners have dispensed with privacy altogether and you can see right through their knocked-out, bare boarded, white painted living spaces to the patio gardens beyond. Every other rooftop is adorned with a satellite disk, thrusting its shiny umbrella into the sky like a victory call. Authentic Victorian tiled paths have replaced crazy paving, plastic sash windows are making a reappearance and the Cortinas and Sierras have been overtaken at the kerbside by BMWs, VWs and Mazdas.

But at no 101, time stands still. Annie pauses at the gate and takes in the weeds pushing their way up through the crazy paving. In the window, Norma's 'best' curtains hang like drunken sailors. They never really looked right again after the ill-fated game of Hide and Seek. The beautiful glass sunburst, Norma's pride and joy, is still there adorning the front door. Annie recalls peeping through the glass that bathed everything in the acid glow of Lucozade wrapping. Now it's grimy and cracked.

Taking a deep breath, Annie turns the key in the lock. A fine film of dust gives familiar household objects an otherworldly feel. The blue melamine table where Norma would read her true romances is set with a china teacup and milk jug and there's even a teapot full of mouldy tea. It seems her grandmother must have left in haste. Or perhaps she was past worrying about the niceties. In the front room, Norma's beloved china shepherdesses are still posturing on the windowsill under a fine dusty coating. On the mantelpiece, the letter offering Annie a place to study psychology at Bristol University is propped up in pride of place, now yellow and curling at the edges. Annie's first pram, an enormous black 'Balmoral' carriage with silver chassis, still blocks the tiny dining room. Norma never wanted to let it go for some reason, so they learnt to live around it.

Her grandmother is dead. Annie shifts the words around her mouth, whispering them in the silent house—but still she can't believe them. For Annie, Norma was the fixed point. Her grandfather Clive died many years before, when she was at university. But her grandma lived on, reading her true romances, following her favourite soaps, angrily cleaning her front porch and even, reluctantly, tending to Clive's patch of garden. Sometimes she'd share a cup of tea with Marcia Grimes down the road. They never got out of the habit of calling each other 'Mrs'. Emily came by on odd occasions, but the visits usually ended badly. For Annie's visits, less frequent over the years, there would always be a plate of her 'favourite' pilchard sandwiches and Battenburg cake. How could grandma have left her without somehow warning her, or saying goodbye?

Norma died, as she had lived, independently. Although the visits dwindled, Annie made it a habit to call every Sunday at 6 p.m. She would imagine the ancient green telephone ringing out in the still house. Norma always picked up before the third ring - it was how Annie knew she was waiting for the call. But last Sunday, it kept on ringing. Eventually, Annie dug out Marcia Grimes, whose number she keeps for emergencies and asked her to go check.

Norma had been found at the foot of the attic stairs. The paramedics thought at first she might have tripped and fell, but it was later confirmed that she'd suffered a massive stroke. The position of her body suggested she was climbing the stairs, rather than descending. 'Why would she be doing that?' mused Annie. 'No one's been up there for years.' The young paramedic she spoke to later, who had been first on the scene, shrugged. Who can account for crazy old ladies, his shoulders seemed to say.

Now Annie is at the foot of the attic stairs, suppressing a shudder as she thinks of her Grandma lying there alone, perhaps conscious and scared. She thinks of all the times she's helped a client to come to terms with death. As a practicing psychologist, she thought she knew the strategies. The times she's sat with a client in her bright consulting room and discussed immortality. Was it all prevarication? Taking a few deep breaths, she heads quickly up the stairs and gingerly pushes open the attic door.

Inside, everything is as it should be. Two single beds, neatly made up as if awaiting someone's arrival. Emily's desk, beneath the dormer window, still with its green plastic reading lamp from Woolworths and a pile of books. Fitzgerald, Steinbeck, Lawrence. Annie marvels again at what a reader her mother was and at how little she managed to do with all that book reading. She did work as a librarian for several years, but that was before Leo decreed she'd be more use in the restaurant. And then she got sick.

Annie is struck by how much the room is possessed by Emily. It was *her* room for a long time, but where are the traces? She pulls open the wardrobe door and out falls all her stuff. In between the scrunched-up anoraks, t-shirts and underwear, neglected dolls and broken toys, she finds relics that bring childhood flooding back. An 'I can swim a width' certificate from 1984, a Polaroid snap of her hula-hooping in the back garden while Grandpa looks on adoringly, an entry ticket to Chessington World of Adventures and more. She recalls that both she and Alaya got sick riding the Speedy Viper.

There's a narrow top shelf above the bulging clothes rail that Annie never noticed before. She clambers precariously on to the swivel chair to take a closer look. All pretty boring stuff. Dusty shoe boxes crammed with old household bills, a heap of Norma's True Romances and pile of ancient school text books which must have belonged to Emily. Annie is tempted to leave them just where they are, but then remembers that someone is going to be responsible for clearing the house. Undoubtedly that will be her. The swivel chair is wobbly so she takes one big swipe at the heap, releasing a cascade of paperwork into the fetid attic air.

Climbing down, Annie collapses on her old single bed and considers the mess she's now going to have to sort through singlehanded. She's starting to wish she'd accepted Ben's offer to tag along and help her with sorting the house. She'd been firm about it being her task and in any case no fun for Phoebe. So now he's having the best time, taking Phoebe swimming and then out for a burger. She pictures her husband tossing their wraith-like five-year-old over his shoulders into the shady depths of the emerald pool. She'll be squealing in terror and delight and when she surfaces, will want him to toss her all over again. She misses them both already.

Then something catches her eye. It's a ring binder the colour of the night sky adorned with silver stars and planets and there's a sticker on the front –*Emily Enderbie's Memory Book.* Inside, sheaves of narrow-lined paper are covered with Emily's tiny handwriting. Annie squints and reaches into her pocket for her reading glasses. She turns to the first page:

'My babies have taken over my life. I'm only 18, it's not fair. One is bad enough, but twins are crazy bad luck.'

It's getting towards dusk by the time Annie reaches the end. When she gets to the ill-timed meeting with Leo Petrakis over spilt eggplants, Emily's first encounter with Ambrosia and lovemaking on Wimbledon Common, the writing stops abruptly. Perhaps Emily left her Memory Book buried at the back of the wardrobe here in Elm Avenue and forgot about it? Surely not. Perhaps she wanted to put that part of her life in a box, wrap it up and forget it and this was her way of doing so. Or maybe she *did* want someone to find her book at some point in the future which is why she stuffed it at the back of the wardrobe, knowing that sooner or later it would come to light.

Annie looks at her silenced phone. She's missed three calls from Ben and one desperate text message. 'Annie, we're worried about you. Just text and let us know you're okay. Phoebe's staying awake for her goodnight kiss.'

'Coming soon. So, so sorry, love. I'm a useless wife and mum. Lots of stuff to tell. Have a stiff drink ready.' She pings her text over and rolls the phone around in her hand. Her instinct is to call her mother right away. But she sits on the urge. Instead, she taps in Ben's number on her mobile. It rings a long time and when he does pick up, he sounds gruff.

'What the hell's going on there? We were expecting you back hours ago. I just finally got Phoebe off. She's very unsettled. She wants her bedtime story and a goodnight kiss from you. I had to tell her...'

'Ben, I am so very sorry and I love you totally. But would you please stop and listen to me just for a moment? Something quite extraordinary's come up. I think I may have found my father. And maybe a sister too. A twin sister.'

'My God. How come? Is this some sort of excuse-for-not-being-here joke?'

'No, Ben. This is not one of my sophisticated psych games, as you call them. It's for real. My mother kept a diary—what she called a Memory Book. I found it in the attic wardrobe behind a heap of papers. That's what I've been doing all afternoon, reading it.'

'Jesus. Shouldn't you call your mother?'

'Well, that was my first instinct. But then I thought again. If she and Grandma have been so anxious to cover this up all these years, they must have had very good reasons. Milly will be obstructive if she doesn't want me to know and try to throw me off the scent. Or she'll beg me not to investigate further. You know as well as I do how good she can be at emotional blackmail. Plus she's ill. Not a good time for her to go digging up demons. It's best if I, we, do it for her and present it in the right way.'

'Hmm. I see where you're coming from. But are you sure this Memory Book is for real? Maybe she made it up. The part about the father sounds sort of plausible. But she could've made up the bit about an identical twin. I remember when I was a child, wishing so hard for a brother that I could almost picture him there.'

'Trust me. I am listening to you and I'm trying not to get ahead of myself. There are so many small details in there that ring true. The really strange thing is that years ago my Grandpa tried to tell me about a twin called Bea. I assumed it was his dementia and Grandma and Milly thought so too. Grandma even threatened to send him to a home if he mentioned it again. I'm beginning to suspect they colluded with each other to keep the truth from me.

'But let's take it one step at a time and start with my possible father. Can you do something for me right now? I don't think I can hold on until I get home. Can you go to your computer and google the name Toby Summerfield? Just see if anything comes up. You could try the electoral register...'

'Okay, Toby Summerfield. That name rings a bell. With a *b,* not an *n*, right? I've a feeling I won't need to look far. Isn't he that leftist journalist? Used to do a lot of campaigning stuff. I think he might edit one of the nationals now.'

'Good God.' Annie can feel her heart, or is it her stomach, doing a flip. 'That ticks a lot of boxes.'

'Come home,' says Ben. 'There'll be a huge glass of Sauv waiting for you. And no recriminations about being late and not letting me know where you were, promise. We'll do this thing together.'

Chapter 40
Annie, 2013

Not for the first time, Annie wishes that her mother would come to live closer by in north London. South Wimbledon is such a long, dark, rattling journey on the Northern Line. And when she steps out blinking onto Merton High Street, she knows she's going to be flooded with uncomfortable memories that won't back off. Ironic how often she encourages clients not to bury bad stuff, but to pull it out, examine it, pick it over. She now understands that Leo is a coercive controller and Dimitri quite simply a bully. But muttering the words doesn't make it any easier when she's standing at the door to Ambrosia engulfed by familiar sensations of panic and dread.

When Emily answers, Annie is struck by how pale and listless she is. Her lips are bloodless and her once-spectacular black hair is collapsed on her head in a frizzy heap. The prospect of a visitor, even her own daughter, seems to overwhelm her.

'Come on in, Annikins.' She opens the door just a crack. 'Unexpected. To what do I owe the pleasure? It's just us. Leo's over at Dimitri's.'

'Thanks Milly.' Such a relief Leo isn't around, or worse, the extended family. Sophia and Dimitri flew the nest years ago. Sophia emigrated to Australia in search of freedom and Dimitri is probably busy bullying his own small family somewhere out Croydon-way.

'Let me get you a coffee.' Emily teeters up the narrow staircase to the Petrakis flat above the restaurant. Why is she walking in that funny way, wonders Annie. Her mother, who is only in her early fifties, seems to be turning into a cautious old lady. Surely Leo's benevolent bullying can't have reduced her this far. Or perhaps she senses something is up? In the little kitchen, Annie can hear her clattering about making way too much noise for coffee for two.

Lurking in the kitchen doorway, Annie clears her throat, a nervous habit. 'Milly, I have something for you.' Out of her plastic shopping bag, she pulls the much-thumbed Memory Book.

A plate of biscuits falls to the floor as Emily reaches for the Memory Book. 'It's mine. Give it to me now. You have no right to keep it. Have you read it?'

Annie nods. 'Believe me, I'm not here to judge you. I just need to understand who I am. I think I told you once, years ago, that I've always felt like half a person. I've assumed it's because I'm missing a father, but perhaps there's more to it than that.'

Emily grabs the book and hugs it to her stomach. Her face is a mask. A toxic blend of anxiety and deception. She says nothing, so Annie ploughs on.

'I found it in the wardrobe. When I was clearing out at Elm Avenue. A week or so ago.'

Still, Emily says nothing. But her skinny hand is plucking at the thin, loose skin on her neck. 'You read all of it?'

'Yes I did, Milly. And I believe my father's name is Toby Summerfield. He doesn't live abroad. He lives right here in London and he was easy to track down as he's pretty high profile. As I'm sure you're aware.

'What's more, I contacted him,' adds Annie. 'I emailed him first off as I didn't want it to be too much of a shock. He emailed right back and suggested we should talk. So we did. By phone, yesterday. He remembers you well and with huge affection.' It had felt to Annie more like love, the way Toby had expressed his feelings, but the word is too big to deal with right now.

'Apparently he had no idea whatsoever that he had a grown-up daughter,' she continues. 'It brings tears to my eyes, the way he reacted. I was quite prepared for him to tell me to piss off. Or accuse me of being a liar. Or simply putting the phone down. But d'you want to know what he said? *Emily and a daughter. My daughter. Can I be so blessed? My cup overfloweth.*

Milly, he loves you. Loved you. What happened?'

'You had no right.' You shouldn't have contacted him,' Emily's chicken-like hands are stretched tight around the book.

'Milly, he's my *father*. Isn't he? Or is he not? If he is, I most definitely have the right.'

Emily chews her lips. 'He is your father,' she admits, finally.

'So what happened, then? Did he dump you?' Annie's only spoken to Toby by phone, but somehow he didn't come over as the dumping sort.

'No. I dumped him. I let go of him. With great regret. I didn't want to drag him down with me. He was going places. I was just a pregnant nobody from the wrong side of the common.'

'But Milly, did you love him?'

'Yes I loved him. I was crazy about him. But love can mean letting go. It was the hardest thing I ever did, stepping out of his life. It was hard for him too, but staying together would have ruined him. And you know what, it was the right thing. Do you know why? Because he never came after me, never tried to find me. His family left the area soon after we split off, then he went off to Oxford. And he never came back. Not for me anyway.'

'So you've spent all these years feeling bitter about him because he didn't pursue you after you dumped him? On what planet does that make sense? He probably thought he was respecting your wishes. Anyway, he wants to see you now.'

'Why? Why on earth would he want to see me now? I'm not his pretty little Emily any more. Look at me.' Emily tugs at her wizened topknot.

'Milly, please. I'm asking you to complete this circle. For me, as much as you. Because there's more.'

'Which is?' Emily bows her head and Annie's sure she suspects what's coming.

'In your Memory Book, you talk of identical twins. My sister, Bea. Is this true? Did—do—I have a twin? Did she die?'

'No, she didn't die. Well, not as far as I know. It's 35 years since I saw her. We put her up for adoption. I was only 18, you see. I couldn't cope with two babies. She was just three months old. Norma told me it would be for the best and I believed her. There isn't a day goes by that I don't regret it. She was a difficult baby, cried a lot. She didn't have your sunny temperament. Norma forced me to choose and I chose you. She led me to believe that we would all have been out on the street otherwise. So, to answer your question, yes, you have a twin. An identical twin. Somewhere out there.'

Annie battles with a sense of almost overwhelming revulsion at the idea of giving away your child. She pictures Phoebe waving from the bay window as she left the house just a few hours ago—and her head swims. Her beloved Grandma, cast in a different mould. And Milly, her mother, who colluded in dispensing with her own child. How can she ever square her love for them both with…this crime.

It was another time, she argues with herself. A different era altogether. Her mother and grandmother are good people who made a very bad call. History is full of such people. Carefully and logically, Annie talks herself down from her outrage and anger.

'Milly, no one is to blame. You were in crisis. Grandma did what she thought needed to be done.' As she says it, Annie can't help wondering if the baby Bea would agree.

'You also need to know that I haven't yet told Toby Summerfield about my missing twin. That is your prerogative. If you decide not to tell him, I'll support you. But I think you'd feel better if you did.'

Emily recoils. 'Who says I'm even agreeing to see Toby?'

'You are, Milly. You know you are. He was the love of your life. I know, I understand, Leo mustn't hear a word of this. Leave it with me.'

Chapter 41
Annie, 2013

The school run is usually a highlight in Annie's day, some quality time with her daughter. Why some parents find it tiresome, she can't imagine. From her pole position in the drivers' seat, Annie knows she can glean all those precious nuggets about her daughter that she won't get by stroking her brow at bedtime and murmuring: *now, darling, tell me about your day.*

Today is different. The traffic is horrendous and Annie can taste the fumes in her mouth, even with the car windows up. Three little girls, strapped up in the back seat, are chattering like magpies. Phoebe is cross because her plait has come undone, Ella has forgotten her PE kit and wants to go back home to get it and one of the words from Lottie's word tin has fallen down between the seats.

'Don't take your seat belt off, Lottie,' Annie warns. 'You'll have to wait until we stop to find the word. Phoebe, I'll re-do your plait when we get there.' She doesn't have a solution for Ella's missing PE kit. So be it.

The joys of being a pilot's wife, she thinks, as she inches her Fiat into the school car park, neatly avoiding a battery of confrontational 4x4s. Quite a few of the drivers are dads, which makes her a little sad because she knows just how much Phoebe would love it if *her* dad could drive her to school more often. Ben rarely gets to do the school run and now he's on often on long haul he's lucky to give Phoebe a bedtime story either. They'd sat up late the night before, going over how Annie might handle today, then he was up again at 4:30 a.m. and on the way to Heathrow for a flight to Dubai.

Getting the girls out of the car and herded into the playground is always a challenge, but when she's finally ushered the three of them to safety, Annie feels bereft. Now there's no one left to hide behind. Pointing the Fiat resolutely in the direction of Hammersmith, she begins the stop-start journey to South Wimbledon. Milly had insisted she'd take the underground, but there was always a chance she'd chicken out at the last minute. Far better to keep her mother captive in the car, even if it does mean a two-hour round trip to collect her.

In the coffee shop opposite South Wimbledon station, Emily is anxiously sipping a cappuccino. 'Annikins, you made it. Good job we arranged to meet here. Leo's a bit suspicious. I told him I was meeting someone from the library and he accused me of being overdressed! I think he suspects I'm meeting a man. Well, I guess I am, in a way.'

Emily is dressed in a simple black linen dress, with a statement necklace the buttery colour of honeycomb. Her hair's arranged in a French plait which cleverly conceals the grey fuzzy bits. Rake thin, she is the picture of understated elegance. By contrast, Annie wears a flared cord skirt, leaf print blouse and open sandals which make her feel like what she is, a mum.

'You look fabulous, Milly. Your carriage awaits.'

Emily arranges her long, thin legs in the pint-size Fiat and they head off into the traffic. 'Hmm. I'm nervous. You know, I haven't seen him in 34 years.'

'I bet you followed his career in the press though.'

'On and off.' Emily gazes out at the hectic street scene. Clearly, she doesn't want to talk. The journey passes in silence and urban clutter gives way to wide avenues lined with handsome Victorian villas shaded by plane trees.

'Is this where he lives?' asks Emily.

'Yes, it's Muswell Hill. Have you been here before?'

'Nope.'

The car wheels spin as they turn into a generously shingled driveway. A foursquare mellow brick villa squats complacently on the loop of the drive that ends in a final flourish at an ornate Victorian conservatory.

'Should we have brought flowers?' ask Emily.

'Nah. I heard they all suffer from hay fever.' Annie jerks the car to a halt at a seemly distance from the house. The front door opens and a middle-aged man peers out: a Panama hat, unexpectedly narrow shoulders, a portly middle. Recalling Toby's wraith-like waist, Emily gulps back the tears.

'What is it? Are you okay?' asks Annie.

'Yes, it's just that he's different from how I remember.'

Toby Summerfield's face looms into focus as they walk together up the drive, shingle scrunching underfoot. 'He has a kind face, Milly,' Annie whispers.

'Yes. He always did. And soft brown hair that I used to push back a lot. I can't see it under the hat though.' Emily seems intimidated. Annie's heart catches to see it. What has happened to her feisty mother?

'Is it okay to park here?' she calls out to Toby, although there's clearly space for at least six cars on the drive. Toby doesn't respond. He's looking at Emily.

'Can this be real?' he asks finally. 'Emily. My Emily. And Annie? My daughter?' There's another awkward silence. Emily seems to have turned to stone and Toby's sunglasses are misting over. Annie searches desperately for some words, anything.

'Yes, Mr Summerfield. It's us and I can't tell you how very, very pleased I am to meet you. At long last.' As a therapist, Annie is painfully aware of the inadequacies of language. She thinks of the nights she lay awake in her narrow bed in Elm Avenue dreaming of her dad the adventurer, doing something important in a foreign land, brave and strong, helping people, saving lives. As she got older, she would look in the mirror and wonder if her dad has a crinkly dimple in one cheek and a tiny bump on his nose, just like she does. Then came the years of anger and resentment. Why did her dad leave them? Had he found another family more worthy of his love? Surely there must be a phrase in the English language more fitting than 'very pleased to meet you'.

Toby smiles and a crinkly dimple appears on his cheek. He extends a hand that somehow melts into a bear hug. Annie takes in his scent of aftershave mingled with skin and fresh linen.

'I'm not Mr Summerfield. I'm Toby. Better still, dad, but only if and when you're okay with it. We have so much to talk about. And of course, you must meet my son Theo. Your brother—half-brother, I guess, to be pedantic. He's in town just now with his mother. My partner Clara. They'll be back later. Sorry, way too much to take on board.'

The words tipple out, one on top of the next. Can the powerful Mr Summerfield, investigative journalist turned editor supremo, really be nervous? Is Clara actually his wife? 'Partner' is an odd word, setting a distance between them. Annie's conscious of over-analysing, as she often does in social situations. Emily still looks stunned as they follow Toby through the dim house into the sunlit rear garden.

'Let me get you some coffee,' he says, as they settle themselves on the patio and strides off without waiting for a response. Annie senses the tension loosen. It's a relief when he's gone.

'Milly, you have to say something,' she hisses at her mother. 'You haven't said a word since we got here. I know it's tough, but he's making an effort and you should also try. I'm here to help, but I can't do everything. Remember, he's my dad. It's a shock for me too.'

Emily gazes blankly at Annie. 'You're right I should behave better. But I don't know how to be around him. I still love him, you see. I knew it the moment he opened the door. I never dreamt I'd feel like that. I'd never have agreed to coming if I'd thought there was the slightest possibility. He looks different, of course and I'm sure he's not the Toby he was before life got to him. But it's his voice. It sounds exactly the same.'

Annie nods. Her eyes are tearing up. 'He's going to be back in a minute. What can I do? How can I help? Would it be best for you if we both just leave?'

'No, no. It would be cruel and in any case I don't want it. I need some time with him. Alone. To explain all the fifty million stupid reasons why I did what I did. And to tell him about Bea. It was a terrible mistake, pushing him away like that and then relinquishing my daughter. I was heartless and misguided. But I was 18 years old, I knew nothing and I thought I was doing it for him.'

'I'll do it, Milly. I'll find a way to excuse myself and give you some time. Make the best of it. Sounds like he's on his way back now.'

Toby emerges with a tray heavy with coffee and cake. 'Oh good, you haven't escaped yet. Sorry it's taken me so long. Clara always hides the best biscuits. Trying to save me from myself.'

He sits down under the parasol, removing his Panama. 'Toby, your hair!' exclaims Emily. 'Where's it all gone?' They're the first words she has spoken.

He rakes his fingers through wiry grey locks. 'What's wrong with it? I had a haircut yesterday. In honour of you coming, of course. I imagine that you're referring to that floppy brown mess that made me look like a puppy dog.'

'It was always hanging in your eyes. I loved stroking it.'

Toby smiles and the single dimple reappears. 'Yes, I remember.'

With the ice broken, conversation moves tentatively forward. Annie has filled him in on the bones of her life in their telephone conversations. She produces a picture of Phoebe and Ben.

'My grand-daughter.' Toby grasps the image as if he'll never let it go. 'Ha, she has the floppy hair too.'

Annie feels herself expanding in the warmth of family. A month ago, she had Milly. Now she has a proper father and perhaps a sister too. For many luckier people, that's the norm. For Annie, it's a delicious luxury to unwrap bit by bit.

Toby and Emily tiptoe cautiously around the perimeter of their history. As they ease themselves back into the past and bring it up to date, they grow less stilted and careful with each other. Annie peeks at her watch under the tabletop. Now would be the time to leave them to get on with it, if she could find an opportunity.

Luck is with her. Just at that moment, a petite middle-aged lady with a blonde bob appears at the French windows. 'Hi, it's me. I'm back.' She steps on to the patio. 'Is this a good time?'

'Of course, of course. Clara, come on out and meet Annie. And Emily.'

'Wonderful to meet you, Annie.' Clara clutches both Annie's hands warmly in her own and then turns to Emily. 'And you too, Emily. We've heard so much about you both.'

Taking two steps back, Emily stares woodenly at Clara, offering a slim, pale hand at arm's length. 'Nice to meet you too.'

There's a heavy silence. 'Clara, I think there are a few things that my mother would really like to talk to Mr Summ—ah Toby—about before we leave. In private. Things I'm sure he'll share with you further down the line but…ah…'

'I quite understand. Emily would like a little time alone with Toby. It's not a problem. Is it Toby?'

'Fine by me. I'm wondering if you've got any more interesting surprises for me now, Emily.' His clumsy attempt at levity hangs in the air like a question mark.

'I'd love to meet Theo,' says Annie in a desperate attempt to move things on.'

'That won't be possible this morning, I'm afraid. Theo's headed off to see his girlfriend. He won't be back until after lunch, mid-afternoon at the earliest.'

So, the implication is, she wants us gone before then. And Theo's girlfriend takes priority over his half-sister. Annie chides herself once more for over-analysing. 'Okay. No worries.'

'But why don't we have a cuppa and a chat indoors? Toby's mum is coming over later and I'm attempting a homemade cake. I'm useless at cooking. Perhaps you can give me some tips!'

She's letting me off lightly, thinks Annie. And she's patronising me—like I'm the sort of woman who bakes cakes. In the twenty-first century? 'I'll do my best,' she promises. Stepping through the French doors, she glances once more at Toby and Emily. He's throwing his arms around and talking wildly in what sounds like a Jewish New York accent. And Emily is laughing. Out loud. She never saw her mother's face lit up like this before.

'What on earth are you doing?' she calls to them.

'He's pretending to be Woody Allen killing a spider. *Annie Hall*. We saw it in 1978 and both loved it.' Emily is still in fits of laughter.

The older generation. What would they come up with next? Annie nods sagely and follows Clara into the kitchen.

Perched on the counter stool, she watches as Clara throws random amounts of butter, sugar, flour and eggs into a mixing bowl. The way she does it looks like anger. 'So sorry for bringing chaos into your life.'

'Don't be. She was his first love. But I'm his last.'

'Of course. She isn't here to raise demons from the past, or meddle with the present. I think she needs to make peace, or perhaps some sort of sense, out of what happened. And I'm not going to pretend I'm not thrilled to find I have a father after 35 years of dreaming of one!' Maybe a twin too, but Annie won't be drawn into that subject with Clara. It's something for her mother and Toby.

Clara gives her a sidelong look. 'I'll be straight with you. I've lived with Emily Enderbie all my life. Toby and I met in our final year at university. I'm an economist. I deal in facts. Toby read English Literature. An incurable romantic. He was on the rebound when we hooked up. Between us stalked the shadow of Emily Enderbie. But I knew what I was taking on. I fell deeply in love with him and he sort of grew to love me. Nothing much has changed on that score. But it works. I micromanage Toby, it's what he needs. He doesn't do chaos.'

'I get it. It would be easier and cleaner for you if we weren't in your lives.' Annie glances out of the kitchen window that also overlooks the garden. Toby and Emily are no longer fooling about. Their heads are bent together in intense conversation. And Toby seems to be stroking Emily's wrist. Annie is glad that Clara's attention is fixed on the cake batter.

'I agreed to today, but that will be it. I know all I need to about Emily Enderbie. How clever she is, how resourceful. How she came from the wrong side of the tracks, worked her way through sixth form and excelled. Then disappeared into thin air. Dropped Toby like a hot potato, causing him no end of trauma. She's the sort of person we don't need in our lives.'

'I understand.' What's more to say? Annie does understand. She adores her mother, but years of experience have taught her to keep a certain distance too. For her own sake.

'You, of course, are a different matter,' continues Clara. 'I may be, by Toby's standards, an unimaginative woman. But I'm not an unkind one. You must feel free to develop a relationship with your father and your half-brother. I'd only ask, for the time being, to do so away from this house. I may feel differently as time passes. Toby may ask you here—I beg you to say no. At least for now. Let's do this one step at a time and see where it takes us.'

'Of course.' Annie is overwhelmed by a sense of sympathy for this stalwart woman. She rises and grasps Clara's floury hands in her own. Clara pulls back. 'Okay, one step at a time.' But her eyes are smiling.

Chapter 42
Toby, 2013

Toby waves energetically until the little blue Fiat turns the corner at the end of his road. Seeing it disappear feels like loss all over again. The smell of over-baked cake is wafting from the open kitchen window and in the herbaceous border, Clara is furiously removing deadheads.

'Don't forget your cake.' He fingers his chin nervously, unsure what to say or even where to begin.

'Oh God. I knew I'd forget that damn cake. I hope your mother likes them well done.' Clara throws down her secateurs and wipes her hands on her hips. 'I guess we should talk. Do you want to talk?'

Toby gazes at her blankly. If asked, he would say Clara is his wife and that he loves her. But a sense of disassociation is enveloping him. Clara seems to be behind glass and everything—the familiar plants and flowers in his garden, the view of the messy kitchen from the sash window, even the cars passing on the road beyond the garden wall—feels surreal. He blinks and pulls himself together.

'Yes. I think so. Is now a good time?'

'Well, your mother's not here till three and Theo probably won't be back for ages so, yes, it's probably the best time we'll get today.'

'Let me get us some more coffee and we can sit out here on the patio.' Toby moves towards the kitchen as if in a dream. It seems to take him ages to find clean mugs and then he has to go back for teaspoons. Meanwhile, Clara has started rapping her fingers on the patio table. He can hear her rings going clunk, clunk against the wrought iron.

'Well?' she asks as he sets down the mugs. She doesn't do small talk—it's one of the first things he likes about her. The low bullshit factor. But just now, a little decorum might help.

'This has thrown up all sorts of stuff for me. Stuff I thought I'd buried. But I think you and I know that wasn't the case.'

'Right. So what sort of stuff? You need to elaborate.'

'I found out some things this morning. Emily is dying.'

When Clara doesn't know how to respond, she has a habit of not making any response at all. It's part of her innate wisdom that Toby has always respected, though it can be disconcerting. She's doing it now, looking down at the tabletop and playing with her rings.

'Are you sure?' she asks finally.

'She left me in no doubt. It was diagnosed a couple of months ago. It's inoperable. Whatever happens, we must keep this between ourselves. She hasn't told Annie yet. Or even her husband, who's called Leo by the way. She will do so soon.'

'I wonder why she told you then.' Toby suspects Clara is secretly relieved that the possibility of Emily posing a long-term threat is now removed. In her place, he would feel the same. And Clara is more pragmatic than he'll ever be.

'Maybe part of her wanted us to know that she wasn't going to be around long to mess up our lives. Or she needed to tell someone and it was easier to talk to me than to Annie or her husband. I don't know how you'd react in that situation. I've never been there myself.'

'I'm sorry.' Clara finally raised her eyes from the table to Toby's face.

'Don't be. It's life and death. Shit happens. She doesn't want to see me again. Ever. I have to respect that.'

A wave of relief passes over Clara's face. 'How do you feel? Are you sad?'

Toby pauses, choosing his words carefully. 'I loved her. Passionately. But notice the past tense. We made a good life, you and I. She was high maintenance. I might not have lived so well and complacently on a roller coaster ride with her. And here we find ourselves, comfy and happy with a wonderful son and a full life. Passion passes with time and what's left after it is what counts in the end. But there's more to tell you…'

'Which is?' Toby sees the tension mounting in Clara's body again.

'Annie had a twin. Apparently Emily's mother, who was a piece of work, persuaded her to give the child up for adoption. The secret would have gone to the grave with them, but for a sort of diary that Emily kept in the time after she split up with me and the babies were born. Apparently, Annie found this Memory Book, as Emily called it, in the family house in Tooting when she was clearing it out. Emily admitted to me that she was out of her mind at the time, she didn't really know what she was doing. It would be diagnosed as post-natal depression nowadays, I guess. Anyway, that evil witch of a mother forced Emily to choose between the two babies and she picked Annie. The other, who was apparently a bit of a handful, was sent off to an adoption agency.'

'My God. So you might have not one, but two daughters?'

'Well I hadn't really thought of it that way, but yes, two daughters. All I could think of was the poor kid being sent for adoption. Her name was Bea. Of course, that could've changed but Annie thinks her adoptive parents might have named her Bea, or Beatrice, or suchlike because they sent her off with a bumblebee hat. Sounds a bit whimsical, but it's the only clue we've got.'

'You say *the only clue we've got*. Are you planning to do something about it? Try to find her? Wouldn't that be opening another hornet's nest?'

'Well, Emily asked me to help. She feels the need to join up the dots of the past. She seems pretty ambivalent about finding the child though. I think she's anxious about the fallout. Obviously, a part of her is worried about how she'll come out of it. How this daughter that she gave away might react to her. But Annie will stop at nothing to find her sister. She's absolutely insistent, according to Emily.'

'This baby—Bea, if you like—is your daughter too. How do you feel about it all?'

'Excited. Sad. Okay, let's be honest, angry and resentful too.'

'Mmm, that's understandable, Tobes.' Clara winds a strand of blonde hair around her finger. 'Have I got this straight? She never said a word about those babies to you. Not a word. She split up with you and refused to see you ever again, right?'

Toby pulls himself back to that dark November night: the wind knocking against his window panes, a clatter of pebbles hitting the sill and then Emily looming out of the blackness, torch flickering. 'She was pretty feisty in those days. I sense now that she was little more than a frightened child. But that's not how she seemed. She scared me, her absolute insistence that we should never see each other again. She told me she was pregnant. And then she came up with this story that I was one in a long line of boys who could have been the father. I never really believed that.'

'And that was it? End of.'

'Hard to believe, but yes, I never saw her again. We moved shortly after and I went off to uni. And this is where my guilt comes in. I tried to tell her I'd support her, I was there for her. But I didn't actually *say* it. I sat down on the wet grass and put my head in my hands. I didn't beg, I didn't even cajole. I just sat there while she told me how it was going to be.'

'Don't be so hard on yourself, Tobes,' says Clara gently. 'Even if you didn't say it, I'm sure Emily knew you were there for her. It sounds like she didn't let you get a word in edgeways. She already had everything planned.'

'No, wrong!' Toby slams his fist down on the table.

'I loved her. I would have picked the stars out of the sky for her. But there was an impediment between us. And it was this. My fucking glittering career. My golden future. She didn't fit into it. I knew it and she knew it. She'd already outstripped me at school. I loved her to bits, but I couldn't have her holding me back. Or a baby.'

Toby's knuckles are white on the tabletop. 'It took me 10 fucking years to work that one out. Yes, I'm angry with myself for being a selfish dick. But I'm also angry with her for lying to me about other boys. For denying me my babies. She told me this morning that she did it for me. So that she wouldn't hold me back. But you know, I think we both were a little selfish in our own ways. I guess that's what being 18 years old is all about.'

'What will you do now?' asks Clara in her considered way.

'I shan't see her again. It won't do either of us any good. I sometimes think we were toxic. But I will, with your agreement, help them search for my other daughter. I've got a contact book bulging with investigative journalists. Even if none of them can help, they'll know other routes to explore. We don't have a lot to go on. I think I'll start with the adoption agency. It probably closed down years ago, but there will be records somewhere, I'm sure of it. We have a clue in the name too. Bea. What an unlikely name. Trust Emily!'

Clara cradles her coffee and gazes reflectively across her garden, dappled in sunlight. 'Of course, I'll support you. Always. What do you think you'd like to do now. Shall I put your mother off? She's due in an hour or so. We could stroll up to the pub? What do you think?'

'D'you know, what I'd really like is to play some music?' Toby rises, pecks his wife on the nose and heads towards the sitting room.

'Your guitar's upstairs on the landing.'

'The piano will do nicely for now.'

He sits at the piano and fingers the keys. Out of nowhere comes a song he loved in the early 90s. Something about a girl who came from Nashville clutching a suitcase in her hand, who found it hard to act normal when she was nervous. He never fully understood the lyrics, but they speak to him always, conjuring up Emily. Now he's crashing down on the keys, the anger and pain seeping through his fingertips. In the garden, Clara continues with her snipping, secateurs flashing silver in the harsh overhead sun.

Chapter 43
Toby, 2013

Finding Bea is like looking for a needle in a haystack. The only clues are her birth name, Bea Enderbie and her birthplace in Tooting. Annie is busy scouring the Memory Book in search of further indicators, but Toby is feeling despondent.

He taps his fingers on the keyboard in frustration. The search is narrowing down to locating the adoption agency, but he'll need input from Emily. Against his better judgment, he picks up his mobile and taps in her number.

'Yes?' She sounds tired and tense. She could do without this sort of emotional minefield when she's also coming to terms with end-stage cancer. Toby isn't at all convinced digging up the past is what she wants or needs. She's doing it for Annie. And possibly for him.

'Emily, I hope this isn't a bad time to call.'

'No time is a great time for me right now, Toby. But what can I do to help?'

'I wonder if you can remember the name of the adoption agency who took the baby? Or anything about it at all. The street it was on. The name of someone who worked there. Anything.'

'So sorry, I know nothing. Norma offered to take her to the adoption agency. She seemed keen to do it and I thought I might break down if I had to leave her there, so I agreed. That morning, I changed and dressed Bea and put her in her Moses basket on the kitchen table as agreed. I heard Norma leaving about half an hour later, but I didn't want to run into them so I stayed upstairs. I lay on the bed with my eyes shut tight and my hands over my ears until I knew they'd be way out of sight. I know, it beggars belief, but I was out of my mind.'

'Hmm. And the date was?'

'October 31, 1978. So the agency must have taken her in on that date.'

There's something really fishy about this. Toby only met Norma twice, but he wouldn't trust her as far as he could throw her.

'And there's nothing else relevant you can recall? Nothing at all. Take a minute to think.'

'Well, there were a couple of odd things, but they're so insignificant. They probably mean nothing.'

'Go for it.'

'Norma was away for an awfully long time. And when she came back, she complained about the underground. She said the journey back and forth on the tube was a nightmare, she was glad she didn't get stuck in the rush hour. It struck me as strange she'd used the underground. She must have travelled some distance. We always walked to the local shops in Tooting. Or we took the bus.

'Another thing. She didn't take Bea's birth certificate with her. I found it later at the back of a cupboard. I felt sure the agency would need it to give to the adoptive parents. I did ask Norma if the agency needed to speak to me, if they required the birth certificate, or if I should sign anything. She closed me right down. I should have challenged her.'

'Emily, please don't worry yourself over this. We will get to the bottom of it. I'll sign off for now. Go and get some rest. Actually, one thing you can help with—do you have a photograph of Bea?'

'Sorry, no. But I do have one of Annie. Clive took one of her on his Polaroid shortly after Bea's departure. Remember, they're twins and as babies they must have been pretty interchangeable on camera!'

'Good thinking. Keep that snap safe. We might need it.'

Toby fiddles with his mobile, checking his emails, texts and finally the weather. It's his way of taking the heat of out a situation that's fast turning sinister. He has a plan, but first he needs to rule out a gruesome scenario that he prays has not played out. He taps 'Jon Ellswood' into his phone and hits the number. It's Saturday morning and the phone keeps ringing, but he's not giving up.

Five years ago, he'd been at his desk considering the merits of two news leads when he got a call from reception. 'It's a Jon Ellswood to see you. He says he knows you.'

'I don't know any Jon Ellswood. Unless I'm losing my marbles at an unconscionably early age.'

'Well, he says he does. And he's very persistent.'

Toby sighed. 'Send him up.'

At least Jon Ellswood had the grace to look sheepish as he entered Toby's office.

'And you are?' Toby extended a hand across the desk.

'Jon Ellswood.'

'Yes, I know that. But what are you doing in my office?'

Jon Ellswood looked like a geek, pale and skinny with huge, black-framed specs that magnified his eyes to Disney proportions. 'I know I shouldn't have done this Mr Summerfield, but I so, so need a job. Nobody wants to take on Oxbridge graduates now. Employers think we're, like, entitled. Living in a bubble. I'm not asking for a job, an internship will do great.'

'What'd you have to offer me?'

'A first from Oxford. Editorship of the student newspaper. A lifetime immersed in crime. I mean, reading about it, not doing it.'

It didn't take Toby long to make up his mind. Jon Ellswood was already a proficient door-footer, for God's sake.

'Fax me over everything you deem relevant. Full CV, references, the lot. If I have any misgivings, I'll let you know. I can only offer you a six-month internship, I'm afraid. If you want to take it up, you start here Monday morning, 9 a.m. sharp.'

'I won't disappoint.'

'How will you finance the internship? Six months, no pay?'

'I'll find casual work any spare time I have, Mr Summerfield. And I'm ashamed to say it, my family is moneyed.'

'I know the feeling,' says Toby. 'It's not a good look. But someday, you may need it.'

Five years down the line, Jon Ellswood is Toby's chief crime reporter. He can work a crime story like a ferret sniffing out prey. Now, he's been offered the editorship of the biggest right-wing rag in the land. The one that celebrates the Cons, lies to the middle classes and gives false hope to the elderly. Toby abhors it, but the job is probably the crown jewel of the newspaper empire. He loses sleep at night at the thought of relinquishing Jon to a morally-questionable future, but he's pleased for him. Now it's time to call in a favour before Jon moves on.

'Jon Ellswood,' says the voice down the line. Years in crime reporting have given Jon Ellswood the opportunity to take on a new persona. The geeky specs are now super-cool and he speaks in the world-weary cadence of a modern-day Raymond Chandler. 'What can I do for you, dude?'

'One last favour, before you move off to that disgusting rag which you know I detest and deplore.'

'Fire away, dude. Anything.'

'Can you use your magic to check something for me? It's historical, something that may or may not have happened back in 1978. Can you check any babies who were abandoned, disappeared, or worse, murdered, in the Greater London area from October 31, 1978, up to the end of that year? I'm not necessarily expecting a positive result. This is more a process of elimination.'

'Consider it done, man. I'm on the case. Greater London's big, but I'll be back to you as soon as.'

Toby's sense of deep unease follows him around the house, into his office and even out running in the park. He doesn't know whether to hope for a positive, or a negative, result and days drag like sleepless nights. Then the call comes.

'Zilch, dude. I can't find a thing. Not for that time frame. I've used all my normal search mechanisms and some more. No abandoned, missing or dead babies at all. Seems like the whole of Greater London was playing happy mommies and daddies in autumn 78.'

'Thanks Jon. And stay in touch. Arrive in my office unannounced any time you like.' Jon laughs and clicks off.

So, it's a dead end. Toby feels a mix of relief and frustration. But he has a plan B. He taps in Annie's mobile number and she picks up immediately, as if she knows it's him.

'Annie. Good news and bad. I'm not really any further forward here. I've had someone do an extensive search of missing and abandoned babies throughout Greater London in the three months from Oct 31 to Christmas '78. Nothing's come up. Nothing for dead babies during that period either.' Toby gulps, but it had to be said.

'So what's the good news then?'

'I have a Plan B. Now it's a little left field and I have your mother to thank for it. But it does actively involve you and I need to know if you're happy with it.'

'I'm desperate to find my sister. There's not much I'd stop at.'

'I guessed that. Well, for Plan B I need a good, high-res full facial image of you. Black and white might work better. Colour fades.'

'Whatever for?' Toby senses a growing scepticism in Annie's voice.

'My plan is to draw a five-mile radius circle of Elm Avenue Tooting on a map. I'm going to compose a missing person poster. We don't have any images of Bea. But you're her twin. So we simply use a picture of you instead.'

There's a long pause on the line. 'Wow. You're right. It's left field, Dad.' Toby just loves the way Annie's new name for him rolls off her tongue. 'What about people seeing the poster and thinking it's me?'

'How many people still know you around there?'

'Not many, I guess. I've been gone nearly 20 years. I bet Mrs Hussein will be on to it, though. She's still around.'

'We'll worry about that when we get to it. Meantime, could you do me a favour and call your mother? I don't want to bother her. Speaking to me unsettles her. I need her to send me the Polaroid picture of you as a baby. Make sure she sends it in a jiffy bag, special delivery. Sounds like there's only one of them. And I need a mugshot from you too.'

Two days later, Toby has the photos. He rises early as Clara sleeps on. He doesn't want her to feel that this business has taken over his life, that she's being pushed out. He creeps down to his study and as dawn breaks, he composes the poster.

MISSING PERSON

Are you, or have you seen, this woman?

'Bea' has been missing for too long. Her family desperately wants her back. If you know Bea, please tell her she is loved and missed. She has a mother and father and twin sister who are waiting to welcome her with open arms. Ask her to call this number: 09908 463824. Bea, if you read this, we are waiting eagerly for your call.

Reading over the copy with some satisfaction, Toby reflects that, if nothing more, a lifetime in journalism teaches you how to use language to emote. He takes a map of London and draws a five-mile radius around Tooting. It takes in a surprising number of suburbs: Balham, Streatham, Wimbledon and even East Dulwich at the outer point. All that's left is to distribute the posters.

He begins bang in the middle of his search area at the Elm Avenue T-junction, trying hard to close down the memories in a box marked: *Don't go there*. He gets two independent newsagents and a charity shop to agree to put his poster in the window. By the time he reaches East Dulwich, he has just two posters left. One goes in a newsagents on Lordship Lane. Perhaps that will do. But he needs a coffee, so he makes his way down North Cross Road. He's a great believer in supporting independent coffee shops.

He finds one with black vinyl discs embellishing the walls and Thelonious Monk belting out of the loudspeakers. That will do nicely. A slim girl with the grace of a deer and scraped-up blonde hair takes his complicated order: a large, skinny Americano with hot milk. What happened to 'coffee'?

'Anything else I can get you?' she asks.

'Well, as you're asking, I have this poster that I'm trying to get in as many windows as possible. Would you be so good as to display it in your window?'

'Of course. No problem at all.' The waitress takes the poster. 'Nice-looking lady. Is she your daughter?'

A jolt like electricity runs through Toby. 'Yes. Actually, she *is* my daughter.'

Chapter 44
Sara, 2013

It's not often an elderly lady of 83 gets an unexpected visit from an unfamiliar gentleman of 85. But Mr Smit has been so persistent. When she hears the doorbell ring, Sara pauses a moment to primp her hair in the hall mirror. 'Oh, you silly octogenarian,' she whispers to herself.

Picking a time to receive a gentleman visitor is more tricky now she lives with Julia, Sean and Jake, when he's around. She'd wanted to be independent and stay on in the Golders Green house when Ernest died. But they absolutely insisted she come here so they could 'keep an eye' on her. 'I don't need keeping an eye on,' she'd wailed, but it makes sense. She couldn't carry on in that big house by herself forever.

It's a calm, happy place here. Julia still has her illustrating work, which helps absorb that troublesome nervous energy. And Sean has finally dropped to part-time at the college—though he's still driven mad by Media Studies. How different it all was when Beatrix was here. Sara recalls the atmosphere, nothing short of toxic, and feels sad. For all of them. It was a grim time.

On the step, Mr Smit is waiting, homburg in hand. He's formally dressed in a black suit with royal blue tie and crisp white shirt and Sara is uncomfortably reminded of an undertaker.

'Ah-ha, Mrs Kaplinski. I thought I'd give you a little time to get to the door. At our age, it's the knees that slow us, isn't it?' He speaks in a guttural Dutch accent that brings the past gusting back at Sara. 'May I come in?'

'Please do.' Sara opens the door an extra crack. What has she got herself into, entertaining a random elderly gentleman in an empty house?

Reluctantly, she guides Mr Smit into the sitting room where he eases himself into Sean's favourite armchair. She'd planned to offer coffee and homemade cake, but maybe it's best to wait until she learns why he's here. Let him say his piece and get it over with. Time for refreshments at that point, if it still feels right and proper.

'Thank you for responding to my letter. I gave the matter much consideration before sending it.' Mr Smit gazes at Sara with very blue twinkly eyes, concealed under a layer of wrinkly flesh. As he crosses his legs, there's a flash of Snoopy sock at his ankles. Sara is beginning to warm to him.

'I have the letter right here.' She'd re-read it several times earlier that morning to make sure she'd go it straight, although it couldn't be simpler:

'Dear Mrs Kaplinski, I write to you because I have news of your cousin, Pieter. This will be a shock to you, no doubt, after all these years. I would prefer to convey this information to you in person and would be very happy to visit you in the UK at a mutually convenient time. I am aware that the clock ticks fast, particularly for those of us who are astounded to find ourselves in our eighties (I am 86)! I do apologise for taking all these years to reach out to you. I tried for a long time and failed. Now we have the internet and it does have some advantages to offer us, as we see!

Respectfully yours.
Abel Smit.'

'It's a lot to take in. But it might help you to make peace with your past,' says Mr Smit. 'As we get older, it's important, no?'

'All my poor family died, I'm afraid. I was the only one left in the house on Nieuwe Keizersgracht after the Germans raided. They used Pieter and me as a sort of bargaining chip. Oma, my grandmother, was forced to choose between us and she chose me. I went into hiding and, at the end of the war when I arrived in England, I made extensive searches for them. But the answer always came back the same. They all perished, I'm afraid, probably in Auschwitz. Dates unknown.'

'Sadly, Mrs Kaplinski, Pieter did die. As we all must, sooner or later. But he did not die until 1944. Not until he'd saved many Dutch lives. He joined Dutch Resistance, you see. And his short life was most certainly not in vain.'

'How can this be?

'Mrs Kaplinski, I will share with you all I know. There's not much to tell, sadly. Pieter's was a short life. But he packed more into it than many manage in a lifetime.

'I met Pieter in summer 1941 and we quickly became friends, being the same age and having a shared goal—to blow Germans to smithereens as English would say. Pieter had jumped a train going East towards the camps. It was an extraordinarily brave act. Many contemplated it, but they did not have courage, either to leap from the train or to leave their families. And they were jumping into the unknown, of course, possibly right into the hands of the enemy.

'In Pieter's case, his family begged him to do it. They wanted to stay together, with the grandparents, he told me. But they thought Pieter stood a chance. He didn't look Jewish, did he? And nor do you, Sara.'

'No, that's right.' She recalls Pieter's searching blue eyes and bright hair. 'We both looked Aryan. A blessing and a curse. But where did he meet you?'

'Right by the railway line for the Amsterdam/Rotterdam train. Where Pieter jumped, there's a steep embankment and the track curves sharply to the left. The train always slows to take the bend. I was crouching at the very bottom of the embankment in tall grass and I heard the whistle blow. Next thing, I saw what looked like a heavy bundle hurtling towards me. Pieter, of course. The bundle continued to roll down the bank until it halted about 30 metres from me.'

'But what on earth were you doing there?'

'Aha, that's a whole other story, Mrs Kaplinski. If you want to hear it sometime, I will tell you. Suffice it to say, I had just joined a resistance cell and was out on a mission involving train lines.'

'But you must have been only 14 at the time, the same as Pieter. You should have been at home with your family.'

'It is a long story, Mrs Kaplinski. I was the middle son in a comfortably bourgeois household, Jewish, of course. My father was a businessman with his own factory in Rotterdam. He was able to keep the Germans sweet, so to speak, because he manufactured certain products that were useful in the war effort. He shut his eyes to what was going on under his very nose. My family thought they were immune, but I knew it wouldn't last. And their complicity disgusted me. Always the rebel!

'So, I decided in my naïve adolescent way to join the resistance. The Dutch resistance was in its infancy, but growing fast. My friend Noah—another Jew—told me of a cell seeking members. We decided to strike out on our own, with the aim of making contact with the cell.'

'But you were only 14?'

'Mrs Kaplinski, you must know very well that 14 years old in Holland in 1941 did not in any shape or form resemble 14 years old in England in the twenty-first century. We lied about our age, reinventing ourselves as 16. I don't believe it would have made any difference, though. These cells were desperate. They would have taken a two-year-old if it was capable of sabotaging a railway line.'

Sara recalls that wretched walk in 1941 through the familiar streets of her own neighbourhood. Eyes lowered, jumping into the shadows, ears on the alert for the thud of a jackboot. Yes, she'd also aged too fast.

'Would you like coffee and cake?' she asks.

'I'll finish what I have to say if you don't mind, Mrs Kaplinski, and then some coffee would be nice. These retellings are painful.' Mr Smit clears his throat.

'I'd been sent out by the cell to inspect the track, to see how best we could sabotage the train line. It was my first-ever mission. Imagine my horror, crouching in the dark with the bundle edging closer towards me. I saw Pieter's blonde head and was terrified, assuming him to be German. Hitler Youth or worse. But he was crying out in Dutch, so I crept tentatively towards him. At first, he was frightened of me too, so I replied in Dutch, explaining I came from Rotterdam.'

'Was he injured?'

'No, no, bumps and bruises and a twisted ankle which troubled him for a while, though he never complained. We sat in the darkness, sharing our stories. A friendship for life was sealed, sadly not a very long life in Pieter's case. I offered to introduce him to the cell and we agreed, implicitly, to stick together. It was a huge relief for me as Noah had lost his nerve and returned to his family. I was feeling very alone at the time I met Pieter.

'It was also a feather in my cap with the cell. Pieter was just the recruit they were seeking. They needed someone to deliver Jewish children safely from their homes to certain rural locations, to go into hiding. Pieter, with his blue eyes and blonde hair, was the perfect escort. He had various guises, but generally he played the part of an older brother accompanying younger siblings home to their parents. We used to joke that he had nine lives, he owned so many fake identity cards.

'All through 1943 he continued with this work. I wish I knew how many children he saved. Many. It was high risk as he was using the public transport system and often changed his appearance. For a time, he dyed his hair brown! Then, in early 1944, he was asked to help with a bigger assignment.

'15 children from the same school had been concealed in an abandoned warehouse on the outskirts of Rotterdam. They were being looked after by two Catholic nuns. Sounds farfetched, doesn't it? You know that's how it was. The kids were between six and 12 years old and, I suspect were *Omdat je een beetje zot wordt.*'

'Going a little stir crazy?'

'Absolutely. There were rumours flying around that the Gestapo was closing in and I suspect the good nuns felt they had had enough. So it was decided to relocate them to remote farmhouses away from Rotterdam. It was high risk. Pieter would assume the disguise of a farm boy, transporting farm implements in a covered wagon from the old warehouse to the farms. The wagon had a false bottom and the children were concealed beneath.'

'I saw Pieter on the morning he set off. He looked every inch the farm boy with his yellow hair poking out of a flat cap. The kids were given strict instructions to be quiet as mice. I gave him a big hug and wished him *Mazel Tov*. That was the last time I saw him. Everything that happened after, I learnt from others.'

'What did they tell you?'

'The first 12 children arrived safe and sound at the farms they were allocated. Pieter had just two farms left to visit and the next drop-off was a brother and sister. The farm stood at a crossroads in the middle of open fields and as the wagon entered the farmyard, three Gestapo officers appeared in a plain black car coming from the opposite direction. They drove into the yard, trashed the wagon and found the children under the false bottom. Everyone, including the farmer and his wife, Pieter and the kinder were ordered on to a patch of land behind the farmhouse.'

'Were they all sent to camps?'

'No, they were shot at point blank range in the head. All of them, including the kinder. Then the Gestapo officers got back in the car and drove off.'

'How do you know this?'

'The farmer's 15-year-old daughter. She hid under her bed. She was lucky. The Gestapo officers didn't bother to enter the farmhouse. She testified against them after the war.'

'My God.' Sara's head is reeling. 'So he didn't die for nothing?'

'Your Pieter was one of the bravest I came across. He had this aura of being both fearless and protective.'

'But what was he *like*? As a person?'

'Funny. He used to say he'd get to kiss some girls before the war was done. Not sure he ever had time for it. Loyal. He talked a lot about the family. Especially you. He loved you all dearly. And profound.'

'Yes, I know all this,' says Sara almost impatiently, thinking of the cave. She needs time alone, just a few moments would help.

'You loved him, didn't you Mr Smit?'

'I did.'

'Please do let me get you refreshments, Mr Smit? Sit right there and make yourself comfortable. I need a few moments.'

'Of course, Mrs Kaplinski. Take all the time you want. I understand, it is a shock. I'm not going anywhere fast with these old knees.'

Chapter 45
Bea, 2013

Beautiful…and how! Beatrix never passes her shop front signage without a frisson of pleasure. Her initials BH are picked out in an ornate font called Lucida Calligraphy, with the other letters in an understated copperplate. Silver on a delicate pistachio green. So elegant.

It's still early, but even at 7:30 a.m. the traffic is humming on Lordship Lane and down here on North Cross Road, the artisan coffee shops are opening their awnings in time for the first wave of commuters. Beatrix lets herself in through the slate grey front door to ready her beauty salon for the day. She'd admit it herself: she's a little OCD. Nail polishes are aligned in a perfect colour gradient and the mirrors and footbaths gleam. Fluffy white towels are stacked in neat rows and the twinkly grey countertop is adorned with copper and glass vases stuffed with fragrant lilies.

When her grandfather Ernest died 10 years ago in 2003, he left Bea a substantial sum of money in his will, with firm instructions to make something of it. She'd left school with modest qualifications and no prospects, but she worked hard at anything she could get to pay her way. Petrol pump attendant, dog walker, store detective, she's done it all. Willy's mum and dad had been good to her, taking her in when she left the family home. She couldn't face going back to Hampstead and being her mother's big disappointment in life.

Her acting ambitions shrunk bit by bit as time passed. Somebody suggested theatrical make-up as a career and she managed to save the money to sign up for a course. Discovering a talent for it, she began to build a reputation tarting up the rich and famous. She still struggles with the client liaison part, but people stop noticing her lack of social grace when they see what she can do with a face. Now she has her own thriving business and can pick and choose her clients.

The salon is a hall of mirrors where they can view themselves from every conceivable angle. In the full-length mirror next to the counter, Bea checks her hair which falls in strawberry-blonde waves past her shoulders. Going blonde was such a thrill after the black years! She'd aimed for an old movie star look and with her full red lips and spiky eyelashes, she might have stepped straight out of a fifties blockbuster. 'Change your disguise and preserve the surprise' was a phrase she learnt at make-up school and she's not forgotten it. Next month she might be a Punk, a Stepford Wife or a Little Girl Lost. Any new look is good for business, just as long as she never looks like Beatrix Howard, whoever that person was.

At 8:30 a.m., Bea's three assistants file in, artfully war-painted and ready for action. Tilly is an Amy Winehouse lookalike, while Emma, who's curvy, is more of a Beyonce girl. Beatrix's favourite is Sally, who's 60 this week and has to work that bit harder. She's making a statement with iron straight grey hair precision cut to her chin and black-framed specs which cover most of her tiny heart-shaped face. Beatrix calls her 'the iron lady'.

'I see we have one of our old ducks at nine.' Sally is rifling through the appointments book. 'Mrs Hargreaves. She's booked you for the works, Bea— pedicure, manicure, hair and make-up. What on earth can she be up to? Surely she's not going to a rave. Not at her age.'

'I think she's off to Cyprus later this week. She has a second home there. Remind me who else we have.'

'It's busy. Tilly has three bookings this morning. A leg wax and two pedicures. Emma has hair and make-up for that TV producer who lives around the corner. I think she's hosting an awards night tonight. You've got another old duck, Mrs Pelham. Full works, same as my Mrs Hargreaves. I wish I had their time and money. Mind you, I'll be an old duck myself soon.'

'You'll never be an old duck, Sally. And Mrs Pelham is a sweetheart, if a bit nosy. I just wish I didn't have to do her in-growing toenails. You'd think that was a job for the NHS.' Beatrix looks at her watch. 'They'll be here any minute.' She checks the footbaths and wipes down the counter once more. 'I guess I'll get Mrs P's life history as usual. I hope she doesn't ask me about my sex life like last time.'

After leaving home, Bea went through a troubling period of confusion about her sexuality and for a long time didn't understand what her body was trying to tell her. Wally had been a complicating diversion. When he'd made it clear her feelings for him weren't reciprocated, she fell into limbo. Now Cyn is in her life and they're loved up and having fun, but she's still coy about the relationship. It's early days. She's certainly not ready to share her new love with the world—just yet. So they both hang on to their own apartments and their own lives, though both sense a change coming.

'Whoops, here she comes. Get out *Hello* magazine—it's her favourite.'

The door chimes and Mrs Pelham trundles through in sensible old lady sandals. Beatrix clocks the thick, cracked soles of her feet and makes a mental note to add an extra dash of Epsom salts to the footbath.

'Mrs Pelham. Delighted to see you. I know the saying goes 'top to toe' and that's exactly how we're going to pamper you, starting with the pedi, then the manicure and finally hair and make-up.' It sounds a remarkably slick speech. Beatrix memorised it by heart.

'Lovely. What a luxury. I can't wait to get the weight off the old feet.' Mrs Pelham settles into her pulsating chair and sets it to gentle rock.

Bea gently removes her sandals from her swollen feet, revealing toes like gnarled tree trunks and yellow fang nails. If this is what age does to your feet, what must it do to other parts of your body? Bea gulps and begins to shave off dead skin. Mrs Pelham throws her head back into the pulsating chair in what looks scarily like sexual pleasure.

'Ah, I needed this, dear.'

'Is this about the right pressure?'

Massaging Mrs Pelham's blue-veined calves reminds Bea of some St Agur cheese she ate the other day. Poor Mrs Pelham.

'Is this a good time to talk, dear?'

'Wouldn't you prefer *Hello* magazine? Or we have lots of others to choose from.' Anything to avoid a conversation about sexuality with a pensioner.

'Well, I do love *Hello*, as you know. But what I need to say is actually very important. A life-changer.'

'Mmm, okay.' Bea is wondering whether to plead sick and ask Tilly to take over, but Mrs Pelham pushes on relentlessly.

'You know that coffee shop a few doors down, the one with the discs on the wall? Where they always play music without words? Well, there's a picture of a missing young woman in there. And she looks almost identical to you.'

'Oh, right.' Bea is barely listening. She's trying to make sure the Royal Purple nail polish that Mrs Pelham favours doesn't touch the backfriend on her big toe.

'Bea, please stop that for just a moment and listen. This is serious. The woman in the picture has straight black hair, just like yours before you dyed it. Her face is *exactly* the same as yours. And what's more, your name is mentioned on the poster.'

'Really?'

'It says something like 'Bea is loved and missed and we are waiting for her call.'

Bea has frozen, the loaded nail brush suspended dangerously in mid-air. 'My God.'

'You look as if you've seen a ghost, dear. Do you think there may be a mistake? Or something more sinister?'

'Neither of those things. I think it may be about my missing birth family.' Bea feels as if she is speaking through an enormous lump in her throat.

'Why don't you go now, dear? Go and see the poster for yourself. Look at Tilly. She's between bookings. Couldn't she take me over? Just until you get back. I'd rather you went to see for yourself.'

'That's incredibly kind of you, Mrs Pelham. It's not something I'd normally do'

'Get Tilly over and go! All I ask is that you let me know what happens next.'

Out on the pavement, Bea takes a few deep breaths, dons her sunglasses and checks her reflection in the salon window. The coffee shop is only a few doors up and there, in the window, is the poster. How has she not noticed it before? The woman in the photo has long, shiny black hair, just like Bea's before she went blonde. She's wearing a slim gold necklace with a tiny star, something Bea—who prefers statement jewellery—would never do. But when you block out everything but the face, they are identical. Right down to the half-dimple on the left cheek.

Bea glances furtively up and down the street to check no one's watching. She might have some explaining to do if someone walks by and sees her gazing at a mirror image of herself in a shop window. She taps the phone number on the poster into her phone and walks fast in the direction of the park.

There's a secluded seat just off the main pathway behind an overgrown hedgerow. Bea sits down and puts her head in her hands, trying to work out what to say. She's bound to screw it all up.

The voice at the other end of the line is male, soft and even, but with a hint of anxiety too. 'Toby Summerfield here.'

'I'm Bea.' What else is there to say? She's simply lost for words.

'Are you sure?' says the voice, not unkindly, but probing.

'My name is Beatrix Howard. Bea for short. I was abandoned as a baby in 1978. I'm 35 years old and my face is identical to the one on the poster in East Cross Road, East Dulwich. How does this person have my face? Do you know about my birth family?' A note of pleading has crept into her voice. It feels like the longest spoken sentence she ever strung together.

'If you are the Bea that I think you are, you have a twin, Annie. A mother too. And a father. Me.' Toby's voice breaks.

'I don't know what to say. Can I see you? Soon?'

'You need to meet your sister and your mother first. Then me.'

'When?'

'I'll contact Annie right now and she'll be in touch to arrange a meeting. Hang on while I scribble down your details.'

'I'm scared this is some sort of prank. Or worse.'

'I promise, it's not a prank. Speak to Annie and you can both take it all from there. You aren't about to run away and hide, are you?'

'Never,' breathes Bea. 'I've dreamt of this all my life.'

Chapter 46
Emily, 2013

Not long to go. Emily gently turns the pages of her Memory Book, breathing in the essence of her teenage self. Eight months ago, the doctors gave her six months, but some days she can still get up, out and about and even down to the local shops with the help of a stick. Today isn't one of those days. She'd prefer to stay in bed, but Toby has been insistent. He simply won't let things be.

Reluctantly, Emily closes her Memory Book. She should put on some make-up, so as not to shock Toby. She fumbles in the dresser for a bright lipstick and applies it to her bloodless lips. As an afterthought, she daubs a crimson blob on each cheek and carefully rubs it in. Gazing at her reflection in the mirror, a harlequin clown with panda eyes and red gash of a mouth looks back at her. Well, too bad. If Toby will insist on disregarding her wishes, he must take her as he finds her.

When she got the call from Annie a fortnight or so ago, she didn't believe it. How could they possibly have found Bea, missing over 35 years? After they'd forwarded the picture, she knew it must be true. She'd told Annie straight that she had no intention of meeting Bea, not after all these years. Not in her position. Annie tried over and over to get her to change her mind, then roped Toby in. 'I think we agreed, no more contact between us,' she'd said. 'And that includes any long-lost member of my family you manage to dig up too.' She was seething with anger at the assault on her hard-won equilibrium.

Since then, she's had plenty of time to examine her feelings and to appreciate how big a part guilt plays in that anger. She's been forced to acknowledge that Bea probably *does* have a right to meet her. But it's going to churn up all sorts of horrible emotions she's too busy dying to deal with. How on earth would she manage a polite conversation with a woman she chose to reject as a tiny baby? This woman who is her daughter, although it doesn't feel remotely like it. Yet

Toby has persisted, gently but firmly and now here he is knocking at her front door.

'Emily. Your friend's arrived,' shouts Leo up the stairwell.

'Can you let him in and show him up. I'll stay on the couch if you don't mind. I'm a bit weak and wobbly today.'

Leo grunts as he descends the stairs. She's given him a short and sanitised version of the whole sad Toby story. Being Leo, he's extrapolated from it only those parts that affect him. He's less interested in the lost baby than in the potential threat Toby poses to his manhood.

There's a tap on the sitting room door. 'Knock, knock. Can we come in?' Leo has adopted a tone of false geniality which Emily finds sickening. In the doorway, 'her' Toby (she still thinks of him as hers, though he hasn't been for 35 years) is clutching his beloved Panama. She still can't get her head around the grey spikes that have replaced his floppy caramel fringe. He's padded out over the years, but seems diminished by Leo who takes up most of the doorway.

'Here's your chap, then. I'll let you get on with it. I don't suppose you have time for coffee?' It's not an invitation and is accompanied by one of Leo's trademark scowls.

'No thanks.' Toby's face is a mask. 'We'll say what we need to and then I'll be out of your way.'

Nodding curtly, Leo turns his elephantine back on them and heads for the door. Once it's firmly closed, Toby edges gingerly towards the only armchair in the room. 'Is it okay if I sit here?'

'Of course.' It's the first time Emily has been alone with Toby for 35 years and—along with her falling hair, scraggy limbs, sore mouth and sense of enfeeblement—it's hard to cope with.

'Your Memory Book?' Pushing on his specs, Toby peers at the faded stars and planets ring binder on the little coffee table. 'I never read it.'

'No.' Emily swallows the unspeakable. The time to read it will come soon enough. 'It's nice to see you, Tobes.'

'You too.' Tension hangs in the air like a blow-up question mark.

'But maybe not such a good idea. And not to be repeated. Leo doesn't like it, for a start.'

'Oh, him.'

'So what was it you wanted to say? That you couldn't say on the phone.'

'It's about Bea. I sense your reluctance to meet her, Emily. But it has to happen. For her sake, if for not yours. It's simply not right to shut your eyes and pretend she doesn't exist. Can you imagine what this might be doing to her? To know her own mother's reluctant to reconnect after 35 years' absence?'

'I suppose so. But look at me. Don't hang your head like that, look me in the face. Remember that line we both loved from *Macbeth*? I'm a walking shadow.'

'I don't see that. I see those searching Emily eyes and that pert Emily nose and those slim Emily hands always fluttering about in the air when you're talking in your absolutely inimitable Emily voice.' Toby pauses as if he's run out of breath.

'You're still pretty irresistible, Toby. But I'll have to consider it. I get good days and bad days. I never know how I'm going to be. You did know, didn't you, that I'm two months beyond my death sentence?'

Toby cups his head in his hands and pushes up his grey spiky hair so that it frames his head like armour. 'You've told Annie, haven't you? And Leo, he knows of course. You can't just shut everyone out of the frame.'

'Of course they both know. It would be hard to hide now, wouldn't it? Look at me, I'm shrinking.' She tugs at her billowing top.

'You need to make peace with the past, Emily. Both you and Bea. Don't delay too long.'

'Give me time, Toby. I promise, I'll keep it in mind.'

'May I read your Memory Book?'

'No. I have a little more to write in it. After that, perhaps I'll give it to you for safekeeping. And to set the record straight, for you, Bea and Annie, of course.'

'Your, um, partner…he seems a little brusque. Is he okay with me being here?' Toby jerks his head towards the door.

'Probably not. He can be a bit of a bully. But his bark is worse than his bite. We've muddled along together for however many years. He wouldn't have been my first choice as a life partner.' Emily raises her head to look direct at Toby. 'But we work with what we have. He's a good provider and he does love me in his own overly protective way. And the sex is good. Not better, but good.'

'He doesn't have a problem with me, then?'

'Yes, probably with you and with any other man who comes within a metre of me. But he has a worse problem right now.'

'Which is?'

'He can't deal with me being ill. He's angry with me for getting ill, angry with himself for not being able to protect me. And angry with the doctors for giving up on me. They've stopped the drugs. I told them to.'

'I'm sorry.'

'Me too, but it's hard to cope with Leo's finer feelings on top of everything else. Actually, I'm surprised he's left us alone so long. He must be going through hell out there, knowing I'm in a room with the door closed, alone with another man.'

As if on cue, there's a rustling at the door and a faint knock. Leo's brought coffee. 'Thought you might need it, mate.' He hands Toby a mug embellished with a Grecian urn.

'So kind. Just what was needed.' Mate is not a Toby sort of word and it clearly unsettles him. He's such a prig, thinks Emily, in a flash of loyalty to Leo. She rolls the thought around in her mind, but it won't stick.

'Cool little restaurant you have here. So good to see the independents still flourishing in this part of London. And Greek too. Magic. I'm an inveterate Greek-island hopper. Do you serve Tomatokeftedes? One of my favourites. A Santorini speciality, I believe.'

Toby is trying ever so hard to be nice, but he's coming over as patronising. Emily cringes. Her husband is not a man to patronise.

'Tomatokeftedes is a new one on me, I'm from Spetses. Never been to Santorini. Anyway, I don't follow the menus closely anymore. My son Dimitri manages Ambrosia and overseas day-to-day running. That gives me more time to keep an eye on the little lady here.' Emily rolls her eyes but Leo ploughs on. 'I'm the owner of course. And once we have Emily up and running again, we'll probably get more involved in what goes on down in the kitchen.'

'Leo, I'm never going to be "up and running" again. I told you. I'm dying. Please let's drop this pretence that one day you'll snap your fingers and everything will go back to normal.'

'Babe, less of the negative talk. You need some good home-cooked food to build you up and lots of TLC. Here, let me plump up the cushions and tuck your blanket in. You'll be right as rain in no time.'

Buried amidst the newly-plumped cushions and tasselled throw, Emily feels like a small, frightened child. 'Leo, you're scared. But I'm even more scared than you. Please face up to what's coming and be brave for both of us. Toby, can you explain to him?' she pleads.

231

'It's not my place.' He turns to Leo: 'All I will say is that I think perhaps Emily is asking for you to acknowledge her illness, its gravity and its inevitable conclusion. And now it's high time for me to leave.' Grabbing his Panama, Toby moves towards the door, but not quite fast enough. Leo is there before him, his huge bulk blocking the exit.

'Are you trying to tell me how to look after *my* missus? When I've been the one protecting her all these years while you were out flogging newspapers? What were you doing all that time she needed you? Living in an attic room at her mum and dad's with two babies to care for and not a penny to her name. Fucking about at *Oxford*. Is that where you were, *mate*?'

'I didn't know. About the babies.' Toby pushes his specs up the bridge of his nose, a nervous habit. 'She never told me.'

'And you didn't take the trouble to find out, did you *mate*? What would it have taken? A phone call? Maybe you could have even slummed it down to south London to check on her?'

'Leo, stop it. Now. Toby, please go. It's okay. Leo loves me. Nothing bad will happen. You've no need to worry.'

'Yeah, that's right, go. You're a past master at walking away, aren't you? So just do it, no backward glances. You're no fucking better than the shit on my shoe.' Leo opens the door and Toby stumbles down the stairs.

Chapter 47
Bea, 2013

Picking up the phone to call Annie was the toughest thing Bea ever did. She's crap at small talk, especially with a disembodied voice. But Annie seemed, instinctively, to get that. Pauses weren't a problem for her, or finding the right words. She didn't rush to fill up spaces. She simply waited quietly until the conversation was good to go again.

They've agreed to meet at a bench in Golders Hill Park. Bea had suggested Tooting Common, but Annie thought it might be too sad. No place feels special enough to meet the twin you haven't seen for 35 years, so Bea guesses it might as well be a park bench as anywhere else. But she's wondering why she agreed to Golders Hill Park. It means going northbound and she worries about running into one of the Howards. She stays in irregular contact, but doesn't want them butting into all this stuff. Not until she knows the direction it's going. No, the big draw northbound is Phoebe.

'I'd love you to meet my partner Ben and Phoebe,' Annie had said. 'Phoebe is thrilled at the idea of an aunty! I don't want you to feel crowded out. But if you like, we could drive over to my place later on in the day so you could meet them. We'll keep it simple and flexible. See how we both feel. What do you think?'

Bea had faltered. 'I'd really love to meet Phoebe. My niece. Can't believe I'm saying it! But I'm not sure…'

'Ben might be a bridge too far on the first date. I totally get it. Don't worry, I can send him off on an errand. Everything's on the table and we'll take things step by step.'

Now it's 8:30 a.m. on the big morning and sunshine is pushing through slatted blinds, casting horizontal bars on the bedroom ceiling. The bed beside Bea is empty, but still warm. Cyn stayed over and she's up already, making coffee. Bea sniffs the aroma appreciatively. Three hours to go. She rolls out of bed and stumbles in the direction of breakfast.

'How you're doing, hon? Big day.' Cyn is cracking eggs into a basin from a great height, the way she likes to do it. She claims it makes them lighter.

Bea loves to watch Cyn cook. Petite and energetic in her flowered kimono, she's in complete control of her kitchen kingdom. It may look like a war zone, with last night's detritus piled in the sink, a heap of scraps for the birds scattered across the countertop and the cutlery drawer hanging open, revealing a dodgy collection of cooks' knives. But Cyn cooks with a mix of confidence and dedication that makes Bea believe in the possibility of falling in love.

'So glad you stayed over last night,' she mumbles. It's still a struggle to express love, need or gratitude, but she's learning.

'Fried, coddled or scrambled?' Cyn rarely looks at you when she's busy cooking. Her sense of purpose is something else Bea admires.

'Fried, please. They always look so nice fresh from the pan, all golden and glittery.'

Cyn makes space at the table and sets out fried eggs, toast and coffee for Bea. 'You're quiet, hon. Are you nervous?' Sitting down opposite, she takes Bea's long, pale hand in her own small, round one.

'I guess.'

'D'you want to talk about it?'

'Mmm. No.' Bea takes a big mouthful of glossy yellow yolk. 'I can't talk about it right now.'

'That's okay, babe. Save it for another time. You haven't lost your appetite anyway. Eat up. You need your strength. What you gonna wear?'

'I don't know. I'm not very good at choosing what to wear for things like this. What do you think?'

'Well, you don't want to scare her off. Look at you—so beautiful, tall and stately. Mind you, I guess she's going to look the same.'

'Her hair's black though. I'm glad now that I dyed mine blonde. It might be really weird if we looked exactly the same.'

'One thing I would say, hon. Don't wear that awful hoodie thing of yours. It's a bit threatening.'

Bea's black hoodie is one of the few bones of contention between them. It pre-dates their relationship by several years. Cyn's nicknamed it 'Bea's comfort blanket' because of her tendency to reach for it whenever she's anxious, angry or upset.

'It belonged to my friend Willy,' she'd explained.

'Well, why not give it back to him?'

'He died of AIDS.'

'I'm not going to wear it,' she says now. 'But I'll probably take it in my backpack. In case of rain.'

'So it'll be your usual symphony in black look? With the hoodie safely hidden away in the backpack. Well, you're going to look adorable whatever—as long as it doesn't rain! You should get going. It's a long old journey to Golders Green and it wouldn't do to be late. Here take this. My low blood sugar buster!'

Bea opens the small package to reveal a carton of apple juice, stick of cheese, apple and tube of Werther's Originals. 'Thanks Cyn. Big hug.'

By the time Bea reaches the ornate iron gates at Golders Hill Park, she's eaten the entire blood sugar buster, including the tube of sweets. Anxiety makes her hungry. Steadying her pace, she heads along the formal pathway towards the bench that Annie has described in detail. It's in a secluded spot, halfway up a grassy bank, shaded by a plane tree. To help her identify it, Bea has a note of the inscription carved into the wood: *In Memory of Adelaide Lewis who loved this spot. 1900-1969.* But what if someone is already sitting on it? How can she check if it's the right bench? Panic strikes Bea as she approaches. There *is* someone there.

Long, long legs in blue jeans, skinny like Bea. Shiny raven hair, straight as a ruler. The woman is huddled over her phone, but looks up as she hears Bea's footsteps crunching on the gravel. Now Bea is less than a metre from the bench and she gazes down into the woman's face, a mirror image of her own. As if in slow motion, she sees the woman's lips moving: 'Hi. It's Bea, isn't it? I'm Annie.'

Chapter 48
Annie, 2013

'Did you put the bubbly in the fridge?' Annie shouts at Ben's disappearing back. She's chopping up red onion and chilli to add to her casserole and her eyes are full of tears.

'All done. And I've swept the front step—along with all the other things you needed doing. Let's see: hoovered the sitting room, watered the plants, even cleaned the downstairs loo. I'm just locating Phoebe's trainers. I thought they were under the stairs.'

'You're an angel. Are you taking Phoebe to the park now?'

Ben fishes a pair of purple and pink trainers with flashing lights from under the sofa. 'Yes, if I can get her to sit down one minute and put these on. Here, Phoebs.'

'I'm sorry, I'm being a bossy pain in the arse. It's just…'

'You're nervous. Understandable. Look, put that whatever-it-is casserole in the oven, then relax and take time to get yourself ready. We'll stay out of the way, won't we, Phoebs?'

'I want to meet my aunty,' Phoebe pipes up. She's heard aunties are givers-of-treats. She hasn't had an aunty until today, so expectations are running high.

'Of course you do, sweetie. It's just that Mummy needs a little time with Aunty Bea. But we'll all be having lunch together. Does that sound good?'

'If I can take my scooter to the park.'

Ben sighs. It's a liability on the pavement. 'Okay, as long as you don't break the speed limit. Come on, let's get going.' He kisses Annie. 'Remember what we said. Keep calm and take it slow.'

Left to her own devices, Annie doesn't know what to do next. The casserole is bubbling away softly in the oven and there's a delectable selection of cheeses piled up on the slate board. Just the salad to do, last minute. She falls back on their saggy sofa and gazes at her domestic universe. What will Bea make of it?

When they moved into their Victorian terrace on what was then one of the shabbier roads in West Hampstead, they knocked down the downstairs walls to create one big space. They retained the narrow hallway with its indispensable under-stairs glory hole and the downstairs toilet and put the kitchen into the L-shaped extension. But everything else is one gloriously messy living space. Phoebe's desk, below the wonky sash window, is drowning in a sea of coloured pens and paper. A precarious tower of Annie's workbooks and papers is building up on the dining chair with wobbly legs that no one ever uses. She notices *The Psychology of the Child* by Jean Piaget on the top and hastily moves it down the pile. Ben's freshly-ironed pilot's uniform is dangling on a hanger from the picture rail.

We are not tidy people, thinks Annie. I should clear up. She pictures Bea, with her manicured fingers and toes and her artfully teased honey hair. What will she make of this? It'll be like straying into a foreign land.

Closing her eyes, Annie tries to breathe, the way she gets her anxious clients to do, expelling all the air from the lungs on the outward breath. 'Relax,' she tells herself. 'This is your sister. It's good stress.' At that moment, the doorbell rings, bang on time. Too late, she realises she never got around to putting on make-up.

Opening the front door with what she hopes is a welcoming flourish, Annie takes two steps back and stares at Bea, the warm smile dying on her lips. 'What *have* you done?'

Bea's honey blonde hair hangs like glossy strips of liquorice, nearly down to her waist—dyed back to its original colour. The effect is unsettling, like looking in a mirror at a distorted image of yourself.

'Wow. You look just like me. Sorry, that was a silly thing to say. Of course you look like me. We're twins. It was just a bit of a shock.'

'You like?' Bea tosses her head from side to side and her ebony locks float in the air. 'I thought how cool it would be for us to look exactly alike. If you don't like it, I can cover it up.' She pulls a black hoodie from her big bag. It doesn't look at all Bea-like.

'It's my comfort blanket,' she explains as if guessing Annie's thoughts. 'It belonged to a very dear friend of mine, who died. I don't carry it all the time. Just on big occasions like this, if I might get stressed.'

'Oh, I see.' Annie thinks back to Phoebe's blankie, a nasty, sick-encrusted square of muslin that wasn't allowed in the washing machine. Phoebe only gave it up a year ago and she still keeps it on a shelf in her room, though it's hidden when friends come round.

'Bea, it's lovely. And amazing that we both look so completely alike.' Annie struggles to regain composure and thinks longingly of the bubbly in the fridge. 'Come on in. Ben and Phoebe have popped down to the park, but they'll be back soon. Can I get you a drink?'

'A soft one, please. Orange juice if you have it. I don't touch alcohol. It used to feel like I was on a constant bender, but I've made a lot of changes. I'm veggie too. Did I tell you that?'

Annie considers the casserole bubbling away in the oven with a sinking heart. It's mainly vegetable, just a little bacon added to perk it up. It shouldn't be too hard to pick out the bacon bits. 'All fine. I hope you like cheese. We have a groaning cheeseboard.'

'Sounds yummy.' Bea glances around her, checking out the various piles of mess, along with the visible signs of family wear and tear. It begins to dawn on Annie: she's on the spectrum. Could she be obsessive/compulsive? If so, an environment like this must be hell for her.

'Lovely space you have here. Lived-in.' Bea has a disconcerting habit of seeming remote and a shade uncomfortably close, at the same time. Like she just arrived from a parallel universe but she clocks you, inside out. Perhaps that's what being a twin feels like.

'Take a seat, Bea and let me get you a juice.'

'Where would you like me to sit?'

Glancing round, Annie realises that every available seat is occupied with something. Phoebe's dolls are littered across the sofa, gazing vacantly in the direction of the TV set. Ben has left a half-built model aeroplane on one armchair and the other is taken up with Annie's laptop. She quickly removes it and pats the cushion encouragingly, bidding Bea to sit.

'Well, this is wonderful. Time with my sister. I never thought I'd get to say that. Did you?' Annie squashes on to the sofa with the dolls. She's taken a big slug of bubbly and it's just the job, the tension ebbing in her abdominal muscles.

'No and I never thought I'd say the word "dad" and mean a real one, either. We've made a date to meet next week. Just me and Toby. Lunch.'

'Hmm, I think you're right, doing us one at a time,' muses Annie as she throws lambs lettuce and rocket into a colander. 'It's all a little overwhelming. And there's such a huge vibe going on between our father and Emily. I felt it when we met up—you could slice the air with it. It just adds an extra layer, you know, makes everything seem so uber intense.'

'Right. I got that. Toby can't wait to meet me. But Emily's dragging her feet. She must feel guilty?'

'D'you think she should?' Annie forces herself to look Bea directly in the eye.

'I do. She abandoned me. What's not to feel bad about? Whatever, I'm desperate to see her. Actually desperate isn't a big enough word. But I'm taking it step by step, especially as she's so sick.' Bea gives a quick shudder. 'Can't wait to meet my niece though. I have something for her.' From her bag, she pulls a chocolate multipack.

Annie cringes. She's not going to say that Phoebe's not allowed sweet things. Certainly not on a multipack scale. She'll have to let it pass, just this once. A key turns in the front door and she lets out a sigh of relief mingled with apprehension. 'Here they are.'

'Aunty Bea!' Phoebe bursts into the room, trainers twinkling. Ben follows behind with the scooter. Suddenly, Annie's tranquil living space feels overcrowded.

'Phoebe, don't crowd your aunt out. Bea, hi, wonderful to meet you at long last. I'm Ben.' He extends a hand, but thinks better of it and reaches down to give her a hug. Bea shrinks back almost imperceptibly. This must be so hard, Annie thinks. If only I could help her out.

'Hey kiddo.' Bea produces the chocolate multipack from her bag and holds it up triumphantly. 'This is for you.'

'I'm not allowed chocolate, am I Mummy? Thank you Aunty Bea. I do love it. But I had to have a filling and now I can't have it.'

'Just this once I think we can make an exception.' Annie sneaks Ben a pleading look. Stay complicit with me, please. 'But after lunch, please Phoebe. Why don't you show Aunty Bea some of your drawings while I serve up?'

In the kitchen, Annie painstakingly fishes every last bit of bacon from the casserole, checking it for taste. You'd never know. The bacon flavour is well and truly drowned out by chilli and fresh herbs. She's aware of murmuring voices in the sitting room, though she can't hear what they're saying over the drone of the dishwasher. She brings lunch through to the table.

With a small stab of jealousy, she sees that Bea and Phoebe are already new best friends. Of course, it's natural, her psychologist self tells her. Bea has novelty value. And the aunt/niece relationship is always going to be very different from the mother/daughter one. She really is going to have to adjust to a more complex framework of family relationships. Ben's an only child and his parents both died some years ago. Milly has never been what you might call an enthusiastic grandma. Up till now, she and Ben have been lucky to have Phoebe to themselves.

'Aunty Bea says she'll paint my nails for me in rainbow colours if it's okay with you. Is it okay with you, Mummy?'

Ben, who's staring intently at the label on a bottle of red wine that Bea produced from her apparently bottomless bag, rolls his eyes. Annie clears her throat.

'Well, if I'm not allowed, Aunty Bea will do my hair in a special style instead. That would be okay, wouldn't it?' pleads Phoebe.

Memories of Norma and her wispy old-lady hair float down the years. Phoebe has thin hair the colour of caramel. 'What about trimming it?' Annie suggests. 'Styling it into a blunt bob?'

'What's that?' Phoebe looks crestfallen and Annie realises she hasn't made it sound very enticing.

'Well, if you had a bob, you could hold it back in one of those rainbow unicorn headbands you love so much.'

'And I think I know just the place to get a unicorn headband,' adds Bea.

'Okay, after lunch let's go. For now, let's eat.' Annie scoops a ladle of casserole on each plate. Just as she's about to sit down to her own, the house phone rings.

'Leave it,' murmurs Ben. 'Eat. It's probably loft insulation again.'

'No, I ought to pick up. You never know.' The trilling of the house phone always makes Annie uneasy. As if the caller has something momentous to say. Why would anyone call you on a landline unless it was something big? It could be good big, of course. It doesn't have to be bad big. But Annie doesn't err on the side of optimism.

'Yes,' she cradles the handset in the crook of her neck in a way she's heard can cause a mini-stroke.

'Annie, it's Toby. Dad.'

'Oh gosh. Lovely to hear you. We have Bea here for lunch. We're plotting ways to get her together with Emily once she's met you. I think they're getting there. Just need to take it gently-gently with Emily. She's a bit up and down.' Annie turns and smiles at Bea, who has put down her knife and fork. An expectant hush hovers over the lunch table.

'Annie, can you sit down a moment?' There's a long pause. 'I'm very sorry to have to tell you that your mother passed away this morning. My darling Emily.' Toby's voice crackles down the line.

Annie turns to face the others, her mouth a perfect O. The handset drops to the floor. 'She's dead. Emily is dead.' Ben, Bea and Phoebe stare back at her. A random gust of wind rattles the sash window. Toby is still speaking into the handset and finally Ben rises, picks it up and takes it into the narrow hallway. In his other arm, he gathers up Phoebe and cuddles her close.

'Yes. Okay, I understand. Yes, I'll tell them. I'm so sorry. Let me talk to them and we'll get back to you later.' Annie hears the handset click off and then she's enveloped in Ben's chest. Phoebe is crying softly into his shirt. All three of them cling together, while Bea looks on.

'I never got to know her,' she says finally.

'No, I'm sorry, Bea. The universe is unfair.' Whose grief is greater, Annie wonders. Mine for knowing her, but not properly connecting. Or Bea's for never knowing her at all.

'Leo found her this morning,' explains Ben. 'She passed away in the night. Leo thinks it's probably a blessing. It could've become very distressing for her if things had dragged on.'

Bea lurches out of her chair and it slams backwards, hitting the stripped wood floor with a thud. 'I can't do this. I can't fucking do it. I never got to see her. Do you know what that feels like? It's best I go. Let you get on with your grief over your mother. I'm sorry for it.'

'I'm so, so sorry, Phoebe,' she adds as an afterthought, stroking the child's teary cheek with the lightest of touches. 'Forgive me.'

Bea rips the black hoodie from its plastic bag and shrugs it on, ramming up the zip and pulling the hood down low over her forehead. Then she is gone. Annie runs to the bay window and sees her striding down the front path, clasping the hood around her face as if fending off an attack. Next door, Mrs Pooley is watering her pocket-sized herbaceous border. Annie sees her opening her mouth as if in greeting and then closing it like a fish out of water. The garden gate slams and Bea is gone.

Chapter 49
Toby, 2013

The day of the funeral is windy, with grey clouds scudding across a low sky. Toby arrives early at the crematorium to secure a seat as far as possible from the area assigned to 'close' family. A run-in with Leo Petrakis is the last thing he wants today. He's wishing he'd agreed to Clara accompanying him. Going solo to a funeral is a lonely business. But it is *his* unfinished business, not Clara's and now it's time to get on with it.

Emily's funeral arrangements were Leo's last grand attempt to control and impress her, thinks Toby ruefully. He would have done it differently. Perhaps a scattering of ashes on her beloved common. He imagines tiny particles of Emily drifting upwards on the wind towards the sun, finally set free. Why they are saying goodbye to a life-long atheist in a chapel, he has no idea.

Inside, the chairs are arranged in a neat semi-circle around what he thinks of as a stage, with its discreet curtain concealing the hell and brimstone beyond. Toby sniffs. Hanging in the air is the acrid scent of white lilies past their peak. And now the organ is striking up a grotesque version of *You'll Never Walk Alone*. Emily would hate it. Actually, no, she'd probably have got the giggles. Toby finds comfort in this as he seeks out the most obscure seat he can find.

Sitting down, he bows his head in what feels like a seemly manner. Cautiously narrowing his left eye, he spots a couple of about his own age enter and take seats at the far end of his row. The woman has the look of an elegant spider, dressed in a riot of black velvet and deep purple satin that falls from her thin frame like drapes. Beside her, the man is dapper with thick silver-grey hair and a close-cropped beard. He looks like a media type. Both smile and wave encouragingly in his direction. Reluctantly, he edges his way along the row. 'Hi. I'm Toby.'

'Oh, we don't know a Toby, I'm afraid. Are you a relative?' The woman extends an etiolated hand.

'No. Not a relative. I'm, ah, the girls' birth father.' Up close, Toby sees that the woman's delicate face has turned pale as milk, throwing a tracery of wrinkles into bold relief.

'You mean, you are Beatrix's birth father?' she asks incredulously.

'Well, yes. But I don't know Bea. I mean, I've never met her – today will be the first time. It's a long story…' Toby trails off. He doesn't know where to start.

The woman fixes Toby with an inscrutable gaze. A deep purple feather adorns her hat and it sways in the draught from the open chapel door. It's mesmerising. 'We are Beatrix's adoptive parents.'

'My God.' Toby feels as if his throat is closing up and he loosens his tie, but it doesn't seem to help. 'Is Beatrix with you?'

'She's arriving separately with Annie. Sadly, we became a little distanced over the years, although we do maintain contact,' says the man, almost apologetically. 'I'm Sean, by the way, and this is my wife, Julia.'

'Toby Summerfield. So pleased to meet you both.' Toby shakes each proffered hand a little too energetically.

'Ah, *the* Toby Summerfield. The boy racer of campaigning journalism, latterly turned media mogul.'

Toby casts about wildly for an appropriate response to what feels like the ultimate character assassination. 'We should talk.'

'Yes, but maybe later.' Sean nudges his black-rimmed Gucci specs back up his nose and studies the order of service intently.

Leo Petrakis comes into Toby's line of vision, ploughing his bulky frame through the chairs. Trailing behind is a whey-faced woman about Annie's age. Clearly his daughter, Sophia. At the rear is a couple. The younger, plumper version of Leo must be his son Dimitri, accompanied by a heavily fecund wife. Toby clears his throat. He must stop this cynical and sneering stuff. He knows it's a defence mechanism to stop it all getting to him: the mournful lilies, the hymns that would be meaningless to Emily and most of all Leo with his air of entitlement and that meaty slab of a body that had loved her.

As Leo and his entourage approach, Toby slumps down in his seat, lowers his head as if in prayer and holds his breath. 'Okay, guys, keep going right down to the front. We're family,' instructs Leo, pausing at Toby's row.

After counting to 10, Toby raises his head warily. The Petrakis family are making themselves comfortable in their ringside seats, but Leo's on his feet glowering at Toby. Any minute now he's going to jab his finger in the air and command me to remove myself, thinks Toby. Good luck to them, they've got a great view of the curtain. Taking a leaf from Sean's book, he scans the order of service obsessively.

There's a rustle at the back and Annie appears, resplendent in a frock of rose silk. Well, she could be Annie. Or might be Beatrix? Toby blinks. Whichever, she is followed by an equally stunning identical other, dressed more conventionally in a tailored, cobalt blue linen suit. Neither wears a hat and coal black hair ripples down each long, elegant back. Toby puzzles over which is which and suspects Bea to be the flamboyant one. His first meeting with her— terrible timing, but everything was put on hold after Emily's death.

Sure enough, the rose red one takes a seat on the other side of the room, while the cobalt blue one makes a beeline for Toby.

'Dad, you came! I wasn't sure.' Annie plonks down in the empty seat next to Toby. 'Bea's here with me.'

'Yes I noticed. I wasn't sure which of you was which when you walked in. But I sort of guessed you were you.'

'You're desperate to meets her, aren't you? It's crazy it's taken this long. But I don't think today's the right time. She's feeling pretty nervous and overwhelmed. Remember, she's dealing with Julia and Sean too. It's all amicable, of course and they are here to support her. But she does seem to find them hard-going.' Annie glances at the Howards who abandoned their original seats to position themselves in the row in front of Bea.

'I get the feeling she's a delicate flower.'

'You're right. I'm only beginning to get to know her myself. My feeling is, she was traumatised by what she discovered about her birth. Odd, isn't it? She was brought up in a much more educated and well-to-do family than mine. Liberal too, kind and caring, from what I can tell. My instinct is, she was scarred by the rejection. She told me she always felt an outsider in their home, even though she didn't find out she was adopted until she was 17. Tread carefully, Dad. I know you can.'

'Should we do something really awful and escape somewhere else after this?' adds Annie. 'Just the three of us? I know Leo asked everyone back to Ambrosia for sandwiches and stodgy Greek snacks. But Bea will find it hard to cope and it'll be hard for me too! Leo and his sidekick Dimitri made my teenage life hell.'

Toby glances up and sees Bea gazing fixedly at him. From a distance, he can't detect if her expression is hostile or yearning. He raises a hand in greeting, but it feels unnatural and she doesn't respond.

'Let's do it. Last time I saw Leo Petrakis, I nearly got my teeth knocked out. I'm probably barred from Ambrosia. No great loss.'

'Fine.' Annie bends and drops a kiss on Toby's thinning hair. 'Are you, okay, Dad?'

'I am now. It's just everything jars. This is not Emily.'

'I know. She'd have found it a hoot. Hold on to that, Dad. That's what I'm doing. There's a pub, the Coach and Horses, up by the common. Do you know it? It's crammed full of horsey things, saddles, horseshoes and whips all over the walls. Dead corny but big, so it's never hideously overcrowded in the week. And there are lots of little partitions, so you can get some privacy. I suspect a lot of people go there for Romantic Assignations.' Annie rolls her eyes, Emily-style. 'Let's meet there.'

'I know it. I'll be there. Find me under the crystal riding crop near the men's toilets.'

The organ strikes up and Annie blows him an extra kiss as she returns to her seat. Leo and Dimitri have gone 'backstage', presumably to help to launch the coffin on its final journey. Toby squeezes his eyes shut and thinks of Emily. The way she would brush his fringe back off his brow, her look of fierce determination in class, rushing to undress each other in his cluttered bedroom, clothes heaped on the floor and apple boughs cupping the windowpane. When he opens his eyes again, he finds tears on his cheeks.

After a mournful rendition of *Oh God! Our Help in Ages Past*, the organ stops abruptly and Leo takes centre stage in front of the curtains. 'Emily was my beloved wife and a wonderful mother to my two children.'

Tact! Toby squirms uncomfortably in his seat and resists the temptation to twist around to see how Annie and Bea are reacting.

'We met later in life, but it was a true union of souls. She devoted herself to me, showing her dedication in so many ways. She was a support in my business, helping with the running of my restaurant in practical matters. I can't imagine my life without her.'

You mean she waitressed and wiped down tables. Toby is now engaged in a physical effort not to stand up and start shouting. But what good would it do Emily?

'She was a kind and attentive stepmother to my two children and a loving grandmother to my son Dimitri's brood,' muses Leo, gazing benignly at the congregation. 'I know she had ambitions. For a time she was a librarian and she once told me that she liked to write. She kept what she called a Memory Book and wrote her last entry the evening before her death. I respected her privacy and never read it. Following its retrieval from her childhood home, it remains under lock and key in the cabinet at Ambrosia, as was her wish. It's lovely to see some of her former library colleagues here in the congregation, along with a couple of her school mates and even one of her old teachers, I believe.'

No mention of her birth daughters sitting right in his line of vision. What the fuck. Toby fingers his tie like a worry bead until it's twisted out of recognition.

Leo continues to intone. 'But what is important is that for Emily, family always came first. Writing was a pastime, as was reading. She loved us all very much and we loved her back.

'Now, if anyone would like to step up and say a few words about Emily, they would be most welcome. I am a man of few words, but perhaps some of you have memories you'd like to share.'

A deathly silence descends over the congregation. Toby rises to his feet, clutching his ravaged tie like a comfort blanket. 'I would—like to say a few words, that is.'

Leo shoots him a look of pure hatred. 'Ah, we're quite short on time. Perhaps we should prioritise close relatives?' There are a few coughs and some restless shuffling, but no volunteers.

'Fine. Please share your thoughts, Mr…?'

'Summerfield. Toby Summerfield. Emily Enderbie was my first love. We met in the late seventies when we were still at school. We became inseparable. And then for some inexplicable reason—the sort only young teenagers crazily in love one second and at war the next—would understand, we split up. I'd like to say a few words about the Emily I knew.

'My Emily was passionate, fearless. She read voraciously. In those days, it wasn't a pastime. She often joked about coming from the wrong side of the tracks, but her instinct for literature was peerless. We'd argue over everything from Kafka to Sylvia Plath. She delighted in outmanoeuvring me! She loved

David Bowie, The Clash, The Sex Pistols, Curtis Mayfield. Musicians who had something relevant, often angry, to say.

'I'd like to set the record straight regarding the religious side of things.' Toby glances meaningfully at the rafters. 'She didn't believe in divine intervention, rather the power of personality. Working hard, staying determined and sometimes getting lucky. Or at least she did in 1978, because that's what she told me.' The congregation laugh nervously.

'Emily was clever and funny and sensitive. She had to fight for what she got, unlike me. I was the entitled one. Perhaps it's frivolous to mention, but she was also beautiful. I can show you just how beautiful.' Toby raises his hand towards the twins, sitting in the back row. 'Here are our daughters, our birth daughters— Emily's and mine. Bea and Annie are the image of my Emily. I lost them for many, many years and I only just found them. I won't let them go again.'

Leo strides up onto the stage, ignoring a wave of murmuring. 'Have you quite finished, *Mr* Summerfield?'

'I think so, Mr Petrakis.'

'Well perhaps, you'd like to remove yourself from the stage then,' he hisses close up to Toby's face so the congregation is unable to hear. 'Do you want to destroy her memory, as a devoted, family-loving wife and mother? What is it you want from us?'

'The Memory Book. Give me her Memory Book and you'll be shot of me. We'll have no reason to cross paths again.'

'Get out of my sight. I'll get you your precious Memory Book. Don't bother coming around for it. I'll have it delivered. Much good it'll do you to find out how she couldn't stand the sight of your smug face. That's why she ditched you, even though she was pregnant.'

'I may be an irreligious man, but I'm not irreverent. That said, I have just two words for you, Petrakis. Fuck off. May your God forgive us both.' Toby turns on his heels and strides down the aisle as the organ strikes up with *What A Friend we have in Jesus*.

Chapter 50
Annie, 2013

Early mornings and lonely nights are an accepted part of being a pilot's wife. Ben warned Annie what she was getting into when they hooked up and she's still more than enough in love with him to accommodate the irregular lifestyle. It's 5 a.m. and he has an early short haul to Charles de Gaulle, then an overnighter from Paris to Schiphol and finally back to London. With any luck, she'll see him again the day after tomorrow.

'Busy day?' Ben is straightening his uniform and checking himself in the mirror. Pilots must look as if they just stepped out of a bandbox.

'Well, just the one client today, but I've cancelled. Once I've dropped Phoebe at school, I've a pile of casework to do. Bea's coming over later this afternoon. She called yesterday, asking to see me urgently.'

'Anything up? Is she okay?'

'Hard to say, but I suspect she's *not* okay. The pub meeting with Toby—sorry, Dad, I keep forgetting—was perfect. Things looked ominous after Dad stormed out of the funeral, but I think Bea was actually quite impressed! The fly in the ointment is that cursed Memory Book. Bea got hold of it a couple of days ago and now she's acting very oddly.'

'How did she get hold of it? It must've been painful for her to read.'

'Toby called me a couple of days ago to say he'd retrieved it from Leo and would pass it on to Bea. He felt it only fair that she should read it, considering how short-changed she's been.' Annie almost adds *by her own mother,* but thinks better of it.

'You've already read it, haven't you? Was it a good idea to let her read it? Especially on her own?'

'I'd have preferred to hold off awhile. There's a lot of negative stuff about Bea, especially in the early section. But Dad was adamant she had a right to read it, warts and all. Milly added another entry, just before she died. I haven't read that—hope it's more positive.'

'Wish I could be around. Sounds like you have a challenging day ahead.'

'Hmm. You know, it's hard to tell how Bea's feeling, especially on the phone. But she didn't sound right. I'll know more when I see her.'

'What about Phoebe?'

'Well, here's the better news. Phoebe's got her first ever sleepover tonight—at Tilly's house. Remember, we discussed it? I'm still not sure if she isn't a little young at six. But it's Saturday tomorrow, no school—and they're both desperate to do it. She has her bag packed already, complete with rainbow Pjs and unicorn slippers.'

Ben laughs. 'I'm pleased for her. And you. You'll have a good, clear day once you've delivered her to school.'

'Yes, but I'll miss her. And you too, of course. Hurry home safe.'

'Always. I should get going. Give Phoebe a big slobbery kiss for me and tell her not to go running away with the unicorns. Fingers crossed for no delays and hopefully see you very soon, my love.'

As she closes the door gently on Ben, Annie is flooded with a deep sense of unease. In an effort not to worry him, she'd held a lot back. She recalls Bea's voice on the phone, shrill, bordering on hysterical. And angry too, as if she judged Annie complicit in her pain. *We need to talk about that book. Annie.*

If only the Memory Book had gone to the grave with their mother. There's that killer verdict on baby Bea: *Bea is my difficult one. She hates the cot and cries bitterly to be lifted out. She avoids my face and I have never yet seen her smile. Annie smiles all the time.* And there's the way Emily is so easily seduced into parting with her. Annie shudders to think of how it might affect Bea. Surely Toby wouldn't have given it to Bea so readily if he'd seen some of the vitriol in there?

Annie shakes herself and goes to the kitchen to prepare Phoebe's packed lunch. Beyond her kitchen window, a weak sun struggles through the clouds, lighting up the London chimney pots in an acid haze. Soon Ben will be flying through that cloud layer into the blue beyond. Settling down at the kitchen table with a coffee, she tries to distract herself with a pile of case notes. But in her head, she hears Bea's words over and over, the mix of pain and anger. *But why would they abandon me and keep you?*

It's a relief when Phoebe bounces downstairs, demanding breakfast and a chocolate bar in her packed lunch. 'Did you remember my sleepover, Mummy?' She's tugging along a little wheeled suitcase in the shape of a pig. 'We're supposed to give this to Tilly's mummy at the school gates.'

'What have you got in there?'

'Well, my Pjs, slippers and teddy. And clothes for tomorrow.'

Annie wants to say *I'll miss you sweetie, please don't go*, but checks herself. She mustn't burden Phoebe with neediness. 'Let's take a quick look through and double check.'

'I've got everything, Mummy. I promise. Even my toothbrush,' Phoebe protests. Too late. The suitcase is opened to reveal a stash of chocolate bars and a bottle of blood-coloured liquid labelled 'grape juice'.

'What on earth is this?'

'We bought it at the corner shop, Mummy. You know, when you said we could walk to the shop together and spend our pocket money. It's for our midnight feast. But Tilly was worried about hiding it...' Phoebe is crestfallen.

'Come here. Give me a hug. You know this is wrong, don't you Phoebe? You shouldn't have bought that rubbish drink and you most certainly shouldn't have hidden it away. But just this once, your secret is safe with me. *Just* this once. Never again! Now off you go and have wonderful midnight feast.'

Phoebe's unusually quiet in the back of the car on the school run. Could she have cold feet about the sleepover? Or perhaps she's feeling guilty? Or confused by mixed messages about chocolate? Annie recalls a key piece of parental advice from her training: *you can't win every battle. Let some things go.* A showdown with Phoebe this morning is the last thing she needs.

The mood changes as they swing into the school car park. Annie hands the plastic pig suitcase with its forbidden contraband to Tilly's mum. 'I'm sorry, there's something in there they shouldn't have. Some C-H-O-C bars and disgusting liquid, masquerading under the name of juice. Just to warn you, they're planning a midnight feast.'

'Got it! You don't need to whisper. They're right over the other side of the playground. Shall we let them have their guilty secret, *just* this once?' Tilly's mum is a kindred spirit.

Annie nods. Thank God for other mums. The ones that get it. We're like an army, she thinks. Licking our small troops into shape, preparing them for the battle that is life. Without the camaraderie, how would we survive?

Back home, she settles back down to casework. Thank God for work, the great tranquiliser—she hardly notices the hours ticking by. Skipping lunch, she makes herself a mid-afternoon cheese sandwich and on the dot of 4 p.m., the doorbell rings.

'Coming, Bea.' An acidic swirling sensation rises in the pit of Annie's stomach. Through the frosted glass panel door, Bea's outline looks threatening. Of course, she has a right to be angry. She *should* be very angry. Annie breathes in and then right out to the bottom of her lungs.

'Bea, welcome. Come on in. Tea? Or is it late enough for wine?'

'No, I don't want tea and I don't want wine either. Had you forgotten? I don't drink it. What I do want is to talk about this!' Bea thrusts the Memory Book into Annie's hands.

'I know, Bea. It must have been awful for you, reading it. But did you read right to the end? I think Emily added more, after she became very sick and we re-discovered you.'

'No, I bloody didn't read all of it.' Bea's face is pale and drawn. 'I read up to the part where *your* grandmother carted me off to the adoption agency 'cos my own mother didn't have the balls to do it. The next part was all about how relieved she was once I'd gone and she was free to enjoy *you* in peace and quiet. For Christ's sake, what'd be the point of reading anymore? I wasn't even in the narrative.'

'Well, I get that. But there were bits she wrote that she was sad about missing you and how she regretted letting you go. Perhaps you should've carried on reading. In fact, we should both read her final entries. I didn't see them either.'

'She was sad. She missed me.' Bea mimics Annie in a high-pitched voice, layered with sarcasm. 'Oh dear. Poor Emily. The so-called mother who fucked up my life. D'you know that every single day of my childhood, I felt a misfit? And every single night, it was like something was missing? As if someone had cut off one of my arms or legs. I guess the bit I was missing was you, *dear* sister.'

'But your adoptive parents seem lovely. The Howards were good to you, weren't they? In some ways, you had a better start than me. Don't get me wrong. You can't replace a birth mother. But you had a lovely big home, a good school and a little brother. And Julia and Sean *love* you. It's so obvious they do.'

'Yes and isn't this fucking weird? I love them too. In my own way. I'm still learning what love feels like. But I never felt *equal* to them. And I never belonged. I hated that creepy old house in Hampstead and the snotty school and

252

even Jake because he was their real child. I was a substitute, until he came along and I became the black sheep.'

'For God's sake, Bea, the picture you're painting is too dark. I had my own problems to deal with too, you know. Emily had a string of boyfriends, then I had to go and live with Leo and his dreadful kids. But at least I had Norma.'

'Yeah, Norma. Well, all I got was Sara and she's crippled inside from the war. She was suspicious of me from the start. Treated me with kid gloves, like I was about to hit her in the face or something.'

Rooted to the spot, Annie clenches the Memory Book in her right hand. Bea's tone becomes even more goading.

'Meanwhile, you were having those lovely sessions with Norma, styling her hair and all that. Sharing secrets. Playing in the garden together in the summer. Norma's best girl, you were. Her prize, Annie. It was you that took all that from me. You. I should hate you. You're always so fucking calm. Why don't you lose it, just for once? Then you'll know how it feels to be an ordinary mortal.'·

Annie feels anger coursing through her veins, a new sensation that she has no idea how to handle. For a nano-second, she hates her sister. 'Here's the cause of all this misery. This bloody Memory Book. Someone should have burned it!' Clutching the book, she raises her right arm and hurls it in frustration across the room in Bea's direction.

Instinctively, Bea lurches out of the book's path as it arcs towards the mantelpiece. She loses her footing and what happens next switches to soundless slo-mo. As Bea falls silently through space, Annie, rooted to the spot, is incapable of stopping the inevitable. There's a shocking crack and a sucking noise as Bea's head slams down on the slate hearth. Pages of the Memory Book are scattered around her like airborne leaflet propaganda. A dark squiggle of blood oozes from somewhere behind her left ear, pooling in an ever-widening red circle on the wooden floorboards.

'Oh my God, Bea! Are you okay? Bea?' Annie bends down and tentatively touches her face. Her sister is completely still.

'Bea, hang on in there. I'm calling an ambulance.' Annie dimly remembers that you mustn't move injured people, but you should try to keep them conscious. Covering Bea in a blanket, she considers propping up her head on a cushion, but decides against it. Instead, she kneels and cups her sister's ravaged head in her hands. This seems to bring Bea briefly back to consciousness. She's mouthing, though it's hard to tell what she's trying to say. It sounds like 'don't tell anyone it's me.'

'What do you mean, don't tell anyone it's me?'

Bea labours to get the words out. 'Don't tell anyone which of us is which. You'll get into trouble - they might even charge you. Claim it was your fault. But it wasn't. So just don't tell anyone which of us is which.'

'That's crazy, Bea. I have to tell them truthfully what happened.'

Bea shakes her head and more blood oozes out of her ear. 'Let's work it out when I'm better. Please, Annie, promise. Don't say anything for now. And don't talk to Sean and Julia about it. Or Toby. Everything will get out of control. It's not just to protect you. I don't want it for me either. All the fuss—I won't cope. It's the way I am.'

Annie sits back on her heels, horrified. What sort of a crazy promise is she being asked to make? But Bea's growing more agitated, slipping in and out of consciousness. 'Don't tell *anyone*,' she whispers again.

'But I can't pretend to Ben and Phoebe that nothing's happened. And I certainly can't conceal my identity from them! In any case, I should take some blame. Of course, it *was* an accident...'

'That's why you mustn't take the blame,' gasps Bea. 'I don't want them sending you away, not now I've found you. Please Annie. Just until tomorrow?'

'Okay, I'll say nothing. Just until tomorrow. Promise.'

Chapter 51
Annie, 2013

Annie calls the emergency services, then crouches on the floor and strokes Bea's damp forehead. 'Stay awake, Bea. Keep talking to me. They'll be here very soon. Hang on in there.'

With every dragging minute, Annie is terrified that her sister will slip back into unconsciousness. And sure enough, as the doorbell rings, Bea's head is starting to loll. Backing towards the door, Annie reminds herself of the promise she made.

'What do we have here?' The room is suddenly crammed with paramedics in high-vis jackets. One of them, who looks underage and has a huge Adam's apple, is hanging back and doing his best to avoid looking at Bea, lying in her dark halo of blood.

The young woman paramedic takes control. 'Don't worry about Will. It's his first call out. He's doing the driving tonight. So can you tell us what happened here?'

'We need to get her in, Belle,' says the third paramedic, an older man closer to Toby's age. 'Get Will to bring the stretcher. Now.'

'Will do, Barry. Hear that, Will?'

While Will's been freaking out at the sight of blood and Belle's been casing the joint for evidence of foul play, Barry's been quietly attending to Bea's medical needs. Two minutes later, a stretcher appears and she's gently lifted on to it.

'We're taking her to Saint Mary's. Do you want to come in the ambulance?' Barry doesn't even lift his head to look at Annie: his concern is his patient.

'Shall I follow on in my car?'

Twisting her head, Belle gives Annie an accusatory stare. 'Hang about. Before we all get ahead of ourselves, there are some details I'm unclear about. How did this *accident* actually happen?'

'She fell and hit her head on the hearth.' Annie considers adding that her sister had swerved and lost her footing, but decides the best policy is simply to answer what she's asked.

'*How* did she fall. Did she trip?'

Annie nods.

'You're twins, right? Can you give me your names?'

There's a tense pause while Annie grapples with her conscience. She should be honest with them, but something holds her back. To break her promise to Bea would feel like a betrayal—and her sister has weathered so many betrayals and broken promises. But Annie also acknowledges in herself the seed of self-survival. She recalls Toby talking to her about his break-up with Emily. *My golden future. My fucking glittering career.* Could she have inherited from her birth father a talent for self-preservation?

Barry's urgent voice cuts through her hesitation. 'Look Belle, if you want to pursue this, can you do it once we have this young lady safely in the hospital? She needs an urgent head scan. She's still slipping in and out. Will, let's get her into the ambulance right now.' He turns to Annie. 'Why don't you come with us. It'd be safer. You've had a shock too.'

'I'm coming. Give me one moment please. I need the toilet.' Annie runs up the stairs two at a time, slams the bathroom door behind her and fishes in her pocket for her mobile phone. 'Hannah, it's me, Annie. Look, I don't want to go into details right now, but could you be on standby to keep Phoebe with you for an extra night? She mustn't worry, just tell her and anyone else who asks that it's a work issue.'

'Not a problem, Annie. I'll think of some plausible excuse to give Phoebe. But you sound terribly worried. Are you sure there's nothing else I can help with?'

'Thank you Hannah, there's nothing. I've got myself into a little bit of a situation and I need to resolve it without things exploding out of control. I have to go now...'

As the line goes dead, Annie pulls the chain and runs downstairs. In the ambulance, Belle is gazing vacantly out of the mud-spattered front window. As they pull away, Annie sees Mrs Pooley from next door lurking behind the privet hedge, her white face peering at them through the slanting rain. Busybody.

'Sorry, sorry. Hope I didn't keep you waiting. How is she?'

'Pretty much the same.' Will switches on the lights and claxon. 'Don't worry. We're minutes from the hospital and we've called ahead, so they know we're on our way.' On the stretcher, Bea is absolutely still. Annie wishes she'd moan or stir—anything to show she's still alive. At the hospital, she's rushed down a long corridor and swallowed by swinging doors. Will and Barry disappear along with her, but Belle takes Annie's arm a little too firmly and leads her to the relatives' room. 'Tea?' she asks brusquely.

'No thank you. I think I'd like to be left alone if you don't mind.'

'I expect you would. So, now are you going to tell me your name and the name of your twin lying there on that stretcher?'

'No. Not for now anyway.'

'Why not?' snaps Belle.

'I promised my sister. We made a promise together. And I'm not going to let her down.'

'You're a piece of work, aren't you?'

'Pardon?'

'You know I'm going to involve the police? It's part of our job if we think there's something suspicious going on.'

'Well in that case you must do that. Because I'm not letting my sister down.'

'At the very least, we need *her* name and date of birth. She's not well enough to supply the details herself and there's nothing on her to make an identification.'

Annie never thought faster. 'Okay, I understand that. It's Emily Enderbie. DOB is October 31, 1978.'

'See, that wasn't so painful, was it? I'll warn you, the police will be more insistent about you supplying your name too, when they arrive. Any pre-existing conditions we should be aware of?'

'Not that I'm aware of.'

'Okay. I'm leaving you here now. You can stay here all night if you want. Or you can get a taxi home. Your choice.' Shoulders set at a self-righteous angle, Belle makes for the door.

The relatives' room is mercifully empty. Arranging her coat on a bench, Annie settles herself into a foetal position and closes her eyes to shut out the windowless room, with its pathetic selection of broken toys, tattered magazines and cracked vinyl chairs. Though nothing can block out the sounds: a cry of agony in the dark, the ominous whisperings of passing medics, urgent footsteps rushing to a patient in need. And then the clatter of cups and saucers as the evening tea trolley makes its way to the wards.

Next thing she knows, Annie awakes from a deep, dreamless sleep, struggling to remember where she is and why. Nothing's changed in the relatives' room: it's the same sickly yellow light, like translucent egg yolk. Annie has no idea how much time has passed. She fumbles for her phone. It's 9 p.m. She must have slept a good two hours. A message from Sean pops up: *So sorry, unlikely back home tomorrow. Hopefully day after. Gale force winds here, flights backed up. Will be inflight when u get this, so don't call me. I'll call u. Hope all okay. Love to u both xxx*

Feeling thirsty, achy and sweating in the hot hospital air, Annie considers what to do next. No one has brought any news of her sister: it's as if they've all forgotten she's there, waiting. Hearing the tap, tap of footsteps advancing along the corridor, Annie shoves on her shoes and pulls on her coat. 'Excuse me. Can you help? I'm waiting for news of a relative.'

It's a young nurse with a gentle, round face. 'Oh dear. How long have you been waiting here?'

'Hours. But what's important is what's happening to my sister. Her name is Emily Enderbie and she was admitted several hours ago.'

'Of course. Let me see what I can find out for you. Meanwhile, let me get you a cup of tea too. You must be parched. My name is Mary, by the way, if you need anything.'

It feels like a lifetime before she reappears and hands Annie a Styrofoam cup of hot water with a tea bag to dunk. 'I've got an update for you. Your sister's only just been admitted to the ward after various scans and tests. The results aren't back yet, or I'm sure someone would've come to find you.'

'How is she in herself?'

'Still very drowsy and a bit confused. But we've made her comfortable. We won't know more until the test results come back which shouldn't be too long as they're marked urgent. Would it be best if you went home now and we call you as soon as there's more news?'

'No, no. I'm staying here.' The horror of what's happened is beginning to recede a little, replaced by a sense of overwhelming guilt at what she has done to her sister.

'Well, you must do what works for you. You're lucky—it looks as if you'll have the visitors' room to yourself tonight. Let me bring a blanket and a pillow to make you a bit more comfy.'

The kindness of strangers. Annie's eyes fill with tears and she very nearly spills out the whole sorry story to the kindly nurse. But that wouldn't do at all. Tossing and turning on the vinyl bench, she drifts in and out of a film reel of distorted images. Norma, staring down at her with eyes like hot coals. A naked baby lying in a bath. Her mother, back from the dead, shouting at her, but no sound emerging from her white lips. At 6 a.m., she surfaces, eases her cramped limbs into a sitting position and combs her tangled hair. If only she had a toothbrush.

Outside on the corridor, the working day kicks into action, but no one seems aware of the dishevelled woman in the relatives' room. Then there's a tap at the door and Mary pops her head round. 'Awake.'

'Sort of.' Annie stifles a groan.

'I'm just finishing my shift. But before I go, I've some good news. Your sister's tests and scans have come back clear. It's a nasty wound and she's had quite a few stitches, but it seems she's escaped more serious injury. My God, she looks like you!'

'Oh thank you. So much.' Annie sinks back on the bench and puts her head in her hands. 'I've been so frightened.' She starts to quiver involuntarily.

'Yes. It was a nasty injury. I'd like to be able to tell you to go right up there and see her now. She's having a cuppa. But I can't do that. There's a question over her injuries, I'm afraid. We've been advised not to let you see her until the police arrive. It seems that the paramedic who attended your sister had concerns about how the injury was sustained.'

'When will the police arrive? You see, I made a promise to my sister. I wouldn't give my name, or hers, to anyone before she—we—had a chance to speak with them. My sister's dealt with a series of lies and broken promises over the years and I'm not going to be just another person who lets her down. I'd like to explain more, but I can't. Not until I've spoken with my sister and to the police.' Annie wipes the tears from her cheeks with the heel of her hand.

'Hey,' Mary touches her arm lightly. 'I shouldn't form judgments in my job. But...' her mobile pings. 'Yes. Oh good. Fine. Right now then.' She turns to Annie. 'The police are ready to see your sister and take statements from you both. I'm gonna take you up there. Sod the end of my shift.'

They take the lift to the third floor and follow Mary down an interminably long corridor to a ward called Gilead. Bea's in the bed closest to the door.

'They've been keeping a close eye on her,' explains Mary. 'But she's making good progress.'

Sitting up in bed with a bandage wrapped around her head and a violet-yellow bruise spreading across her cheek where her face hit the hearth, Bea doesn't look too good. But her face lights up when she sees Annie. 'I'll go and tell the constable you're ready to talk to him. He's waiting by the nurses' station,' says Mary.

Police constable Ryan Melish is a burly redhead with a confident manner. 'Now ladies, it's high time we got to the bottom of what's been going on here. So I suggest we begin by asking the injured party what happened.'

'That's fine,' Bea pipes up from her high white hospital bed. 'I didn't want to give my sister's name until I was sure I could clear up any confusion over what's been going on. Could you get out your notebook, or whatever it is you use and make notes while I tell you what *did* happen.'

Bea can be very persuasive when she wants to be. Constable Melish produces a report sheet. 'So you are Emily Enderbie, DOB 31/10/78 and this is?' He turns to Annie.

'Before I give you my details, I have to make an admission. I lied about my sister's name last night. A terrible thing to do. What is it you call it? Perverting the course of justice? But I'd made a promise to my sister. So when we got to the hospital, I said the first name that came into my head. Which was our mother's name, Emily Enderbie.'

Scratching his head, Constable Melish makes a big show of striking out the name he's just added to the report sheet. 'So you are? And this is? He nods towards the bed.

'My sister is Bea Howard and I'm Annie Harrison, although my maiden name was Enderbie. And we are, as you can see, twins.'

'Hmm. You're quite right about perverting the course of justice. That alone is an offence for which you may be charged. However, let's get the details entered up correctly. Then we can get down to what happened.'

'I can explain that quite simply. I was being very annoying and in frustration my sister picked up a heavy folder and hurled it across the room. If it was anyone's fault, it was mine for being annoying.' Bea lies back against the pillows, exhausted.

'Well, that's how you see it, Miss Howard. But it's not necessarily how it would be viewed by the prosecution service. Do you have anything to add, Miss, sorry Mrs, Harrison?'

'No, it's exactly as my sister described. Except I shouldn't have lost my temper like that and hurled the book across the room. It was very wrong of me and I should take the blame. It's certainly not my sister's fault for 'being annoying'. But ultimately, yes, it was all a ghastly accident.'

'Was there any intention to harm Miss Howard when you threw the book at her?'

'Truthfully, no. The anger I felt was not specifically directed at my sister. It was at the universe for being so messed up.'

Constable Melish looks a little quizzical, but continues questioning. 'What about you, Miss Howard? Is it your belief that your sister intended to harm you? Or was it, as she suggests, an unfortunate accident?'

'Let me tell you this. I will not support a case against my sister. She meant me no harm. Now please leave us alone and let me rest.'

Constable Melish looks from one sister to the other, sighs and taps his biro against his teeth. 'Right. I think we can close down this incident. But ladies, might I suggest that in future, you keep your sisterly tiffs under control? Mrs Harrison, never lie to the law again or you may not be treated so leniently. Miss Howard, I do hope you are fully recovered soon.' Bea and Annie stifle giggles at the sight of Constable Melish's indignant retreating back.

'Hey sis. Come sit with me for a while. I won't break,' says Bea, patting the bed. Annie envelops her in a huge hug. 'I'm so sorry, Bea—words can't express it. Can we put all this behind us and take our time learning to be sisters now?'

Bea nods. 'Please. It's what I want, too.'

Chapter 52
Toby, 2013

How does anyone, ever, know what's the right thing to do? What the heck, thinks Toby, as he heads the car off the South Circular towards the urban maze of Tooting Bec. In the back are his wife, Clara, possibly the most stoical woman in the world, and son, Theo. And in the boot are two huge plates of pilchard sandwiches and a Battenburg cake. Clara's a self-confessed cookaphobe who'd never even heard of a Battenburg cake, but somehow had managed to produce the goods.

'How're you feeling today?' She touches Toby's hand gently where it rests on the steering wheel.

'Yeah, better. It was a bad shock seeing that newspaper report, but I'll get over it. Emotions were bound to run high after the funeral. It's not surprising everything boiled over. Keeping the accident a secret was simply Bea's way of trying to protect Annie. She didn't want to lose her sister all over again. Annie knows that. All's well that ends well and I sense they're closer than ever.'

'I forgot to ask. Are the Petrakis family coming?'

'Leo was asked, but impolitely declined on behalf of them. I've a feeling it's the last we'll see of them. Annie, certainly, has no intention of keeping up ties.'

'I wonder how the newspaper got hold of all that stuff. Pretty shocking. Almost as if someone was spying on the girls in Annie's own home. You can't even have a domestic without the press getting hold of it these days! Have you any idea where they got the story from?'

'Ha, as it happens I do know. I called the paper and got through to an old contact, who did a little investigating. And guess what? That old busybody, Annie's neighbour Jasmine Pooley, called up the paper, reported the incident—and even provided them with a meaty quote. So much for sticking your nose where it's not wanted...'

As the car peels off down Elm Avenue, Toby is assailed with memories. Stealing kisses from Emily on the number 11 bus. Picnics on the common, sprawled on the coarse grass, making two chocolate bars and a shared can of Coke last all afternoon. Hiding behind a privet hedge, clutching each other, sinking to the ground in a needy embrace as Norma walked by on the pavement.

It had been his mad idea to throw the family gathering at Elm Avenue and now it's his responsibility to make it a success. The house lies empty, waiting to be sold. He'd hired a man-with-a-van and, with Annie's help, set up a couple of trestle tables and some chairs and added some rugs and cushions for kids who wouldn't mind sitting on the floor. Everyone's chipped in with seventies-style catering ranging from classic cheese and pineapple hedgehogs and sausages on sticks to a delectable black forest gateau baked by Cyn.

'Remind me again who's coming?' asks Theo, unhooking his headphones.

'Well, your half-sister Annie, partner Ben and their daughter Phoebe. I think that makes Phoebe your half-cousin? And your other half-sister Bea with her partner Cyn. And then there'll be Bea's adoptive parents, Julia and Sean and their son Jake. Plus Julia's elderly mother Sara and her new man Abel. And us of course, along with your Aunt Chloe—we're meeting her there. That makes 14, I think?'

'How the heck can the old lady be in a new relationship? She must be at least 80!'

Actually, she's 83. And her partner Abel is even older. Survivors, both of them. Maybe you'll hear their incredible story sometime.'

'Wow, 83 years old. That's awesome. And Bea is bi, right? Her partner's name—is it short for Cynthia?'

'Correct.' Toby's looking for a space in the line of 4x4s parked in Elm Avenue. 'She's a lovely lady. And a dream cook.' As he edges the Volvo into a tight slot, Julia, Sean and their son emerge from a monster off-roader. You couldn't miss Julia, looking more like an exotic bird of prey than ever as she flutters about helping Sara and Abel out of the car.

'Good to see you again. Bea's going to love this.' Sean extends a hand which Toby pumps a shade too vigorously. Boy racer of campaigning journalism indeed. Hard to imagine this silver fox of a man raising his flesh and blood. Arm in arm, Sara and Abel follow. Julia and Jake are still on the pavement, engaged in intense conversation.

'Don't worry about them. Like peas in a pod, those two. Julia's probably fussing about the cupcakes she was planning to bring. She's a rubbish cook and sadly they didn't rise so she left them at home. Or Jake's asking who's the cool dude with the uber expensive headphones. Would that be your son?'

Toby nods. They exchange pleasantries as they walk down the crazy-paving path to Norma's pride and joy, the sunburst front door.

Inside, everyone's busy introducing each other, exclaiming, retelling the extraordinary story of the twins separated at birth and now reunited. Annie and Ben are handing around bubbly, while Phoebe helps Chloe with sausage rolls, sandwiches and cake.

Bea arrives last, leaning in slightly on her partner Cyn and wearing a bright bandana to conceal the patch where her head was shaved. Like a game of statues, everyone stops whatever they were doing. A brief moment of silence is followed by a slow clap coming from the bay window, with Theo bravely trying to break the ice.

As the clapping gathers momentum, everyone is whistling, shouting 'Go Bea!' and pushing their way forward to be first to greet her. Annie rushes protectively to her side. 'Listen up, everyone. My sister hates a fuss. Give her some space. Please do.'

But a slow smile spreads over Bea's face. 'Are you really *all* my family?'

Sean steps forward and puts a protective arm around his adoptive daughter. 'All of us, Bea. Some by birth right. And others, like us, acquired along the way. But make no mistake, we all love you.'

'Love you too, Dad. And Mum.' Bea enfolds Sean and Julia in a big hug, then makes a beeline for Annie. 'Sis? We're good, aren't we?'

'More than good, Bea.'

'Can I have a moment, everyone?' Not for the first time, Toby wishes he had a more commanding voice. In his hand is a heavily-edited extract from Emily's Memory Book. When he holds it up, a hush descends over the room.

'So pleased to see you all here today. An empty house is an odd choice for a family party, I know. But to celebrate the memory of Emily and welcome Bea to the fold, 101 Elm Avenue seemed the perfect venue. We're just lucky it didn't sell for a million before today! We're also fortunate that, in our search for Bea, we've somehow managed to acquire a huge extended family. Nothing in the world, in my view, matters more than family. Bea probably now has a bigger one than she'd imagined in her wildest dreams! We all love you, Bea. Welcome.'

Toby continues: 'When our girls were tiny babies, Emily started to write a sort of diary, or record, of her life which she called her Memory Book. She added to it intermittently over the years. The last entry was made shortly before she died.

'I'd like to read you an extract from the late seventies, around the time Emily was coerced into giving up Bea. I know "coerced" is a strong word, but that is my sense of it: that my Emily was not in a position to make a reasoned judgment and so the decision to abandon Bea was made for her. I think these words convey just how deeply Emily cared for Bea and how much she was a victim of her times and circumstances.'

Toby opens up the doctored extract and begins to read:

'Bea's little fists wave furiously in the air as she demands love and food. She loves me to stroke her back and tickle her tummy. What have I done? After she'd gone, I jumped into bed and huddled the blankets into a nest. Underneath the pillow was a Babygro she'd worn the day before. I held it to my face and breathed in the Bea-like smell. I've heard people say that you never know what you had till it's gone. Since Bea was taken away, I've just sat here in my room feeling cold and empty. Wish I could cry, but it's like I've turned to stone.

I got an old hatbox from the top of the wardrobe and put in everything that would remind me of her: one Babygro; a soft yellow caterpillar that she'd taken a liking to; a hairbrush which only she used because she had more hair than Annie. I wished I'd kept the woolly Bea hat. I wrote 'Bea' on the hatbox lid in big letters, lifted Annie out of the cot and we both kissed it. Sort of kissed it, in Annie's case. We put it right at the back of the cupboard, like a time capsule.'

Toby clears his throat and looks up. 'So there you have it. A snapshot of Emily's feelings for her baby. She loved you Bea, but perhaps she didn't quite realise it in time. She was too young, too frightened and everything was stacked against her. Me included. I should have fought harder for her, for you girls. But I was young too and intent on following my dreams.

'Now, that's quite enough of the past. Drinks, everyone. And do help yourselves to a slice of Cyn's amazing forest gateau.' Toby has spent a lifetime exploiting the power of language: enhancing, distorting, re-inventing. He never put his skills to better use than now.

As the party starts up again, he taps his wife on the shoulder. 'Clara, would you mind? I need to do something at the house. Nothing you need worry about, but it's urgent, or I wouldn't leave the party in full swing.'

Clara's deep in conversation with Annie and gives her husband only a cursory glance. She's accustomed to his erratic behaviour and has trained herself not to question it too deeply. 'Theo's having a great time. I don't think he'll be too thrilled about leaving just yet. I'd like to stay on too. Taxi?'

'Come with us,' urges Annie 'We've space for you and Theo. Ben will be more than happy to drop you off. Good, that's sorted. Off you go, Dad, on your mystery mission.'

Epilogue
Toby, 2013

The sky is darkening and the street lamps are lit by the time Toby reaches the sanctity of his own driveway. As the car scrunches to an abrupt halt, he reaches over to the glove box to pull out a plastic folder which has been pushed to the very back. It contains the final extract of Emily's Memory Book, carefully separated from the rest.

On the passenger seat beside him is the Memory Book itself, in its battered stars and planets cover. Inside, the pages are ragged, some are coffee-stained and others bear spots of Bea's blood. He's about to pick everything up and carry it indoors, but decides against it. Too poisonous.

Instead, he steps into the hall and, without switching on the lights against the gathering gloom, goes straight upstairs. In the big pine cupboard on the landing he finds his gardening clothes in their normal place. Hastily, he changes and runs back downstairs for his wellingtons. He needs to get this thing done before Clara and Theo arrive. Feeling guilty, almost criminal, he takes some matches from the kitchen drawer.

The remaining light in the garden is fading fast, illuminated by a soft orange glow from his bedroom window. He forgot to turn off the light, but no matter. Taking a spade from the shed, just in case, he trundles down to the compost heap at the very bottom of the garden. On top is a pile of tinder dry twigs and dead leaves, perfect for starting a fire. He checks that everything's in order and returns to the car.

Easing himself into the driver's seat, he picks up the folder to read Emily's final memory once more. He's read it before—when he took the Memory Book from the house in West Hampstead after helping Ben clear up. But he needs to be absolutely clear he's doing the right thing. It's entitled *Emily's Last Memory.*

267

Dear reader, this will be my last entry. Every day, there's some new hurdle for me. My hair is falling out, my muscles are wasting—even my teeth feel strangely loose in my mouth. My time is up.

It's 35 years since I started this Memory Book, but feels like a million. Today I re-read my first entry:

This will be my Memory Book. Or it could be a diary. It can actually be whatever I want it to be. I'm not sure anyone will ever read it. I might put it in a box and make it a time capsule when I'm done with it. Or there again, I might hide it under the bed or behind the wardrobe and someone will find it in about the year 2000! Whatever, I'm sure if I write down all the stuff that's going around in my head, I'll feel better.

Well, I made it way past the year 2000, but I haven't always been faithful and attentive to you, dear reader. I grumped at you, told you things I regret and for years at a time I totally neglected you. I was a frightened little girl, way over her head. But now I want to set the record straight, to be truly honest, for the people I touched and loved and harmed.

Norma was my bad start in life. She never properly loved me, not as a mother should. I shan't dwell on it: Norma and Clive are both long gone. But I'd like it to be known that I spent my childhood looking for love. Lately, I've begun to wonder if there was something in Norma's history that made her incapable of loving me. Clive too. Could it have been the war? I shall never know. I wish I'd tried harder to find out.

When I met Toby Summerfield, I was hungry for love. Toby filled me up in every imaginable way—physically, mentally, emotionally. Toby, if you are reading, know this: you were the love of my life. It's a profound regret that I walked away from you. But then you didn't run after me, did you? I have an idea why. Remember that time on the common when you said that one dropped exam grade made no difference to you, but top marks all around might change my life. You meant to be kind, but underneath the sweetness I heard another message: nothing, but nothing, would stand in the way of your glittering future. Not even me. Did you dare disturb the universe, though you loved me dearly? Sadly, you did not.

Annie, sweet Annie. I always loved you from afar. Nobody could have tried harder, but something stopped us making a real connection. For a long time, I thought it was the trauma of having to make a choice between you and Bea. Then I was jealous of your growing relationship with Norma. And I know you never fully forgave me for staying on with Leo, effectively choosing him over you. It was my moment of not daring to disturb the universe. Annie, you are the one good thing that Toby and I made together.

Leo, we were meant as an escape route, each for the other. But I trapped you with my demons and you controlled me through coercion. Did you ever, really, understand a word I said? About the books I loved? The ambitions I had to bury when I was wiping tables? But did I make any effort to help you to confront your past? To assuage your insecurity? What a waste of three decades. I'm sorry for it, Leo.

Bea, you are the hardest to address. I'd like to be able to tell you that I loved you, as mothers are meant to love their daughters. But the truth is, I never knew you: I didn't get the chance. My feelings for you are bound up in guilt and pain. Norma forced me to make a choice between you and Annie, insisted that I put one of you up for adoption. You were a difficult baby, unsettled and needy, so I chose to relinquish you. I am sorry for this, from the depths of my heart. I should have stood up to her, tried harder to keep you. I suspect I had postnatal depression, something people know a lot more about now than they did then.

As soon as you'd gone, I realised I'd made the most terrible mistake. I should have tried harder to get you back but I was in a terrible place for months and barely knew what I was doing. Then it was too late. And now you've made a reappearance in my life, I am reluctant to meet you. I truly believe that, for both of us, it's better not to revisit the ghosts of the past, especially as I don't have long to live. Better that you continue to enjoy the love and care of your adoptive family (I hear they are lovely people) than to try to renew a relationship that has never really existed. At least you found me and now it's time to cut the cord.

Toby stares, deep in consideration, out of the car window for a long time when he's finished reading. A light rain has left a smattering of drops on the windscreen. Switching on the wipers, he focuses on the whine, whine as they stroke the screen clear. It will soon be too wet to start a fire. Taking the Memory Book and folder under his arm, he stomps back down the garden in his ancient wellies, bundles a handful of twigs and dead leaves into his small firepit and sets them alight.

269

First, he rips up Emily's Last Memory folder and, bit by bit, feeds it to the crackling flames. There are no regrets, only an overwhelming sense of relief in relinquishing the toxic words to the blaze. Sitting back on his haunches, he pokes at the fire. He's rewarded with a yellow flare as the flames lick the wounded memories, hungrily. When the last curling page is reduced to hot ash, he picks up the Memory Book, stroking the shiny moons and planets and sniffing it as if it still bears Emily's scent. This is much harder to let go. Should he make a time capsule for it, as she might have wished? No, it's done too much damage already. He hurls it resolutely on the dying embers. The flames lick hard again, consuming the Memory Book, reducing it to ashes.

Toby stays rooted to the spot until he's quite sure that the Memory Book is no more. Car headlights beam into his drive and he hears the voices of his wife and child. Now, all the lights are going on in the house and silhouettes of his beloved family appear in the big kitchen window. He turns and, with a light step, makes his way to join them.

END